Driftless DECEIT

SUE BERG

LITTLE CREEK PRESS®
AND BOOK DESIGN

MINERAL POINT, WISCONSIN

Little Creek Press®
A Division of Kristin Mitchell Design, Inc.
5341 Sunny Ridge Road
Mineral Point, Wisconsin 53565

Book Design and Project Coordination:
Little Creek Press and Book Design

First Printing
August 2022

Printed in Wisconsin,
United States of America

Follow Sue on Facebook @ Sue Berg/author
To contact author: bergsue@hotmail.com
To order books: www.littlecreekpress.com

Library of Congress Control Number: 2022913394

ISBN-13: 978-1-955656-31-3

Cover photo: Perched, La Crosse, Wisconsin © **Phil S Addis**

This is a work of fiction. References to real places, events, establishments, and organizations
in the Driftless area are intended only to provide a sense of authenticity. They are used fictitiously
and are drawn from the author's imagination to enhance the story.

ACKNOWLEDGMENTS

To my readers:
Thank you for supporting my work, coming to library book talks,
recommending my books to others, contacting me on
Facebook with your comments and suggestions, posting
reviews on Amazon and Barnes & Noble, and purchasing
my books at your local bookstore.

To my family:
You keep everything real!
Without you, my life would be so empty!

To others:
Every book has a multitude of people who deserve recognition
for their part in the creative and publication process. In no
particular order, I would like to thank the following people for
their role in the Driftless Mystery Series: Heidi Overson for
your stellar editing and revision suggestions; Beth Harris for
accompanying me on many of my book talks; Phil Addis
for his iconic photography of the Driftless region; Alan Berg
for encouragement, love, and support; Kristin Mitchell of
Little Creek Press for wisdom and advice about the
publishing process; and to my Facebook fans for your kind
words of praise and your loyalty in buying my books.

And finally:
"...Clothe yourselves with compassion, kindness, humility,
gentleness, and patience. And whatever you do, whether in word or
deed, do it all in the name of the Lord Jesus, giving thanks to God
the Father through him." Colossians 2:12 & 17

2021 WISCONSIN BOOKSHELF WINNERS!

Driftless Gold & Driftless Treasure

from *Isthmus Magazine*, reviewed by Michael Popke

What readers are saying about the first two books in the Jim Higgins Driftless Mystery Series:

DRIFTLESS GOLD

Outstanding! Superb!
~Rich, Prairie du Chien

...developed this legend into a great story.
~Lona, Cassville

Interesting and captivating mystery.
~Dave, Eau Claire

An irresistible tale of lost treasure and the scoundrels
who will do anything to get their hands on it.
~Jeff Nania, author of the Northern Lakes Mystery series

Deeply engaging and absorbing.
~Bill, Viroqua

DRIFTLESS TREASURE

A story of avarice, revenge, and Middle East intrigue in
a setting of charming riverfront villages, friendly people, and the
steep rugged landscape of Wisconsin's Driftless Region.
~Harold Thorpe, Wisconsin author

Romance, love, faith, history, suspense, crime,
shock, resolution—it's all here!
~Heidi Overson, Driftless area writer

Submerges you in the beautiful Driftless area and pulls you
in with murder and stolen treasure. Page-turning!
~Alexandra "Birdy" Veglahn,
Birdy's Bookstore, Holmen, Wisconsin

OTHER BOOKS BY SUE BERG

Solid Roots and Strong wings—A Family Memoir

The Driftless Mystery Series:

Driftless Gold

Driftless Treasure

Driftless Deceit

FOREWORD
THE DRIFTLESS REGION

The name *Driftless* appears in all of the titles of my books because this region of the American Midwest where my novels take place is a unique geographical region, though relatively unknown. The Driftless Region—which escaped glacial activity during the last ice age—includes southeastern Minnesota, southwestern Wisconsin, northeastern Iowa, and the extreme northwestern corner of Illinois. The stories I write take place in and around La Crosse, Wisconsin, which is in the heart of this distinct geographical region.

The Driftless Region is characterized by steep forested ridges, deeply carved river valleys, and karst geology, resulting in spring-fed waterfalls and cold-water trout streams. The rugged terrain is due primarily to the lack of glacial deposits called drift. The absence of the flattening glacial effect of drifts resulted in land that has remained hilly and rugged—hence the term *driftless*. In addition, the Mississippi River and its many tributaries have carved rock outcroppings and towering bluffs from the area's bedrock. These rock formations along the Mississippi River climb to almost six hundred feet in some places. Grandad Bluff in La Crosse is one of these famous bluffs.

In particular, the Driftless portion of southwestern Wisconsin contains many distinct features: isolated hills, coulees, bluffs, mesas, buttes, goat prairies, and pinnacles formed from eroded Cambrian bedrock remnants of the plateau to the southwest. In addition, karst topography is found throughout the Driftless area. This landscape was created when water dissolved the dolomite and limestone rock resulting in features like caves and cave systems, hidden underground streams, blind valleys and sinkholes, and springs and cold streams.

About eighty-five percent of the Driftless Region lies within southwestern Wisconsin. The rugged terrain comprising this area is known locally as the Coulee Region. Steep ridges, numerous rock outcroppings like the Three Chimneys northwest of Viroqua, the classic rock formations of Wisconsin Dells, and deep narrow valleys contrast with the rest of the state, where glaciers have modified and leveled the land.

The area is prone to flooding, runoff, and erosion. Because of the steep river valleys, many small towns in the Driftless Region have major flooding problems every fifty to one hundred years. Farmers in the region practice contour plowing and strip farming to reduce soil erosion on the hilly terrain.

Superb cold-water streams have made the Driftless Region a premier trout fishing destination in the country. A variety of fish, including brook and rainbow trout, thrive in the tributaries of the Mississippi River system. The crystalline streams are protected by Trout Unlimited, an organization that works with area landowners to maintain and restore trout habitat. In addition, abundant wildlife such as deer and turkeys provide excellent hunting for the avid sportsman.

La Crosse is the principal urban center that is entirely in the Wisconsin Driftless Region, along with small cities, towns, and numerous Amish settlements. Cranberries are grown and harvested in bogs left over from Glacial Lake Wisconsin. At one time, cigar tobacco was grown and harvested throughout the Coulee Region, but foreign markets decreased the demand for Wisconsin-grown tobacco. However, tobacco barns or sheds are still found throughout the landscape and are an iconic symbol of a once-thriving industry. The region is also home to Organic Valley, the nation's largest organic producer of dairy products, organic vegetables, and fruits, particularly apples. Winemaking and vineyards have popped up in recent years, and apple production continues to be a staple in the Driftless economy.

After describing the area's geographical features, you can see why Wisconsin is the perfect setting for a mystery series! It's a wonderland of unparalleled geographical beauty, impressive wildlife, and friendly, memorable people. Enjoy! ◘

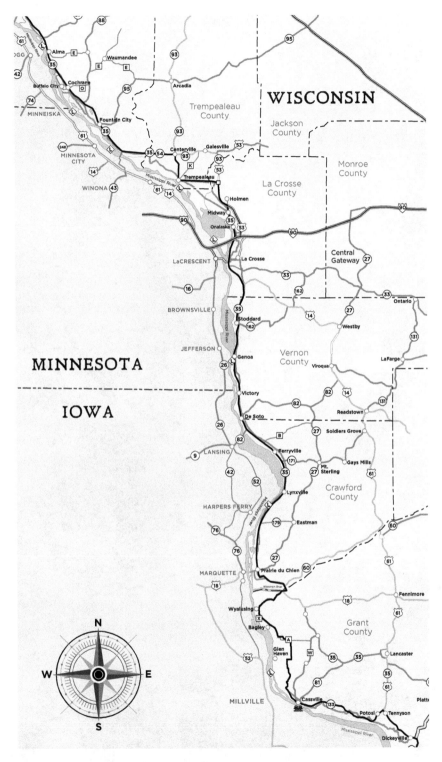

FRIDAY EVENING,
MAY 10

1

The orange sun was sinking toward the horizon, the blue sky airbrushed with swirling masses of orange, pink, and red. The Mississippi River flowed silently in the distance, a dark brown ribbon snaking its way south, meandering here and there, picking up speed and power as it traveled. Barges and boats noisily blared their horns with intermittent blasts. The temperature grew cooler, and Juliette pulled her dirty, loose sweater tightly around her shoulders. She dreaded the dark hours of night ahead with her small granddaughter, Lillie.

Here in Tent City, the center of the homeless population on the northern edge of Riverside Park in La Crosse, Wisconsin, they were relatively safe. However, outbursts and arguments from other residents sometimes punctuated the hours of darkness.

"When are we going to find Bapa?" little Lillie intently questioned her grandmother, Juliette, while they rested on one of the park's benches. "Does he know we're here? When will we get to see him?"

"Hush now, Miss Lillie. We just arrived yesterday," Juliette reminded her. Her illness heightened her sense of insecurity, and she was filled with a deep, dark despondency. Her rasping cough filled the night air, and shivers prickled her skin. The pain in her lower back built into agonizing spasms, leaving her weak and shaken. Although it seemed horribly selfish, she prayed that her death would come swiftly and soon.

"I'm hungry, Grandma," Lillie whined. Her vivid blue eyes were large with want and malnutrition. Her T-shirt, smudged with yesterday's dumpster food, was covered in grime. The little girl's ringlets of blonde hair were dark with grease and sweat from the weeks they had been on the road traveling to La Crosse. Her flip-flopped feet dangled from the bench, making her look like a poster child from a third world poverty-stricken country.

"Here, here now," Juliette groaned, trembling from her coughing spell. She pulled a discarded sandwich from the pocket of her sweater. She'd found it lying on the cement near the back entrance of a nearby restaurant. With quivering hands, she handed it to the innocent child. Lifting a bottle of water from her tote bag, she unscrewed the top and offered Lillie a drink. The child gobbled ravenously at the stale sandwich, gulping drinks of water between bites.

After a few moments, Juliette gently grasped Miss Lillie's hand and led her into the wooded area beyond the International Gardens, where they had spent the day loitering and resting. "Come on, now," Juliette said, her guttural voice laced with pain. "We need to find a place to sleep for the night."

Lillie began crying, a pathetic whimpering that Juliette hated to hear. The sick woman was all alone and desperately ill, and it was hard to bear the suffering of such an innocent child. She hoped she could find her brother, Jim, before she passed away.

Juliette was convinced her death was near. She'd been sick too long without medical care, and everything seemed to be crashing down around her. Still, she was sure she would have died months ago without Lillie to care for and defend.

Last night a vivid dream of an angelic being came to Juliette, and she found the comfort more welcome than she cared to admit. In the velvety darkness of the night, the angel sang to her. *I am a poor wayfaring stranger traveling through this world below. There is no sickness, no toil, nor danger in that bright land to which I go.* The resonance of the heavenly voice soothed her like a mysterious balm. For just a few precious moments, she was pain-free. The haunting melody lifted her to another world filled with hope and light—an assurance that the Lord had not forgotten her desperate needs. A peace washed over her, easing her agony and freeing her from the incessant loneliness that weighed her down.

One more night, Lord. Just one more night so we can find Bapa, she prayed silently. Juliette smiled at the nickname Lillie had assigned to Jim—Bapa. She refused to call him anything else even after Juliette had tried to correct her.

They found a patch of tall grasses near the jogging trail that skirted the homeless community. Falling into the grass, Juliette patted it into a kind of natural mattress. She was so tired. In her last act of kindness for her precious Lillie, she pulled a thin blanket from her bag and pulled her granddaughter close, groaning in pain as she covered the little waif with the blanket. The inadequacy of her provision for the child filled her eyes with tears. As darkness descended, the woman and child fell into a restless, wounded sleep, waiting for the morning and another chance for hope. ◙

SATURDAY,
MAY 11

2

The fishing lure plopped on the surface of Timber Coulee Creek and floated gently along the rippling current, bobbing and dipping in the stream. Lt. Jim Higgins, chief investigative officer at the La Crosse Sheriff's Department, was reveling in the uninterrupted solace of nature. The wooded foliage on the hillsides and along the creek was beginning to pop with green, and the heavy, sweet scent of lilac filled the air.

Racing over exposed rocks in the stream, the sound of the gurgling creek filled Jim with a deep sense of contentment. He noticed the sting of sunburn on his nose and forehead as he adjusted his Ray-Ban sunglasses. Fumbling around in his backpack, he found the sunscreen and swabbed some across his face, ears, and arms. He took a hat from his backpack and plopped it on his head.

Jim continued to amble down the creek in his camo waders, his Badger hat shading his striking blue eyes from the intense morning sunshine. Moving athletically, he climbed up and down the banks casting and retrieving his line with a casual expertise that belied his recent conversion to the sport of fly fishing. As he maneuvered in and out of the clear, cold water, he thought back to the morning's events and his wife, Carol.

Dawn was just beginning to find its way into the darkened recesses of the bedroom on Chipmunk Coulee Road. Carol, now in her ninth month of pregnancy, slept sprawled on her side, her nightie barely concealing her expanding tummy. Jim smiled at the prospect of a baby. When he thought about it, it seemed so absurd. Carol had been divorced for over twenty years, and Jim lost his wife to cancer two years ago. This was the second marriage for both of them. Carol was forty-two, and he was fifty-two. Never in any world they'd inhabited in their imagination or in the bedroom had they expected to find themselves pregnant.

Believing that Carol's perimenopausal symptoms would make pregnancy impossible had been their first mistake. Her pregnancy had taken a considerable amount of time to adjust to. There'd been a few arguments, a weak attempt to lay the blame at one another's feet. However, as the months passed, the disbelief and bewilderment had gradually turned to joy and now, in the past few weeks, excited anticipation.

This morning, Jim had tried to get out of bed and dress quietly. He wanted to get an early start fishing near Coon Valley, where some of the best trout streams in Wisconsin offered unparalleled relaxation. But Carol's ears were tuned to him and his movements. Opening her eyes, she rolled on her back in a lazy motion.

"Hey. You headin' out already?" she asked, her voice raspy with sleep. "Kinda early, isn't it?"

Jim leaned over for a kiss, but she pulled him down beside her. They cuddled up together, and Carol rested her head gently on his shoulder.

"I can't sneak away anymore," Jim said in his deep baritone voice, nuzzling his nose into her brunette hair. "Your ears are fine-tuning for this baby. New mothers hear every squeak and squawk their babies make."

Carol grabbed his hand and held it to her swollen belly. Jim could feel the urgent kicks and tugs rippling under her skin.

"Active little thing," he said, giving her a tender kiss on the temple.

"Just like his daddy," she said. "When are you going to be home? Dr. Lockhart told me at my last checkup I might go earlier than June. I'm measuring farther along than she thought. And I wouldn't want you to miss out on the whole event," she said, anxiety lacing her words. Her brown eyes scanned Jim's face as she ran her fingers through his blond hair, now flecked with graying streaks.

"Honey, I'm going to Coon Valley, not the moon. I'll have my cell," he said seriously, "but don't call me except in an emergency, okay?" Staring into the cool blueness of his eyes, she felt the rising panic in her chest subside. Those eyes tugged on her heart strings like no other.

Kissing him passionately, she said, "Well, there's a little something I need before you go." His eyebrows arched, and he grinned.

"That's the reason you're in the condition you're in right now," he teased, responding to her with a kiss of his own. "You better settle for a nice back rub and a shower."

"Oh, come on. I miss our little early morning romps," she said impishly.

"You are such a devil," Jim said, grinning. "But I think we better shelve that idea," he said, running his hand over her taut tummy.

Standing in the creek in his waders, Jim reached for his phone, deciding his hours of relaxation in the verdant greenery of Spring Coulee would have to come to an end. Patting his pockets, he groaned when he realized he'd left his cell in the truck. He'd promised Carol the new crib for the nursery would be assembled by evening, and he knew better than to upset her organizational mojo. Glancing at the position of the sun in the sky, it was time to go if he was going to be home by noon.

He loaded his gear into the back of his Suburban, swung onto the road from the designated turn-out for fishermen, and worked his way over the gently rolling hills of the Driftless Region of southern Wisconsin. After several weeks of cold, rainy weather, the spring sunshine had finally arrived in force. Its strength increased daily, warming the earth until the temperatures consistently hovered around seventy. Puffy cumulus clouds leisurely floated against the powder blue sky. Jim powered down his window, leaned his arm on the frame, and drew the clean air deeply into his lungs.

Hooking up with County Highway K, he breezed around a huge tractor and corn planter, waving out the window while negotiating a wide berth. A female bobwhite and her brood fluttered hurriedly across the road, disappearing into a patch of brush. Farther down the road, he noticed Gladys Hanson hobbling to her mailbox. He slowed, pulled up beside her, and rolled down his passenger window. Gladys gave him a quick wave of the hand and a mannerly smile.

"Beautiful day, huh?" Jim commented, smiling, a dimple denting his right cheek. He leaned toward her.

"Shouldn't you be home with Carol? She's due any day, isn't she?" Gladys said with a put-on sense of indignity, her wide bosom filling the truck window. Her flowered dress was covered with an apron that looked ancient and was speckled with flour. Snow-white curls framed her wrinkled face, and she wore an expression of someone who had no interest in pretense or social posturing.

"I'm heading home right now," Jim said, feeling like he was reporting to his mother.

Hiding a grin that was fighting to get to the surface, Gladys asked, "You been fishin' again?"

A guilty expression crossed Jim's face. "Might be my last chance in Timber Coulee for quite a while."

"Does Carol know you're fishin'?" Gladys asked persistently.

What is this? The Inquisition? he thought. "Absolutely. She's all for it," he stated, feeling like a kid who got caught with his hand in the cookie jar.

"Well, you let me know when she has that little one." She pointed at her buxom chest with her index finger. "I don't do Facebook and all that other nonsense. A phone call from you will do," she said seriously.

"You got it, Gladys. I trust you'll spread the word to the other ladies at Hamburg Lutheran Church when the event happens," he said, pointing a finger at her.

"Those old windbags can find out for themselves," she said abruptly.

Jim threw his head back and laughed. He could always trust Gladys to give him her honest opinion with a twist of humor. Turning serious, he asked, "Can I count on your prayers?"

"Always. Been praying ever since I found out about this ... *expectation,*" she said, her face flushing pink. She gazed at Jim with her attentive hazel eyes. Her voice softened. "I'm praying for you every day."

Jim nodded his head, and his blue eyes misted. "As I thought you would. Thank you, Gladys. Gotta go!"

He lifted his hand in a hurried goodbye and sped down the blacktop. Driving up Chipmunk Coulee Road, he turned into the driveway. Carol was on her knees in a flowerbed by the front entry, digging in the dirt and transplanting perennials. She glanced up expectantly when he rolled up to the garage. Jim climbed out and walked up to her.

"Hey, whadda ya doin'?" he asked casually.

I'm sweating. That's what I'm doing, she thought irritably. Her garden gloves and the knees of her jeans were covered in black dirt. She stuck her trowel in the soil, leaned back, and placed her gloved hands on her jeans, her swollen belly resting on her thighs.

"Well, I'm trying to get some gardening done before this baby comes. By the way, did you realize your phone is turned off?" she asked, giving him a frazzled look. Her brunette hair, normally carefully coiffed, was in disarray. She pushed a few loose strands away from her face with a gloved hand.

Jim reached in his pocket. "Sorry, I guess I didn't notice," he said sheepishly, retrieving it from his jeans pocket.

Carol gave him a sideways glance. "Really?" she asked sarcastically, tipping her head.

"Honestly, honey, I didn't know it was off," he said, holding out the phone.

"You're supposed to call Luke at the morgue," she said. Jim looked puzzled. "He wouldn't tell me a thing, and I pressed him," she finished. She made an effort to stand. Jim reached out and pulled her up.

"Ooof. It's getting harder to do that," she complained, a frown creasing her forehead as she laid a hand on her distended belly. "I'm heading for the shower. Would you be sweet and make some sandwiches while I clean up?"

"Sure. No problem."

"Don't forget to call Luke," she reminded him as she waddled down the hall to the bathroom. "Then this afternoon, you've got to get that crib put together."

Jim began rummaging through the refrigerator, searching for sandwich fixings and placing them on the counter. In the middle of grabbing the mayonnaise and mustard, his phone vibrated in his pocket.

"Jim Higgins."

"Chief, it's Luke down at the morgue." Luke Evers was the La Crosse County Medical Examiner and Carol's boss. He continued. "Just wanted to let you know a jogger found a body near Riverside Park this morning. It's a set of unusual circumstances. I want you and Carol to come down here in the next couple of hours. Can you do that?" he asked, his voice taking on an anxious tone that Jim found unusual.

"Carol? Why Carol?" he asked, confused. "What's she got to do with this?"

"It's hard to explain over the phone. Can you promise me you'll come down, say by two o'clock?" he asked again, more impatient this time.

"Can't you just tell me right now and save Carol the hassle of the drive into La Crosse?" His voice had taken on a brusqueness of its own. "She's pretty uncomfortable."

"No, I'm not telling you over the phone. You both need to come down—by two or so," Luke ordered, his own voice echoing Jim's irritated tone.

Jim sighed loudly. "All right, if you say so. We'll be there." He stood in the sunlight of the kitchen, wondering what could have happened that would require both of them to head to the morgue. *Maybe it's Matt. Probably wandered into the park after a gig and died of a massive coronary,* he thought.

Matt Donavan was Carol's ex. His country/rock band, Mississippi Mud, was known throughout the area and was a wildly popular tri-state entertainment act. He was also notorious for his hard partying and escapades with women. Jim shook his head. *Who knows what happened. Sometimes life is stranger than fiction.* He started making a couple of sandwiches. Over lunch, Jim explained the odd request from Luke Evers to Carol.

"He wants us both to come downtown?" she questioned, making a wry face. "I've got a million things to do, Jim."

"Yeah, I know. I tried to tell him that, but he was acting really weird," Jim commented, taking a bite of his sandwich. Carol frowned and pushed a lock of hair behind her ear.

"Can't imagine what that could be," she said suspiciously.

"Me, either," Jim finished. "I have no idea what this is about. I'm not even going to speculate." *I just hope it isn't something about Matt,* he thought. He couldn't imagine any other reason that Carol's presence would be required. His sense of uneasiness grew. *This is not what Carol needs when she's about to deliver a baby.* ◖

3

Jim and Carol entered the ground floor of the Law Enforcement Center on Vine Street in La Crosse at one-thirty in the afternoon. Weaving through the maze of hallways, they came to the coroner's office toward the back of the building. Jim noticed the quietness of the place when Carol opened the clear glass office door.

Sarah Evers, Luke's wife, was in the family waiting area off to the left with a little blonde girl at her side. *That's odd,* Jim thought. Usually, children that young were shielded from any exposure to the morgue. He wondered who had screwed up this time. Jim recalled the cryptic phone call from Luke, and sweat broke out along his hairline as he tried to get a handle on his unexplained anxiety.

Carol's eyebrows shot up when she saw the little child in the waiting room. She crooked her finger at Sara, who got up and came over to Carol and Jim. "Who's little one is that?" Carol asked. She placed her hand protectively across her stomach. Jim noticed she'd been doing that a lot lately.

"I think I'll let Luke explain the situation. She's safe with me, for now," Sara explained.

"Come on," Jim said, grabbing Carol's hand. "Let's find Luke."

They walked through Carol's office area to the door marked

Theater #2. They found Luke standing next to a corpse that had been pulled from the refrigerated storage cabinet. The body lay on a gurney covered with a clean white sheet. Luke looked up when he heard the doors slide open. He noticed that Carol appeared bloated and uncomfortable.

Pointing to the waiting room, Carol asked, "Luke, why is that little child here? You know—" but Luke stopped her before she could start on a complete harangue.

"Don't say anything, and don't go off on me," Luke ordered, holding up his hands. His voice was tight and tense. Carol's eyes widened. "Let me explain this situation first. It's very unusual. Then I'll try to answer your questions."

For reasons he couldn't understand, Jim's stomach clenched in an anxious spasm. "Go for it. We're listening," Jim replied seriously, laying a hand on Carol's arm when she appeared ready to ask more questions. Sam Birkstein, a member of the sheriff's investigative team, was standing in the far corner. He waved listlessly, giving Jim and Carol a weak smile. Jim wondered why Sam was here.

"I've only done a cursory examination. An autopsy and full DNA workup will be done as soon as possible, but I can tell you a few things to bring you up to speed," Luke explained. He carefully folded back the white sheet until the face was exposed. Jim studied the face carefully, expecting it to be someone they both knew. It wasn't.

"The deceased is a white blue-eyed female approximately sixty years old. Height—five feet, eight inches. Weight—about one hundred twenty pounds. I believe she's been homeless for some time. She exhibits all the signs: low weight, aging well beyond her chronological years, dirty skin, hair, and nails. Her clothes were in tatters, and her shoes have seen a better day. Her personal effects were minimal—no purse or wallet, just a large tote bag with various scraps of clothing and trinkets and another document I'll explain in a minute."

Jim shifted impatiently on his feet. "I still don't see what this has to do with us," he said, running his hand through his hair. "I don't know this person." His hand flopped back to his side.

"I'm getting to that," Luke said, his voice patient and steady. "She was found dead in Riverside Park near Tent City. There are no defining wounds or injuries that would explain her death. She doesn't appear to be a drug user. Instead, I believe she suffered from some acute disease, possibly cancer or tuberculosis. More on that later, after I make a detailed blood analysis and complete the autopsy. From her core temperature, I'm guessing she died sometime yesterday, maybe toward evening ... say between eight and ten o'clock."

"I hope someone is working the scene?" Jim asked, shifting his gaze to Sam in the corner.

"I called Sam because I couldn't reach you. He got the crew over there," Luke said, which explained Sam's presence. Jim felt guilty when he thought about his turned-off phone. Luke glanced back and forth from Carol to Jim, his eyes staying a beat longer on Jim, knowing the news he was about to tell him would rock his world.

Shuffling uncomfortably under Luke's serious gaze, Jim felt uncharacteristically exposed and vulnerable. He crossed his arms and glanced down at the body. The victim looked peaceful despite being homeless, which Jim knew could add years to anyone's life. She appeared almost relieved—like life had been long and hard, and now her burdens were over.

Luke began again, his tone firm and clinical. "That's about all I have as a preliminary physical assessment. But there are some other things I need to tell you about." Sam nervously watched Jim and Carol from his corner.

Jim waited. Carol leaned toward him and asked, "Honey, could you get me a chair?"

"Oh, I'm sorry. I should have thought of that," Jim said apologetically. Luke grabbed a chair near a lab table and offered it to Carol. She sat down, smiling weakly.

"The victim was found with the little four-year-old girl you saw with Sarah in the waiting room. In fact, her crying led the jogger on the park trail to investigate the situation. The child was noncommunicative when she was found except for her inconsolable sobbing. The only word she kept repeating was 'Grandma.' Sam brought her here, and we fed her and tried to clean her up a little bit. She was pretty dirty. She was in shock and seemed confused and disoriented. So far, she still hasn't talked."

"Oh, my Lord, that's awful!" Carol responded, locking eyes with Jim. He offered his hand, and she held it tenderly. "The poor little thing!"

"But the main thing is ... " the coroner stumbled as if he were at a loss for words. He started again. "The main thing is the certificate found in the victim's bag. It appears to me to be an official notarized document—like a will." He stopped again and locked eyes with Jim. "But I'm no expert. You'll have to check it out."

"Right. Go ahead, Luke," Jim encouraged. He'd never seen the coroner struggle with his composure like this. In his line of work, Luke had seen just about everything: murders, suicide, drowning, fire victims. His stumbling apprehension now was unnerving.

From a tray beneath the gurney, Luke pulled out an official-looking piece of paper enclosed in a large transparent baggie. He'd obviously read it earlier. Summarizing its contents, he began to explain. "This is the last will and testament of ... Juliette Lindvig Marquart Olson." At the sound of the name Lindvig, Jim's posture stiffened, and his eyes widened in alarm.

"Did you say Lindvig?" Jim asked softly.

"Yes. Is that important?" Luke asked.

"Could be. That's my mother's maiden name," Jim stated.

Luke shuffled on his feet. "Well, the document states she's your sister. It identifies the little girl as your great-niece, who prefers to be called Miss Lillie. The little girl's mother, your niece, died of a drug overdose when Lillie was a baby, and Juliette has been caring for the girl as best she could. In the document, she designates you as the child's guardian and asks that you raise Lillie as if she were your own." Luke placed the document back in the bag and handed it over to Jim, his hand shaking ever so slightly.

Jim slowly raised his arm and took the baggie. He didn't examine it. Rather, it hung limply at his side.

"There's a news article about you folded inside the will," Luke added.

Carol stood up and wrapped one arm around Jim's waist, her eyes staring at Luke in disbelief. The silence dragged on. Jim seemed frozen, unable to move. In the corner, Sam was waiting for someone to say or do something.

Jim heard his voice, but he didn't recognize it. "The name … Lindvig. That's my mother's maiden name, but I—I don't have a sister. This is impossible," he sputtered. He glanced desperately at Carol. "I only have a brother—David—in California." His hand waved in a confused gesture. The quiet in the morgue was unsettling. "I only have a brother," he repeated, trying to convince himself. "There's got to be some other explanation for this," he said, staring at Luke as if he had the answers.

"I can understand that this is a shock," Luke said evenly, meeting Jim's stare. The incongruity of the situation propelled Jim into confusion and alarm.

"I don't have a sister," Jim repeated with conviction, his voice echoing off the ceramic tiled walls. "This is impossible," he repeated, his voice a little louder. Rattling the bag in Luke's face, he said, "Either this is some humongous mistake, or it's an incredibly tasteless joke."

Disengaging from Carol, he turned to her, laid one hand on her shoulder, looked squarely in her eyes, and said in desperation, "Carol, tell him. Tell him that I don't have a sister."

Carol laid her hands on Jim's chest. "Let's take it easy, honey," she said calmly. Turning to her boss, she continued, "Luke, we need to get to the bottom of this. Quickly. To my knowledge, Jim only has one brother. And I absolutely believe him."

"This is crazy," Jim whispered, his eyes exhibiting a vacant stare as he gaped at the body on the gurney. Weaving slightly, the bag still dangling from his hand, his eyes zeroed in on Luke again. "If I had a sister, then how come I don't know about her at age fifty-two?

Do you have an answer for that?" Jim asked, his voice increasing in volume.

"Jim, honey," Carol said softly. "You need to settle down. Luke is not the enemy." Seeing that the situation was going off the rails, the coroner took control before Jim could respond.

"Let's go into my office. Sam, can you get us some coffee?" he asked, moving Carol and Jim gently out of the examining room into his adjoining office. Sam sprang into action, disappearing briefly.

Jim plopped in a chair, flipping the baggie on Luke's desk. Carol lowered herself slowly into another chair next to Jim. Luke sat behind his desk. Reappearing with a tray of piping hot coffees, Sam distributed the drinks silently. Then he stood against the wall, keenly observing the drama unfolding before him.

"I can understand this is a shock," Luke started again, sipping his coffee and examining the document in front of him. He lifted his eyes and noticed their disbelieving expressions.

"That doesn't even come close to describing it," Jim stated seriously. Luke dipped his head as if agreeing with him. Jim turned to Sam.

"Sam, I want you to start investigating this. Go down to Riverside, check out the homeless that are living in that area, and see if anyone has talked to this woman and child. Go to the shelters, Salvation Army, and the other ones. Get a photo of her before you go. See if anyone recognizes her." His voice and demeanor seemed to have returned to normal, and giving orders stabilized his emotions.

"Right, Chief. I'll canvas the area and see if anything turns up," he said. He waved as he exited the office.

Jim nailed Luke to the wall with a piercing gaze. "So how soon will DNA testing come back so we can verify the validity of these claims? A couple of days?"

"I put a rush on it, so I'm thinking maybe we'll know for sure by late Monday." He felt more comfortable now that he was on familiar medical ground. "Genetically speaking, if the woman is your sibling, you'd share anywhere from thirty-eight to sixty-one percent of DNA.

On the other hand, Lillie would share about twelve percent of your DNA if you are truly her great uncle." He stopped, letting Jim absorb the statistics. "But in the meantime, we still have a problem. What are we going to do with Lillie?"

Jim blew out his cheeks in a pent-up sigh. Carol dropped his hand and stood up. "Let's go meet her, Jim," she suggested.

Jim got quickly out of the chair. "Well, this whole day has gone head first into the ditch anyway. We might as well," he said, resigning himself to the uncomfortable facts.

Carol gave him a sympathetic look, and he hung his head. "This is unbelievable," he mumbled. Then he turned back to Luke. "Let me call somebody at Social Services and give them the details of the situation. See what legal ramifications might be involved if we take Lillie home until this mess gets straightened out."

Carol sat down again while Jim phoned his contacts in Social Services about the legalities of fostering Lillie. When he finished, he placed his phone in his shirt pocket, grabbed Carol's hand, and they walked to the waiting area. Standing outside the door for just a moment, they watched the petite, impish girl concentrating on her picture.

Sarah noticed them observing Lillie. "I was just trying to keep her busy," she said. Lillie was madly coloring on a piece of white paper, her attempts a jumble of vibrant circular scribbles. Gripping a crayon, she scrutinized Jim and Carol with wide-eyed wonder. Jim could see she was a darling child if a bit rough around the edges at the moment. Her blonde curly shoulder-length hair needed washing, and her clothes were ragged and quite dirty. But her petite face held angelic blue eyes, which strangely reminded Jim of his daughter, Sara, when she had been a child. Lillie's dimpled chin and cupid mouth were frozen in sober concentration. She put her crayon down, stepped forward shyly, and put her tiny hand in Jim's. "Grandma said you'd come, Bapa," she said.

There was an uncomfortable silence. Jim's stomach clenched with an unfamiliar angst, and he briefly closed his eyes. *This just gets worse and worse.*

"Who's that?" Lillie asked, pointing at Carol, still holding Jim's hand. "She's got an awful big tummy."

Sarah lifted her shoulders in a shrug, a grin spreading across her face. "Go figure. I couldn't get her to talk," she informed them.

Jim was dumbfounded. *Out of the mouths of babes,* he thought. He was keenly aware of Lillie's warm, little hand enclosed in his. He realized that this child seemed to know about him. *This whole thing could be the ruse of some poor demented soul who was planning on committing suicide and needed a place to unload the child.* Maybe the dead woman had observed him, followed him, or read about him in the paper. He did have some local notoriety for solving difficult cases. He groaned inwardly. *Why me, Lord?* he asked, staring at the ceiling.

Jim stooped down, then sat on his haunches in front of Lillie. She gazed into his eyes with a wisdom that seemed uncomfortably precocious for her age. *That's what happens when you live on the street,* he thought. He reached over, took Carol's hand, and pulled her toward them.

"This is my wife, Carol, and her tummy is big because she'll have a baby very soon," he told Lillie.

Lillie's mouth formed a little "o," and her eyes drifted from Carol's belly upward to her pretty face and dark hair. She gazed at her with an innocent stare while Carol smiled at her. Lillie turned to Jim, studying him with intensity.

"Are you going to take me to your house?" she asked seriously. "Grandma said you would."

Well, you can't go back on the street, Jim thought. He stood and said, "I'm checking into that."

Seeing that Jim was about to leave, Lillie whimpered, "You'll come back, Bapa?" Tears flooded her eyes and spilled onto her pale cheeks.

Jim gently lifted Lillie into his arms. "You're safe now. We'll be back in a little bit, and then we'll make a plan, okay?" he said, his blue eyes connecting with the child. *Blue to blue,* he thought uncomfortably. He felt his heart tug in his chest.

"Promise?" she said hopefully.

"Promise," Jim said, but all the while, he was thinking, *What are we getting ourselves into?*

Carol sat in the waiting room, watching Lillie color while Jim made some more frantic phone calls. Finally, he motioned Carol back into Luke's office. Faxing the document found in the homeless woman's bag to Judge Benson and the district attorney, they had agreed it was an official will. A La Crosse County social worker emailed a Temporary Guardian Petition Form to the morgue office.

"Honey, are you sure about this?" Jim asked Carol, his hand poised above the petition form. He searched Carol's face, doubtful she could be serious about taking on a four-year-old when their own baby was due any day.

"Well, the timing certainly isn't perfect, but we can't just fling the poor child into the welfare system given the options. She's had enough trauma already. Abandoning her goes against everything you and I believe, Jim. So yes, we'll deal with the fallout as best we can." Carol leaned over and kissed Jim's cheek. "Don't worry. We'll be fine."

Plans were formalized. Carol and Jim signed the guardianship papers in Luke's presence, and he notarized them and put the official La Crosse County seal on them.

"Well, as of 3:11 p.m., you are officially the temporary guardians of Lillie Marquart. The statute runs out in sixty days. You can revisit the issue at that time. I'd say congratulations, but somehow that doesn't seem like the appropriate response," Luke said sheepishly.

"Thanks for your help, Luke," Carol said. "I guess I'm going to be a mother of two, not one."

"Can this day get any weirder?" Jim asked huffily.

"Probably not," Luke answered. ◙

SATURDAY EVENING,
MAY 11

4

Throughout Jim's years as a cop, his wages were modest, but he and his first wife, Margie, had managed to save quite a nest egg through discipline and frugality. He'd worked hard at his job and been promoted several times. Margie had saved and budgeted. When his wife died of breast cancer over two years ago, finances were the last thing on Jim's mind. He lived from day to day and seldom even checked the balance in his checking account. Thank God for automatic deposits. They made his life simple.

Since his recent marriage to Carol a year ago, they'd combined their resources, and the end result was impressive. As office manager of the La Crosse County Morgue, Carol's job paid well by Midwestern standards. She had contributed a sizable nest egg, which considerably strengthened their financial landscape.

Some months ago in February, Jim and Carol began seriously discussing a baby's implications on their household and lifestyle.

"We either have to build on a bedroom or two or remodel the basement into an apartment," Jim had suggested. Time was ticking by, and he knew how hard it would be to retain the services of a building contractor in the spring.

"So you think we should build an apartment in the basement for what reason?" Carol asked, mystified, sipping a cup of peppermint tea on the couch.

"Well, after you have the baby, the apartment downstairs will be a great space for the twins when they come and babysit. And it will be a great retreat for guests," Jim explained.

Carol was puzzled. She tucked a lock of hair behind her ear. "So we're building this apartment for weekend guests?" Carol asked, trying to understand Jim's reasoning.

"Maybe. I was hoping you could help me think it through," he said hurrying on. "We've got the exposed south side of the house that faces the patio. Putting a sliding glass door that opens to the patio would work well, and a private entrance from the garage could be built. The basement is wide open. We can configure it any way we'd like. I'm pretty handy. I can do some of the finish work, trim and baseboards, which would save us money." He paused, seeing she was having a hard time with the concept. "We don't have to decide yet. Just think about it."

"It sounds like *Home Improvement* times ten," Carol said sarcastically.

By March, the plans were completed, a builder was hired, and construction began. The mess drove Carol crazy, but they were both very pleased with the extra space when it was finished. Thanks to Carol's decorating expertise, the one-bedroom apartment with a luxury bath was elegant yet understated. An open concept living room and kitchen area was bright with natural light from the patio door and an egress window in the bedroom. In addition, light tubes brought sunlight from the roof to the darker interior areas of the basement. Limestone accent walls, light gray cabinetry, recessed lighting, and sleek granite countertops were understated but gracious. Jim laid limestone in the corner of the living room and inserted a small wood-burning Franklin stove. Using her online shopping expertise, Carol found discontinued yet comfortable furniture pieces to put the final touches on the space.

Now, after the escapade at the morgue, Jim stood in the late afternoon sunlight that streamed into their living room, phoning his daughter, Sara.

"Hi, Dad! What's up? Is the baby here?"

"Hi, sweetheart. No, not yet. Listen, something's come up that Carol and I want to discuss with you." *You'll never believe it,* he mused. "I know it's short notice, but we wondered if you'd like to come over for dinner tonight? I'll grill."

"Love to. Time?"

"Sixish?"

"I'll be there."

By five-thirty, Carol had managed to bathe and dress Lillie in some new play clothes and a new pair of sneakers they'd picked up at Target. Digging through the boxes of junk in the garage's rafters, Jim found a container of the twins' old toys. Lillie was enthralled with her new Elsa doll from the movie *Frozen* they had bought for her.

Jim lit the charcoal on the grill. They'd picked up ribeye steaks at Festival on the way home. A simple tossed salad and baked potatoes would accompany the steaks. The crunching of gravel on the driveway and a short blurp of a car horn told them Sara had arrived. Charging through the front door, she inspected Carol. Each week of the pregnancy, she'd seemed to expand a little more.

"Hey, how's it going?" Sara asked. Her blonde hair and crystal blue eyes gave ample evidence of her Nordic roots. She beamed a high wattage smile. Carol walked up to her, giving her an enthusiastic hug. Suddenly, from around the corner, a bright-eyed little girl appeared. Holding Elsa under her arm, Lillie smiled shyly and took stock of Sara.

"And who have we here?" Sara asked, stooping down to gaze into Lillie's blue eyes.

"My name is Lillie, and I'm staying with Bapa and Carol," she said intelligently. There was silence. Carol watched Sara's confusion playing across her face like waves on a turbulent lake. She could understand the feelings. They were still trying to wrap their heads around all that had happened since lunch.

"I see … Carol?" Sara said, cocking her head at an angle, although it was obvious she really didn't understand what was going on.

"It's a long story that I think we'll tell you *after* dinner," was all Carol would say, giving Sara a perceptive glance and a wink.

"Gotcha," Sara said, reading Carol's expression perfectly.

After dinner, when dusk began to descend, Carol corralled Lillie into a bedtime routine. After a change into pajamas, a banana, and bedtime stories, she finally slept, exhausted from the emotionally draining day.

Out on the patio, Jim had built a fire. The coals glowed and gave off waves of warm, relaxing heat. The sun was just slipping down over the horizon, and the air grew chilly. Close by, the unexpected hooting of a long-eared owl penetrated the stillness of the growing darkness.

"Excuse me?" Sara said incredulously after Jim had filled her in on the afternoon's revelations. "This is either a fairy tale in the making or a horror story. Which is it?" she asked pointedly, sitting forward in her chair. She simply could not wrap her head around it. *Since Mom died, you get yourself in the most bizarre predicaments,* she thought.

"I haven't decided yet," Jim said. "I don't know." He sat in the Adirondack chair near the fire pit, sipping absentmindedly on a Leinie's beer.

"And I thought having a baby when you're fifty-two was crazy," Sara mumbled.

"There's that, too," Jim agreed. Sara had rarely seen her father perplexed except when her mom was dying. Now she noticed his sagging shoulders and worried expression. Carol slipped out of the patio door and joined them. She leaned down and tenderly kissed Jim. Sitting down carefully, she folded her hands across her expansive middle, enjoying the warmth of the fire in the coolness of the evening.

"Has your dad asked you yet?" Carol inquired, glancing at Sara over the coals.

"Asked me what?" Sara responded. Carol lifted her eyebrows tellingly as she looked at Jim.

"I just filled her in on the afternoon's events," Jim told Carol. He turned to Sara and continued explaining. "Before all this stuff happened today, we intended to use the basement as guest quarters—a place where you could stay when we needed an overnight sitter. I know this probably won't come as a surprise, but this whole scenario with Lillie's arrival and the baby about to be born any day has left us in a tailspin. It's totally unfair to ask you, but we wondered if you'd consider moving in immediately and using the basement as your own apartment. That way, when the baby comes, you can be right here when we need you," Jim finished. Sara stared open-mouthed at the suggestion. Jim hurried on. "It's okay if you want to think about it for a few days."

An inscrutable expression crossed Sara's face. She was silent for a while, considering her options.

"If you don't like the idea, I can totally relate," Jim finally said, frustrated. "Like I said, none of this is what we had planned."

"Hold on, Dad. Hold on," she said hurriedly. "Calm down. I can see where it might work. School ends next week, and then I'll be relatively free. I would be willing to consider it, but I can see the need to set up some boundaries for it to work. I want my autonomy, and I'll need to respect your privacy and family time. But we might be able to work something out that's agreeable to us all."

"Really?" Carol said, her voice hopeful for the first time that day.

"Yeah, really," Sara said, smiling broadly. "The apartment is gorgeous. What's not to like?"

"See, honey? I told you she was a great kid," Jim said proudly. He stopped and said seriously, "But you *will* be paying rent."

"And I *will* be charging you for babysitting," Sara retorted, grinning at Jim.

"She is truly her father's daughter," Carol remarked, a warm smile spreading across her face. ◙

SUNDAY,
MAY 12

5

Sam Birkstein pedaled over the gravel surface of the La Crosse River Bike Trail in the bright spring sunshine, his legs churning as he headed northeast toward West Salem. Bucolic farmland rolled by as he enjoyed the beauty of the coulees and bluffs. Here and there, he encountered herds of Holstein cows grazing in knee-high grass in contented bovine bliss. In desperate need of exercise, he reveled in the vigorous workout that made his breath quicken and blood pulse in his limbs.

His mind wandered back to the events at Riverside Park yesterday. Since he'd joined the investigative team almost four years ago, he'd rarely seen Higgins come unglued, even in dangerous situations on the job. The developments yesterday, as shocking as they seemed to be on the surface, now seemed less threatening in the brilliant sunshine.

All in all, he thought Carol and Jim had handled the bombshell well after the initial revelation. Better than he would have. But the mysterious woman found in Riverside Park was an enigma that made Sam squirm with misgivings. Where had she come from? Was she really Higgins' sibling, or was that just a ploy to place the child in a safer environment? Who was she? Why did she die?

He'd spent most of Saturday afternoon and the early evening hours checking out the homeless population near Riverside Park and the Mobil Oil property—a sixty-five-acre natural area where the La Crosse River meets the Mississippi. Despite walking through the tent city at the north end of Riverside Park where the woman had been found, his interviews with some residents were discouraging. He understood how people could fall off the face of the earth without anyone being the wiser. He'd scoured the marsh trails. Then he'd visited several shelters within the city limits. None of the transients he'd met recognized Juliette. Yesterday's lack of clues left him frustrated.

"I don't know that lady," an older black man said, intently studying the photo on Sam's phone. Shaking his wizened head back and forth, he continued. "I never saw her before. You say she had a little girl with her?" He squinted up at Sam, his demeanor guarded, his eyes suspicious.

"Yeah. The little girl was blonde. We're trying to figure out when they arrived in La Crosse and find anyone who has seen or talked to them," Sam explained, watching the black man carefully.

The black man's tent was surrounded by bikes in various states of disrepair. Parts and tools were scattered around the wooded site. Other tents and hand-constructed shelters dotted the shady grove. Cardboard and wooden pallets seemed to be popular building materials. Small fires smoldered, and clothes flapped uneasily on impromptu lines tied from tree to tree. Once in a while, Sam caught sight of other people moving around, tending their fires, and cooking simple meals.

"How long have you lived here?" Sam asked the old man, taking in the surroundings. *This would be the last place I'd want to live,* he thought.

"I come up here from Charleston in April. I been trying to establish a bike business, but it's tough goin'," he said. Sam could see the sadness and despair in his eyes. "But I believe in workin' hard, and I like to use my hands."

"That's good," Sam said, trying to encourage him. A tense silence followed. "Well, if you hear anything, you can call me at this number. Take care out here," he said, handing him his card. He wasn't even sure the man had a phone.

"I'll do that," the black man replied. Sam doubted he'd hear from him again. No matter who he talked to in these shifting communities, he felt he was being stonewalled. Without any real leads, he called a cop friend from city police for some help.

"Rory? It's Sam Birkstein."

"Hey. How's things in your world?" Rory asked.

"I need to call in a favor," Sam said without answering Rory's question.

"Sure. But you'll owe me a coupla beers Friday night," Rory suggested. Sam could imagine his friendly smile on the other end.

"No problem. You might have heard of the homeless woman that was found dead over in Tent City by Riverside."

"Nope. Don't know anything about it. Been off-duty this weekend."

"We're trying to find witnesses who might have talked to her or who have information about her. We think she was homeless, but we're not really sure about that. She had a four-year-old girl with her. I know you work pretty closely with that population. I was just wondering if you could ask around. I've tried, but I seem to be hitting a brick wall," Sam finished, letting out a sigh.

"The homeless population is very cautious. Their trust levels are pretty low, but I know a lot of them on a first-name basis. I'll check around and let you know. Might take me a while."

"Hey. I appreciate it, but sooner is better than later," Sam said.

"I hear you. Oh, by the way, you got a name for this homeless woman?" A moment went by. "Sam? Are you there?"

"Yeah ... For right now, just use the name Juliette."

"You mean like Romeo and Juliette?" Rory asked, his curiosity piqued.

"Yeah, like Romeo and Juliette," Sam said. *More like Jim and*

Juliette, he thought. "I'll send you a photo. And thanks, Rory."

"Sure. I'll let you know if I come across anything."

Sam stopped at a turnout on the bike trail where a rough wooden bench sat in the shade of a soft maple. Dismounting, he pulled a water bottle and an energy bar from his backpack. A breeze wafted through the leaves, causing a rippling sound, evaporating the sweat on his face. He sat down and began munching his snack.

He wished he could get past the ache in his chest and the frequent thoughts about Leslie Brown, another detective he'd worked with in the department. He realized now that he'd taken her presence for granted. He still couldn't fully accept that she was really gone. Their final conversation several months ago kept replaying itself in his mind at the most inopportune times—like now when he was supposed to be relaxing. His thoughts returned to that difficult parting conversation many months ago.

"You're what?" he'd asked, standing in her apartment. His mouth fell open in astonished surprise.

"I'm taking a job with ICE in Chicago. It's too good to pass up, Sam."

"I can't believe you didn't tell me," he said, his voice wavering in disbelief, notching up in volume. Paco, her black lab and constant companion, growled a low warning.

"Well, I'm telling you now," she said quietly. "Please, don't be mad. We'll still see each other." But it was a lame promise, and Sam guessed that would never happen. Leslie squirmed uncomfortably as he continued to stare at her wide-eyed.

"I knew it," he finally said, wanting to lay the guilt on her. "I knew when things started getting serious, you'd run away." He was huffing now, and the tightness in his chest made him feel like he was suffocating. He turned in a little compact circle, coming back to face her. "God, I must be the stupidest chump on the face of the earth," he sputtered. "How dumb could I be?"

"Please don't say that. You're wonderful, Sam," Leslie said. "You told me once that God has a plan for my life. I believe that this job is part of that plan. This is an opportunity of a lifetime. You've helped me in so many ways. Please don't—"

He rudely interrupted her. "I fought for you!" he yelled furiously, not hearing a word she'd said. "I defended you and protected you from that killer, Wade Bennett!" He made a wide curving gesture with his hand. "Do you even care about that?" Tears stung his eyes.

"Sam," she said tenderly. "I didn't ask you to do that, but I ..." She reached and grasped his hand, but he pushed it away and stepped back from her a few feet. By now, tears were glistening in his dark hazel eyes.

"Don't ... " he said, holding up his hand. "Don't do the apology tour. I don't want your sympathy," he said roughly. They stood in the imposing silence, avoiding eye contact.

"I'm sorry, Sam. I never meant to hurt you." By now, Leslie was crying, too. Sam watched her carefully, taking a measure of her words, noticing her tears.

"Maybe ... maybe you're sorry. But you'll never be as sorry as I am." He leaned toward her, kissed her tenderly on her cheek, pivoted, and walked out of the apartment.

He drove aimlessly for a couple of hours until he found himself down by the river. He sat in his car as the engine ticked and cooled in the frigid January air. He thought about going into one of the local establishments and getting wasted, but he knew that would only delay what he would feel tomorrow. Instead, he got out of his car and walked through Riverside Park, oblivious to the weather, the cold, the people, or anything else.

In his mind, he railed against God; Leslie; her abusive boyfriend, Wade Bennett; and everything else that had led him to fall in love with her. His thoughts rumbled around in his mind like a tumbleweed rolling across a desert. He wore himself out with criticism and anger. And then, he drove home and curled up in bed, sobbing until he finally slept.

The loose waves of dark hair stirred in the breeze and brought him back to reality. He closed his eyes, reveling in the peace and

SUE BERG

quiet. He knew he had to move on. His juvenile hopes that she'd return were unrealistic. She was gone. She'd made her choices. He had to find a way to accept that and get on with his life.

He suddenly remembered he hadn't prayed for her for many weeks. Maybe he really was accepting her absence. Now, instead, he prayed for himself. *God, I need your help. What about the plan for my life? What about that, huh?* ◘

MONDAY,
MAY 13

6

The peaceful routine that Carol and Jim usually enjoyed in the morning was fast receding in the rearview mirror. Jim was sure it was a thing of the past. *Where did my second cup of morning coffee go? What about my time to read the newspaper?* he asked himself. *You should've thought of that when you were making mad, passionate love to your wife without any protection, getting her pregnant at forty-two.* On top of all that, Miss Lillie arrived on Saturday, and their world had turned upside down—again. Jim supposed this was the beginning of their new normal.

He showered, and during his morning shave, Miss Lillie wandered in and out of the bathroom asking questions.

"Bapa, why do you have whiskers?" she said, clutching Elsa under her arm.

Jim took another swipe with his razor, watching Lillie tilt her head in four-year-old fascination.

"Don't know. That's just how God made me, I guess," he said patiently. While he dressed, the questions continued.

"Why do you have to be all dressed up so fancy?" her little voice squeaked.

"Well, I'm a detective, and these clothes are what I'm supposed to wear to work." *Of course, that doesn't include Sam,* he thought, frowning to himself.

"Who says?"

"My boss."

"Who's that?"

And on and on and on. Jim had forgotten how many questions a four-year-old could dream up.

At the breakfast table, they ate their scrambled eggs and toast, accompanied by Lillie's nonstop chatter. If speaking was any indication of intelligence, then by those standards alone, Lillie could be considered brilliant.

With the unexpected arrival of another child, Carol was feeling overwhelmed by all the things she still wanted to complete before their baby arrived, so she'd decided to begin her maternity leave a little early. Today she'd have to clean out the craft room and convert it into a bedroom for Lillie.

Saturday night, Jim tried to get in some serious reading before going to sleep. Nothing relaxed him more than an exciting, fast-paced story. He'd been looking forward to a new novel in the Nathan Caslin detective series by JM Dalgliesh. But the changes they'd been through the last few days were still too new.

"Jim, do you think I should start my leave Monday?" Carol asked, laying down her magazine. Decisions had to be made, and that required discussion. He turned over the corner of the page in the novel, laid the book on his nightstand, and gave his full attention to Carol. Pulling her close, he gently caressed her bulging bump.

"Just take your leave, honey," Jim counseled her. "You've got a great boss, and you've been training that new girl for two weeks. Luke'll be fine with it. For Pete's sake, he was there when this whole thing went down with Lillie," Jim said. "Besides, you've got a gazillion days of personal leave. Situations like this are what they're for."

Carol nodded in agreement. "Yeah, I know. You're right," she said, but apprehension lingered in her remark.

"What's wrong then?" Jim asked, kissing her hair.

She blew out her cheeks in frustration. "I don't know ... " Jim waited. "Do you think I'll be a good mom?" she asked softly.

"Sweetheart, I couldn't think of anyone who'd be better," Jim said.

"Well, this whole thing is kind of overwhelming—first our baby coming any day, and then Lillie appearing on our doorstep. It's the kind of the stuff you see on *Dr. Phil.*"

Jim chuckled. "It is pretty unbelievable. I hear you, hon. But God didn't give us children so we'd fail. He gave us children because He knew we were the ones they really needed. And there's no denying that Lillie needed a soft landing somewhere."

"Mmm, she is a beautiful child, isn't she? I think I'm going to go to sleep with that thought in my mind." She reached up and gave Jim a tender kiss. "We'll be fine."

"Yes, we will," he agreed. Carol rolled over, and soon Jim could hear her regular breathing. He picked up his novel again.

Now, as the morning light streamed through the dining room window, Jim finished his coffee and carried his dishes to the dishwasher. Lillie trotted behind him like a little puppy dog.

"Bapa?"

"Yes, Lillie."

"Will you come home again?" Her question traveled like an arrow into Jim's heart.

He knelt down uncomfortably, his knees creaking. Gazing into Lillie's eyes, he said, "Of course I will. Are you worried I might not come back?" Carol was standing next to the counter listening.

"That's what happened to Grandma, and now I'll never see her again."

The poignancy of the moment made Carol cringe inwardly as she bit her lower lip. Jim's eyes locked on Carol. Lillie's glistening tears reminded him of the sad journey that had brought her to their doorstep. He held both of her tiny hands in his.

"You're safe here. I'm sad for you that your grandma went away. But we're going to make sure you have everything you need."

Lillie scooted into Jim's arms, burying her head in his crisp shirt. *She's certainly found her way into our hearts,* he thought, hugging her tightly. *Could we let her go even if we find out the will isn't real?*

"Okay. Time for a fist bump and a kiss," Jim announced, untangling himself from the hug. He'd read somewhere that establishing little rituals with kids gave them a sense of stability and security.

Lillie enthusiastically followed Jim's example. He grinned at the sloppy, messy kiss she gave him and discreetly wiped his mouth on his sleeve. Carol smiled, watching the scene.

"I love you, Bapa."

"Be a good girl today," Jim added. ◘

7

The parking lot of the Law Enforcement Center on Vine Street was humming with activity as Jim stepped out of his Suburban. Bikers whizzed by uncomfortably close to live traffic. Other law enforcement personnel were arriving, locking their car doors and heading into the building. The sound of a distant ambulance siren pierced the bustle of morning traffic.

Jim stopped a moment and tipped his head upward toward the warm sunshine, stretching his muscles in a backward leaning motion, enjoying the fragrant morning air—a mix of blooming lilacs and recently mown grass. He set out across the parking lot.

After the shocking news he'd learned about the possibility of an unknown sibling on Saturday, Jim was struggling with the fact that he might really have a sister. *Unbelievable.* Stepping out of the elevator on the third floor, Jim was greeted with one of Emily Warehauser's radiant smiles.

"Good morning, Chief. No baby yet?" she asked, looking up briefly from her computer.

"Not yet. Listen, when Paul and Sam arrive, send them right into my office," he ordered in brisk fashion, not stopping to chat as he usually did. He turned, walked down the hall, entered his office, and quietly closed the door.

Under her breath, Emily mumbled, "Expectant parents. Go figure."

In his office, Jim flipped his phone open and dialed Jensen Family Counseling Services in Holmen. After a greeting and introduction, Jim asked to speak to Vivian Jensen, Carol's psychologist sister and owner of the business.

"Do we have a baby?" she asked breathlessly when she came on the line.

"Sorry to disappoint. No baby yet. But I do have other news," Jim said seriously. "You might not believe what I'm going to tell you."

"Now you *are* scaring me," she replied, her voice tight with tension.

"This will take more than a phone conversation. I know you have patients, so could we meet for lunch?" Jim heard the rustling of papers and muffled voices. Finally, Vivian came back on the line.

"Sorry, I'm just checking my appointment book. How's one o'clock at Red Lobster sound?" she asked.

"Perfect. See you there."

Jim shut his phone and leaned back. Truth be told, these latest family developments were taking their toll. He wasn't sleeping well, and his anxious thoughts sometimes left him in a tailspin. Vivian would understand, and she could advise him about Lillie.

That little girl is a conundrum, Jim thought. He didn't exactly know what she'd experienced when Juliette died at Riverside Park or where their homeless travels had taken them. But he knew she was traumatized. Her recent fears and comments were proof of that. He didn't want to push the child to confide in him, but he hoped Vivian could suggest a direction.

A quiet knock on the door interrupted Jim's thoughts. Sam appeared, and Jim waved him in.

Dressed in dark blue dress slacks and a tailored dress shirt and tie, for once Sam looked like the professional he was supposed to be. Despite their conflicts over the department's dress code and his outrageous attire, which frequently sent Jim into fashion convulsions, Sam had proven his mettle in a couple of recent difficult cases. Jim found himself relying more and more on his quick mind and keen analytic thinking.

He noticed Sam's serious, sad demeanor. It was like a cloak of depression had wrapped itself around him since Detective Leslie Brown had departed for Chicago. They all missed Leslie, but Sam had been the most affected. He'd been especially quiet and reserved since her departure. A song floated into Jim's head. *Please help me mend my broken heart and let me live again.* Jim was pretty sure Sam wouldn't even know who the Bee Gees were.

"Nice shirt," Jim said casually, his eyes scanning his threads.

"Thanks. So how was the weekend with Miss Lillie?" Sam asked, lifting his eyes to meet Jim's gaze. He pulled a chair over to the desk from the corner of the office and sat down.

"Nonstop questions. I forgot that it's four-year-olds who really run this world. I bet I've answered two hundred questions since she came on Saturday." Jim let out a pent-up sigh.

Sam smiled. "Sounds to me like a detective in the making."

"I hadn't thought of it that way," Jim said, disgruntled. Another knock at the door.

Paul Saner strolled into the office and plopped down in another chair in front of Jim's desk. He looked chipper and rested. He'd been shot last November in a raid near the tiny town of Avalanche in Vernon County, and his recovery had been long and painful, both physically and emotionally. He finally seemed to have turned a corner, returning to work at the end of February. Jim was keeping tabs on his sessions with the department's psychologist. Paul been faithful about attending, and Jim hoped it was helping.

"Morning, guys. What's up?" Paul asked, sipping on a steaming cup of coffee.

"Lots of stuff, most of it unbelievable," Jim mumbled as he unfolded the facts about the victim found in Riverside Park near the Mississippi River.

"Say what? She's a sister you never knew you had?" Paul asked, dumbfounded. His eyes widened, and he held his coffee cup in mid-air. "How's that work?"

"Good question. How does that work? I don't have a sister that I know of, so I don't see how it's possible, but ... " Jim's voice trailed off. Turning in his office chair, he gazed out the window, brooding.

Sam filled in the details, continuing the narrative. "I spent a good portion of the weekend trying to find someone in the homeless community who knew Juliette and Lillie or had seen them arrive.

Nothing. So I guess now it's up to Luke and the DNA report. That'll give us some answers."

"How you doin' with all this, Chief?" Paul asked pointedly.

Turning back to face them, he blew his cheeks out in a huff. "Well, how would you be doing after discovering you may have a sibling you knew nothing about, you gain custody of a four-year-old, and your forty-two-year-old wife is pregnant and ready to deliver any day?" Jim asked, his voice gruff, his blue eyes flashing. He straightened his tie, then ran his hand through his gray-blond hair. "Let me know how you'd handle it," he finished impatiently, crossing his arms over his chest.

"Okay. Okay. I get your point," Paul said, taking a sip of coffee.

Sam spoke up again, still in the investigative mode. "I checked Tent City, Chief, and the Mobil lot and the shelters Saturday afternoon and evening. The homeless are a reluctant crowd—pretty tight-lipped. Didn't get any hits on Facebook. I asked a cop friend to check in with his regular sources. He's going to let me know if he finds anything out. I also checked Twitter and Snapchat, but there was nothing there either. I updated the post. We might get something. We'll see what happens."

"All right. This morning I want you guys to check transportation into the city—taxis, buses, and trains," Jim began. "She could have driven here, too, but I doubt it. She had to get here somehow. Someone must have seen her." Shifting topics, he asked, "How are we coming with our evidence for the Bennett case? The trial is set to start in a couple of weeks," Jim reminded them, checking his calendar.

"We're plugging along," Sam reported. He returned to their original line of inquiry. "What about Lillie? Would she have remembered anything about their trip to La Crosse?" Sam asked.

"I'm sure she would, but I haven't pushed her on that subject," Jim said. "First of all, a four-year-old's version of reality can be pretty skewed, and I need to give her a little time to absorb everything that's happened to her before I start ... quizzing her." Jim struggled with the idea of questioning a little child. There were limits to his investigative sensibilities.

"Well, she's our only witness right now," Sam reminded Jim.

"I know. That's what bothers me," Jim said softly. "That's why we've got to find somebody who's seen Juliette or talked to her. So you guys work on how she arrived in La Crosse, and I'm going to dig into her background. I'll start downstairs at the Clerk of Courts."

The two detectives stood and started toward the door. Sam turned back.

"What about closed-circuit cameras down by the park?" he said.

"Worth a try. You might see her coming or going, maybe getting off a bus or getting out of a cab," Jim hypothesized. Then he thought, *Not with twenty-seven cents in her pocket.*

"We'll check it out," Paul said. "Good luck on your end."

"Yeah, I'll need luck ... or something like it," Jim said.

Jim spent half an hour of research in the Clerk of Courts office downstairs on the main floor of the law enforcement and county government facility. He located his birth certificate, but none was on file for a Juliette Lindvig.

Back in his office, he searched the Vital Records Service of the Wisconsin Department of Health Services. There he learned that when children are adopted, their birth certificates are impounded by the state and are not available for viewing without a written request. He downloaded a form that would allow him to view Juliette's adoption information and birth record.

Then he went on the internet using search engines specifically related to finding lost siblings.

On a site called *The Seeker,* he was able to locate a Juliette Marquart who lived in Wausau, Wisconsin. An address and phone number were listed, but it was disconnected and no longer in service when Jim tried the number. He phoned the Wausau Police Department, and they referred him to Officer Darryl Hines, a liaison between the police and Social Service system. Jim explained his dilemma and asked him to visit the address and find out what he could. Any information would be helpful.

Sighing with frustration, he leaned back in his chair. His cell chirped.

"Jim Higgins," he said, his weariness coming through.

"Hello, Lt. Higgins. It's Leslie," a soft voice said shyly.

Jim sat up, then leaned over his desk, his elbows resting on top.

"Leslie. Nice to hear from you. What can I do for you?"

"Well, I'm in sort of a bind. The ICE job is not what I expected. I won't bore you with the details, but I really miss working with a team. Frankly, I miss the investigative aspects of being a detective. So there are two things I need your help with," she said, stalling for a moment, "if you wouldn't mind."

"Sure. I'll help in whatever way I can." Jim rubbed his hand across his face impatiently.

"First, is my job still available, or has it been filled?"

"No, it hasn't been filled. The wheels of government move slowly."

"Do you think there's a chance Sheriff Jones would hire me back?"

Jim thought carefully before he answered. "I think I can create a rationale for re-hiring you. I can try and plead your case with Jones, justifying your absence as leave due to injury on the job. I can try anyway. But you have to be sure this is what you really want. Administration isn't going to be happy if you come back only to leave again in six months."

"Oh, I understand that," she said, sounding hopeful.

"So, what's the other thing?" Jim asked. *I already know—Sam.*

"Sam and I didn't part on good terms. In fact, he was very hurt and angry. Since I'd have to work with him again if I came back, I wondered what you thought would be the best way to find out if he can handle the situation ... " she trailed off.

"Well, technically, he has no choice. If you're hired back, he has to work with you. But on a personal level, that may be harder than you think, especially if he resents you or there are hard feelings between you."

"So, what should I do?" Leslie asked.

Kiss and make up, Jim thought. Then he reminded himself, *It's none of my business.*

Instead, he said, "Let me do some checking first to even see if there's a possibility you can come back. If you can, then I'll approach Sam and see how he reacts. Or you can show up and test the waters yourself, but I'm going to shoot straight. I'd love to have you back, but I don't want to lose Sam in the process. So before you make any firm commitments, make sure you know what you're in for."

"Yes, I get that. I'll wait to hear back from you, sir," she finished.

"Can I leave a text or message?" Jim asked.

"Sure, and thanks, Chief."

"No problem."

Checking the time, Jim flipped his phone shut. *More sticky personal problems I don't really have time for,* he thought. He grabbed his suit jacket, closed the door, and headed to Red Lobster in Onalaska for lunch with Vivian.

The day was gorgeous. Temperatures close to seventy-five, puffy cotton ball clouds floating in a crisp blue sky, lawns and trees greening up. The sandstone bluffs that towered over La Crosse were shimmering in the early afternoon sunlight. At Bluffside Golf Course, Jim could see golfers teeing off. People were driving carts around the course in seemingly random patterns. Pedaling furiously along Losey Boulevard, a biker clipped along, weaving through traffic, his jacket flapping wildly in the wind.

When Jim arrived, Red Lobster was bustling and packed with the local lunch crowd. He went in and secured a table. Vivian arrived a few minutes later, sliding into the booth opposite him.

"Sorry. I'm late," she apologized, catching her breath.

"No, you're fine. Let's order, and then I'll explain my dilemma," Jim said, taking charge.

When their food arrived, and Jim was sure they wouldn't be interrupted, he filled Vivian in on the weekend's events. Throughout his account, she said nothing. She ate, sometimes shaking her head in disbelief at the series of events that had brought Lillie to their doorstep.

"This sounds like something on one of those goofy Jerry Springer reality shows," she finally commented, holding a skewered shrimp mid-air. Her eyes behind her gold-framed glasses were wide with astonishment.

"That's what Carol said. You can't make this stuff up." He sighed wearily. "So here's my problem—or I should say *our* problem. Lillie probably witnessed Juliette's death. She knows more than she's saying. We're pretty worried about the trauma she's been through, being homeless and all." Jim's forehead wrinkled with a frown of concern, and his face was dark with worry. He'd loosened his tie, and Vivian noticed his exhausted look.

She leaned back from the table, pushing her plate away.

"Don't force her to share until she's ready," she advised. "Lillie has been through a significant upheaval in her little life. From all your descriptions, she's exhibiting the classic symptoms of a traumatic event: fear, crying, insecurity, and clinginess. That's understandable considering what she's been through."

Jim nodded in agreement. "She's just so sweet, Viv," he said tenderly. "Although she never shuts up," he finished with a wistful smile.

"From your description, she sounds like a cherub. But don't be surprised if she shows an uglier side at some point. She may turn aggressive and be quite naughty." Vivian smiled. "But you're an old hat. You know the drill—assure her of your love and be consistent in discipline. Carry on with your normal activities. She'll need lots of reassurance, and keep your promises so you can rebuild her sense of trust."

"Thanks, Viv. She's really latched onto me. I hope she can bond with Carol, too. Eventually."

"So you're taking this guardianship seriously?"

"If Lillie is blood family, then Carol and I will do our best to love her and raise her."

"How's Carol feel about that? Are you sure this is what she wants?"

Jim thought for a moment. "I think she's totally on board, but we'll have you out for a meal so you can meet Lillie and talk to Carol about it."

"And you need to have a few sessions with one of my staff if Juliette is really your lost sister," Vivian said assertively.

Jim waved his hand in a flippant toss. "I'll be fine."

"Jim, don't minimize this," she warned in a serious tone. "You may uncover some family secrets that will be quite unpleasant. Just promise me you'll take it to heart and get help if you need it."

Jim grew quiet. Then he nodded and said softly, "Yeah, I will. At least I have Carol in my corner."

"Yes. Yes, you do," Vivian said. "And that factor alone is a huge plus." ◘

8

By four-thirty, Jim had exhausted his efforts to gain any more knowledge about his sister. He was about to pack up and leave when his phone buzzed.

"Jim, it's Luke. I have the DNA and preliminary medical exam results. Do you want to come down, or do you want it over the phone?" Silence. "Jim?"

"Just let me have it," Jim said nervously.

"Juliette is your half-sister. I didn't mention it to you, but I took the liberty of taking a DNA sample from Lillie, too. She's related as well—probably your great-niece."

Jim slumped in his chair, letting out an ominous groan.

"There's more. You ready?"

"Go ahead. Let's hear it."

"Juliette was in the last stages of pancreatic cancer. She would have been in terrible pain at the end without proper pain medication. Frankly, I don't know how she took care of Lillie and arrived in La Crosse in one piece. That was an amazing feat of strength and determination on her part." He paused for a moment. "I'm sorry to give you this tough news," Luke said sympathetically. "One more thing. Juliette's remains? What should I do about that?"

"Send her body over to the Mortenson Crematorium. I'll call them and explain the situation."

"Right, Chief. Anything else I can do?"

"Yeah, call Carol and tell her, will you? I'm just leaving the office, and I don't like to talk on my phone when I'm driving. She's waiting to hear." A few moments of silence followed. "Thanks for your help, Luke."

"Sure. Let me know when the baby arrives," he said, trying to be positive.

"Will do."

Although Jim dreaded the phone call, he opened his cell and dialed his older brother, Dave Higgins, in Stockton, California. The phone rang several times and went to voicemail. Jim listened carefully, then left a nondescript message asking his brother to call him later that evening.

Jim sat in his office, ambivalent thoughts bouncing around in his head. When he finally came out of his stupor, he was amazed to feel the wetness on his cheeks. It was creeping up on five o'clock. He grabbed his suit coat, flung it over his shoulder, walked out of the office, and climbed on the elevator. The drive south on U.S. Highway 35 was busy with end-of-the-day traffic, but Jim didn't notice. He was a thousand miles away, wandering in the rooms of his memory.

The days of his childhood on his parents' farm in Glen Dale Coulee near Blair seemed as clear in his mind's eye as if they had happened yesterday. Reflections like a black and white movie film rolled along in his mind—playing in the creek with his brother, Dave, catching crawdads and watching them posing defensively with their miniature pincers in the air, and climbing trees. Hoisting boards aloft with a rope and pulley, he and his older brother engineered the construction of a lofty tree fort. In his dad's machine shop, the brothers had learned valuable hands-on skills that they still used every day. Jim recalled his mom beckoning them for supper after evening chores in the barn. Her tender kisses at night and her eloquent prayers for their safety and salvation so long ago seemed to speak to him now. He could almost hear her lilting Norwegian way of talking, her love expressing itself in a word and a touch.

He didn't remember turning onto Chipmunk Coulee Road or driving up his driveway. When he walked into the house from the garage, Lillie's excited cries of greeting brought him back to reality with a snap. He scooped her up and held her tight, smelling the baby shampoo in her hair and her tender skin. *My flesh and blood,* he thought, tears suddenly springing in his eyes.

Putting her down, Carol walked into his arms. She kissed him firmly.

"I'm here for you, honey. We're going to figure this out," she assured him, her brown eyes sympathetic.

Jim felt a tugging on his pants and heard a demanding little voice.

"Hey, what about me?" Lillie pouted, stomping her little foot.

Jim picked her up. "How about a triple hug?" he suggested.

"Comin' right up," said Carol, enjoying Lillie's squeals of delight when Jim nuzzled her with his whiskers. "Supper in fifteen minutes. Meatloaf and mashed potatoes."

"Sounds great," Jim said, smiling for the first time that day.

Shortly after seven that evening, Jim's cell rang.

"Dave?"

"Yeah, what's going on? You usually don't call me during the week."

"Well, some things are happening on this end that I'm having a hard time reconciling in my moral framework."

"This coming from a cop? That doesn't sound good. What's up?" Dave said.

"Did you know we have a sister?" Jim asked.

The silence was complete until Dave finally said, "What's this all about? Tell me."

Jim proceeded to fill him in on the DNA results from Juliette, the appearance of Lillie, and the subsequent legal affairs that landed

SUE BERG

her in Jim and Carol's care. But weighing heavier on Jim's mind were the ambivalent feelings he had about the secrets their parents had kept from them.

"I never thought I'd say this, especially to you," Jim said, "but this is one instance where being single might be an advantage in the general scheme of things."

"How so? You've always enjoyed your marital bliss, right?"

"Yeah. But when age starts creeping up on you and you find yourself in a time frame more appropriate to a thirty-something, it tends to stop you in your tracks," Jim explained. "Expecting a baby at fifty-two and having a four-year-old materialize like a genie out of a bottle can warp your sense of things to some degree."

"You'll be fine. Look at it this way—you've been there and done that already."

They talked a while about the odd circumstances that had catapulted them into a past they thought they both knew.

"Hey, you'll call me when you find out more details, right?" Dave asked.

"Absolutely. Take care, brother," Jim finished. He quietly shut his phone and walked toward the bathroom to help Lillie get ready for bed.

During the night, Jim was startled awake. By what, he wasn't sure. A dream? A noise in the house? Something had roused him from the first decent sleep he'd had in a week. Listening in the dark, he heard soft breathing, then a little hiccup.

"Bapa, I'm scared," Lillie squeaked. She'd obviously been crying. "I miss Grandma."

Jim reached over and turned on the light. Lillie squinted her eyes shut protectively. Carol sat up, confused.

"I'll deal with this," Jim said, gently pushing Carol back down and covering her shoulders with the quilt.

"Elsa's gone. She's lost," Lillie whimpered, "just like Grandma."

Throwing back the covers, Jim picked up Lillie, carrying her into the makeshift bedroom.

"Well, if Elsa's lost, then we've got to search for her. She's got to be here somewhere," he whispered, peeking under the pillow and turning back the sheets. Searching under the bed, Lillie shouted, "There she is!" Jim retrieved the doll and tucked Lillie back in bed, pulling up the lightweight quilt. Jim shut off the bedside lamp, the night light giving the room a warm ambient glow.

"I saw her when Grandma died," she said softly as Jim reached down to kiss her.

"What do you mean—you saw her?" Jim asked curiously. A prickle of goosebumps raised the hair on his arms. He sat on the bed next to her, his arms on each side of her little body. Lillie stared up at him.

"She came for Grandma. She had a pretty dress, and she was very beautiful. She sang a song, and then she took Grandma's hand. That's when they left, and I was all alone." Tears spilled onto Lillie's cheeks. Her eyes were like pools of blue sadness. She began to cry softly. A shiver ran up Jim's spine.

"Well, you're not alone anymore. I was here when you needed me tonight, wasn't I?" Jim asked.

Wordlessly, Lillie nodded her head. "Will you always be here, Bapa?"

Thinking back to Vivian's advice, Jim thought, *Be careful what you promise.*

"I will try to always be here for you, Lillie." He kissed her again, taking in her scent.

"Promise?"

"Promise."

"Night, Bapa."

"Night, Lillie."

When Jim returned to bed, Carol rolled up against him, moaning in her sleep. Jim kissed her hand tenderly as she flopped her arm over him. He lay awake for a while, trying to absorb all the changes they'd been through. Lillie's revelation was surprising in an oddly comforting way. *Angelic beings?* Jim truly believed they existed. Was that what Lillie had seen?

After a few moments, the warmth of Carol's body, the lingering smell of Lillie's skin, and the soft rain on the roof made him drowsy. Deep sleep washed over him like an ocean wave as he drifted off. ◘

TUESDAY,
MAY 14

9

The sunny days that had pushed temperatures to nearly seventy degrees on Monday afternoon disappeared overnight. A steady drizzle fell until it was gradually replaced by tiny raindrops. By noon, thundershowers were expected to blanket the entire southwestern corner of the Coulee Region. A haze of blue-gray fog swallowed the river and substantially reduced visibility on the roads. The murky atmosphere did nothing to slow traffic. Drivers continued to weave erratically in and out of snarl-ups, desperate to reach their destinations.

Jeremy Bjerkes, senior partner of the Bjerkes and Oates Funeral Home on Fifth Street on the south side of La Crosse, sat at his desk in the early morning, periodically gazing out his office window, waiting patiently for his new intern to arrive.

Layne McNally hailed from De Soto, just down the river below Genoa. His credentials from Des Moines Area Community College were impeccable—a solid A student who displayed a friendly yet serious demeanor. He had finished the requirements for a bachelor's degree in Mortuary Science, graduating with honors on April 26. Fulfilling an internship was the only thing left before he could take his state boards and become a full-fledged licensed mortician.

In addition to his college achievements, Layne's high school references fairly glowed and leaped from the pages. An Eagle Scout and honor student all four years at Luther High School, his recommendations included enthusiastic praise from his wrestling and baseball coaches—an all-around classy kid. Jeremy just hoped all the hoopla came with a solid work ethic.

The stress of comforting shocked, grieving families trying to come to terms with the death of a loved one required a particular kind of mental toughness balanced with a compassionate nature. Not everyone could do it. Layne's recommendations, what Jeremy considered the fluff of inflated opinions from teachers and professors, wouldn't go far when it came to the grunt work required to prepare a body for viewing and burial. Mortuary work frequently involved odd hours and trips to out-of-the-way places, picking up bodies in various states of decay. Furthermore, death rarely occurred during regular business hours and at predictable intervals. It was either feast or famine. The profession was certainly not for the fainthearted.

As he waited for Layne to arrive, Jeremy thought about his conversation earlier in the morning with his business partner, Lyle Oates.

"What kind of a question is that?" Lyle had asked suspiciously, lowering the *La Crosse Sentinel* a notch. Beneath his outdated knit suit jacket, his beer gut stretched his polyester dress shirt until he looked like a stuffed synthetic blimp. His tie hung at a funny angle, and he smelled like he hadn't showered in several days. Grizzled whiskers sprouted on his cheeks and chin, and his hair needed trimming—not the image a professional businessman should be projecting to the public.

"It's a valid question. Are you considering retirement?" Jeremy repeated, his eyes hardening as he confronted his partner. Lyle continued to stare over the top of his newspaper with contempt.

"Lyle, you're sixty-two," Jeremy reminded him. "Most people your age begin to at least think about retirement. Some start playing a little more golf or go fishing one or two days a week to ease into it.

Or maybe you could volunteer somewhere in town. I'm just trying to help you consider your options."

Jeremy turned his attention again to the required state paperwork on his desk. The bureaucratic rat race never ended. Lyle lowered the newspaper he'd been reading and laid it on the sofa next to him. He crossed one leg over the other, resting an ankle on his knee. His mismatched socks stuck out as his dress pants rode up over his ankles. Jeremy rolled his eyes at the sight of the socks. He hoped they could have a civil discussion and make some important business decisions, but that didn't seem likely.

When Lyle failed to respond, Jeremy said, "You're not going to live forever, you know."

"I know that, you twit," Lyle said rudely.

So much for civility, Jeremy thought. He often wondered how Lyle could be so pleasant to their customers and be such an ass to him. He tried again, locking eyes with Lyle, challenging his crotchety attitude.

"So, what are your plans?" he asked calmly. "This new intern looks very promising, and if he works out like I hope he will, I may offer him the opportunity to join the business as a partner."

Lyle poised tensely on the edge of the couch. Suddenly he leaned forward in an aggressive move. "You can't do that!" he said loudly, his face reddening.

"Yes, I can. And I will," Jeremy said firmly, his eyes flat with resolve. "Lest you forget, I have fifty-one percent interest in the business; you only have forty-nine. I have every right to protect the future of Bjerkes and Oates. I'll be fifty years old this July. I'm going to need some help around here when you decide to retire."

"Stop saying that word!" Lyle snarled, his irritation reaching a peak.

"What? Retirement?" Jeremy questioned, a sly grin crossing his lips. "Well, how about this word—termination? How do you like the sound of *that* word? After the last disgusting drunken escapade when you shaved off Mr. Grindle's mustache that he'd had for the last twenty years and his wife had a hissy fit, I could have fired you. I *should* have fired you. Thank God his family was understanding and didn't take us to the cleaners, although they did get a significant discount on their bill."

"Do you always have to throw all my failures in my face?" Lyle shouted, jumping to his feet. "I told you I've been goin' to AA for the last month. The next thing you know, you'll be getting a breathalyzer machine in here so you can perform random breath tests. Balls, what a friggin' joke this place has become! A guy can't even have a beer once in a while!" Lyle turned and headed to the main lobby, spewing profanities and cursing as he blasted through the front door.

Jeremy sighed. *If we could just have a civil conversation, it would help.* He lifted his head and glanced at the gloomy fog outside. A compact, dark blue Nissan Leaf pulled up under the entrance's canopy to the funeral home. A young, well-built man jumped out of the vehicle, flipped his car keys in his pocket, and walked energetically through the front door. Jeremy stood up and walked to the main lobby, stepping forward and thrusting out his hand.

"Welcome to Berkes and Oates, Layne. We're so glad to have you here." Layne's face broke into a welcoming, friendly smile, and his handshake was firm with self-confidence.

"Good to be here, sir. I'm looking forward to working with you," he gushed.

The exuberance of youth, Jeremy thought. *That's what we need around here.* "Come on. Let me show you around the place, and then you can move your car into the visitor's lot."

By nine-thirty, Jeremy and Layne had finished the tour of the mortuary facility. Layne was attentive and asked interesting and challenging questions. After he'd moved his car, Jeremy decided to put him to work preparing a female from one of the nursing homes who'd been brought in late last night. Her viewing and visitation was scheduled for Thursday.

Jeremy walked back to the business office to the left of the main entrance. It was quiet. He was looking forward to completing the paperwork he'd started earlier that morning. He'd put it aside when the argument with Lyle arose.

At 9:57 a.m., the door to the front entrance of the funeral home swished open. Jeremy looked up and was about to greet the visitor. Instead, the visitor pulled out a Sig Sauer 9mm pistol and shot Jeremy Bjerkes twice in the heart. *POP! POP!* Jeremy gasped. The look of shock on his face was replaced in the next second with the look of someone quite dead. He slumped over his desk as if he were taking a nap. An audible sigh escaped his lips as he expired.

In the next few seconds, Layne McNally opened the side door of the office, startling the visitor with his unexpected presence. The assailant shot Layne in the chest, although his aim was off since he hadn't anticipated anyone else being there. As Layne fell to the carpeted floor, the perpetrator walked over and shot him once more through the head, making sure he was dead. He didn't want any witnesses.

The visitor looked around, tucked the pistol in his jacket pocket, turned, and left through the front entrance. The time was 10:02 a.m. He walked down the blacktopped circular drive to the side funeral home parking lot, climbed in a non-descript black vehicle, and exited the rear driveway into the alley. Making his way past the funeral home, he drove through the alley, turned left on Fifth Street, and merged into traffic on U.S. Highway 35, which paralleled the Mississippi River. He drove south out of the city limits.

It wasn't until he drove into Goose Island Park above Stoddard, Wisconsin, along U.S. 35, that his hands started to shake, and sweat began pouring down his face. He pulled over into a turnout, throwing the car into park.

"Oh, God, what have I done?" he asked himself. His voice seemed to ricochet around in the car's interior. He leaned his head on the steering wheel for a moment to steady himself. Then, opening the car door, he walked to the edge of a backwater pool. For just a moment, the enormity of his actions left him gasping in horror.

He feared he was hyperventilating or having a heart attack. The extreme wickedness of what he'd done threatened to override the incongruous relief in eliminating Jeremy Bjerkes. *Now Gloria will suffer as I have,* he thought.

Too bad about the other kid. He didn't even know who he was. That wasn't supposed to happen, but it was over and done with. Too late now.

Reaching in his jacket, he felt the solid weight of the pistol. His fingers grasped the handle, and he looked around in panic as he pulled it from his pocket. Then with wild abandon accompanied by intense fear, he flung the pistol as far as he could into the backwaters of the river. It plunked in the water unceremoniously, leaving arcing ripples on the surface.

He tried to pray then, to ask God to forgive him, but the words seemed to hit a brick wall and echo back, leaving him empty without any sense of absolution or relief. He turned and walked slowly back to his car. He was oblivious to anyone who might be watching him. To his knowledge, nobody was.

It had to be done. You've suffered enough. You had no other choice. It had to be done, he told himself. *Justice had to be served.*

He started the car, turned around, and drove out of the park. **◘**

10

Leslie Brown lay on her back in bed at her parents' house in Decorah, Iowa. It was early morning, and the light was beginning to filter into her bedroom. She stared at the familiar cracks on the plastered ceiling. There was the spider web that had held her attention as a child when she was trying to work through a problem or had been sent to her room for some infraction of family rules. And over there were two parallel lines topped with an oblong circle that looked like a giraffe's neck. The cracks in the ceiling had sparked her imagination much like the night sky's constellations did now. They'd been her companions throughout her childhood, participants in the good and the bad moments.

The walls of the room were still decorated with her athletic awards and other paper ephemera from high school—a kind of silent time warp. Regional and state track medals, certificates of appreciation for her years as a Big Sister, newspaper photos of her induction into the U.S. Army, and a story by a local reporter about her work as a military dog handler—most of it stuff her mom had kept. Now here she was, right back where she'd started. She let out a nervous sigh. How could she screw up her life so completely?

Leaving a job she loved in the beautiful Driftless Area of Wisconsin was the first mistake. Despite being at the La Crosse

Sheriff's Department for only a year, she'd grown close to the other members of the investigative team. Her relationships with them reminded her of her friendships in the military, forged in dangerous, trying times. She was sure the indelible bonds between them would last a lifetime.

Lt. Higgins was tough and professional. His reputation was well-known and earned when he'd solved some baffling cases that drew national and international attention. He'd shown extreme kindness and patience toward her, especially when dealing with her lingering issues of PTSD from her military service in Iraq. Even though he was a demanding boss, there were times when he felt more like her dad.

Then there was Paul Saner. Although they weren't particularly close, his teasing and cajoling reminded her of an older brother who might get ticked at you but always had your back when the chips were down. Leslie could empathize with his recent experience of being shot. She understood the long, tough road to recovery; many of her soldier friends had similar scars. Lots of them had not made it back home to American soil.

Sam. Just the thought of him filled Leslie with remorse—and longing. She missed his quirky sense of humor. His decency. His warm kisses. She'd hurt him. Badly.

He'd been the only man she'd ever known who'd really respected her and hadn't tried to take advantage of her. Empathizing with the sexual abuse she'd endured from her former boyfriend, Sam had lifted her to a place of hope—a place where she could respect herself again. He'd restored her belief that God loved her and cared for her. And what had she done? Left him in a lurch for a job she ended up hating. She let out an agonized groan and pounded the bed with her fist. *I am so stupid and bullheaded,* she berated herself.

Throwing back the covers, she grabbed her sweats and started dressing. Paco, her faithful black lab, watched her, panting with anticipation. The dog had a preternatural ability to sense the nuances of her moods. They'd been to hell and back again together. He barked loudly now, whining as he waited for their morning exercise routine to begin.

"Ready for a run, boy?" Leslie whispered, fondling his ears and caressing his head.

Paco woofed, turning in an anxious circle. Clipping his leash on, Leslie headed down the hallway and used the bathroom. Then she bolted outside with Paco, who energetically yelped his approval.

Warming up along Mill Street, where her parents lived, they jogged up College Drive crossing the Upper Iowa River, which ran through the heart of Decorah and formed the western edge of the Luther College campus. The waterway was still and hushed, a hazy fog lying just above its surface. Reflecting a picture of serenity, a pair of wood ducks swam slowly in the stream, their heads pivoting, the male resplendent in his colorful plumage. Being the bird dog he was, Paco stopped along the trail, assuming a pointer position. Leslie tugged on his leash, and he bounded forward, nose to the ground.

The trees were bursting with lush hues of green. Apple blossoms, resembling snowflakes, drifted from the trees and landed in the grass beneath them. Leslie headed for Dunning Spring Park, which had originally been the site of an 1850s grist mill. Now it was a recreational area of trails culminating in a waterfall that cascaded down a cliff of limestone and granite.

As she ran, she thought about forgiveness. Would Sam forgive her for running away when her growing love threatened to overwhelm her? Why couldn't she trust him? Could she love him the way he deserved to be loved? Could she forgive herself for crushing him with disappointment, leaving him angry and hurt?

Pounding along the dirt trail through the park, she picked up speed. If she couldn't forgive herself, then she'd push herself to new athletic limits—anything to forget the stupid mistakes she'd made when she'd left Sam behind. Her shoes angrily slapped the pavement as she ran along the river.

Arriving back at the house, she showered and was eating a light breakfast of yogurt and granola when a text arrived on her phone.

Hi. Job still available. Apply online. Just a formality. Call for details.

Let me know your decision. Higgins

She closed her eyes, feeling relief and gratitude to Lt. Higgins. At the same time, she was unsure of the reception she'd get when she returned. *Well, there's only one way to find out,* she thought. *La Crosse, here I come. Ready or not.* Still, this was no time for a victory dance. She had a lot of fences to mend. ◙

11

Emily appeared at Jim's office door at ten minutes after eleven Tuesday morning, an expression of panic and concern shadowing her face. "Chief, you need to call Sheriff Jones immediately. I just heard it on the scanner. It's bad, sir. Really bad," she said anxiously, her eyes big with alarm.

Jim picked up his cell and dialed the sheriff.

"Davey. Higgins here. What's up?" he asked.

"Double homicide at Bjerkes and Oates Funeral Home. 545 Fifth Street off Mormon Coulee Drive. I need your team here. Now."

"Be there in ten minutes."

Jim closed his phone, grabbed his suit coat from the back of the chair, and ran down the hall.

"Sam! Paul!" he yelled.

The two detectives appeared in the hallway, concerned with the tone of Jim's voice.

"Grab your stuff. Double homicide off Mormon Coulee. Let's go!" Jim ordered.

They ran through the hallway, scurried down three flights of stairs, and trotted to Jim's Suburban in the parking lot. Jim flew out of the parking lot, negotiating the traffic in the heavy rain. Thunder rumbled, and a few flashes of lightning ripped through the darkened sky. Rain pooled at the intersections, and cars splashed through the puddles spraying water across the road.

The place was swarming with law enforcement vehicles, ambulances, and police when they arrived at the funeral home. The La Crosse County Medical Examiner's van was parked prominently under the front entrance awning. Ducking under the yellow crime scene tape, the team approached the front door. Inside they noticed Luke Evers, medical examiner and coroner for La Crosse County, in the funeral home office. He was kneeling over a young man. The carpet was soaked in blood, forming a red irregular halo around the victim's head. The other victim, a middle-aged man, sat at his desk, eyes partially opened, his head resting on the desk at a funny angle. Noticing Jim, Luke interrupted his work and walked over to the team.

"Double homicide. A UPS truck driver found them and called it in," Luke said, glancing back at the scene. "She's right over there," he said, pointing to a young woman in a brown UPS uniform who was being interviewed by a city policewoman. The young female courier appeared pale and distraught.

"So, what do you think happened here?" Jim asked, slipping blue footies over his shoes.

"Don't know. That's your job," Luke said, an exasperated sigh escaping his lips.

"Can I have a look?" Jim asked Luke. Luke nodded.

Jim walked into the office, went around the desk, and leaned down to better view the victim. He knelt closer, noticing the position of the body. 'Bout my age, he thought. *Nice looking guy.* His half-open eyes stared into oblivion. Jim grimaced at the puddle of blood that had dripped on the chair and pooled on the carpet, coagulating into a dark clot at Jim's feet.

"I think the shootings occurred mid-morning, probably around nine-thirty or ten," Luke began. "My initial speculations are that someone walked in while Mr. Bjerkes was seated at his desk. It appears that he was completing paperwork for the state. He never even got out of his chair, which makes me think he might have known the perpetrator. He didn't feel the need to stand for a formal greeting or never got the chance. Happened too fast. He was shot twice in the chest," Luke said rather dryly, his arms crossed over his white jacket.

Jim nodded his head in silent agreement, then walked over and knelt down by the second victim, avoiding the blood stains on the carpet. He groaned at the wounds in someone so young, now very dead. The kid's whole life went up in smoke before hardly getting started. Jim thought of his twins, John and Sara, who were about the same age. Violence ended so many dreams.

Luke continued talking as he walked over and stood closer to Jim. "I think this guy, Layne McNally, surprised the shooter by coming through the side door. He seems to have dropped right where he was shot. Once in the chest area, then in the head. Whoever did the shooting obviously wanted no witnesses. But I think Layne was collateral damage. Jeremy seems to be the one who was targeted. That's what I'm thinking at this point."

"One shooter?" Sam asked, feeling queasy at the scent of the blood. He swallowed the bile rising in his throat.

"Ninety-five percent it's one shooter. What a waste," he said, depressed at the gruesome sight. "I'll have more information later." Luke turned away from the trio of detectives and went back to his work.

Jim and his team left the office and stood in the entry. Hearing voices, they turned and focused their attention on Sheriff Davy Jones, who stood further down the corridor. Jones lifted a hand in greeting and waved the trio over as he walked toward them.

"I have city officers securing the scene here," Jones began explaining, waving his arms in different directions as he talked. "More officers are going door to door to all the surrounding homes and businesses. There are no closed-circuit cameras on the premises, but there is one at the used car dealer right on the corner of Fifth and Mormon Coulee. We might be able to get license numbers of vehicles who were in the vicinity during the shootings."

"Where's Tamara?" Jim asked. Tamara Pedretti was the chief of police for the city of La Crosse.

"Out of town at a family funeral," Davy said. "Listen, here's what I need from you. I need you to go to De Soto and talk to Layne's family. Establish their whereabouts at the time of the crime. Then someone needs to interview Lyle Oates, Jeremy's partner in the business. Here are their addresses."

"Sure, we'll get started," Jim said, taking the information from the sheriff.

By early afternoon, Sam and Paul had located Lyle Oates on a stool at the Cavilier Court Bar several blocks north of the funeral home. The bar was a local mom and pop tavern—just one of about one hundred fifty bars in the city limits. *And they wonder why we have addiction problems,* Paul thought.

Sam noticed the local dart ball schedule and other events plastered on the wall next to the window in the front entryway. The place smelled stale, heavy with the smell of spilled beer. When Paul and Sam asked about Lyle, the bartender pointed him out with a tip of his head. Approaching him as he sat by the bar, they flashed their IDs and invited him to a corner table where they all pulled out chairs and got comfortable.

"Mr. Oates, are you aware of the events that took place at the funeral home this morning?" Sam began. His eyes moved over the older man. His rumpled clothing and unshaven face made a poor impression for someone in the funeral business. Sam leaned away from him when he smelled the rancid alcohol from his stale breath.

"What events? You mean a funeral?" Lyle asked, clueless, trying to focus his eyes on Sam. "We didn't have any visitations or funerals scheduled." He looked rough and was well on his way to a binge drinking event of some sort.

"I'm sorry to have to tell you that your partner, Jeremy Bjerkes, and another man, Layne McNally, were shot to death about mid-morning at the funeral home," Sam said matter-of-factly. Sam discreetly picked up his pen, preparing to take notes.

Lyle's eyes bulged in shock. He slowly set his beer on the table. Motionless, he tried to wrap his mind around the words. His eyes moved back and forth between the two detectives. Leaning forward, he cradled his head in both of his hands.

"Mr. Oates? Are you all right?" Paul asked, concerned.

"I … I … can't believe that. I just talked to Jeremy this morning. This … this is unbelievable!" he sputtered, lifting his head and staring into space.

Sam didn't think his reaction was put on. He seemed truly shocked.

"Tell us what you talked about this morning," Sam said. "What time was this?"

"Umm … I was at the office about nine o'clock," Lyle started. "We discussed my possible retirement, although we hadn't made any real decisions yet."

"Who was Layne McNally? An employee?" Sam asked.

"Sort of. He was just starting his internship. In fact, today was his first day on the job. Poor kid."

"Do you know anyone who would want to harm Jeremy?" Sam continued.

Lyle shook his head, confused at the turn of events. "No, no. He was very well liked in the community. Coached baseball at the university, was a good strong Catholic and sponsored little league teams. I … " His voice tapered off to nothing. His disbelief was palpable.

"So, where were you at about ten o'clock this morning?" Paul asked. Sam continued taking fastidious notes.

"I think I left the office about nine-fifteen," he said. He thought a little more, his eyes drifting upward, then coming back to meet Paul's gaze. "Yeah, yeah, it was about nine-fifteen. It was before Layne arrived. I never met the kid. He was supposed to come around nine-thirty."

"What did you talk about this morning with Mr. Bjerkes?" Sam asked, getting back to the retirement issue. Lyle stared at Sam, concentrating, trying to remember. He hesitated. Sam noticed and thought, *They argued.* Lyle made a wry face and began to explain.

"Well, we've been having this ongoing discussion about my retirement. My *possible* retirement. This morning I kinda lost my temper and walked out," he said, letting out a pent-up huff.

"Was there something more to it than that?" Sam probed, his hazel eyes roaming the bar and coming back to Lyle.

Lyle slumped in his seat. He suddenly seemed to sober up. *Murder. Is he capable of it?* Sam thought. *Anyone is capable if pushed hard enough by threats or if circumstances and emotions run amuck.* Lyle studied Sam, his rheumy eyes watering with tears.

"I've had a drinking problem the last few years since my wife died. Jeremy threatened to fire me if I screwed up again," he said. There was a moment of silence. "I've embarrassed Jeremy and our clients more than once when I made some major errors in judgment."

"What kind of errors?" Sam asked.

Lyle frowned. He hated to admit his screwups. "I shaved off a client's mustache that he'd worn for over twenty years. When his wife saw him in the casket, she barely recognized him." He cringed at the memory of it. "And I've been drunk at a number of visitations and funerals. I've been going to AA, but I fell off the wagon recently," he finished, embarrassed. "I guess that's evident since I'm in a tavern drinking, for God's sake."

"Okay. One more thing," Paul said. "Can anyone testify to your whereabouts between nine-fifteen and ten-thirty?" Paul asked.

"No. I went home for a while—I live alone—and then I came here at noon," Lyle informed them. "Maybe some of my neighbors saw me come and go. I don't know. You'd have to ask them."

"Anything else you want to tell us?" Paul asked.

"No, not really." Lyle slumped back in his chair, still reeling from the news.

"Please don't leave town, Mr. Oates. We may have more questions for you later," Paul said as he slid his card toward him across the table.

Sam wrote down Lyle's address and cell number. They left the tavern and walked to Sam's Jeep. "Whadda ya think? Is he telling the truth?" Sam asked, glancing at Paul as he wove through traffic.

Paul lifted his shoulders in a shrug. "I think what he told us so far is the truth. But this conflict with Jeremy sounded kind of serious. Whether it's a reason to kill someone, I'm not sure. And we'll have to wait to see if the financials tell us anything. If anything is off, Higgins will find it," Paul said.

"Or you will. You usually get that job. He seems to pass the financial stuff off on you," Sam said somberly.

"God, I hope not." Paul peeked at the sky, the rain continuing in a steady downpour.

"You can always hope, but you'll probably end up with the numbers." ◘

12

Jim had visited the two murder victims' families by five o'clock that evening. *I'll never get used to doing this,* he thought. He supposed that was a good thing. Driving north up U.S. 35 from De Soto, he could still see Layne McNally's parents' stunned faces and blank, shocked expressions as they sat on their leather couch in the living room.

"He had everything to live for," his mother wept. "He was so excited to be starting his career. And now it's over before it even began," she sobbed. Mr. McNally gripped his wife's hand and pulled her closer to him. Tears streamed down his face, but Jim could see the anger building behind the tears.

He waited, giving them time to get a grip. Their painful journey was just beginning.

"Mrs. McNally, I'm wondering if you could just go through this morning's events at home. What Layne did this morning. His demeanor. What time he left the house. That sort of thing," Jim began quietly. "It might give us some clues to get us started in our investigation." He'd pulled his memo notebook from his suit coat and prepared to write down his observations.

Mrs. McNally stopped crying. She steadied herself, laid her hands in her lap, and began in a hesitant voice. "Well ... Layne

SUE BERG

got up about seven o'clock, showered, had breakfast with us, and messed around with his brother and sister. You know, teasing and teenage stuff—what they'd seen on Facebook, Twitter, and YouTube. They got in a heated discussion about *The Bachelor*. Stuff like that." A faint smile crossed her face as she remembered how they'd gathered around Layne's phone. "He seemed excited to be starting his first day of work. He left here about nine," she said thoughtfully.

Jim could see she was trying very hard to remember the details of the morning. "Did he mention anything that was bothering him? Did he have an argument with anyone that you know of? A girlfriend, maybe?" Jim asked gently.

"He didn't have a girlfriend. Everybody loved Layne," his father said. "He just came home a couple of weeks ago from college. Graduated with honors. It felt ... " he choked up and waited a minute, "so good to have him home again."

Jim reviewed their story, clarifying the details, but he could see they had shut down emotionally. They were bereft and dazed, in a sea of grief. However, their family seemed very strong, normal in all the right ways. Jim asked a few more questions, but he could tell by their wooden responses that shock and numbness were moving in.

"I'm so very sorry about your son," Jim said, leaning forward, grasping Mr. McNally's hand. "I want you to know that our department is totally focused on finding your son's killer and bringing whoever did this to justice. I'm so sorry this happened," Jim repeated softly.

Mr. McNally's eyes were pools of shocked disbelief and sadness. "I appreciate that, but it won't bring our son back," he said.

"No. No, it won't," Jim agreed. "If you think of anything, please call me. Sometimes the littlest detail can be very important in figuring out what happened or who might have done this. Here's my card if you think of anything else." Jim slid his business card across the low coffee table, rose from his chair, and quietly exited the house.

A heavy feeling settled in Jim's chest on the drive back to La Crosse. It was a familiar sensation, and he recognized it as the beginning of righteous anger—that slow-burning emotion that was his companion during murder investigations. Anger could be useful if it doesn't get ahead of you. It had to be harnessed much like a seasoned rider who curbed the strength of a powerful horse. It was just one tool at his disposal, but it had helped him catch killers before.

As he drove toward home, he reviewed another interview he'd had earlier in the afternoon with Gloria Bjerkes, Jeremy's widow. She agreed to meet him at Rosie's Cafe on the south side. When he entered the restaurant, she waved him over to a table in a corner near the window. He sat down opposite her. While they exchanged greetings, Jim spent a long moment studying her.

Mrs. Bjerkes had a pixie haircut. Although it was shorter than Jim liked, the style was attractive on her. It gave her an impish appeal. *A replica of Mary Martin in Peter Pan,* he thought. In combination with her deep hazel eyes and high cheekbones, she was attractive in a curious way. She wasn't beautiful, but she was interesting.

Gloria's shocked, frozen expression was sufficient evidence that she was flabbergasted at her husband's murder. After introductions, Jim began focusing on the timeline of the morning, trying to uncover motives and possible suspects.

"So your husband had a normal morning?" Jim prompted.

"Yes. A shower, breakfast. Read the paper until seven-thirty. Left for work. Called me about eight to ask the time of our son's baseball game this afternoon. He plays on the middle school team at Logan, but it was canceled because of the rain."

"How old is your son?" Jim asked politely.

"He's eleven. We had him right after we were married. Jeremy was already forty when he was born," she explained. "Some people thought we were nuts to start a family at that late stage of the game, but Trevor is a wonderful kid. He's really going to miss his dad." She began softly crying.

Jim swallowed, briefly closing his eyes. *You have no idea. Forty's pretty young to have a baby. Try fifty-two.* He waited for a bit.

"Did he seem upset this morning in any way?"

"No, not at all."

Since the morning's events appeared normal, Jim tried a different line of questions. "Can you tell me about your husband's relationship with his business partner?" Jim asked, watching her face carefully. The waitress came with fresh, hot coffee.

Mrs. Bjerkes took a sip of coffee and leaned toward Jim, giving him a rather coquettish glance that was not lost on Jim. He could see some guy who was bored with his marriage falling for her smoldering sexuality. She gave him a smile, running her tongue across her lips. "What were you saying, Lieutenant?"

Jim prompted her again. "Your husband's relationship with his business partner?"

"You mean Lyle Oates?" she asked innocently, batting her long lashes. Jim nodded. "Oh, Lyle. What a fruitcake! He causes more trouble than he's worth." She reached for a Kleenex from her purse and dabbed her cheeks with the tissue. Jim thought it smacked of pretension. For someone who'd just lost her husband, she had uncanny control over her emotions, bouncing from sorrow to seduction in seconds. Her gaze shifted to the window, the rain steadily pattering on the glass. She began again.

"Well, I guess that sounds rather unfair, doesn't it? I mean, when Jeremy and Lyle started the business twenty-five years ago, it was a good arrangement. They must have gotten along. You wouldn't start a business with someone you didn't like, would you?" she asked, focusing her big eyes on Jim.

"I don't know. I'm not a businessman. I'm a detective." Her lingering gaze made Jim feel like a worm being scrutinized by a hungry robin. He fought the urge to squirm. Despite his outward control, she did give Jim ideas that were embarrassing. He leveled his blue eyes on her and calmly asked, "Were you married when your husband began his career in the funeral business?" He felt as if he was missing some innuendo lurking beneath the surface.

"No, I guess I should explain that. Jeremy and I have only been married ten years. Our relationship began while he was still married to his first wife, Julie. We had been seeing each other for quite a while before she figured it out. Most men never leave their wives because of an affair, but Jeremy was way ahead of his time. When his wife caught us together, he stood up to her and divorced her." A smirk of triumph and pleasure briefly passed over her features.

More like the wife kicked Jeremy to the curb, Jim thought. He stayed silent, consciously keeping his expression neutral. The silence stretched on.

"You were telling me about Lyle, the partner," Jim reminded her, his tone flat and businesslike.

"Oh, sorry. Lyle has had a pretty serious drinking problem the last few years. Jeremy came close to firing him more than once. His screwups with some of the clients were notorious, but Jeremy could smooth things over. It wasn't good for their business reputation. My husband was hoping Lyle would just retire. But whenever they tried to discuss that, it ended in a knock-down, drag-out fight."

Jim made a mental note to ask Sam and Paul about their interview with Lyle. Then, not trusting his memory, he wrote *Lyle* in his notebook. *Relationship with Jeremy? Problems?*

"Were there any financial difficulties with the business that you know of?" Jim asked.

"Not that I was aware of, but I really didn't have anything to do with the funeral home."

"Where do you work?" Jim asked.

"I'm a physical trainer for the university's athletic department. I design cardio and weight training programs for many of the athletes. The workouts are personalized and tailored to the specific sport they participate in. And I help them recover if they're injured," she explained.

I'll bet you do, Jim thought sarcastically. Instead, he said, "Must keep you busy." *No wonder she's so buff.* Immediately he was ashamed of where his mind had taken him, but he didn't dismiss her responses. Out of nowhere, the word *predator* came to him.

"I enjoy what I do, if that's what you're wondering," Mrs. Bjerkes said, studying Jim's face.

It was a comment that begged an explanation. Jim ignored it. He had the distinct impression she considered this interview a game of cat-and-mouse. The grieving, shocked widow was conspicuously absent now. She was concentrating on her prey.

Jim cleared his throat and straightened his tie. "And where were you this morning between nine o'clock and ten-thirty?" he asked.

She studied his face and said, "Well, I was in my office. My secretary will confirm that. Here's my card," she said, handing the card to Jim, their fingers touching briefly. *Boy, I'll bet she has a heyday with college guys,* Jim thought. *The woman is an expert at dropping subtle, sexual come-ons.*

"Please call if you think of anything else that might be helpful," Jim said, getting up from the table. "Just ask for my secretary, Emily Warehauser."

"Oh, I will, Lieutenant Higgins. I will," she said. But underneath, Jim felt he was being played. And that was unacceptable. ◘

WEDNESDAY,
MAY 15

13

The classroom on the third floor of the La Crosse Law Enforcement Center was warm for an early spring morning. Someone had pushed open a couple of windows to let in some cooler air. Jim could hear the bustle of traffic outside on Vine Street. A car horn blasted, and a gravel truck rumbled by. The smell of warm asphalt lingered in the room.

A couple of city police officers sat together at one table. Others were scattered about the room, some standing, some sitting on the edge of the tables. Luke Evers, the medical examiner, was conversing intensely with Sam and Paul, their heads bobbing in agreement as they talked. They glanced in Jim's direction a couple of times. Sheriff Davey Jones leaned back in a chair near a window, observing and taking in the general mood of the crowd, zeroing in on the attitudes of the tight-knit group of detectives. Jim knew this was more than a perfunctory interest on Jones' part. Jeremy Bjerkes had been a life-long acquaintance of the sheriff's. Both had graduated from the same high school class and played Legion baseball together. The sheriff and Jim exchanged a glance, and Jones gave Higgins a small nod.

Pushing off from his relaxed pose against the wall, Jim walked to the front of the room. The whiteboard was his mute companion, its white surface somewhat empty right now, hinting at the lack of information about the case so far. Jim hoped that events, suspects, and motives might be displayed in some coordinated fashion by the end of the day. He'd been listening to the different theories and bits of information floating around the room. Now he stood in front, commanding their attention.

"So, ladies and gentlemen," he began as he cleared his throat. Private conversations gradually stopped. "After eavesdropping on a few conversations, it looks like we have one possible suspect. Is that what you're telling me?" Jim asked the group of police officers in front of him. A couple more city police drifted in as the meeting began.

"Well, sir," Sam spoke up, "Lyle Oates had an ongoing argument with Jeremy Bjerkes about his retirement." Sam glanced at his notes. "From his own account, he said, 'I kinda lost my temper and walked out.' That was about half an hour before the shooting, if he's to be believed."

"Well, that might be a motive," Jim said.

Sam continued. "From noon on, he was at the Cavalier. Before that, he claimed he was home during the morning hours. We questioned his closest neighbors. One was at work, and the other two were out doing errands between nine-thirty and noon on the fourteenth. Nobody saw him come home. So there are no witnesses who can corroborate his story about returning home after his argument with Jeremy at the funeral home, Chief."

"All right. I get that," Jim conceded. "We don't know enough about the business's financial status yet to know if there's anything wrong there. We'll dig into that in the next couple of days. Both victims' wallets were still on them when they were found, so a robbery doesn't seem to play into this. What about closed-circuit cameras?" Jim nodded to another cop who'd raised his hand.

Officer Mike LeLand spoke up. "We were able to view the closed-circuit video from the used car lot on the corner of South Avenue and Mormon Coulee Drive during the time frame of the shooting. Sixty-two vehicles passed by the car lot from nine-thirty to ten-thirty when the UPS driver called in the crime at 10:16 a.m. We're getting a list together of the years, makes, and models. But the camera is a side view, so we won't have access to any license plate numbers unless they turned north. Southbound traffic would be out of camera range. You couldn't view the license plates from the front either. But we'll keep working on it."

"Good. You do that," Jim said. "I want a squad car parked along South Avenue tomorrow during the hours the shooting took place. Any cars similar to those on the closed-circuit cameras should be stopped and questioned. Many times people drive the same routes to work each day. They may recall something important about that morning. There's also the possibility that the murderer could have walked to the funeral home and left on foot." Jim stopped briefly, looked around the room, and continued. "What about the neighbors adjacent to the funeral home? Did any of them see anything during the time frame of the murders?

City police officer Mindy Fauske raised her hand. Jim acknowledged her with a lifting of his chin. "We canvassed the area immediately after the crime." Mindy stood and walked to a city map of the vicinity surrounding the funeral home and began pointing. "The only resident that remembers anything from that morning was a Mrs. Walsh. She recalls seeing a blue car leaving the driveway into the alley that borders her property at about nine-thirty. I checked with Mr. Oates. He does drive a blue Pontiac. Either no one else was close enough to notice anything, or they were at work during the incident."

"Let's keep pushing that. Luke, what can you tell us about the victims?" Jim asked. He stepped aside and leaned against the wall, feet crossed, head down, his classic listening pose.

"Both victims were shot with a small 9mm pistol, possibly a Sig Sauer model or one of the P938 series that are popular for personal protection right now. Mr. Bjerkes was shot twice through the heart. Two very accurate shots passed through the atriums causing massive internal bleeding and stopping the heart instantly. The downward trajectory of the bullet indicates Mr. Bjerkes was seated at his desk when he was killed. He never even had the opportunity to stand to greet the killer. Or he may not have felt the need to stand, which raises the possibility that he knew the person who'd walked into his office. Maybe a friend or colleague. At any rate, he was shot when he was seated at his desk. I believe he was the first to be killed. Remember, this is preliminary—a complete autopsy will follow, but it may take a couple of months."

Luke referred to his notes and then continued. "I believe Mr. McNally entered the office from the side door, startling the killer, who got off one shot which hit Layne in the left side of his chest. The bullet entered the left lung and lodged in his back in the seventh rib on the left side. He would have collapsed from the first wound, and then the shooter shot him in the head at close range above his left ear. That would have killed him instantly. Unfortunately, I think McNally was collateral damage. I don't believe he was the intended target, but that's conjecture at this time. It's my best guess with the evidence I have right now."

The room had become extremely quiet. Pin drop quiet. That wasn't unusual. The tension in the room was always noticeable when the details of homicides were reviewed. After waiting a few moments, Luke continued. "We recovered all four bullets, three from the victims' bodies and one embedded in the floor under Mr. McNally's head." Luke and Jim exchanged a glance. "That's it for now, Jim, unless there are questions."

"Any fingerprints anywhere?" Paul asked.

Jim began to tell what he knew. "The CSI techs are still processing what was found. Nothing unexpected yet. But a piece of red ribbon about four inches long was found in front of Bjerkes' desk by the crime scene crew," Jim said. "In talking to the second shift cleaning crew who vacuumed on Monday night, they claim they would have seen the ribbon when they cleaned the office since the carpet is a beige color, and it would have shown up and been quite conspicuous.

They didn't notice it Monday night. So we believe that the ribbon may have dropped out of the killer's pocket Tuesday morning when he pulled out the pistol. That's one theory anyway."

This piece of news caused a ripple of excitement throughout the group.

"Any DNA from it?" Sam asked.

"The lab is in the process of extracting what they can from it," Jim said. There was a brief silence. From the side of the room, another voice piped up.

"That's good news, Jim. Any other suspects?" Sheriff Jones asked.

Jim thought back to his interview with Gloria Bjerkes. His instincts told him something was off-kilter with her. He could still feel her eyes moving over him like he was fair game. But he needed to do some more legwork before proposing a theory.

"No," Jim said. "Anything else, people?" Not hearing any more comments or questions, Jim clapped his hands in a cheering motion. "Good work, everyone. Keep digging. Follow your instincts," he said loudly over the scraping of chairs and the rising buzz of conversation. Jim motioned Sam to follow him to his office. He walked in and sat behind his desk. Sam followed behind.

"Could you close the door?" Jim asked as Sam walked in.

"Sure," Sam said, his stomach cramping with nervousness as he quietly shut the door.

"I'll get right to it then," Jim said, resting his elbows on the arms of his chair. Seeing Sam's anxious demeanor, he softened his tone. "Don't worry—you're fine. No faux pas in your attire." He paused, realizing he wasn't being very clear. "Grab a chair."

Sam pulled up a chair and sat down. Jim continued. "Look, it's about Leslie. Apparently, she's been unhappy at the Immigration and Customs job in Chicago. It isn't what she thought it was going to be." He stopped briefly, gauging Sam's reaction.

"So what? She's the one who wanted to leave," Sam said, trying to appear unaffected by Jim's news. He leaned back in his chair, his ankle resting on his knee nonchalantly.

"She's reapplying for her position on the team," Jim commented.

Sam continued to stare at Jim, but he lowered his foot and sat up straight. Meeting Jim's gaze, he said, "I don't care." A pause. "What's this got to do with me?" he asked, but Jim could hear the edge of anger that had crept into his voice. "Besides, if this is about the team, then where's Paul? Did you talk to him, too? In fact, why isn't he in here right now? He's just as much a part of this team as I am. Don't you think he deserves to know what's going on around here?" Sam said loudly, his voice ratcheting up, challenging Jim's authority.

"I can see you're angry," Jim said calmly, ignoring Sam's attempts to deflect the attention elsewhere. *His red flags are popping up all over the place,* Jim thought. *So much for not caring.*

Jim waited patiently. Sam made a huffing noise. "You have no idea how she treated me," he said darkly, "after all I did for her. What a bunch of bullshit."

"I'm giving you a fair warning," Jim said, standing and hardening his tone to match Sam's. "If you can't get along with Leslie, then I will fire both of you, despite the fact that I think you're both extremely talented at this job. You need to consider whether you can put aside your personal differences and continue to work as a team and serve the public effectively. If you don't think you can do that, then I have no choice. You both will have to go. Unity on a team like ours is top priority. We have to have absolute confidence that we will have one another's back in any situation." *I'm preaching again,* he thought, *but he'll have to deal with it.*

Jim could see Sam was conflicted, but he couldn't tolerate anything except the very best from each person on his team. To accept less was to sacrifice the standards and principles that kept the public safe and helped them solve crimes.

By now, Sam had stood up. He faced Jim and put his hands on his hips defiantly. "I've been pretty depressed since January, but can you honestly say I haven't given my job one hundred percent of my effort?" Sam asked angrily, pushing back.

Jim thought for a moment. "I'm sorry about the falling out you had with Leslie. Romantic involvements with people at work are fraught with difficulty. That's why we discourage them." He paused a moment collecting his thoughts. Sam relaxed a little, but his surly attitude was just below the surface. Jim went on. "But you're right. I know you've been upset since Leslie left, but I can honestly say your work has not been affected."

"Well then, there's your answer," Sam said, turning, hoping he could leave.

"No, that's not the answer." Now it was Jim's turn to be angry. "Have you ever considered giving Leslie another chance?" Sam stared at Jim as if his mind had left the building.

Jim sat down and held Sam's stare.

"So you're saying I should forgive her?" he asked incredulously. Coming from a self-proclaimed Christian, Jim didn't see what was so novel about that idea. *Christianity 101*, he thought. *Forgive us as we have forgiven others.*

"People are flawed, Sam. They make mistakes. They screw up. They have baggage. It doesn't mean we throw them on the scrap heap of human failure and write them off. Besides, you're in love with her," he finished. He leaned back, waiting for the roar of denial.

"In love with her?" Sam asked softly, his mouth hanging open. With Sam's supposed innocence on display, Jim had a fleeting idea of the attraction women could have for someone like him.

"Yes. It's obvious to anybody who watched you when you were with her that you're in love with her. So you can be petty and immature, or you can be a man, admit it, and do something about it." *God, I wasn't going to get involved,* he thought. *Too late now.*

"Can I go now?" Sam asked roughly, his seething anger barely contained.

"Yep. Just wanted to make sure we were on the same page. We understand each other and the situation, right?" He caught Sam's eye and pointed at him.

"Perfectly, sir," Sam said crisply, meeting his gaze. He turned and left the office.

Jim groaned. He hoped things would work out, but it didn't look promising if Sam's attitude was any indicator. ◐

14

By one o'clock, the search at the Bjerkes and Oates Funeral Home had started. Two city police officers, along with Paul and Sam, began going through the premises with a fine-tooth comb, emptying drawers, investigating the contents of file cabinets, and searching for evidence of contacts, clients, or business associates who may have had a conflict with the funeral business. The funeral home's financial records were confiscated and delivered to the third floor of the law enforcement center. The crime scene crew continued working the scene, meticulously gathering physical evidence.

"You okay?" Paul asked Sam, noticing his unusually reserved disposition.

"Fine," Sam snapped, slamming a file cabinet drawer shut.

"You're not your usual talkative self," Paul commented, flipping through a pile of papers taken from Jeremy Bjerkes' desk.

Sam roughly opened one of the file drawers in the funeral home office. "Just got some news that doesn't make me too happy," he said, taking out a stack of file folders and plopping them on the counter.

"Oh, yeah? What's that? Goodwill closing?" Paul asked, still flipping papers, occasionally stopping for a closer glance.

"Not," Sam spit sarcastically. He waited a moment and then said, "Leslie's comin' back."

Paul stopped shuffling his stack. He stared at Sam. After a moment, he said, "Well, you should be a happy man then. Maybe you can quit walking around with your lip hanging on the ground."

"What is this? Some kind of conspiracy?" Sam said, letting out a huff. "First Higgins, and now you."

"No, it's not a conspiracy, but you either pony up or shut up," Paul said, hardening his tone. "And you better decide which it is before Leslie gets here."

"I don't believe this!" Sam complained, bringing his clenched fist down on the top of the files.

"Listen. You're not the first to get dumped on the curb," Paul continued on a roll. "You either accept it and move on, or you reconsider your options. And moving into a cave where you've been the last six months is not allowed in the adult world—unless you want to be a monk."

"What? So now I'm immature and self-centered?" Sam said.

Paul stuffed his pile of papers back in the file and locked eyes with Sam. "I'm not going there. It is what it is."

While Paul and Sam continued rifling through the funeral home records in stony silence, Jim decided to visit the athletic training facility on the La Crosse university campus. He walked across campus and entered the front door of the Trameney Athletic Training Center. In the center's spacious office, he was greeted by a pert, enthusiastic woman sitting at a slick, modern desk. The reception area was decorated with paintings of Wisconsin artist John Schultz—landscapes of barns and flora and fauna of the Mississippi River.

"May I help you?" she asked cheerily.

"Yes, I'd like to talk to Mr. Bates. I realize I don't have an appointment, but something of a serious nature has come up, and I wondered if I could see him," Jim said pleasantly.

"Oh, he's very busy," she said. Then she leaned forward, throwing a furtive glance at Mr. Bates' door. "A staff member's husband was killed yesterday. We're all just sick about it," the young girl moaned, laying her hand along her neck. "Mr. Bates' schedule is really quite hectic today."

Jim flipped open his credentials. The young girl paled when she looked at his ID.

"Mr. Bates? Could I talk to him, please?" he asked with a little more grit in his voice. Just once, he'd like to walk into an office and not feel like a third-class citizen who didn't understand the ins and outs of office procedure. *Like I'm some kind of terrorist ... or idiot.*

"Oh." The young secretary's forehead wrinkled with a little frown. "Let me see what I can do. Just wait here." She stood up, stepped from behind her desk, and disappeared down a hallway where several offices were located on both sides. Jim could hear her shoes clicking a staccato beat as she walked down the ceramic tile corridor.

Jim waited next to the counter for ten minutes. He refrained from checking his messages, choosing instead to go over the questions he had been thinking about asking Bates. Finally, the girl reappeared and said briskly, "This way, please, Lieutenant."

Jim was escorted into the office of Donald Bates, the athletic director for the university. The office was on the third floor of a huge multi-million dollar facility that housed four gymnasiums, six weight training rooms, an Olympic-size swimming pool, and a variety of other rooms designed and equipped for specific sports like gymnastics.

Bates' office was understated but decorated with real leather furniture, dark walnut bookshelves, a matching walnut credenza, and walls that were sporadically but tastefully decorated with original artwork. Jim loved river art, and one of a stunning, smoky river scene by local Wisconsin artist Linsay McKintosh aroused his artistic admiration. He noticed the huge windows that looked down on Taron Hall and the Alumni Visitor's Center. Across the street, the Hiram Stapleton field house occupied an entire city block. Both men sat down—Bates in his leather executive chair behind the desk and Jim in an expensive wingback situated in front of the desk. After introductions, Jim got right to it.

"I'm wondering, Mr. Bates, what kind of an employee Mrs. Bjerkes has been?"

Bates smiled widely. He was a short, stout man with a friendly face, deep-set eyes, and a full head of thick dark hair. His brown eyes glowed warmly as he began. "Oh, her evaluations every year come back glowing. She's an excellent employee—very knowledgeable in her field."

Jim paused. "That's not really what I'm asking." Bates' forehead creased. "Has she ever been disciplined in any way while working with university students? Were any student complaints ever filed against her?" Jim felt a chill that had nothing to do with the room's temperature.

Bates seemed perplexed. His eyes lost some of their friendliness and warmth. "I'm not sure what you mean, sir."

Jim shifted in his chair and crossed his legs. "I mean just what I asked. Has she ever been disciplined for inappropriate behavior involving university students? Sexual liaisons with students? That type of thing?"

Mr. Bates took a quick inventory of the detective. Jim could feel the boxes being ticked off. There was a long silence. Finally, he answered, "No. Not to my knowledge ... no. That is quite an accusation about someone you hardly know, detective."

"So you are confident that when I examine Mrs. Bjerkes' employment records today, I won't find anything of a disciplinary nature in her files?" Jim asked.

Bates paled considerably, his mouth turning downward in disapproval. "Personnel files are private and are treated as such. I'm not sure you have the right to review her records, Lt. Higgins." He was suddenly nervous, and he flicked a lock of hair away from his face, swiping his hand across his forehead.

Jim uncrossed his legs and leaned forward toward Bates' desk. "I have every right according to Wisconsin State Statute 103.13 to look at employee records as it relates to a crime we are investigating. In case you hadn't heard, Gloria Bjerkes' husband was shot in cold blood yesterday while he sat at his desk at the Bjerkes and Oates Funeral Home." He let the gravity of the event sink in. Then he continued. "I'd hate to think you were lying to a police officer. Or are you unaware of Mrs. Bjerkes' history?" Jim's blue eyes blazed.

Jim knew he was taking a huge gamble that Gloria Bjerkes could be involved in questionable sexual behavior with college kids; he just hoped his gamble would pay off. He still hadn't been able to get his mind off the way she'd leered at him like he was a fine piece of meat. It disgusted him, although he knew plenty of men who would have taken it as a compliment. His first impressions weren't always right; he'd been mistaken on occasion. He just hoped this wasn't one of those times. Staring at Bates, he noticed a fine layer of sweat on his face and neck. *She's guilty of something if Bates' condition is any indication,* he thought. *He looks petrified.*

Jim stood abruptly in front of the desk. "I'll wait in the lobby while you prepare copies of Mrs. Bjerkes' entire employment record since she's been here at the university. Don't take too long. I'm trying to find a killer." Jim turned and walked briskly down the hall, taking a seat in the outer reception area. His cell vibrated in his pocket. He was still seething at being obstructed and hindered in his investigation when he answered.

"Higgins," he said gruffly.

"Hi. Do you have time to talk?" Carol asked quietly.

"Oh, hi, sweetheart." He softened his voice. "Everything okay?"

"Yes, Lillie is just playing in her room, and then we're going for a walk down by the creek."

"Good. So what's up?"

"An officer from the Wausau Police Department called. A Darrel Hines. He wants you to call him back. He said he has some information you requested." She gave Jim the number.

"Okay, I'll call him. See you tonight. I should be home by six. Love you."

"Love you, too."

The same girl sitting at the reception desk approached him

fifteen minutes later with a thick file folder. Jim flipped it open—the employment records for Gloria Bjerkes dating back to 2007. He smiled graciously and left the office. Throwing the folder on the front seat of the Suburban, he drove through traffic back to the Law Enforcement Center. He thought back to his interview with Mrs. Bjerkes.

After years of dealing with and evaluating people's personalities and quirks, he'd developed a sixth sense about things swimming below the surface. Innuendos. Undertones. Allusions. That sense was alive and tingling now like a nerve twitching from an electric shock. Something about Gloria was off, and he intended to find out what it was.

Stepping off the elevator on the third floor, he wandered to the coffee pot. He was about to sit down at his desk with a steaming mug and Gloria's records when there was a timid knock at his door.

"Hi, Chief. I'm back," Leslie Brown said, walking in energetically and extending her hand. She seemed fit and healthy. When she'd left six months ago, she was still recovering from torture and abuse by her former boyfriend. The team had rescued her from certain death, and in the process of recovery, Jim believed Sam had fallen in love with her.

Jim grabbed her cool hand in his and said, "Well, you're lookin' great, Lez. I hope you're ready to go to work. We've got a lot on our plate."

"I heard about the double homicide downstairs in HR. Everybody's talking about it. What do you want me to do?"

"Why don't you get settled back into your digs?" he suggested. "Then—" Leslie waved her hand quickly.

"Everything's pretty much the same as when I left it. I retrieved a laptop downstairs," she pointed to her briefcase, "so I'm ready to dig in."

"All right. That's great." Jim said. He dove into instructions, firing orders. "Call City Police and talk to Mike LeLand. Get a list of the cars on the closed-circuit camera from the corner by the funeral home. We can't see all the plate numbers because of the camera's angle, but for those numbers we can see, get the owners' names from the DMV. Set up interviews with those who were in the vicinity the morning of the homicides. See if any of them noticed anything specific."

"I'll get right on it, sir." She turned and left.

Jim dialed the Wausau number Carol had given him earlier. He located the officer, Darrel Hines, but he was conducting a traffic stop.

"I'll call you back in fifteen minutes," he promised. True to his word, he called.

"I went to the residence you asked about," Darrel said. "The house has fallen into disrepair. It looks pretty tough. No signs of recent activity. So I went to the courthouse and did a title search. The house was foreclosed in May 2016. The owner was a Mrs. Juliette Olson."

"Keep going. I'm listening," Jim encouraged, scribbling notes on a scrap of paper.

"While at the courthouse, I did a birth certificate search for Lillie as you requested. She was born October 19, 2013, at Ascension St. Clare's Hospital here in Wausau to a Sandy Lindvig. She was the unmarried daughter of Juliette. Sandy was addicted to meth, although she claimed to be clean when she had the baby—this is according to a source of mine in Social Services—and Sandy signed over custody of Lillie to her mother shortly after her birth. Sadly, Sandy died of an overdose on April 23, 2015."

Jim took a deep breath. A bone-deep sadness had crept in, and he couldn't shake it. He was familiar with the scenario. He'd seen enough sorrow, destitution, and abandonment surrounding meth to last a lifetime. And it was only going to get worse.

"Thank you, Officer Hines. I'll take it from there."

His chair creaked as he leaned back and studied the ceiling. He'd do more investigating at home tonight. He wished he knew what to do with the ambiguous feelings he had about all of this. It felt like he was creeping through an emotional minefield, waiting for another explosive discovery to rock his world again, but he couldn't afford the time today to investigate his family's history. It would have to wait. With resignation, he returned to the employment files of Gloria Bjerkes and began reading. ▣

SUE BERG

15

Leslie pulled her blue Prius into the driveway of a red brick duplex located below Grandad Bluff on Cliffwood Lane late Wednesday afternoon. The apartment building was well-cared for. Black shutters graced the large windows in front, and attractive shrubbery filled the space around the small portico leading to the dark red front door.

Leslie had found it hard to locate affordable housing in La Crosse that accepted pets. When she'd given her two-week notice at ICE a month ago, her mom began searching immediately for housing on the internet. Through her persistent efforts and contacts, she'd located this older, but well-maintained duplex for rent. The fact that Leslie was a veteran had helped.

The duplex was in a quiet residential neighborhood, and although it wasn't close to the hiking trails of Myrick Park like her other apartment had been, this one was within walking distance of Hixon Forest. Leslie could exercise with her dog, Paco, on several trails in the park that ran along the bluff and through the woods.

Her dad's truck with a U-Haul trailer attached was parked along the street. Walking over to the truck, her dad rolled down his window.

"I hope you have some help," he said grumpily.

"There's not that much in the trailer, Dad, and Slumberland is supposed to be coming with the living room and bedroom furniture at five," she explained, patting his arm. "So let's get going. I have the key."

In less than two hours, Leslie's apartment was stuffed with boxes of her belongings. The containers were stacked along the walls, and the furniture that had been delivered was assembled and positioned in a casual arrangement. With the last of the bulky items moved, she hugged her dad goodbye. He gave her a tin of chocolate chip cookies, then drove down the road with the empty U-Haul trailer rattling behind him.

Closing the front door, Leslie sagged against it. Reflecting on her first day back on the job, the open-armed welcome she'd anticipated had been absent. Higgins seemed especially stressed and harried. Paul and Sam were out doing a search at the funeral home where the murder had taken place. So she buried herself in her office with a list of vehicles from the closed-circuit camera video, then called the DMV to identify the owners from the license plates she could identify. That had taken a good portion of the afternoon. Since she was technically not getting paid until tomorrow, she cut out early and stopped at Festival Foods and Wal-Mart to buy groceries and other housekeeping essentials.

Now in the silence of her new digs, she felt a strange combination of excitement and trepidation. She had hoped to connect with Sam if for no other reason than to get her stomach flutters under control and the awkwardness of seeing one another again out of the way. That hadn't happened. Now her anxiety about confronting Sam again ramped up.

Paco wandered throughout the apartment, sniffing and smelling. He roamed over to her, and she reached down and thumped his side, petting his large, intelligent head. Begging for affection, he looked up at her with warm brown eyes. His wet, pink tongue swiped Leslie's face, his tail wagging enthusiastically.

"Well, if I don't get together with Sam, I guess you're still the alpha male in my life," she said to Paco, who cocked his head at her and whined.

She was in a rhythm of organizing and unpacking forty-five minutes later when her doorbell rang. Her landlord had promised to stop over and make sure everything was okay. Expecting him, Leslie walked around boxes, bubble wrap, and wadded newspapers strewn on the living room floor, grabbed the door handle, and opened it wide. Her mouth gaped in surprise.

"Sam," she said, taking in his presence. She closed her mouth with a gulp.

Sam stared. "I heard from Higgins that you'd arrived. I ... " He seemed at a loss for words. He looked away, then tried again. "I just wanted to say that I acted very badly when you left in January. I'm sorry." She thought he looked older, more seasoned, less innocent. *You did that to him,* she thought.

"I shouldn't have sprung my news on you so suddenly. It was totally unfair of me," she said nervously, her hand still resting on the doorknob.

"Do you need some help?" Sam asked, peeking around her at the mess on the living room floor. "I'm not really good at this domestic stuff, but I can lift and move."

"Oh, I'll do that," she said with a wave of her hand. Seeing his disappointed expression as if she'd dismissed him, she quickly added, "But you could come in and have something to drink. Maybe order a pizza."

"I'd like that," he said, a faint smile creasing his lips.

Sam walked in and sat on the leather couch. His heart was banging in his chest like a junior high kid with a major crush. Paco sidled up to him, his tail wagging hesitantly, nuzzling Sam's hand until he gave him a friendly tug on the ears. Stretching his arm along the back of the couch, he said casually, "You've upgraded to some new furniture."

Leslie hurried into the kitchen. "Yeah, I guess you could say that. I don't want to think about my credit card balance next month. Ouch!" She came out with refreshments, handing him a beer. Sitting down on the leather recliner opposite him, she sipped on a glass of wine.

They talked a while about the double homicide that had just happened yesterday. Sam retold the story of Higgins' supposedly lost sister found dead in Riverside Park and the four-year-old great-niece now living with Jim and Carol.

"Wow! How are they handling that?" Leslie asked.

Sam noticed the soft waves of her blond hair. Her blue eyes were the same deep mysterious wells he'd remembered. She was trim and fit in her blue jeans and T-shirt.

"I've never seen the chief come unglued like that," Sam said seriously. "He's fine now, I think, but it's been a big shock. We're still not really sure she's Higgins' sister."

Suddenly, it became quiet as if they had come to an unassailable brick wall. All the inconsequential prattle had been said. The wall that had kept them apart before still stood between them. Imposing. Formidable. Impregnable.

Sam didn't know what to say or do. All he knew was the vulnerability and trust that was so crucial to moving on was missing. It kept them from being truly honest about their feelings for one another. *Don't be the chickenshit you know you are,* he thought. *Lay it out there. What have you got to lose?* He remembered Higgins telling him to be a man. *Yeah, right.*

"Leslie," he began after a painful lag in the conversation. She watched him, her trepidation swimming below the surface, scrunching her eyes shut briefly. Sam continued. "I need to say something."

"Yes?" She was gripping her wine glass, her fingers entwined tightly around the stem. *Boy, I hope she doesn't throw it at me,* Sam thought. *I'll never live it down if I come to work tomorrow with stitches and a shiner.* Leslie held her wine glass in mid-air.

"Well, I guess I'll just say it ... " He leaned forward, resting his elbows on his knees. "I love you. I think I've loved you for a long time. When you left, I didn't know what to do. I was really angry and hurt, right to the core. I thought I could move on, and it might have worked if you wouldn't have come back, but seeing you again … " Sam sighed loudly. "Well, I can't deny what I feel for you." He leaned back into the couch, waiting, wondering what was going to happen.

Leslie noticed his soft, curly hair. His deep hazel eyes. The goodness and sincerity that welled up from somewhere within him. She set her wine glass on the end table, got up, walked over to him, and pulled him to his feet. Sam noticed the slight pink blush on her cheeks and her lips, those blue, blue eyes. He stood in front of her, holding her hands, waiting for the verdict. He'd put it out there. He was either going to be imprisoned in his love and desire for her or be freed to express it. *Here it comes. She's going to tell me to get lost,* he thought. *I can always write a book—The Insider's Guide to a Loser's Love Life.*

He closed his eyes for a second, then opened them wide. She leaned in and kissed him, tenderly at first, exploring, wondering.

But Sam was done with safety. He was done with the expected gentlemanly thing. His hands reached for her face, and he returned her kisses fervently, moving from her mouth to her neck and back to her lips. Wide-mouthed kisses full of unabashed passion. She pulled him down the hallway. Stopping at the bedroom door, she turned to him and whispered, "I've loved you ever since that stupid sting operation when we played husband and wife."

Stepping into the bedroom, Sam realized they'd reached the tipping point. Leslie pulled the shades, throwing the bedroom into a comfortable dim haze. Fumbling behind himself, he found the doorknob and pushed the door shut.

The next morning, he woke early as was his custom. He'd had this daydream before—the dream where he would wake up with Leslie's skin pressed to his. Now it was real. He leaned into her naked body, taking in her scent. Could this really be happening? He replayed the lovemaking again in his mind. Such sweetness. Such passion. Such release. Then the nagging guilt moved in. He could almost hear his dad, the Lutheran pastor, asking him what in the world he was doing.

He lifted his head and glanced at the clock on the nightstand, quickly dismissing the unsettling ramifications of his decisions—5:32 a.m. Paco scratched at the door. Sam slipped from bed, found his clothes, and left the bedroom, closing the door quietly. Paco growled low. But then he recognized Sam, and his tail began to wag happily.

"Well, buddy. I think your place of male domination is over. There's a new kid in town," he whispered, fluffing Paco's ears. ⬛

THURSDAY,
MAY 16

16

The sun peeked over the horizon at 5:33 a.m. Its golden rays spread warmth to a growing world of vegetation—the brilliant green panorama of leaves and grasses which thirstily drank up the heat and energy like a sponge soaking up spilled milk. The river traffic was already on the move. Barges as big as a football field rippled the dark water, heaving and pushing their cargo up and down the great waterway. Bobbing like corks in the current, fishing boats dotted the area under the big blue bridge that arched magnificently across the Mississippi River, its occupants casting and reeling with enthusiasm, hoping for a strike from a walleye or northern. Overhead in the blue sky, two bald eagles soared high on heated thermals, lazily drifting, their wings outstretched, their brilliant white heads scanning the earth, searching for a morning meal.

An hour later, ten-year-old Bobby Rude stood on the riverbank near Goose Island Park, casting his fishing line into a deep backwater pool and watching the bobber. A painted turtle sunned itself on a weathered gnarled tree trunk that lay partially submerged in the backwaters of the Mississippi River. Bobby had used that trunk many times to get out over the water, giving himself more room to cast, getting away from the brush that always threatened to tangle up his line and tackle. Fish loved to hunker down in the watery branches of the submerged tree. Bobby had caught many fine wide-mouth bass, crappies, and yellow perch there.

He plopped his line and bobber in the water. He glanced at the discolored bruise on his forearm. This morning it was a dark purple color. He cringed when he thought about the drunken stupor his father had been in last night. Weaving and crashing his way into the farmhouse, he stumbled on a chair leg, fell hard on the kitchen floor, and lay sprawled in a heap. Just another bruise he'd earned trying to help his father get to bed and sleep it off.

If he could just quit drinkin', our lives would be a lot better, he pondered. He thought about his mom's wisdom: You can't help people who won't help themselves. He knew the truth of that now.

He'd missed several days of school this spring for a variety of reasons. First and foremost, his mom had left. He woke up one foggy winter morning in March, and she was gone. He knew he'd never get over the empty closet where her clothes had been. Sometimes, when the humidity was just right, he could walk into the closet and smell her Pink Peony perfume. Since then, whenever he thought of his mom, he thought of that bare closet and the way his heart felt. Empty. Empty with the wind blowing through it.

Usually, Bobby spent his nights alone while his dad sat on a barstool at the Tip Your Hat Tavern in Genoa. After his mom left, Bobby tried to keep things going. He swept the kitchen floor, washed and dried the clothes, and made simple meals like hot dogs, frozen pizza, bologna sandwiches, and scrambled eggs. He'd even learned how to make French toast. He wasn't going to give Social Services a chance to come visiting and snooping, threatening to remove him and put him in a foster home.

He missed his mom every day, and when he slipped into a sad mood, he made chocolate chip cookies—the clumps of dough you bought in the frozen food aisle at Walmart. With a bellyful of cookies and a couple glasses of milk, the ache in his chest went away, and he could sleep at night.

School was a pain, albeit a necessary one. Even his alcoholic dad had told him you wouldn't get far in life without an education. The only two things he liked about school were Miss Higgins and books. Worksheets were stupid. Math was stupid. Art was stupid. But Miss Higgins was beautiful—so kind and patient and smart. Her blue eyes and sleek blond hair were a sight for sore eyes to an eleven-year-old motherless child. She smelled really good, too. Miss Higgins spent hours after school helping him with his homework and encouraging his interest in literature.

Bobby reached into his backpack and felt around for the book until he found it—*Rascal* by Sterling North. Miss Higgins had given him her tattered copy to read. He was honored that she shared it with him. Running his fingers over the cover of the book, he noticed it was faded, and the pages inside were well-worn and dog-eared. She told him the main character, Sterling, was from Lake Koshkonong along the Rock River in southern Wisconsin. The story had been her favorite in the fifth grade.

"You remind me of Sterling," Miss Higgins told him yesterday during free reading time.

"Really? Why?" Bobby squinted up at her.

"Well, he lived alone with his father for one thing. Just like you," she'd explained. "And Sterling loved nature, botany, zoology, and history."

"Did he like fishing?" Bobby asked her.

"Oh, yes. And the best part was that his dad let him build his own birch bark canoe right in their living room!" Bobby's eyebrows shot up in surprise. "Do you think your dad would let you do that?"

Boy, that was a stupid question that only had one answer—not in a hundred million years, Bobby thought. But he loved Miss Higgins for caring enough to find books that suited his boyish interests.

Now he lay back in the tall canary grass and nestled in. Opening the first page, he read, "It was in May 1918 that a new friend and companion came into my life: a character, a personality, and a ring-tailed wonder."

Bobby continued to read for an hour. The real world slipped away, and he lost himself in the world of Sterling North—life along marshes and creeks, adventures with raccoons, bike rides, fishing, and building canoes. Eventually, the busy morning traffic on U.S. Highway 35 reached his ears and nudged him back into reality.

Bobby thought back to Tuesday and the strange man who'd stood almost where he was lying right now. He seemed very upset. What had happened that made him so sad? And what had he thrown into the river with such force and anger?

Bobby was glad the stranger hadn't seen him hiding around the bend among the tall bullrushes. His skin prickled with fear and apprehension when he thought about the danger he'd been in. Whatever the stranger had done, Bobby was sure it wasn't good. When he recalled those events, he wondered if he should tell someone. The trouble was he didn't know the man. He'd never seen him before. Still, telling someone would lessen his worry. *Maybe I should tell Miss Higgins,* he thought. ◨

17

At eight-thirty on Thursday morning, Sam arrived at the office on the third floor of the law enforcement center. Emily Warehauser sat at her desk, perky and neatly dressed in an emerald knit dress that hugged her shapely figure. Sam walked down the hallway to his cubicle, made himself comfortable at his desk, and began word processing his report about the search at the funeral home and the interview with Lyle Oates. His phone burred in his pocket.

"Sam Birkstein," he answered.

"Sam, Rory here."

"Yeah, how're you doin'?"

"I'm good. Hey, I found out from one of my homeless sources that Juliette and the little girl were first seen in Riverside Park early Friday morning. Then I checked at Grand River Station and found out that a Greyhound bus attendant remembered them arriving late Thursday night. He identified Juliette from the picture you sent to my phone. They probably slept in or around the station that night, then got their bearings and moved to Tent City."

"Great. I knew you'd get better results than I would. Thanks, Rory. And I owe you," Sam said.

"No problem."

Sam got up from his desk and walked down the hall to Jim's office. Leslie was sitting on a chair in front of Jim's desk. Dressed in a pale pink sweater and dark brown trousers, she wore a simple strand of pearls and earrings that matched. She looked chic and professional as always. Turning, she stopped her narrative. "Good morning," she said, giving him a shy smile.

"Hey. How's it goin'?" *Just be cool and detached,* he coached himself.

Jim watched the exchange, thinking Sam and Leslie seemed rather comfortable with each other—unlike the warring factions he'd anticipated. No emotional bombs were being thrown from the trenches. *Fine by me,* he thought. Now when he studied Sam, he noticed his mood had improved considerably since yesterday. He was almost happy. *Go figure. Kids nowadays.*

"So what's up?" he asked Sam.

"Juliette and Lillie were first seen in Riverside Park on Friday, according to a Tent City resident. And a bus attendant at Grand River Station identified them and remembered them coming in on Thursday night."

"Okay. That's good to know." Switching topics, Jim asked, "Any earth-shattering news from your search of the funeral home?"

"No. But we brought the financial records back, and Paul's going through those in the next few days," Sam explained.

"A boring but necessary job." Jim leaned back, still surprised at the cooperative vibe between Sam and Leslie. *Could it be Sam had actually taken his advice and forgiven Leslie as he'd suggested?* Then another thought. *Could they have had a romantic interlude?* Who knew. Maybe both things happened. All he cared about right now was that they could be effective as members of the team.

"Anything else?" Jim asked.

Sam shook his head. "Other things are still being worked on."

"Keep me posted," Jim said. "I'm going to study the employment records of Gloria Bjerkes, and then after lunch, Leslie and I are going to conduct some interviews." Speaking directly to Leslie, he said,

"Be back here about one o'clock. Until then, get the notes of all the neighbors who were interviewed. See if anything pops out at you." To Sam, he said, "Leslie will give you the names of the drivers of those cars on the car dealer's camera. I want you to call each one. Hunt them down and see if they noticed anything at the funeral home. Check with city police. Find out if they spotted anything on the other surveillance cameras in the area."

"Got it, Chief," Sam said. After he'd left, Leslie stood to leave.

"Everything okay, Leslie?" Jim asked innocently. "You settled in?"

"Yes, sir. Everything's just fine," she said. Jim shrugged to himself as he returned to the piles of files on his desk. Leslie walked briskly down the hall to her office. Sam was sitting in a chair near the door, and he got up and pushed the door shut. Pulling Leslie into a hug, he kissed her long and tenderly. She pulled away.

"Sam, we can't do this at work. It's not professional," she said, a warning in her voice, but she'd enjoyed the kiss. Sam could tell.

"Professional? I guess we're supposed to be professionals, aren't we? Sorry, but if you weren't so beautiful, I could control myself," he retorted, smiling.

Leslie walked to her desk, picked up the list of car owners, and pushed it into Sam's chest as she opened the door. "Have a nice day," she said, a sardonic look on her face.

"You, too," Sam said, waving over his shoulder.

In his office, Jim turned to his laptop, searching his emails for anything from Vital Records. Seeing one that had come in late yesterday, he clicked on it and opened the attachment. The birth certificate for Juliette Lindvig stared back at him. Glancing over it, he noticed the date: June 24, 1958, and his mother's maiden name, Sonya Elise Lindvig.

His stomach clenched when he noticed the details on the birth certificate. *What? How was this possible?* Glancing further at the document, he saw another box checked: Parent: Single.

He sat back, letting out a pent-up groan. He stared over the top of his computer monitor, watching the traffic along Vine Street moving at its sickening furious speed. His mind was going at the same speed. *This doesn't make sense. Why would my mom have kept this from me? This is crazy!* He tried to reason out the unreasonable, and then he remembered Vivian's warnings about family secrets.

He zeroed in on the document again. Nothing else seemed out of place. The birth certificate appeared standard in every other way.

He noticed another attachment and clicked on it. It was the adoption papers for Juliette. On September 2, 1958, George and Mary Marquart from Wausau, Wisconsin, adopted Juliette. Scanning the certificate, he noticed Lutheran Social Services had facilitated the adoption. A name caught his eye. Gladys Hanson was the social worker who had fostered Juliette until the adoption was finalized. She was a faithful member of the Hamburg Lutheran Church where Jim attended, and she had been Jim's rock-solid friend through all of his ups and downs. In addition, Jim knew she frequently and faithfully prayed for him. He was reeling from everything he'd learned. He'd heard about people with hidden pasts; he just never thought his mom would be one of them. He glanced at his phone. The time was slipping away; he'd have to deal with this later.

But he couldn't quite leave the surprising discovery behind. He sat at his desk in a daze, thinking about all he'd learned. *A moment in time. Your life revolved around a moment in time when everything could change*, he thought philosophically. He had no idea when that moment had happened for Juliette, but one decision in the past made by his mother had separated Juliette from her biological family. It was unthinkable.

Finally, his phone rang, jerking him into the present. Two murders were screaming for his attention. Answering the phone, cradling it between his ear and shoulder, he printed the birth certificate and the adoption papers and slipped them into the top drawer of his desk.

He finished a conversation with Luke Evers, and then he turned his attention to Gloria Bjerkes' employment records and began to read.

18

Genoa, Wisconsin, located south of Stoddard along U.S. Highway 35, was a charming river village populated largely by Italian American citizens of the Catholic faith. The short narrow streets and charming older homes and stores built beneath the bluffs created an allure that still attracted tourists and sportsmen who were fascinated with life along the great and mighty Mississippi River. Despite its small population, the village sported a variety of interesting places to visit—the Old Tool Shed Antiques, the Big River Inn Hotel, and Rudy's Bar and Grill, known for their great hamburgers.

In addition, perched beneath a huge jutting sandstone bluff, the red brick complex of St. Ignatius Parish in Genoa included a church, rectory, and an elementary school which served the needs of the Catholic community, although religious interests seemed to be waning. A sign of the times. Like most parochial schools, St. Ignatius struggled to pay its teachers adequate salaries. They frequently lost their educators to the lure of public education jobs that offered higher wages, attractive insurance packages, and retirement plans.

Father Jordan Knight dug fervently in his little plot of land behind the rectory at St. Ignatius Parish and Catholic School. Digging holes and plopping tomato and pepper plants in them, he hoped his small attempt at greening up the earth would help slow global warming. He chuckled to himself. Most of the people in this parish didn't believe the scientific reports about the earth's precipitous slide to destruction. "It's all fake news!" he'd heard a number of parishioners argue. He'd simply walked away, shaking his head at their ignorance.

Father Jordan was thirty-five years old but had already served three parishes before landing in this winsome little community. Here, unlike his other callings, he was a jack-of-all-trades: pastor to the congregants, administrator of the school, and head honcho in securing donations and creating fundraising opportunities.

There were fringe benefits to his job, however. Mrs. Zabolio, his neighbor, kept him well fed with her homemade lasagna, tangy fettuccine with Parmesan chicken, and sweet chocolate almond biscotti. It was enough to make you think you'd died and gone to heaven. He chuckled now as he recalled her latest philosophical ramblings.

"Why are we wasting time trying to recruit our good Catholic boys to the priesthood? Look at you! Such a handsome lad. You should be married and producing a big family. Nowadays, nobody wants a big family. Two children? What's that but a good beginning? Why do they stop there? In my opinion, more husbands and wives should be in the bedroom at night instead of watching TV."

Father Jordan laughed heartily, placing his hand on Mrs. Zabolio's shoulder. "Maybe I should put your advice in the parish newsletter," he teased. "By order of Mrs. Zabolio, all married congregants are to have sexual relations without protection at least three times weekly until our Catholic population reaches the desired peak levels."

Mrs. Zabolio threw back her head and cackled, her white hair flying in the wind. "I dare you, Father. I dare you to do it!" Then more seriously, she said, "There was a time that no good Catholic had less than four children. I had eight, the Lord be praised. I remember the days when ten and twelve children were the norm."

"Well, Mrs. Zabolio, I think those days are over. Now, most

couples both work outside the home," Father Knight commented.

Mrs. Zabolio made a sour face. "What about the old saying, 'Many hands make light work'?" she grumped. "A big family teaches lessons you can't learn when you're only one of two."

"I can see that neither one of us is going to win this argument," he said judiciously.

In the heat of the afternoon, Father Jordan spent time in his study praying, meditating on scripture, and preparing his homily. Today, he had a staff meeting with the teachers to fine-tune ideas for next week's school picnic. It would also coincide with the 110th consecutive year St. Ignatius School had been serving the Genoa area. It would be an event ripe with the possibility of generous donations.

At three-fifteen, the school buses were loaded and ready to depart. They pulled out of the parking lot, little hands waving and energetic voices calling goodbye to the classroom teachers on bus duty. In the small library after the buses had gone, the teaching staff gathered wearily, notebooks and pencils in hand, for a final session with Father Jordan. Activities, volunteer lists, and schedules were finalized for the All School Family Picnic on Saturday, May 25. The meeting broke up at four-thirty.

Sara Higgins strolled casually down the hall to her classroom. Bobby Rude was sleeping, scrunched in a beanbag chair in the corner by the window. Sara shook her head, watching him doze. The well-worn copy of *Rascal* lay propped open on his chest.

Bobby had a sharp, inquisitive mind, but she worried about his general health. He had clean clothes, and his daily hygiene seemed adequate for a ten-year-old boy, but this week had been a rough one. He'd only attended school Wednesday afternoon and today. And today, he'd been late—again.

She leaned down and gently shook Bobby's shoulder. His eyes popped open, and he wiped the drool from the corner of his mouth.

"Bobby, you didn't get on the bus," she said, worried. "Come on, get your things. I'll give you a ride home, okay?"

"Sorry, Miss Higgins," he said apologetically. He popped out of the squishy chair. His brown hair curled around the collar of his plaid flannel shirt, and he hoisted his pants up with a jerk.

"Are you getting enough sleep, Bobby? Getting to bed at a decent time every night?" Miss Higgins asked, probing about his general welfare.

"Yeah. Well, most of the time anyway. It's just that sometimes I dream about my mom, and then I don't sleep too good." His brown eyes misted suddenly with tears.

"I know. I dream about my mom, too," Sara said wistfully. "I still miss her every day."

"Do you think my mom will ever come back?" The young boy's face reflected so much sadness. Sara felt her heart lurch with empathy.

"Mmm, I don't know, Bobby. It's hard to tell. Maybe one day she will," Sara said. "Listen, I need to get home. I'm packing, so I can move into my new apartment this weekend."

"I'll get my backpack from the hall," Bobby said, turning and disappearing.

Sara straightened her desk and glanced at her plans for Friday. Satisfied that everything was in order, she walked to the door and shut out the lights.

Bobby was waiting for her at the car. She unlocked it, and he climbed in, buckling his seat belt. As they started down the main street of Genoa, he turned to her, his eyes full of questions. She glanced over, smiled, and then turned her attention back to driving.

"Miss Higgins?" he asked quietly.

"Yes, Bobby."

"Have you ever had a secret that you couldn't tell anyone?"

Oh boy. I was afraid this might happen one day, she thought. "Well, everyone has some secrets. Secrets can be fun if they're good, like a present that's a surprise for someone's birthday. But secrets can make us anxious if they're sad or bad. What kind of secret do you have?"

Bobby stayed silent. He felt safe with Miss Higgins, like nothing could hurt him when he was with her. He glanced at the river. Its surface reflected a million sparkling diamonds of light. He loved the river, except for the other day.

"Do you have something you want to tell me?" Sara asked after several moments of silence.

"What do you do if you saw something scary, but you—"

"Has someone hurt you, Bobby?" Sara interrupted, alarmed. "Threatened you?"

"No. No. I … It's hard to explain." He shook his head. "Never mind. It's probably nothing," he said, growing quiet.

Sara scolded herself. Patience wasn't her best trait. Now Bobby had shut down. She aimed her car up the rutted driveway to the little white house sitting near a limestone bluff above the river. The view was spectacular from here.

As Bobby opened the door to get out, Sara said, "You know you can tell me if you need help with something. I'll always listen, and together we'll try to do the right thing, Bobby." At that moment, Bobby thought Miss Higgins had the kindest eyes of anyone he knew.

"I know," Bobby said, pushing the passenger door shut. "Thanks for the ride."

He scrambled up the driveway and across the lawn, climbing the three steps on the side of the house. He turned and waved. Sara waved back, reversed the car, and drove back down to the main highway.

What was Bobby going to tell me? Whatever it was, he's worried about it. Since he'd begun attending St. Ignatius School in January through the generosity of a Catholic sponsor, Sara fretted about his home life. An alcoholic father and a mother who had deserted him left him bereft in the world, without an advocate. She sighed when she thought of all the pain he'd endured in his young life. All she could do now was let him know she was there to listen. She hoped he would trust her enough someday to share his secret. ◘

19

The Bjerkes' residence was located in Dunwoody Estates, a relatively recent high-end development on the south end of La Crosse, just barely within the city limits. The home was a sleek, angular structure that featured a huge, exposed limestone chimney that soared through the front face of the house. Large trapezoid windows on either side of the chimney let in abundant light, and a custom front door was carved with an intricate design of leaves and enchanting floral motifs entwined together around a frosted oval window. The lawn was pristine, trimmed and manicured, and the abundant shrubbery around the house was expertly pruned. *Nothing ticky-tacky about this place,* Jim thought.

Leslie leaned forward and pushed the doorbell.

"Quite the place, huh, Chief?" she said softly.

"I didn't think the funeral business was that lucrative," he said, his eyes scanning the exterior of the building.

The door opened. Gloria Bjerkes gave Leslie a cool stare as she held up her police ID and introduced herself. Gloria's eyes wandered over Leslie's head to Jim. She gave him a conspiratorial grin as if they had a secret.

"Oh, Lt. Higgins. You're back." She looked at Leslie with a scrutinizing gaze. "Please come in." They walked through the generous entryway and were ushered into an open, airy living room. A limestone fireplace rose to the ceiling leaving Leslie and Jim kinking their necks upward to get a better look. Sunlight played off the textured walls and rich walnut floors. Hanging from the vaulted ceiling, a huge glass and chrome chandelier in the center of the room warmed the area. The walls were adorned with original oil paintings, and a few shelves on either side of the huge fireplace were decorated with collections of colorful pottery and books. Rather than feeling cold and impersonal, it felt inviting and relaxing.

"You have a lovely home, Mrs. Bjerkes," Leslie said diplomatically.

"Thank you. We didn't build it. Dr. Lars Woodman had it built in 2001 when this area was developed. We bought it from him three years ago," Gloria said.

"Woodman, the heart surgeon at Mayo?" Jim asked with interest.

"Yes, he's my father, actually," Gloria stated, laying her financial credentials out there.

"My first wife, Margie, served on the hospital advisory board with him. She thought very highly of him," Jim explained. "Your home is really something. It's beautiful," he said, impressed in spite of himself. *People and their pedigrees. Old money. That explains it. Not a house most morticians could afford,* he thought.

"Thank you. Please make yourself comfortable while I get some beverages," she said. Gloria retreated to the adjoining open kitchen area returning in a few moments with saucers, cups, hot water, tea bags, and a carafe of coffee. As Gloria poured the drinks, Jim was thinking about the discoveries he'd made in reviewing her employment records at the university.

Accepting a steaming cup of coffee and taking a sip, Jim noticed it was a delicious exotic brew with a hint of chocolate. Leslie opted for tea. They chitchatted for a few minutes. Then Jim began the interview.

"Mrs. Bjerkes, in reviewing your employment files, I noticed several disciplinary notes and a few student complaints that I'd like you to explain, if you can," Jim began, sounding more like a lawyer in a courtroom than a detective conducting an investigation.

The friendly atmosphere that had dominated their welcome suddenly seemed to evaporate.

Gloria held her coffee cup mid-air, then slowly lowered it to the saucer in front of her. "What do you mean?" she said, her voice tense. Her eyes searched Jim's impassive face for a clue. "I thought employment records were private. How did you get access to them?"

"During a murder investigation, we have the right to examine various information, employment records being one of many sources," Leslie informed her. "We'll also be looking through the financial records of the funeral home." Gloria focused her attention on Jim, ignoring Leslie. The flirting disposition was gone.

Jim continued. "In 2013, you were called before a university advisory board that reviews student complaints about instructors. In that meeting, three students," Jim flipped open his memo pad and glanced at it, "Steven Hanratty, Joel Engstad, and Ben Johnson, all claimed you made sexual advances toward them during some exercises you were demonstrating. Apparently, they were recovering from recent injuries in gymnastics and wrestling, and you were providing therapy. Is that correct so far?" Jim finished, giving her an icy blue-eyed stare.

Jim could see the wheels of Gloria's mind turning and grinding out a rationale for the accusations. Leslie watched Gloria's reaction, noticing the tension in the room had become rather hostile. She recognized the practiced rationalization of the inappropriate behavior. She'd been the victim of sexual and physical abuse at the hands of her old Army boyfriend, Wade Bennett, but this was the first time she'd ever seen a woman display it.

When she spoke, Gloria's voice was cold, and her demeanor was frosty. "That little fiasco was a concerted attack on my character and integrity as an athletic trainer. You do know those three students later recanted. They said they made the whole thing up. Were you aware of that?" Her eyes were jumping in her head.

Jim could have cared less if they'd recanted or not. He'd experienced Gloria's innuendos and sexual overtones. He had a feeling their accusations were probably true. She'd tried to come on to him, for Pete's sake. If they'd recanted, then he intended to find out why—from the victims.

"Well, yes, I did see that in your files. But how do you explain their original concerns? It takes some nerve to accuse a college professor of sexual abuse and face a board of college officials. So you're telling me they fabricated the whole thing?" Gloria blinked rapidly and continued to stare at Jim. "For what? Attention? Notoriety? Some college dare? What?" Jim asked, driving his concerns home. "Making up those specific incidents seems pretty far-fetched to me." Jim had read the details of the abuse the students shared, and he was sickened by the violations Gloria had visited on her students.

"I couldn't tell you why they did it," Gloria shot back. "Immaturity? Stupidity? Can I help it if they found me attractive?" Her voice had gone shrill. "The fact is they fabricated the incidents, and it thoroughly embarrassed me. I spent months and thousands of dollars in lawyer fees to clear my name and reputation," Gloria said, a blush rising from her neck and traveling to her cheeks. "I was dismissed for a time from my position. The whole stupid thing was preposterous—and totally false!" *Apparently, she's not used to being challenged,* Leslie thought. Jim waited, letting the quiet hit its mark. Finally, after several uncomfortable moments, Gloria filled the empty space.

Letting out a long sigh, she said, "Some of the exercises I recommended could be considered controversial among certain therapy circles. When I analyzed their injuries, I recommended specific exercises to strengthen their muscles. I suppose I might have touched them occasionally in guiding them through the exercises, and they misinterpreted it," she finished defiantly. *If you keep talking, you're going to hang yourself,* Leslie thought.

"So if we question these students, they'll tell us it was all a big misunderstanding?" Leslie asked, her blue eyes locking on Gloria.

"Why are you interrogating me about something that happened years ago?" she yelled angrily. "You should be trying to find my husband's killer!" Her face was flushed, and her eyes were flashing with pent-up frustration.

Jim thought her hysterical defense was interesting. "As you probably know, Mrs. Bjerkes, spouses are always the first suspects we look at when investigating a murder," Jim said calmly, his baritone voice even and neutral. "That's an uncomfortable reality you'll have to face."

"What? You're investigating me?" Gloria screamed, jumping out of the chair. Her arms flew out from her sides in a defensive posture. "This is ridiculous!"

"Mrs. Bjerkes, we are simply asking you to clarify the conflicting reports in your employment record," Leslie said softly. "We're giving you a chance to tell us the truth."

"I've already explained that," Gloria snapped, dismissing Leslie instantly. "There's nothing more to say. This line of questioning is very upsetting!" She waved her arms and pointed at Jim. "I'm trying to plan my husband's funeral, and you have the gall to come in here and accuse me of murder. This is unbelievable!" she said, revving up for another diatribe.

Jim held up his hands. "Mrs. Bjerkes, no one is accusing—"

But Gloria interrupted him. "I refuse to speak to you without my lawyer present. Please leave," she said emphatically, pointing her finger to the door.

"Sure, we'll leave," Jim said reasonably, rising from the couch, "but the next time we question you, it will be at the Law Enforcement Center."

"With my lawyer present!" Gloria finished triumphantly, her eyes glittering.

Silently Jim took stock of the house and the trappings of a comfortable, wealthy life. He'd met more than his share of spoiled brats. He was in no mood for her antics.

"That's your call," he stated firmly with gritted teeth. Stepping around her, he straightened his tie and followed Leslie to the massive front door. They stepped out on the flagstone entrance, and Gloria slammed the door behind them. The door rattled on its hinges. Jim and Leslie exchanged a glance.

"I know," Leslie said, rolling her eyes. "I need to track down those students and see what they have to say."

Jim nodded. "The sooner, the better. Let's go over and talk to Jeremy's former wife."

Driving across town on Losey Boulevard, they turned left on Mississippi Avenue and drove up to a small but well-kept bungalow. Jim wondered how many doorbells he'd rung in his career. Plenty. Here he was again, pushing another button. Leaning against the wrought iron railing, he waited for someone to answer.

"So you found a place to live?" Jim asked Leslie while they waited by the front door.

"Yes, a duplex over on Cliffwood. Nice place. Sam came over last night, and we—" she began explaining, but a rattling at the door interrupted her account.

Just as well. I don't want to know, Jim thought to himself.

"Mrs. Priebe?" Jim asked, flashing his ID and giving her a dimpled smile.

"Yes, thank you for calling ahead. Lt. Higgins, right?" she asked, her eyes drifting to his odd colored hair, a mix of gray and blond. Jim nodded.

"This is Detective Brown," he said, pointing to Leslie, who flashed her ID.

"Please come in," Mrs. Priebe said. She held the door open and motioned Jim and Leslie into a welcoming but rather dark living room. Leslie and Jim found a place on the couch. Opening the window shades to let in more sunlight, Mrs. Priebe sat in a wingback chair next to a small fireplace. She was a handsome woman with dark coiffed hair, warm hazel eyes in a round face. She was dressed casually in a pair of capris, a colorful blouse, and sandals. She looked at Jim expectantly.

"So, what is it you'd like to know, Lt. Higgins?" she asked quietly.

She was an oasis of peace and calm compared to Gloria's petulant attitude an hour ago. Jim cringed when he thought about her tantrum. He began. "First of all, let me say how sorry we were about the death of your former husband."

"Thank you. We've been divorced for over ten years, but I never wished Jeremy any ill will. I just wasn't willing to share him with another woman." She retained her composure, but that wasn't surprising to Jim. His previous conversation on the phone with her was gracious, and now she appeared more than willing to cooperate.

"I can understand that. So can you tell me about your interactions with his current wife, Gloria?" Jim asked, not knowing the response he'd get.

"Gloria? Well, I'm sure by now you've got her number. Being a detective and all, someone as perceptive as you would not be at a loss to figure out what makes her tick," Julie said, her eyebrows lifting imperceptibly.

"Granted, but could you tell us what your experience has been with Gloria?" Jim persisted, his voice kind. "I'd like to hear it from you."

"Sure. It's simple. She stole my husband. I don't curse or speak deceitfully about people, Lieutenant. But she's a philandering witch. I think the term today would be sexual predator, although we usually use that term in reference to men, not women." Although her placid expression had not changed, her voice had become hard and uncompromising.

"I'm sorry that happened. How did they meet?" he asked, taking notes.

"Jeremy was an assistant junior varsity baseball coach at the university. They met at some function on campus and began an affair," she said, her voice sad.

"You called her a predator. Why?" Leslie asked.

"She set her sights on Jeremy and pursued him without a

backward glance. It didn't matter that he was a married man. I walked in on them at the funeral home," Mrs. Priebe said. "Once I'd discovered their fling, it became apparent that Gloria was neither ashamed about it nor willing to give him up. She called constantly and wouldn't take no for an answer. I persistently asked her to leave us alone. I wanted to make my marriage work, but she was relentless in her pursuit of my husband, and she didn't give up until I'd agreed to a divorce."

"Is there anything at all that you can tell us about Jeremy's current marriage?" Jim asked.

"I have no idea what kind of marriage he had with Gloria. I do know they left the parish at St. Ignatius in Genoa a couple of years ago. There was a rumor that some issue had come up between them and the priest there. I couldn't tell you anything more than that. When Jeremy and I divorced, I lost all contact with him since we didn't have any children. I didn't see him until about three years ago when we happened to run into each other at Target." She lifted her hands in a gesture of frustration. "Sorry I couldn't be of more help," she finished weakly.

"You mentioned a priest. Do you know what this rift with the priest was about?" Jim asked, puzzled.

"No, and I wouldn't take it as fact. People like to talk and spread gossip. I try to distance myself from those types," Mrs. Priebe stated.

"Do you attend St. Ignatius?" Jim asked.

"Jeremy and I were married there and attended regularly throughout our marriage. But once the divorce went through, and Jeremy and Gloria kept attending, I couldn't go back. It was like they were rubbing the affair in my face. It was too painful," Julie explained. "I not only lost my husband, but I also lost my church family."

"That must have been a difficult time for you," Leslie said softly.

"Yes. Yes, it was very difficult. I remarried, but my husband Arnold died from cancer two years ago." She paused a moment, then continued. "I've moved on. All you can do is pick up the pieces, forgive as best you can, and live the life God gave you." She smiled. Jim totally agreed with her philosophy. That's what he'd had to do after Margie died.

After a few more minutes of clarifying her contact information, Jim and Leslie stood and walked to the front door. Turning at the doorway, Jim said, "If it's any consolation, Mrs. Priebe, I intend to find Jeremy's killer." He handed her his card. "Please call me if you think of anything that might be helpful."

"Thank you, sir. I will," she replied and quietly closed the door.

As Jim and Leslie drove across town and returned to the Law Enforcement Center, Jim thought about what he had learned about Gloria. Why was he so bothered by her? He'd had plenty of contact with questionable characters during his years in law enforcement. What was it about Gloria that raised his suspicions about her possible involvement in her husband's murder?

Was it the thin veneer of social status and wealth that Gloria projected in an effort to protect her reputation and position at the university? Or was it how she'd used her position and status to troll for victims who would have a hard time resisting her? Jim harrumphed to himself. He didn't know yet, but when he thought about the deception and lies Gloria had already displayed at the afternoon interview, he knew one thing: Gloria Bjerkes would continue to be a suspect in the investigation of her husband, Jeremy, and his assistant, Layne McNally. ◘

20

Meanwhile, across town, Paul was digging through the financial records of the Bjerkes and Oates Funeral Home. He leaned back and sighed. He wasn't spotting any financial irregularities in the mortuary records. Getting out of his chair, he limped painfully down the hall to Sam's cubicle.

Sam had spent the afternoon calling and interviewing the owners of the cars who were on the closed-circuit camera at Lagerstroms' Quality Used Vehicles on the corner of Fifth and Mormon Coulee Drive.

"Hey, find anything interesting?" he asked Sam, leaning on the door frame.

"Well, of the vehicles we could identify by license plate numbers, all but four of the owners hadn't even heard about the murder. How is that possible in a small town like this?" Sam asked, looking at Paul.

"If you don't listen to the news or go on the internet, I suppose it's possible, but they don't sound like anybody I know." Paul rubbed his leg, grimacing a little. It was throbbing again today.

Sam noticed the gesture but didn't pry. "What about a text? Wouldn't you hear about a local murder from a text on your phone?"

"Not everybody has a cell phone, Sam. My parents don't. They just have a landline, and I talk to them quite a bit," Paul said. "And believe it or not, they do know what's going on."

"They don't have a cell phone? Really?" he asked, surprised.

"What about the other four drivers?" Paul said, slightly irritated, moving on.

Sam reviewed his interview notes. "Two people were on their way to work and never looked at the funeral home lot. Drove right by—too distracted by their busy morning agenda to notice. Another lady, Janet Grotte, says there was a blue car—probably Lyle's—and another red SUV in the parking lot when she went by. I called Gloria, and she said Jeremy owned a 2016 red Jeep Grand Cherokee. So that confirms that Jeremy's and Lyle's vehicles were at the funeral home that morning." Sam stopped briefly.

"We're down to one other car. What about that one?" Paul asked wearily.

"This gets interesting," Sam commented. "A college student, Melissa Turner, was driving down Fifth Street about 9:55 a.m. When she got closer to the funeral home, a cat ran out in front of her car. She braked hard to miss the cat, almost coming to a complete stop. Then she watched the cat run into the funeral home parking lot. According to her, a sporty blue car was also in the lot—probably Layne's Leaf—and a black older model car was sitting next to it." Sam glanced at Paul. "Whaddya think about that?"

"Could be the killer's vehicle," Paul said hopefully. "The timing's right. Was she sure about the time?"

"Yeah, she said she glanced at her dashboard clock and remembered it was 9:55. So I asked her to go online tonight and see if she could find a car that resembled the one she saw and give us a call tomorrow. It's a super long shot, but it's better than nothing." Sam stood and stretched his arms to the ceiling. "Also, the UPS gal said there were only three cars in the lot when she arrived to deliver her packages at 10:15. If the killer drove a black car, obviously, he was already gone by then." Sam grabbed his suit coat off the back of the door. "Man, I need a run tonight. Too much desk work today."

Still leaning against the door frame, Paul asked, "So, how're things with Leslie?"

"Fine. We worked out our differences," he said a little too quickly, casually slipping into the suit coat.

Suspicious, Paul said, "No kidding? You were in a pretty nasty mood yesterday. What changed?"

Sam got a faraway look in his eyes. He rubbed his neck and ran his hand through his hair.

After a few awkward moments, Paul said, "Oh, I get it." He studied Sam, who seemed embarrassed but *happy.* "I get it now," Paul repeated, smiling, his arms crossed over his chest.

"It is what it is," Sam said, cool and collected.

"A word of warning: You better watch it around Higgins. He has a sixth sense about stuff like that even though he doesn't say anything," Paul reminded Sam.

Throwing his hands in the air, Sam said, "Hey, he told me we had to find a way to get along. I found it." ◘

21

A s the sun's rays slipped across the carpet in the living room, Carol collapsed in the black swoopy chair. She pulled the lever as the footrest lifted her swollen feet. Keeping up with Lillie was a full-time job. Carol's back ached, and her feet and ankles were swollen. *A four-year-old's boundless energy and enthusiasm for life are awesome to behold and impossible to keep up with when you're nine months pregnant,* Carol thought, groaning.

She was glad she had dinner in the oven. Lillie played quietly on the living room floor. She cuddled Elsa as she watched the *Frozen* video again. "Let it go, let it go," the lyrics repeated, the music filling the living room. Carol closed her eyes for what seemed like just a minute.

"Bapa! Bapa!" Lillie yelled, running from the living room and clamoring into Jim's arms. Carol jumped at the interruption, then attempted to maneuver her way out of the chair, but Jim was too quick.

"Hey, beautiful! You stay right there," he said, leaning down and giving her a kiss. "You look exhausted. I'll get dinner together. Lillie can help me," he explained, looking over at the little girl who was fascinated with Carol and Jim's kisses. He found the remote and flicked off the television. He loosened his tie and laid it on the end table.

"How come you always do that kissing stuff?" Lillie asked, tapping her little foot on the floor.

"Kissing shows you love someone," Jim said. He grabbed Lillie and swung her into the air, planting a kiss on her tender cheek.

"Hey!" Lillie said, pouting, her face scrunched in a scowl. "You got whiskers," she said grumpily.

"And you need to help me in the kitchen," Jim said, plopping her back on the floor and crooking his finger at her.

While Lillie talked nonstop and peppered Jim with unending questions in the kitchen, Carol reflected on the week that had gone by like a flash. Lillie was like a tidal wave that had washed over their predictable, domesticated lifestyle. She defied explanation, refused to be ignored, bounced off the walls with endless energy and curiosity, and had thoroughly and completely invaded their hearts. The only thing that put a damper on everything was the information Jim kept uncovering about Juliette.

" ... not only that, but my mom must have had a kid out of wedlock. Can you believe that? And Gladys Hanson fostered Juliette until she was adopted. Can this story get any more twisted?" Jim murmured. His face was lined with sadness as he chewed another bite of roasted chicken. "I ... I just don't understand it," he stewed.

"Maybe you better take Vivian up on those counseling sessions," Carol suggested wisely, sipping her iced tea.

"I might eventually, but I've still got to talk to Gladys Hanson. She's got to know something about this whole deal. There has to be some more stuff she knows about this, isn't there?" His blue eyes were puzzled with facts he couldn't accept.

Carol laid her hand over Jim's. "I'm sorry that you had to find this out about your family. But one good thing came out of it," she said, gazing at Lillie as she chased her peas around the edge of her plate with her spoon.

"Yeah," Jim agreed, "that's one thing we can agree on," his eyes softening at the impish little child who now occupied a treasured place in their family.

When bedtime stories were finally finished, Carol and Jim were both scraping the bottom of the energy barrel.

"Tell you what," Jim said slyly, "you start a bubble bath while I clean up the kitchen. And then I might join you."

"Oooh, that sounds too good to pass up," Carol said, walking down the hall to the spacious master bath.

Before Margie, Jim's first wife, had died of breast cancer, Jim had built her an extravagant master bath suite complete with a soaking tub that featured a window above it so she could view the stars. After lighting candles in the windows, Carol filled the tub with French bath salts and bubble bath, then lowered the lights to dim. Slipping out of her clothes, she lowered her aching body into the warm, soapy water, luxuriating in the quiet, watching the stars twinkling in the night sky overhead.

After fifteen minutes, she was ready to give up on Jim when he tiptoed into the bathroom wearing only a towel. Carol watched him longingly as he let the towel fall to the floor. He climbed in the tub, sidling up to her from behind, groaning with the pleasure of the warm, sudsy water.

"It's not nice to tempt an extremely pregnant lady with your gorgeous body," Carol said, pouting.

Jim chuckled softly. "Well, don't worry. We'll be back into the swing of lovemaking again within six weeks of the birth," Jim said, kissing Carol's head. His hands drifted to her swollen belly.

"Six weeks? Says who? You're not the one who's having this baby, big guy," Carol admonished him. Then with a hint of anxiety, she asked, "You'll be there for the birth, won't you, Jim?"

"Honey! Of course I'll be there. Don't worry," Jim said, trying to keep the annoyance out of his voice. "We've already discussed this many times. Sam, Paul, and Leslie can handle any emergency that might present itself." He kissed her neck tenderly. Carol leaned back and laid her head on his chest.

"Well, now you've got this big double murder going on, and I don't want you to miss out. I can imagine some huge crisis that will take you away at just the wrong moment," she said, getting drowsy.

"I. Will. Be. There." A few moments of silence followed. "Do you believe me?" Jim asked softly. "Sweetheart?" But Carol had fallen asleep. He leaned back and enjoyed the peaceful quiet, the stars flickering above him, letting the thoughts that crowded his mind drift away. ◘

FRIDAY,
MAY 17

22

Father Knight's forehead creased with worry as he sat in the darkened interior of his office. He was still trying to solidify his guest list for the school picnic and celebration. One hundred and ten years of continuous Catholic education in the small community of Genoa was something to be proud of. He wanted as many living priests who had served in Genoa to be there. So far, there were five coming. And he expected Father Skip Howard—the last priest at the parish before he came—to respond to his phone call and email invitation. So far, nothing. He'd try again this morning after vespers.

Seven brave, faithful congregants attended vespers. The prayers and chanting filled Father Knight's heart with worship and a closeness to God he couldn't explain. His small group seemed to gain a sense of peace and purpose from the daily service. Sometimes they celebrated the Eucharist, but not today. This morning Father Knight wanted to finish contacting the honored guests for the picnic to confirm their plans to attend.

"So, how are the plans coming along for the school celebration?" Mrs. Zabolio asked as she stepped into the bright sunshine and clasped Father Knight's strong hand.

"I just have to nail down a few details, and then we'll be ready," Father Knight said smiling.

"Come over for afternoon coffee. Three o'clock. Cannoli and Zibbibo?" she said, her bright eyes hopeful.

"How could I refuse?" Father said sweetly, although he had no idea what Zibbibo was. He really didn't care. Whatever Mrs. Zabolio gave him to eat was always delicious. "I'll be there."

Now he sat at the ancient walnut desk in the cozy parish study, attempting another call to Father Skip Howard. Father Knight was aware of the scandalous reports swirling through the congregation when Father Howard hurriedly left Genoa for a congregation in central Wisconsin. But Father Knight really didn't want to know all the sordid details. He was hoping they would fade into the background.

When the young priest had arrived at St. Ignatius, there was a sense of deep hurt and division among the congregation. Although his carnal side wanted all the gossipy details, he was devoted to Christ. His calling was to spread the Lord's message of reconciliation, peace, and love. He refused to listen when people tried to unload their opinion about the rift. Only in the confessional did he allow his congregants to confess their sins so they could be released from their burdens. Still, no one had mentioned Father Howard in all the confessions he'd heard so far.

He leaned back in the old walnut chair with the phone to his ear. The boards on the seat of the chair creaked uncomfortably, protesting against his weight. Finally, on the third ring, a deep male voice answered.

"This is St. Jerome's Catholic Parish. Father Skip Howard speaking. How may I help you?"

"Father Howard. I've been trying to reach you. You're a hard man to get a hold of. It's Father Knight at St. Ignatius in Genoa." There was a foreboding silence. Father Knight asked again, "Father Howard, are you there?"

"Yes. Yes, I'm here. What can I help you with?" he responded, his voice losing some of its friendliness.

"Did you get my email about the school picnic and celebration?

Many have insisted that you attend. You've had such an influence here."

"The email must have gotten lost in cyberspace. I wasn't aware of the event. Can you fill me in?" he said, the iciness still there.

Father Knight gave him the details. After checking his calendar, Father Howard agreed to come.

"I have a meeting with the bishop at the Guadalupe Shrine that morning, so I'll drop by the school before driving back north."

"Wonderful. I'll spread the word," Father Knight said.

"Oh, no. Please, don't. Let it be a surprise," Father Howard insisted.

"As you wish." Father Knight conceded. "I'll leave it ambiguous, and then when you show up, it will truly be a surprise."

By three o'clock that afternoon, Father Knight was seated at Mrs. Zabolio's kitchen table. A bright floral cloth enhanced the setting of white luncheon plates and fine silverware. Fresh cream-filled cannoli sat on a beautiful ceramic tray, and two small glasses were filled with Zibbibo, a rich sweet Italian wine meant to be served with desserts.

Mrs. Zabolio picked up her glass and lifted it to Father Knight. He did the same.

"Cin, cin," she said, smiling sweetly. "Straight from Sicily."

"To your health," Father Knight said, lifting his glass.

"A cannoli for you and one for me," Mrs. Zabolio said as she served the delicate treats.

"Now tell me, is Father Skip coming to the celebration?"

"Can't say for sure. It's still up in the air," Father Knight said.

"Well, there are many who wish he'd just stay away. With all the rumors surrounding him, I can understand their sentiments." Father Knight felt his stomach cramp in anxiety. He stayed silent, hoping the subject would be drowned in whipped cream and wine.

Mabel licked her lips, anticipating the sweet rush of sugar from the cannoli.

"And this double murder at the funeral home. What a tragedy!" she exclaimed, shaking her head. "Jeremy Bjerkes was such a nice man. He attended St. Ignatius Parish with his first wife, Julie, for many years. Then his divorce. And later, his argument with Father Howard. Such a sad way to part," she finished.

"These cannoli are fantastic," Father Knight said, licking whipped cream from his upper lip.

"Help yourself," Mrs. Zabolio encouraged. "And I can understand if the topic of Father Howard is off limits for you. Acqua passata no macina piu."

Father Knight looked puzzled. "An old Italian proverb, maybe?"

"Yes. The loose translation: It's water under the bridge," Mrs. Zabolio smiled. "Another cannoli?" ◘

23

Sam and Paul finished their sub sandwiches and washed them down with bottled water.

Paul chewed thoughtfully, then offered Sam a chocolate chip cookie and leaned back in his desk chair.

"Did you hear anything back from the girl who saw the black car?" Paul asked, brushing a piece of stray lettuce from his tie while crumbs from the cookie dusted his shirt.

"Oh, you mean Melissa Turner?" Sam asked. "She called between college classes. She said after looking at full-sized vehicles on the internet last night, the closest one that fits the picture of what she thinks she saw is a Chevy Impala. Said it had fancy chrome wheels, so it's probably a newer model."

"Boy, that's pretty specific for just one glance," Paul said skeptically. "You and I both know witness testimonies can be wildly inaccurate. Remember that extortion case last year?"

"I know, but I'm just doin' what I'm told."

"You've got to be more independent than that, Sam. Higgins expects you to strike out on your own and uncover stuff," Paul reminded him.

"The last time I did that, a huge dog bit me in the ass. I am going to Mexico Fiesta, that restaurant on Oak Knoll Road, and that fireplace and patio store next to it after lunch. I'll check out their surveillance cameras." Brushing crumbs from his mouth, he got up and threw his trash in the basket, turning to leave. "In the meantime, I'll keep plugging through those surveillance tapes."

"Good. Go get 'em, bud," Paul said, frowning. "I'll be stuck here wading through the numbers."

Back at the office, Sam began checking videotapes from local businesses adjacent to the funeral home when he noticed a black car streak across the screen. Stopping the video, he replayed it. A black Malibu. No license plate.

"Crap. I thought maybe we had something there for a minute," he mumbled. "Another dead end." But he kept looking.

While Sam and Paul were occupied, Jim decided to call his daughter, Sara. He couldn't imagine the skill set required to corral the rambunctious energy of twenty fifth-graders. He remembered some of the escapades he'd been involved in as a fifth-grader, and it made him grin when he recalled them. Even though it was just after lunch, Sara answered her cell on the second ring.

"Hey, Dad. What's up?"

"Hi, honey. How's your day going?" Jim asked, eating a carton of raspberry yogurt at his desk.

"The kids are just having some free reading time. Did you need something?" she asked, stepping out into the hallway, leaving the door open.

"Just a question. What do you know about the last priest who left St. Ignatius? The one before the new guy you told me about."

"Not much. I don't attend church here, so I wasn't privileged to get in on the gossip, but I can tell you it was pretty divisive. Lots of people threatened to pull their kids out of school if Father Skip didn't leave. I know there were many meetings with the local bishop, and the next thing I knew, he was gone."

"Father Skip? Last name?" Jim asked, taking notes.

"Father Skip Howard."

"Who's the priest there now?"

"Dad, what's this about? Are you investigating something?"

"That's my job, honey. Name?"

"Father Jordan Knight."

"I'd ask you for a phone number, but that might be pushing it," he said cautiously.

Sara recited the number. "Hey, about this weekend. John and Jenny are going to help me move. Are you going to be around?"

"Should be unless Carol has the baby. Gotta go. Thanks." And he clicked off. ▢

24

Detective Leslie Brown waited in line at a local coffee shop close to the university. The place hummed with activity and had an energetic vibe fueled by caffeine in the form of mochas, lattes, and other exotic concoctions. She stood by the counter, overwhelmed with the choices. *It's just coffee with a lot of fluff,* she thought.

Grabbing her Americano, she headed to a booth by the window where Steven Hanratty was sitting. She'd already followed up with the other two victims, Joel Engstad and Ben Johnson. Both lived out of state now—Joel in Colorado and Ben in Utah. Neither added much information that she didn't already know.

Steven, however, agreed to meet with her during his lunch break, where he worked in the corporate offices at Kwik Trip. He wore dark dress slacks and a casual knit shirt with the convenience store logo over the pocket. Leslie could see from his physique that he prided himself on staying in shape. Steven's natural swarthy good looks, his fit, muscular body, and open and accepting demeanor would make him a good catch for someone. *Gloria must have had a heyday with this guy,* she thought.

As they sipped their coffees, Leslie began her interview.

"Have you worked at Kwik Trip long?" she began.

"Going on three years. I bounced around at some other places and finally landed a job here. They're a fantastic company. The work seems to be never-ending, which provides great job security."

"That's important ... job security," Leslie agreed.

"I think it is. What about you? Been a detective long?" he asked.

"A couple of years."

"Good job security?"

"As long as people keep being stupid and breaking the law, I'll always have a job," she said matter-of-factly. Steven chuckled.

"So, what can I help you with?" he asked.

Leslie hated to burst his enthusiastic bubble. "Gloria Bjerkes." Steven's eyes snapped to her face. "I'd like you to tell me about the incident when you were under her care for physical therapy," Leslie asked, carefully watching his reaction. Steven visibly paled. He inhaled a big breath, stared upward to the ceiling, then lowered his eyes to meet Leslie's gaze.

"I was hoping I'd never have to revisit that part of my life. I'm still trying to put that behind me." He seemed to expect a reprieve, but Leslie simply waited. After a few moments, she explained.

"Sorry. We're investigating the murder of Jeremy Bjerkes and Layne McNally," she said. "Your experience may be pertinent to the case. Take your time. I've suffered through sexual abuse. It's never easy to tell your story, but if it's any consolation, I've been there. I understand how difficult it is," she said, leaning back in the booth and getting comfortable. Seeing that he was struggling to get started, she repeated, "It's okay. Just take your time." She watched him gather his thoughts. A mask of pain clouded his handsome features as he began recalling the incident.

"I was a gymnast with the UW team back in 2007. Early in the season, September, I think, I had a bad fall from the vault and tore my hamstring. Some other athletes told me Gloria had helped them recover from their injuries so that they could finish their season. I went to see her, and after studying the doctor's report, she agreed to take on my therapy program."

Steven looked embarrassed. Leslie felt his anguish and understood his inclination to avoid discussing the experience. After all, the stigma of sexual abuse had kept a wall of shame between her and Sam for a long time.

"At first, it was just touching and massaging. I interpreted it as necessary to the therapy. But soon it moved to very intimate … " His voice drifted off. Shame and embarrassment overwhelmed him. "Let's just say she knew what she was doing."

"What did you do to stop it?" Leslie asked. Steven's jaw flexed in anger.

"Obviously, not enough," he said bitterly.

"Hey, don't beat yourself up. The only one who gets hurt is you," Leslie counseled, her blue eyes full of empathy.

Steven continued. "At first, it seemed flattering—you know, an older woman spending her time and attention on someone younger. But then it started changing. She became very demanding. She wanted complete exclusivity. She just wouldn't leave me alone. She stalked me on Instagram, sent me multiple text messages during the day, and called my apartment. She was relentless in her pursuit. I lost my girlfriend over it."

"How long did your relationship with her continue before you reported it?" Leslie asked.

His eyes drifted upward as he remembered the time frame. "Probably six weeks, but we had many intense encounters that resulted in intercourse. She wanted more, but I couldn't deal with her manipulative, controlling behavior. It was like being in the clutches of a black widow spider." He paused. "Well, that's probably not a good word picture, but you get the drift."

Leslie nodded. "According to reports, we understand you recanted your account of these incidents. Why did you do that?" Leslie asked, taking careful notes.

"Threats. She'd show up and be standing out in the hallway after one of my classes. She wouldn't say anything; she'd just follow me and stare a hole in my back. She showed up on Third Street and bar-hopped until she found me. Then she'd sit and stare at me while I was with my friends. You wouldn't believe the things she did until I finally got so sick of it that I went in and claimed it was all a big hoax, a dare from some friends. If I ever see her again, it'll be too soon for me. She is one very sick individual." Leslie understood completely.

"Did she ever threaten you with legal action?"

"No, but I knew she was wealthy and would pull out the big guns if I didn't back down."

"I'm sorry this happened to you, Steven," Leslie said with heartfelt empathy.

"She tried to ruin my life," Steven said through clenched teeth, "but I won't let her. She's not going to bring me down," he said with a determination that impressed Leslie. After a few moments of silence, he went on. "One thing about her is that she carefully selected her victims. Other athletes went to her for therapy and had no problems, and she helped them on a professional level. But then there were guys like me and Joel and Ben who got selected for her special treatment."

"That's her predatory instinct at work," Leslie said. "The sex didn't mean that much; it was all about the hunt and conquest and control. Thank you for talking to me. This will be very helpful in our investigation," Leslie finished.

They chatted a while more. Steven had a good job and had been able to maintain a serious relationship with a girl he really seemed to care about. They shook hands, and when Leslie left, he gave her a clumsy hug.

As Leslie drove across town, Hanratty's confessions triggered Leslie's own memories of abuse. She understood the victim mentality and how difficult it was to rebuild your life and stay positive.

Steven was seeing a therapist just as Leslie did. She hoped he could continue to recover and pursue his dreams.

Her relationship with Sam had definitely turned a corner, but Leslie knew she would always struggle with her sexual self-image.

SUE BERG

With counseling, she'd learned to view her abuse as only one part of her life. Her therapist had taught her the value of a word picture. Tears welled up in her eyes when she thought of that image. Her therapist had challenged her to imagine her life as an intricate, colorful quilt made up of vibrant squares of rich color, some light, some dark. Her abuse no longer dominated her life story. It was a part but not the whole.

Through a lot of hard work, she had rebuilt her beliefs about who she was. Continually reminding herself how far she'd come, she knew that Sam was one big reason behind her progress. When he looked at her, he saw the multi-faceted person she was. He loved her for who she was and the growth and progress she'd made. He respected the maturation that had happened in her life, which added to her self-confidence.

In the Vine Street parking lot, she squeezed her Prius into a cramped spot between two huge pickups, mulling over what she'd learned about Gloria Bjerkes. She definitely fit the description of a female sexual predator. Gloria used her position at the university to search for victims—in her case, young men at the height of their sexual prowess. She'd hunted them down relentlessly, keeping them psychologically captivated, playing with them like a cat plays with a mouse. Leslie didn't know whether she was involved in her husband's murder. Only time and evidence would tell. But Leslie's blood boiled when she thought of her rapacious sexual history.

Who else would fall victim to her games before she was finally stopped? Leslie wondered. ◘

25

The late afternoon sun cast a golden glow on the surface of the Mississippi River until it burned like a glowing stream of fire. An egret stood stock-still at the river's edge in the shallow water. Its feathers were brilliant white against the lush green foliage along the marshy expanse next to the highway. Jim gave a wide berth to a group of bikers pedaling furiously along the highway decked out in colorful gear and helmets. Strung out along Great River Road, they reminded Jim of beads on a gaudy necklace. Further on, Wegner's fish market was busy, the parking lot filled with vehicles. A sign reading "Smoked Catfish" hung haphazardly from a red post near the road. *If I wasn't so busy, I'd stop for some of that smoked fish,* Jim thought.

Genoa's Lock and Dam #8 came into sight, stretching expansively across the river, steady against the current. Its smokestack poked into the sky, and leisure boats and a barge waited patiently at the lock. Jim turned off the main highway to the left and drove into the village.

Genoa was an old river town set beneath the towering bluffs along the Mississippi. The first white settler, David Hastings, arrived in 1853 and soon, under his entrepreneurial spirit, Hastings Landing

SUE BERG

became a vibrant steamboat stop on the river's route. Many of the buildings date to the Civil War era. It still had a laid-back Huck Finn feel to it. The construction of brick and stone structures along the bottoms of the steep sandstone bluffs was a testament to the perseverance and audacity of its early Italian immigrants.

Jim turned left on Walnut Street, stopping in front of the St. Ignatius Church and rectory. Getting out of his Suburban, he sauntered along the shaded sidewalk and stopped at the entrance of the rectory. The sound of children's voices from the school playground farther down the street wafted to him on a breeze. He was just preparing to ring the bell when the front door opened. Father Jordan Knight greeted him.

"Hello, Lt. Higgins. I've been watching for you. Please come in," he said, smiling warmly.

Jim took stock of the priest. Friendly, deep-set, hazel eyes in a tanned face, an aquiline nose, a full expressive mouth, and a shocking head of dark unruly hair all combined into something Jim would describe as warm and charming. *Handsome in a rugged way*, he thought. Jim guessed he was about thirty-five years old.

They exchanged a handshake and proceeded to the darkened study immediately to the right of the front entry. Finding a club chair in the corner, Jim sat down while Father Knight sat behind his desk. His study was filled with a wall of bookshelves crammed with the expected religious tomes: *The Ignatius Study Bible, Catechism of the Catholic Church, The Documents of Vatican II,* and a ton of other spiritual reference works that were unfamiliar to him. The place smelled musty with a faint odor of Brut cologne that lingered in the air.

"So, are you related to Sara Higgins? She teaches at our school," Father Knight began.

"Yes, she's my daughter," Jim said graciously.

Father Knight smiled easily, displaying wide white teeth. "She's one of our finest educators. Always has the kids' best interests in mind."

"That's good to hear. I think she was born to be a teacher."

"She seems to have found her calling." Father Knight paused for a moment. "So what brings you to St. Ignatius, Lieutenant?"

"We're investigating the murder of Jeremy Bjerkes and Layne McNally. From talking to Jeremy's former wife, Julie, I understood that he was a member here until recently. I was wondering if you could shed some light on why they left the parish."

Father Knight's face darkened. "Oh, that all happened before I was assigned here. I've heard rumblings in the congregation and bits and pieces of conversations, but I've really tried to remove myself from all of that gossip."

"Fresh start and all that?" Jim asked, curious.

"Yes, something like that. I will tell you that the congregation has been damaged by whatever happened between Father Howard and the Bjerkes. There were some deep wounds, but I think some healing has taken place since my time here, which I'm thankful for."

"Spiritual wounds can be very painful and take years to heal," Jim remarked.

"How perceptive, Lt. Higgins. Are you … ?"

Jim finished the sentence. "Of the Lutheran persuasion. Luther didn't apologize, so I won't either."

Father Knight laughed heartily. "Well, thank you for your honesty." There was a lull in the conversation. "I'm sorry I couldn't have been more helpful, but—"

"I understand your position. You have a duty to protect and nurture your people. No offense taken, Father," Jim said, although he was disappointed he'd come to a dead end so quickly.

"There is a person you might wish to talk to that I would trust to keep your conversation confidential. I could call her," he said.

"Would you? That would really be helpful," Jim said. *Maybe my trip won't be wasted after all.*

Father Knight removed his cell from his trouser pocket and stepped into the hallway, where he talked quietly for a few minutes. Coming back into the study, he glanced at Jim and chuckled.

SUE BERG

"Mrs. Mabel Zabolio lives right next door." He pointed out the window to a little cottage-like house a few hundred feet away. "I'd trust her with my life, plus she's one of the best cooks in town and keeps me well-fed; it saves on groceries. She's willing to talk with you," he finished, smiling. "She'll be very discreet."

Jim got up from his chair by the window. "Thanks for your time and the lead. I appreciate it," he said sincerely, shaking the priest's hand again. Jim left the rectory and cut across the lawn, turning onto the sidewalk and coming to the house's front entrance. Mrs. Zabolio was waiting for him on the front steps. Her white flyaway hair made her seem harmless, but Jim sensed a razor-sharp intelligence beneath her friendly countenance. Jim felt somewhat awkward until she pressed her small warm hand into his.

"Well, I can see the family resemblance," she said, her eyes bright with curiosity.

"Pardon me?" Jim said, feeling stupid.

"Your daughter, Sara. She has your eyes and your bearing. Such a lovely young woman. She does so much for the children at the school."

Despite his training to remain neutral and open-minded, Jim immediately took a liking to Mrs. Zabolio.

"Thank you. I think she's pretty special, too," he said, giving her a wide dimpled smile.

Mabel invited him into her tiny house. Every corner was crowded with the trinkets of a lifetime of collecting. Somehow in the time from Father Knight's call until Jim's appearance at her door, she had made coffee and laid out almond biscotti on her coffee table in the living room. Jim felt welcomed like an honored guest.

"Please sit down. You've probably been chasing criminals all day. Let me pour you some coffee," she suggested. Jim smelled some kind of lavender sachet as she handed him a steaming cup. He laughed inwardly at the concept people had of detectives. Cloak and dagger images had never fully disappeared from the profession. *No thanks to you, Sherlock,* he thought. He sipped the coffee. It was delicious. He helped himself to a biscotti.

"Hmm. I try not to indulge in sweets too often, but these are really good," he said politely, crunching his first bite. "Thank you."

"You're welcome. My house is sort of a revolving door. With eight children and their spouses and thirty-five grandchildren, I'm never alone very much. I do my rosary early every morning before the commotion of the day begins." She smiled benevolently at Jim. "I open my eyes to His presence in the morning and close them with His presence at night."

Jim's mouth gaped open. "Did you say thirty-five grandchildren?" The shocking statistic left him holding his cup mid-air.

"Yes, my husband and I used Psalm 127:4–5 as a guide for planning our family. Do you know the verses, Lieutenant?" She tipped her head in a questioning gesture.

"Not that particular passage," Jim commented, grinning.

"Like arrows in the hands of a warrior are sons born in one's youth. Blessed is the man whose quiver is full of them. They will not be put to shame when they contend with their enemies at the gate," Mabel recited in a strong voice.

"A very good statute to live by, I'd say," Jim said softly as he studied Mabel.

"Yes, Don and I thought so." There was a quiet pause. "Well, we've gone on long enough about me. How can I help *you*?" Mabel asked. Suddenly, she was all business.

"I'm investigating the double murders of Jeremy Bjerkes and Layne McNally. You may know about it," he said, setting his cup down.

"Oh my, yes. I've been keeping informed on the internet," she said, her voice quick and lively. "A terrible crime committed in broad daylight. The heart is desperately wicked. I'm sure I'm not telling you anything new," she finished, studying Jim's handsome face.

Jim's eyes sparkled with admiration. Mabel obviously understood human nature. "I had a conversation with his former wife, Julie, and she mentioned something about an argument Jeremy had with the former priest at St. Ignatius."

"Father Skip Howard?" Mabel asked, frowning.

"Yes. Can you tell me anything about that?" Jim slipped his memo pad out of his pocket.

"I can tell you what I know. The meaning and interpretation I'll leave to you," she said wisely.

"Certainly. I understand." Jim leaned back on the couch and crossed his legs, preparing to listen.

"First of all, let me say that Father Howard is a fine priest." Mabel began. "His problem is that women find him quite irresistible. He has a rakish appeal with the ladies, I'm afraid. Forbidden fruit, as they say."

Jim nodded, hiding a grin, trying to maintain his serious composure.

She tilted her head. "Some women are very attracted to what they can't have. You must run into that in your line of work, Lieutenant," she said seriously.

Jim nodded in agreement, thought of Gloria and her unabashed advances on him, and then refocused his attention on Mabel.

"When Jeremy divorced, he began occasionally bringing his new wife to Mass. Of course, he was concerned his son be raised in the Catholic faith. So his wife, Gloria, faithfully brought him every Saturday to CCD, our Catholic education program."

"Like our Lutheran Sunday School?" Jim asked.

"Yes, exactly," Mabel said, smiling at the parallel example. Then she turned serious again. "Well, being next to the rectory, I couldn't help but notice that every Saturday while the boy was at the church, Gloria would walk to the rectory and meet with Father Skip. Usually, the deacons recommend any counseling or anything of a confessional nature be conducted at the church office. But it seemed Gloria had some kind of special privileges." She stopped for a moment. Her piercing eyes locked on Jim. "Do you understand what I'm saying?"

"Well, unless you actually witnessed them being intimate—

having intercourse—it's all conjecture, isn't it?" Jim concluded calmly, his blue eyes intently studying Mabel's petite features.

"Of course, I understand that. You're interested in concrete proof, not gossip," Mabel said. Jim nodded. "I didn't see anything of that nature. I'm not a peeping tom, after all. But I did observe a number of their goodbyes on the rectory steps, and I can tell you that their relationship was more than a priest to a congregant. The way she touched his hand, the looks she gave him ... Well, if I didn't know better, I'd say she was a woman used to getting her way. I don't think there was a religious bone in Gloria's body, so what she was doing with a priest all that time left me wondering and suspicious." Although Mabel continued to appear unflappable, an angry undertone in her voice made Jim sit up and take notice. "The temptations of the devil can take some very interesting and alluring forms," she concluded.

"No argument there. One more question. Based on what you just told me, do you think Bjerkes' son could be Father Howard's?"

"Jeremy and Julie couldn't have children. I prayed with her frequently about a family. But it never happened for them." She nodded her head sadly. "I couldn't tell you about the son. I suppose DNA would have to be used to determine that. Right?" she asked, her eyes bright with curiosity.

"Right. Any other impressions?" Jim asked.

"No, not really. I always liked Jeremy. I thought he was a decent man," she said wistfully. "I hate to see these families broken apart by divorce ... and now murder. That poor child."

Jim conversed a while longer with Mabel. Finally, the topic was exhausted, and it was time to leave. He stood, feeling gigantic in the small room. He extended his hand to Mabel and then covered her hand with his other one. "Thank you so much for your time. You've given me a lot to think about," he said. "And it will all remain confidential, I promise you."

"So am I an informant now?" she asked, teasing him with a grin while gazing into his blue eyes.

Jim laughed. "Yes, you are now officially an informant. And a very delightful one, too."

Mabel walked him to the door. The temperatures had rocketed up, and Jim could feel the heat through the screen door. He walked down the sidewalk, loosening his tie, then turned to wave goodbye to Mrs. Zabolio. Before getting in his Suburban, he removed his suit coat and threw it in the passenger seat. Buckling himself in and donning his sunglasses, Jim turned out from the shaded side street into the late afternoon sunshine. His cell buzzed.

"Higgins."

"Chief, I've updated the board with all our pertinent information," Paul stated. "Are you coming back into the office?"

"If nothing earth-shattering has been discovered, I thought I'd head home. I've been in Genoa at the rectory. What time is it now?"

"It's ten after five."

"In that case, I'm heading home, but if everyone's available, we could meet tomorrow at nine and go over what we've got."

"I'll check and let you know."

"Sounds good." Jim shut his phone and tucked it into his shirt pocket. Somehow for all the legwork they'd been doing, nothing seemed promising. But he continued to believe that someone somewhere may have seen some inconsequential event that meant nothing to them but would lead the team in a new direction.

It's time for a news conference, he thought. He couldn't count the number of times that normal citizens' observations had helped break a case open and provide new leads. If no one came forward with information, then it was time to put on the gloves and go another round with Gloria. He felt an involuntary shiver move up his arms. Something about her bothered him, and he intended to find out what it was. ◘

SATURDAY,
MAY 18

26

Sam rolled over in bed. Leslie was lying next to him, and she slowly opened her eyes. A subtle grin spread across her face.

"What's so funny?" Sam asked, cuddling up to her, kissing her neck. "Mmm, you smell so good." The kissing continued. Leslie giggled as she ran her fingers through his thick, dark hair. "You didn't answer my question," Sam said. "You're smiling about something."

"What? You can't figure out what that would be?" Looking into Sam's eyes, she couldn't believe how far they'd come—the talks they'd had. She was sure understanding each other would take a lifetime, but the trust and love that had developed with Sam this week was unlike any other relationship she'd ever had before.

"I never knew that trust could be this easy," Leslie said seriously.

Sam rolled on his side and tucked his arm under his head. "You have to be worthy of trust. Relationships can't be sustained without it. And along with trust comes risk. At some point, you've got to dive off the diving board. That can be scary, but look where it got you," he said softly, his hazel eyes luminous with feeling.

"Yeah, look where it got me. Committing adultery with a pastor's son," she said, raising her eyebrows at the suggestion, propping another pillow under her head.

"Well, there's a topic we haven't discussed yet," Sam said, but his eyes were dancing with humor. He kissed her tenderly, then urgently.

Leslie returned his kisses, rolling on top of him. "And I don't think you're in the mood to discuss it now," she said.

"You got that right, baby," he said, his hands caressing her back.

Later, after they'd both had a run in Hixon Forest with Paco, Leslie's black lab, Sam stood in the sunlit kitchen scrambling eggs and making French toast.

"What time does the chief want us there?" Leslie asked, looking up from her phone.

"Nine," Sam answered. Paco, ever vigilant, lounged at Leslie's feet under the kitchen table with his ears pricked as if he could understand their conversation.

"My interview with Steven Hanratty yesterday was interesting."

"In what way?" Sam asked. Leslie smiled. He frequently asked a simple question, but he was always after whatever was swimming beneath the words. That quality would make him a great interrogator someday.

"It's the first time I revealed my experience of abuse to another person. I hope it helped him tell his story, or at least made him realize there are a lot of us who have been hurt like he was."

"Does sharing make you feel stronger?" Sam asked, bringing her a plate of eggs and toast.

"Yes. Every time I share, I feel the past retreat just a little more. And I feel a little freer to live my life without defining it by my experience of abuse," she said as she squeezed syrup on her French toast.

"That's great. Isn't that kinda what AA is all about?" He leaned down and tenderly kissed her temple.

Leslie shrugged and said, "I don't know anybody in AA."

Sam said, "So what do you think about Gloria Bjerkes? I haven't met her yet." Sam sat down at the table and dug into his eggs. The coffee pot gurgled on the counter.

"Oh boy. That's a loaded question." Leslie crinkled her nose. "She's a ... I don't know. She's a bad operator. She certainly fits the description of a female sexual predator. She's intimidating and rich. Quite a combination along with her questionable history."

"Can you prove it, though? Didn't these guys she supposedly abuse claim it was all a big practical joke done on a dare or something?" Sam remarked, a puzzled expression on his face. "And besides, how many college guys do you know who would refuse sex? Even if it was with an older woman?"

Leslie pushed her plate away. "If they had any moral fiber—and that's a hard thing to come by these days—they'd refuse. And yes, they did recant, but if Hanratty's telling the truth, which I believe he is, then she's very dangerous. I would have no trouble believing she could orchestrate her husband's murder," she finished, pointing her fork at Sam. "Maybe she put out a contract on him."

"Whoa! Now there's a thought. But you've gotta prove it. You know Higgins." Then, he mumbled in a low mocking tone, "Evidence, people. Evidence."

"Can't convict criminals without it, Sam. Maybe we should put some surveillance on her,"

Leslie said, thinking out loud.

"Surveillance? On our department's budget? That won't happen," Sam scoffed. "With the new governor at the helm, the state's going to direct money back into education, roads, and social programs. We'll have even less to work with than before. You wait and see," Sam said, disgusted with the political landscape.

Leslie glanced at the clock and pointed to it, saying, "Finish up. It's eight-thirty. We need to get crackin' if we're going to be on time." ◘

27

"But Dad, you promised you'd help me move!" Sara said, her voice ramping up in volume. "John and Jenny skipped out. They're doing some planning stuff for the wedding. I can't do this all by myself!"

Jim wove in and out of traffic on U.S. Hwy. 35 on his trip to the law enforcement office.

Someone honked their horn and flipped him off as they accelerated past him. He hit his brakes, knowing he shouldn't be on his phone while driving. Trying to keep his cool, he accelerated and roared past an old codger in a Ford crew cab pickup.

"Listen, honey. I'll be home no later than eleven. Maybe I can recruit Sam and Paul to help. You don't have that much stuff, do you?"

"Just a whole U-Haul short trailer," Sara said huffily. "And my car is stuffed to the brim."

Jim envisioned mountains of boxes, piles of clothes, and household goods surrounding and swallowing his newly refurbished basement.

"Well, maybe this is a good time to dejunk," he suggested, changing lanes again.

"Daaad! Really?" Sara screeched.

"Calm down," he said in an authoritative voice. "Listen, you drive up to the house and park. Do not let Carol convince you she can carry stuff in. She is not supposed to do any heavy lifting. I will be there by eleven with bells on," Jim said, getting frustrated.

"Okay. Eleven. See you then." Sara clicked off.

Roaring into the law enforcement parking lot, Jim noticed Paul and Sam had already arrived. He jogged into the building, walked into the elevator, and punched the button for the third floor. The door slid open, and he quickly walked down the hall past his office to the large classroom. Sam, Leslie, and Paul were sitting in front of the large whiteboard, talking softly, pointing and discussing theories.

They looked up as he hurried in.

"Hey, Chief. You look a little rattled," Sam commented, noticing Jim's panicked expression.

"Women," Jim said, shaking his head. Leslie's eyes widened. "Sorry, Leslie. Not you," he said sheepishly.

"Here's what we've got, Chief," Paul began. Jim propped his butt on the edge of a table while Paul reviewed the evidence they had.

"The murder weapon, a small-caliber pistol—possibly a Ruger, which we didn't find—was used on both victims. Four bullets, all located at the scene of the crime. Three were found in the victims, one embedded in the floor. No fingerprints of an intruder at the scene. A possible sighting of the killer's car, but the details are sketchy at best. Could be a black Impala, but there are hundreds of them in the city, so that's not much help."

Jim interrupted. "I don't care if there are two thousand Impalas. We need to find that car."

Paul held up his hand in a wait gesture. "We have two suspects at this point. Lyle Oates, business partner with a drinking problem, who claims he was home during the shootings but admitted to a heated argument with Jeremy the morning of the murder. None of his neighbors can confirm his presence at his home between nine-fifteen when he left the funeral home and noon when we found him at the bar. The second possible suspect, the spouse, Gloria Bjerkes says she was—where?" Paul glanced at Jim for clarification.

"I checked. According to her secretary, she was in her office when the murders took place," Jim said.

Paul wrote her alibi on the board next to her photo. He had a gift for summarization that was helpful, especially when it came to evidence. Jim could see Leslie was thinking.

"Leslie? What are you thinking?" he asked brusquely.

"After our interview with Gloria on Thursday and my follow-up interview with Steven Hanratty, I have a gut feeling that Gloria's involved *somehow*," Leslie said.

Jim noticed the motives under Gloria's name were all punctuated with bold question marks. Leslie continued to theorize.

"What about a murder for hire? Is she capable of that?" Leslie paused, then fired more questions. "Did Jeremy find out about a random lover Gloria had, and he threatened him, causing a crisis? Did the jealous lover snuff out Gloria's husband to shut him up? After interviewing Steven Hanratty, I know that Gloria is capable of some sophisticated criminal activity, including murder, and she has the tendencies of a sexual predator. Any chance we can do some surveillance on her? See what she's up to?" She blew out her cheeks in a huff of frustration.

"Not yet," Jim said. He focused his gaze on Sam. "What about the cars coming out of Fifth Street at the corner of Mormon Coulee Road the morning of the murder?" he asked.

"I checked the closed-circuit videos from the cameras at the businesses in the area, but they're too far away, and the angle's wrong. Kind of a dead end." He shrugged his shoulders apologetically. "The only lead is the black Impala."

"Were there any black vehicles on the videos? Did you check for that?" Jim asked.

"There was a black pickup and the black Malibu, but I'll check again," Sam said.

Jim switched his focus back to Paul. "What about the financial condition of the business?" he asked.

"The business looks solvent based on what I've seen so far. They have a steady influx of clients, and the profit/loss seems healthy. They were making good money, but they're not over-the-top wealthy if that's what you're asking. The business seemed to be well managed."

Jim studied the whiteboard. At some point in every investigation, he felt like pitching it out the nearest window. Questions swirled in his mind as he reflected on the data they'd collected. How could two men be shot in cold blood in broad daylight and leave so few clues? There had to be something they were missing. The temptation to pound his fist through the middle of the white space was almost irresistible. He breathed deeply and realized his team was staring at him. *Leadership. They're waiting for you to say something,* he thought.

"All right. We're doing everything right so far. We just need to keep digging. We're going to re-interview Gloria and Lyle here— on our turf—on Monday. We need to rattle some cages. There's still something swimming below the surface. Motivations are hazy at this point. We know Jeremy and Lyle were experiencing some business conflicts about Lyle's upcoming retirement. We need to explore that angle when we talk to him again. Today I learned from a confidential source that Gloria may have been having an affair with a priest from Genoa."

Sam thought about his dad, the Lutheran pastor. Imagining him in a torrid love affair sent a shiver down Sam's spine. A picture of two naked bodies entangled on a bed popped into his brain. He shuddered. To think about his dad in a situation like that seemed impossible to him, but he wasn't naive—it did happen occasionally. "A priest! Holy Moly. That's an ugly can of worms," Sam said.

"It happens," Jim said candidly, echoing Sam's thoughts. "Wouldn't be the first time." He paused as he thought through his strategy. "Paul and Sam, I'm going to send you up to Stanley on Monday to interview Father Skip Howard, the former priest at St. Ignatius in Genoa. Check into his relationship with Gloria. See if you can uncover anything there. Something might break loose," he finished.

"Right, Chief," Paul said, getting up to stretch.

"Anything else?" Jim asked, waiting for their responses. The feedback and insights seemed puny, but they were moving forward. The group began to break up.

"One more thing," Jim said. The team eyed him attentively. "My daughter's moving into our basement apartment today, and I need some help. Brats, hamburgers, and beer after we're done?" he said, looking hopeful.

"I'm in," Sam chirped up.

"Me, too," Leslie responded.

"Let me call Ruby. Is it okay if she brings Melody?" Paul asked.

"The more, the merrier," Jim said, turning to leave. Walking through the parking lot outside, Jim whipped out his phone and called Carol, explaining the lunch deal.

"That's fine," she said. "I've got brats and hamburger in the freezer I can unthaw. If you stop and get buns and beer, we're good to go."

"I can do that. Is Sara there yet?" Jim asked. "Man, what's wrong with her? She was having a fit this morning."

"She's just driving in with the trailer. You better make haste, my lord," Carol said, laughing.

"Be there in twenty minutes ... my lord," Jim said, rolling his eyes.

By one o'clock, all of the boxes, clothes, and other cargo belonging to Sara had been carried into the gleaming new apartment, thanks to the team's help. Sam and Leslie spent time looking the place over, impressed with its layout and the obvious decorating expertise of Carol.

"She really has a way with colors and textures, doesn't she?" Leslie said to Sara.

"Yep. She is one sharp lady. She wouldn't be married to Dad if she wasn't." Sara took a big breath, then hurried on. "Of course, there's always the topic of unprotected sex, but we won't go there," she said, smiling wickedly. "Neither one of them was too smart on that front. But you won't get me to remind Dad about that error in judgment."

"I agree. That would be dangerous territory," Leslie said, smiling.

Lillie came charging down the basement stairs. "Sara, Bapa says it's time to eat."

"Okay, Miss Lillie. We're coming," Sara said. When she turned to continue her conversation with Leslie, Lillie interrupted.

"No more talking!" she said, stomping her foot. "Bapa says NOW!"

Sara did a mock salute, much to Leslie and Sam's delight. "Aye, aye, captain. After you," she said, making a sweeping gesture toward the stairs.

The group sat on the shaded patio and enjoyed lunch over grilled brats, hamburgers, and lemonade and beer. Carol was eliciting Ruby's advice about breastfeeding, and Paul and Jim were talking La Crosse Logger baseball.

"You see that young pitcher from Superior? Vandehuse. Man, he's good," Paul remarked. "Pitched a no-hitter the other night. Course, it's early in the season. He hasn't come up against Duluth yet. I hear they're really tough this year."

"Haven't gotten to a game yet. Sitting on bleachers isn't Carol's cup of tea right now. But let me know when you have an extra ticket, and I'll go with you," Jim offered.

Sam watched Leslie conversing with Sara about teaching, kids, art, and a multitude of other topics. Sitting in an Adirondack chair, he noticed a red-headed woodpecker climbing a gnarled tree trunk in the shaded yard. Lillie tapped his arm, her eyes inquisitive. Sam thought, *She's got the chief's baby blues.*

"Hey. Is she your girlfriend?" she asked him boldly, pointing to Leslie. "Do you ever kiss her?" Alarmed by Lillie's candid questions and accusing finger, Carol came over and leaned down to make eye contact with her.

"Lillie, it's not polite to ask questions like that," Carol said gently.

"And we don't point at people."

"Why not?" Lillie's little voice squeaked, looking directly at her. Carol smiled.

"Yeah, why not?" Sam asked, playing along, an impish grin creasing his face.

"Don't encourage her, Sam," Carol said in a low voice. By now, everyone had turned toward the trio and were listening to the ongoing commotion.

Trying again, Carol said, "Well, some things we keep to ourselves. Kind of like a secret, but a good secret." It was a weak attempt at pacification, and Lillie pounced on it.

"Oh, you mean like when you and Bapa take a bath together with the lights out," Lillie said. "You mean that kind of secret?" She turned her innocent blue eyes to Jim.

For an instant, the quiet was deafening. Jim was aware of the breeze through the trees, the leaves making a slight whispering sound. *O Lord,* he thought. He tilted his face skyward and closed his eyes. *There are no more secrets to tell.* He could hear Paul stifling a laugh next to him. Lillie's lips began to quiver. She stared at Carol, her huge blue eyes filling with tears.

"I'm sorry, Mommy," she said in a wobbly voice.

Carol's heart skipped a beat. It was the first time Lillie had called her mommy. She looked at Jim, her eyes sparkling. "It's okay, baby. That's a good secret that just isn't a secret anymore." She pulled Lillie into a hug.

"You must have quite the love life, Chief," Paul said, glancing at Jim.

"Yeah. I've been channeling my inner Kevin Costner," Jim said, embarrassed. Then he started laughing.

"Must be workin'," Paul said, joining in.

Sara leaned over to Leslie. "As I said, two intelligent people who are madly in love do some pretty crazy things."

"Sounds like fun to me," she said, winking. ◘

MONDAY,
MAY 20

28

Steven Hanratty woke up with a banging headache, ten stitches in his head, and a couple of bruised ribs. He grimaced as he tried to roll out of bed. Flopping back on his pillow, he pushed the call light. For a moment, he'd forgotten how he'd arrived at the hospital ER. Then it all came flooding back to him in nightmarish detail.

After a couple of beers with some friends on Sunday evening at his favorite neighborhood hangout under Hedgehog Bluff, he'd decided to head home. Strolling down a darkened side street, he aimed for the general direction of his car, feeling a mild alcoholic buzz. Out of the blue, two heavyweight wrestling types pounced on him from behind and began pounding him. He vaguely remembered returning a few well-aimed punches and kicks, but then he lost his balance and fell, sharply hitting his head on the curb. The hoods gave him a few swift kicks in the ribs before he passed out. Later, one of his friends parked nearby found him unconscious and brought him to the hospital.

He fumbled through the items on the nightstand near the bed until he located his phone.

Finding Leslie Brown's contact information, he dialed her number.

"Sheriff's Department. Leslie Brown. How may I help you?"

"Hey, Leslie, it's Steven Hanratty."

"Yes, Steven. Is there something I can help you with?"

"Yeah, you can find the two thugs who nailed me last night outside of Lenny's and put me in the hospital," he said, frowning, the bright sunlight revving up his headache.

"What? When did this happen?" she asked, alarmed. "Did you call the police?"

"It happened about eleven," he answered, his voice raspy and irate. "And yes, I called the police. They came to the ER and questioned me, but the street was too dark. I couldn't identify them, but I'm sure they were Gloria Bjerkes' toads."

"Are they releasing you soon?"

"Not until the blood is gone from my urine," he said wearily.

"I'll call you back," Leslie said, clicking off. She got up from her desk, walked quickly to Jim's office, and lightly tapped on his door. He was on the phone, but he waved her in. She took a chair and waited. Jim looked at Leslie when he'd concluded his call.

"Steve Hanratty was pummeled last night outside of Lenny's. He's in the hospital at Gunderson," Leslie curtly informed him.

Jim slammed his hand down on his desk. "What the … ?" Jim reined in his temper. "Most likely the work of Gloria's inner circle, although she'll never admit it. Did he report it to city police?"

"Yes, he did. But it probably won't go far. It was too dark. He couldn't identify them," she explained. "But they were thug types, according to Steve."

Jim swiveled in his chair. "Gloria's not scheduled for her interview until one-thirty, right?"

Leslie nodded. "Maybe a little surprise is in order," Jim said, still gazing out at the overcast sky.

Leslie asked. "What do you have in mind, Chief?"

Jim walked past Leslie to the outer office as she trailed behind him.

"Emily," Jim said, leaning over the counter, stony-faced.

"Yes, sir?" she asked, looking up from her computer.

"Get hold of Judge Benson's office and find out the earliest I can come and see him this morning. Tell him it's a rather urgent matter in the double Bjerkes-McNally homicide case," he ordered quietly.

"Will do, Jim," she said briskly, picking up her phone.

Turning to Leslie, he leaned on the counter. "Nothing like a little fuel to get the fire going."

In the meantime, Paul and Sam left for Stanley. Traveling up State Highway 53 to I-94, Paul skirted around the eastern edge of Eau Claire, then picked up State Hwy. 29 and traveled east to Stanley. Fields of hay whizzed by the window alternating with clumps of dark green woods. The land was flatter here; the glacier had done the work of grinding and smoothing out the hills. Good farmland. Every once in a while, a creek tumbled through woodsy land bursting with spring foliage.

Stretching out along the highway, clusters of farm buildings huddled together on plots of gently rolling land—barns, pole sheds, and huge four square houses built when large families were the norm and not the exception. Holstein cows chomped on the first blades of spring grass, lounged in fenced cow yards or hungrily grazed in open pasture. Rumbling over unending acres with huge dual-wheeled planters and tractors, farmers planted corn and soybeans in dark fields mixed with corn stubble. The smell of humus and manure drifted on the air, and every once in a while, the detectives crinkled their noses at the pungent odor. Every seven or eight miles along the highway, small-town America made its presence known with a main street, four or five churches, a few school buildings, and maybe a hospital or a Walmart, interspersed with local businesses.

Paul turned off Hwy. 29 onto Main Street in Stanley. Using GPS, he coasted to a stop beside the curb in front of St. Jerome's Parish on Third Street. The rectory was shaded by huge maple and oak trees, which spread their branches over the mid-century clapboard house. The neighborhood had a sedate, established feeling. Now during the forenoon, it was quiet, but Paul could imagine that after school and in the evenings, it would be lively with kids on bikes, families taking their babies for a stroll, or front porch conversations between neighbors.

"Seems pretty quiet. Sure hope this Father Howard is around," Sam commented, climbing out of the truck, stretching to get the travel kinks out. "That's his name, right?"

"Yeah, Father Skip Howard," Paul repeated, walking briskly up the sidewalk that led to a set of cement steps and a front door. Paul pushed the button, then noticed the small sign written in bold black marker: "If no answer, please check the church office."

Sam leaned against the wrought iron railing, chewing on his lower lip.

"Ring it again," he told Paul, slightly irritated.

Suddenly, a man waved at them across the lawn as he approached. Coming closer, he hollered, "Can I help you?" He was dressed in blue jeans and a black and orange T-shirt with the Stanley Orioles logo emblazoned across the front.

"We're looking for Father Skip Howard," Sam said.

"You found him," the priest stated. Sam could see how people would be drawn to him. A ruddy complexion, deep-set azure eyes, and a head of reddish-brown hair styled in a carefree mop that fell over a high forehead. His smile was wide and friendly, his body trim and fit. *Looks a little like JFK,* he thought, *or Robert Redford.*

Paul flipped open his badge, as did Sam. A chill seemed to fall over the priest's face, and his demeanor clouded with anxiety for an instant. It was so subtle it would have been easy to dismiss it, but Paul noticed. It wasn't a figment of his imagination.

"We'd like to talk to you if we could. Somewhere private, maybe," Paul said.

"Sure, let's head inside to my study. Follow me," he said, waving them around to the side of the house. He used a side entrance through the garage, went up a few stairs, and breezed into the large, roomy kitchen. A square oak table and four matching chairs stood in the center of the room. Older cream-painted cupboards lined two walls, and a white ceramic sink sat under the window facing the church. Ruffled curtains imprinted with a coffee cup pattern moved gently from a breeze coming through the window. The aroma of bananas and lemon Pledge lingered in the air.

"Coffee?" he asked over his shoulder.

"Sure, if it's no trouble," Paul remarked. "Actually, we can sit right here at the table if that's all right with you."

"Makes no difference to me." He motioned them to the wooden chairs and started the coffee.

Paul and Sam sat down while he found mugs in the cupboard. "So, what's this all about?"

"We're investigating the murders of two La Crosse residents," Paul began. "Jeremy Bjerkes and Layne McNally were shot to death at the Bjerkes and Oates Funeral Home on the south side of La Crosse last Tuesday morning about nine-thirty. You may have heard about it. Could you tell us where you were on Tuesday morning last week?"

Father Skip leaned against the countertop, studying the floor. He let out a long sigh.

"Let me get my calendar from my study. I see so many people each week that it's hard for me to keep track."

He left the room briefly and returned with a spiral-bound calendar appointment book in his hand. He flipped back to Tuesday, running his finger over his notes. "It's kind of my diary," he muttered to himself. "Yes, in the morning, I visited my dad at Hillview Nursing Home in West Salem. My sister lives there. I stayed with her Monday evening. Then after a visit with my dad on Tuesday morning, I drove back home and arrived here at about one-thirty." He snapped the book shut and poured three mugs of coffee, setting one in front of each detective. Grabbing a mug in one hand and his calendar in the other, he sat down at the table.

"Your sister's name?" Sam asked, writing in his memo pad.

"Genevieve Stamper," he answered. "She lives right in West Salem."

"How long did you serve the St. Ignatius Parish at Genoa,

Father?" Sam asked.

"I was there from 2005 until I left in the spring of 2014—about nine years."

Paul took over. "We understand that Jeremy Bjerkes was a member of St. Ignatius. What can you tell us about him?"

"Oh, he came to church regularly when he was married to Julie, less faithfully after they were divorced. Seemed to be a nice guy. I worked with him coordinating funerals for St. Ignatius members.

He was very good at what he did. Very professional and caring."

"We understand that there was some kind of rift between you and the Bjerkes. Could you tell us about that?" Paul asked.

Father Skip's brow furrowed, and he seemed to retreat inside himself for a moment.

"Father?" Paul repeated, dipping his head toward him slightly.

"Well, to be very honest, we didn't have any issues when he was married to Julie. But after he was divorced … " He stopped talking, noticing Paul and Sam's confused expressions. He started again. "It's a Catholic issue that involves divorced congregants. I adhere to the teachings of the church on this topic, but … well, in Jeremy's case, because he was divorced, he could not receive Holy Communion. Some priests are more lenient about this issue, but I'm what you might call the old guard. Jeremy became quite upset when I refused to serve him the Eucharist, and he left the church and didn't come back."

"What year was this?" Sam asked.

Father Skip thought a moment. "I would say about 2013 or so."

"Did you know his second wife, Gloria?" Paul continued.

"Yes, she usually brought their son to CCD on Saturday mornings."

"CCD?" Paul said with a slight shrug. "Sorry, I'm not Catholic."

"Confraternity of Christian Doctrine," Sam said, watching Father Skip's reaction.

"Oh, another believer?" Father Skip asked, smiling.

"Yes, of a sort. My dad's a Lutheran pastor," Sam explained.

Father Skip's smile faded slightly. "We studied Catholic beliefs in confirmation," Sam continued. "Luther's Ninety-Five Theses nailed to the Wittenburg church door and all that stuff. Luther was quite the religious revolutionary,"

"Could we get back to it?" Paul asked, glaring at Sam. "Describe your relationship with Gloria, please."

"My relationship?" Father Skip shrugged his shoulders nonchalantly. "She was faithful to bring her son to CCD."

"There seem to be some inconsistencies in what you're saying and what people in your parish thought went on between you and Mrs. Bjerkes." Father Skip focused his attention on Paul. "Didn't Mrs. Bjerkes see you regularly every Saturday morning while her son attended ... ?" Paul looked over at Sam.

"CCD," Sam said, taking a sip of coffee. He noticed a shadow of anger cross the priest's face. Father Skip began to explain.

"Gloria was going through a rather difficult period in her life, and she came to me for some spiritual counseling and reassurance. Apparently, some nasty rumors surfaced from some college athletes about her physical therapy techniques. Very ugly stuff that threatened her position. She was very upset about it." Father Skip glanced back and forth at the two detectives.

Paul asked, "What about the rumors that you two were having an affair?"

Father Skip visibly tried to control himself. He rubbed his palms on his thighs, sucked in a deep breath, and then spoke in a calm, measured cadence. "I assure you those rumors were terribly hurtful to Gloria and to me. It's one of the reasons the dioceses moved me here. I lost my ability to minister because a very vocal and strident group in the congregation started vicious rumors about me, and apparently, they're still continuing to spread misinformation. There's a reason why scripture says the tongue can start a forest fire," Father Howard said. His voice had ramped up. His nostrils flared, and his face turned pink with irritation.

"James 3, Verse 5," Sam quoted.

SUE BERG

Father Howard nodded. "You've learned your lessons well, detective. But as I said before, those rumors were wicked and completely untrue."

"We'll take your word for it, Father. For now," Sam said quietly, his hazel eyes holding Father Skip's stare. "Would it be possible for me to use your bathroom?"

Father Howard frowned. "Oh, sure. First door on the left down the hallway," he said, pointing.

Paul talked a while more, reconfirming Father Howard's position about his relationship with Gloria. They talked some baseball trivia and reviewed the upcoming Brewers season. Paul drank down the last of his coffee and stood. He offered his hand to Father Skip. "Didn't mean to upset you, Father. We're just doing our jobs," he said, turning to leave. Sam rejoined him and nodded to Father Howard.

"Of course. I understand," he said contritely, shaking Sam's hand.

Paul and Sam let themselves out and walked to the truck parked along the shaded street. It was a perfect spring day. The sunshine was warm without being stifling, the trees and grass were a verdant green, and the air was punctuated with the scent of flowering crabs and purple lilacs. Paul was quiet on the way back to La Crosse. Finally, he spoke up.

"Whadda ya think?" he asked Sam, looking over at Sam.

"Father Skip? Mmm, I don't know. Couple of things struck me as odd."

"Like what?" Paul asked.

"Wouldn't you remember that you visited your dad a week ago? Why'd he have to look it up in his appointment calendar?" Sam asked. "That doesn't sit right with me."

"Yeah, that is a little strange ... kinda like he anticipated being questioned," Paul said. "What else?"

"I grew up around religious people. My dad, for starters. Usually, the church hierarchy puts safeguards in place when pastors counsel their congregants. They may have an elder sit in or another family member. Normally the church governing body discourages counseling in their homes. Sometimes, a pastor's spouse is nearby, or they might look in on them while having a session. Being aware of their appointments, spouses sometimes call during the counseling session to check on them and make sure everything is okay. I know because my mom did that for my dad. Sometimes pastors keep their office doors open and make sure the janitor is around the corner."

"You're kidding me!" Paul said, his eyebrows raised in surprise.

"No, I'm not kidding. Think about it," Sam said, unwrapping a Snicker's candy bar and taking a bite. "Accountability. That's a necessary safeguard in the church. A pastor or priest is a person who is trusted implicitly. More than one congregation has gotten rid of a pastor they didn't like by starting a rumor that their fearless leader was having an affair with someone. My dad knows quite a few clergy who had to leave the profession because their reputations were ruined by malicious gossip."

Sam observed the scenery rolling past his window. He went on. "Of course, sometimes the rumors are true, unfortunately. Jim and Tammy Faye Baker, Jimmy Swaggart, to name a few of the more famous who've bitten the dust because of affairs. And then there's the sexual abuse scandal within the Catholic church."

"Well, I did notice his car in the garage. Not a black Impala," he said, disappointed.

"No, it wasn't, was it?" Sam said absentmindedly. "But I think we need to check out his alibi with his sister in West Salem. Something about that didn't seem quite right." Sam felt in his jacket pocket and pulled out a baggie. "But we'll have his DNA on file when we get back."

Paul grinned. "Hair?"

"Got it from the shower drain," Sam said seriously.

"That'll work," Paul replied, smiling.

Sam continued staring out the windshield, observing a bank of gray clouds building in the west.

He couldn't help but notice how Father Howard's hand started shaking when Gloria was mentioned.

There's something about Father Howard and Gloria, he thought. ◘

29

By one-thirty, Jim and Leslie stood outside an interrogation room at the Law Enforcement Center on Vine Street. Inadequate lighting in the hallway made the rain outside seem even more dismal. Approaching the door to the room, Jim turned to Leslie.

"We've got to maintain our upper hand," he said quietly. "She'll be much more careful about her answers with her lawyer present. But you hop in whenever you want to. Okay?" he asked, his hand resting on the doorknob.

"No problem, Chief. We've dealt with some nasty ones before," Leslie answered, putting her game face on. She couldn't help but notice Jim's attire. He'd dressed carefully for the interview. A conservative but expensive light wool navy suit coat, dark gray slacks, a pale blue dress shirt, and a dark blue Salvatore Ferragamo tie emblazoned with tiny bicycles and flowers. *The blue effect,* she thought. Leslie was sure the tie alone cost well over a hundred fifty dollars.

"Nice tie, Chief," she said, her blue eyes scanning his expensive threads.

"Thanks. Got it in Paris," he said with a wink. "You know, dress to impress."

"You're going to try to impress Gloria? Good luck with that. I don't think it's worked so far."

"Hey!" Jim said, offended. "She already came on to me!"

Leslie shrugged. "Does Carol know that?" she asked. Jim did a double-take. "Ready then?"

"Let's do this," Jim said seriously, opening the door.

As Jim swung the door open, the scent of heavy perfume—some sandalwood variety—assaulted their sense of smell. The fragrance permeated the small room and immediately gave Leslie a nagging headache. Jim glanced briefly from Gloria to her attorney, Vincent Palachecky.

Gloria was dressed conservatively in a light gray suit with a simple pale pink blouse and a classic strand of pearls at her neck. For all practical purposes, she appeared to be the grieving widow. *If only she didn't have those hard snake eyes,* Jim thought. The hostility rolled off her in waves. Her attorney sat scrolling on his phone but looked up briefly when Jim and Leslie introduced themselves. Palachecky gave them a pasty smile, turned off his phone, and tucked it in his pocket. His cheap suit and comb-over hairstyle did nothing to ingratiate anyone to him.

Jim checked the video camera to see that the green light was on. After formal introductions, he pressed the START button, recited the Miranda rights, and began the interview.

"Mrs. Bjerkes, could you tell us about your involvement at St. Ignatius Parish in Genoa?" Jim began, his baritone voice smooth and easygoing.

"St. Ignatius?" Gloria said, playing dumb. She blinked slowly. Jim wasn't sure whether it was an act or the question had caught her off-guard.

"Yes, St. Ignatius. You and Jeremy attended there regularly until recently. Isn't that correct?" Jim continued. He was relaxed with his hands clasped in front of him, his elbows resting on the table.

Leslie stood against the wall, observing.

"Yes, we attended there until 2014 or so," she said. Her eyes traveled to the right, then drifted back to Jim. She took in his expensive clothing. "Nice tie," she said, grinning. Jim ignored her.

"Why did you stop attending church?" Leslie asked.

Gloria glanced at her as if she were a cockroach that needed to be stomped on. "Well, it was really more to do with Jeremy and the church's teachings. Something about divorced people not being able to receive communion. Something archaic that I didn't understand," she said with a dismissive wave of her hand.

Leslie continued to probe. "How would you describe your relationship with Father Skip Howard?" Jim gave her an approving glance.

"Father Howard encouraged us to bring Trevor to CCD every Saturday. I usually drove him there and waited until he was done. Then I brought him home again," she explained.

"Your relationship with him?" Jim reminded her.

Gloria's eyes hardened. "Sometimes, I would counsel with Father Howard. That was when I was going through a hard time at the university. But you already know all about that, Lieutenant," she said, the sarcasm unmistakable. "You seem to have my life all figured out." Mr. Palachecky laid his hand lightly on Gloria's sleeve. She moved away ever so slightly.

"Yes, I do know about that. Since we spoke last time, it's come to my attention that rumors were circulating in the parish that your relationship with Father Howard was adulterous," Jim stated dryly. "How would you respond to those claims?" Jim gave her an icy stare.

Despite the gentle reminder from her lawyer, Gloria all but ignored him. Her face was as cold as marble, all hard angles. She leaned forward threateningly, and with her index finger, she rapped on the table as she articulated her answer. "Those allegations are nothing but damned lies," she retorted, her voice tight with anger and malice. Jim let the silence that followed do its work. Then he started again.

"We've spoken with Steven Hanratty a number of times over the last few days," Jim continued. "He claims you threatened him, followed him, and harassed him with texts and phone calls. He says you even stalked him on Third Street, bar-hopping until you found him. Is that true?"

Mr. Palachecky leaned over and whispered in Gloria's ear.

"I refuse to answer that question on the advice of my attorney," she said icily.

"That's your decision, of course, but we're going to talk to him again after he gets out of the hospital today," Leslie replied, her voice tight and professional. "It seems Steven had a little run-in with a few thugs after he told me about his abusive incidents related to your therapy. You wouldn't know anything about that, would you?"

"No comment," she said, continuing to stonewall, this time without a reminder from her lawyer.

"Let's see now. Let me get this straight," Jim said, his voice dripping with condescension. "Accusations of sexual abuse related to your job at the university, stalking and intimidation of a university student who was sexually abused—"

Gloria rudely interrupted. "*Alleged* sexual abuse, Lieutenant," she hissed. "Those allegations were withdrawn."

"Rumors of an adulterous affair with a priest," Jim continued smoothly as if he'd never been interrupted. "My, you've been busy, Gloria. Should we include orchestrating the murder of your husband on that list as well?"

"Are we finished with this charade yet?" Gloria asked sarcastically, leaning back against the chair, crossing her arms over her breasts. At that moment, she reminded Jim of a cornered rattler, tightly wound and ready to strike.

Jim leaned forward, his blue eyes burning. "Oh, we're far from done, Gloria," he snarled, his voice ratcheting up. "I will follow up every lead, interview every witness, and uncover every piece of evidence in this county and beyond until I am convinced beyond the shadow of a doubt that you are not somehow involved in your husband's murder. I'm not there yet, but, believe me, I'll get there. Until that time, you will remain my prime suspect in the murder of your husband, Jeremy. Are we clear on that?" he asked, bringing his hand down hard on the table. It was silent for some moments.

"Perfectly clear, *Lieutenant*," she answered quietly. A subtle smile creased Gloria's pink lips. Glancing at Mr. Palachecky, she stood. "I think this interview is over."

"Not until we have a cheek swab for DNA," Jim said firmly, standing to face her. Jim looked over at Palachecky as he handed the lawyer the official paper. "Court-ordered by Judge Benson."

"You've got to be kidding me! This is outrageous!" Gloria screamed, the spittle flying. Her eyes were dancing in her head. "He can't do that, can he?" she yelled at her attorney.

"I'm afraid he can," Mr. Palachecky said seriously, studying the document. "At this point, as your lawyer, I recommend you cooperate."

"And I'm sending an officer to get a DNA sample from your son, Trevor, today, as well," Jim finished.

"What?" Gloria raged, standing suddenly, her chair scraping the floor loudly. She spewed a volley of profanity Jim's way. Her lawyer touched her arm again, but she jerked forcefully, throwing him off-kilter, storming through the door, her stilettos clicking ominously on the tiled floor. An officer blocked the hallway and led her to the lab while she sputtered threats and insults under her breath. Mr. Palachecky followed meekly behind her. The interrogation door slammed with a bang.

"The lady knows her cuss words," Leslie commented dryly.

"She knows a whole lot more than that," Jim said, loosening his tie. ◘

30

Jim sat at his antique desk in his study Monday evening after dinner and tried to ignore the PBS kid's show, which was turned up way too loud. As the sound drifted down the hallway, Carol appeared at the door and leaned against the frame.

"Come here, babe," Jim said, gesturing to her. "How're you feeling today?"

Carol waddled toward him. "Like a hippo. Like an elephant. Like a walrus. Like—"

"Okay. Okay. I get it," Jim interrupted as she came up behind him and wrapped her arms around his neck.

"When is this baby going to come?" she complained.

Jim clasped her hands and asked, "What did Dr. Lockhart say today?"

"If I don't deliver before next Wednesday, they're going to induce me. Somehow that didn't sound like a good thing," she commented, leaning her chin on the top of Jim's head.

"It isn't. You want to start naturally if you can. Your labor will be smoother," Jim said.

"Well, la-di-da. Look who's the expert."

Jim rolled his eyes as he got out of his chair. Guiding her into the hallway, he said, "Listen, you go take your shower. I'll tuck Miss

Lillie in and read to her," Jim suggested. "Go to bed and read, or something."

Dragging herself into the bathroom, she blabbered, "Or something? How about jumping jacks? A jog around the block? Swim a mile? Is that something?" The bathroom door slammed shut. Jim grimaced and went to wrangle Lillie into her pajamas.

By ten o'clock, Carol had been sleeping for an hour. Jim showered, pulled out his British detective novel and read until eleven. He got out of bed, tramped through the dining room, and stood on the front steps listening to thunder rumbling in the west. The air was heavy, and the humidity made it hard to breathe. Fingers of brilliant white and yellow lightning sizzled in the sky, precursors of the disturbance to come. More thunder growled. The trees seemed ominously still.

Jim hoped this baby would get here soon, although not half as fervently as Carol. He thought some more about Gloria Bjerkes and the interrogation. Gloria and Father Howard. *Huh. The more they uncovered, the more likely a secret relationship would probably surface. Gloria is a snaky character,* he thought. *Definitely a sociopath and very self-absorbed.*

He turned and went into the house, secured the door, walked down the hall, and quietly crawled in next to Carol. He reached over lightly and covered her exposed arms. She mumbled a little. He lay there thinking about all the changes they'd been through in just one year.

A wedding at the International Gardens, their very romantic Paris honeymoon, boat trips down the Mississippi River finding uninhabited islands, camping under the stars. And all the lovemaking. Of course, that led to where they were now, probably the oldest pregnant couple Dr. Lockhart had ever had. Lillie is another miracle, although sometimes he had to pinch himself as a reminder of the reality of her sad little life. Finding out he had a sister. He never knew she existed until last week. *Still have to talk to Gladys Hanson.* His thoughts jumbled together, surfacing, then sinking from sight like the anchor of a boat. Finally, he slept.

Later that night, Jim was roused when Carol spoke close to his ear.

"Jim. Jim," Carol said softly, rubbing his arm.

He jerked suddenly and sat up, disoriented by the lamplight from the nightstand. He was sweating. *Was I dreaming?* he thought.

"What's going on? What time is it?" he asked, confused, squinting in the light. He glanced at the clock: 1:45.

"You need to get up and get ... " Carol stopped talking and sat on the side of the bed. She began panting, breathing hard.

Jim jumped up, searching for his jeans. He was fully present now. "You should have woke me up earlier," he said, chiding her.

"Oooh. This is a strong one," Carol groaned, panting. "We need to go now!"

Jim continued scurrying around, finding a shirt and his boat shoes. "What about Lillie?"

Sara stuck her head around the door frame. "Got it covered, Dad."

"Your bag?" Jim asked, his hair tousled and wild.

"Already in the car," Carol explained, throwing her head back, still panting, a light sheen of sweat on her forehead.

"Contractions? How far apart?" he asked, throwing on a golf shirt.

"About six minutes."

"Okay, I'm ready. Let's go, honey. Into the car," he said. Grabbing the overnight bag and taking Carol's hand, he led her into the garage.

Jim eased the Suburban onto Chipmunk Coulee Road. The threatening storm that had been farther west had arrived in force. Sheets of rain pounded the car. Spreading its webbed fingers across the night sky, the lightning flared in orange and white bursts. The wind blew through the trees, creating swirling vortexes, loose leaves landing on the wet, shiny pavement. Carol squeezed Jim's hand as the contractions came and went. A couple of times, she let out a subdued cry. *Driving too fast,* Jim thought. He slowed down when he reached U.S. 35. Very few vehicles were on the road. In ten minutes, he pulled the Suburban under the canopy outside the emergency room at Gundersen Lutheran. Helping Carol inside, he went back out and parked the car.

By the time Jim found Carol's room on the obstetrics wing, she was in a delivery bed. Dr. Lockhart was giving orders, checking Carol's progress.

"How we doin', doc?" Jim asked anxiously, his eyes widening as Carol let out an anguished groan. She was flushed, and the hair around her face was saturated with sweat. Jim eased up to the edge of the bed and grabbed Carol's hand.

"She's dilated to eight. We're going to give her a little something to take the edge off. Another half-hour, maybe sooner, she can start pushing. Take off your shoes, put on that gown, and climb in bed behind her to support her. You can feed her some ice chips," Dr. Lockhart said, looking over her half glasses. Between contractions, she praised Carol for getting through the majority of her labor at home.

"You're doing great. We'll have a baby pretty soon," she said.

"Good, because I'm getting really tired," Carol panted, taking hold of Jim's hands, leaning up against him, dozing while she waited for another contraction. A nurse continued to check the fetal heart monitor attached around Carol's stomach.

"How's the heartbeat, Doc?" Jim asked between contractions, worry reflected in his eyes.

"Just how I like it. Strong and steady," she said. She gave Jim and Carol a thumbs up.

True to Dr. Lockhart's prediction, a half-hour later, Carol began pushing, and within twenty minutes, the baby was born. Dr. Lockhart looked over Carol's draped figure.

"You've got a little boy."

Carol gushed tears of joy. Jim kissed her and cried. A nurse placed the swaddled baby into Carol's arms, and she cooed and talked softly to him as Jim watched, mesmerized by the miracle of life.

SUE BERG

"Hey, Henri with an i," he said, softly stroking his little hand. The baby turned his head at the sound of Jim's voice.

"Oh, Jim, he's just perfect," Carol said as she began crying again. They enjoyed some uninterrupted moments with their new little son. Outside, the storm had passed, and the sky was clear. The horizon was just beginning to turn a light pink, spreading out over a bank of pale yellow clouds.

Jim glanced at the clock and saw it was three-thirty in the morning—too early to call anyone with the news. When Carol was back in a clean bed, Jim nestled in with her as little Henri nursed for the first time. Jim thought it was the most beautiful thing he'd ever seen. Carol looked at him, her eyes glowing with love.

"Well, we did it," she said, huddling over Henri, touching his little cheek. Jim glanced at her, puzzled.

"Did it? Yeah, we did it alright." Then tenderly, "And look what we got," he said, leaning down to place a gentle kiss on his son's cheek. "Little Henri."

"No, I meant we defied the odds," she explained.

"Well, they weren't the same odds as Abraham and Sarah of biblical fame, but yeah, I guess we survived," he said, suddenly sleepy. "I'll call people later. It's too early yet," he said as he nodded off.

"Later is just fine," Carol said, cuddling her newborn son. ◘

TUESDAY,
MAY 21

31

Paul Saner whipped his F-150 Ford truck into the parking lot on Vine Street at 7:55 a.m., hoping that Sam was already upstairs. *Lover Boy better not be late,* he thought. Avoiding puddles in the parking lot, he greeted a few people from downstairs and walked into the building with them. He rode the elevator up to the third floor and stepped out to a bunch of women crowding around Emily's computer.

"Hey, what's going on?" he asked, curious.

"Jim and Carol had their baby early this morning. Take a look," Emily encouraged.

Paul leaned over the counter, gaping at the images. "Looks healthy," he said.

"Well, you didn't think he'd be anything but, did you?" Emily questioned, sounding irritated.

"He's a Higgins, after all."

"Name?" Paul asked, still studying the infant's features.

"Henri with an i, Paul Higgins, born at 2:56 a.m., weighing in at seven pounds, twelve ounces."

Paul gave Emily a startled glance. "Really? Paul?" he said, sounding surprised.

"Paul who? Is that the guy who beat up Steven Hanratty?" Sam asked, walking up to the counter. Leslie followed close behind.

"Where'd you come from?" Paul said, confused.

"The elevator," Leslie said.

Sam asked, "What's going on?"

Emily repeated the birth announcement. Leslie and Sam gawked at the photos. "Jim might come in at noon. He's not sure yet," Emily informed them as they huddled around her computer.

"Carol's doing all right?" Leslie asked.

"She did just great, according to Jim," she answered, beaming. "Such a classy lady."

"All right, you guys," Paul said, pointing to Sam and Leslie, "we need to get some stuff done."

"You in charge now?" Sam asked casually, his hands in his pockets.

"Not really." He started down the hallway. "We'll meet in my office in fifteen minutes."

"Sounds like he *thinks* he's in charge," Sam grumbled.

"Get over it," Leslie huffed, taking off down the hall.

By nine-thirty, Sam and Paul were making their way across town, heading to Lenny's Restaurant and Bar. They parked in the nearly empty lot under a large maple. Walking into the bar, they flashed their IDs. Lenny, the bartender, was busy washing and stacking glassware.

"We're wondering if you can help us. A customer of yours Sunday night was attacked out on the street after leaving here. He said the two guys were a couple of thugs—wrestling types. We wondered if you noticed anyone in here that night who was keeping an eye on Steve," Paul explained.

"He says he left here about eleven." Paul scrolled through his photos, then handed his phone to Lenny, who studied the photo of Steve Hanratty.

"Recognize him?" Sam asked, studying Lenny's face carefully.

"Yeah, he was here. You look familiar, too," Lenny said, pointing to Sam.

"I've eaten here a couple of times. Your bacon-wrapped shrimp are great," Sam said.

Paul sighed. "So ... did you notice a couple of beefy guys hanging around here that night?"

"Well, there were a couple of guys at the bar who left the impression they could rip a sink off the wall," Lenny said, still wiping glasses. "Huge shoulders, no neck, and biceps like a side of beef. Fat, but muscular underneath."

"Names?" Sam asked.

"I don't remember, but my wife might. She's better with names than I am, and she was bartending with me that night. Just wait a minute."

Lenny threw the towel over his shoulder, walked back to the kitchen, and returned with his wife. They resembled Mutt and Jeff—he was a bean pole, and she was short and round with a pretty face. Her name was Shelly.

Sam and Paul filled Shelly in on the details of the attack. She listened, nodding her head often, and then she described her conversation with the two thugs.

"The two guys at the bar were Tweedle Dum and Tweedle Dee," she said in a dead-serious tone. There was a moment of disbelieving silence. Shelly continued to stare at Paul and Sam.

"Excuse me?" Sam finally asked, his voice insolent. "You're talking to the police. Let's get serious here. We need real names."

She pushed her hands in a downward motion. "All right. All right. Calm down." She scowled at Sam. "I know them from West Salem wrestling," she said as if that explained things. Noticing the detectives' vacant stares, she went on. "Their real names are John Tweed and Delbert Tweed. But somebody started calling them Tweedle Dumb and Tweedle Dee in junior high, and it stuck. The Tweedle twins." She continued to stare at Paul and Sam. They gawked at her, unwilling to believe her familiarity with local celebrities. "They were Wisconsin state heavyweight and middleweight wrestling champs in 2005." She held up her hands in a stick-'em-up pose. "I kid you not."

"So, where can we find them?" Paul asked, scratching the side of his nose.

"Where else? West Salem," Shelly said, giving them a dubious stare. "Did you say you guys were detectives?"

Sam turned on his heel and was out the door as Paul waved over his shoulder and yelled thanks.

Climbing into Paul's truck, Sam slouched in the seat, cracking open the window. Paul climbed in and pulled out of the parking lot. He noticed Sam's peeved attitude.

"What?" Paul asked. "What's the matter with you?"

"That was total bullshit," Sam sputtered under his breath.

"Well, bullshit or not, we're going to West Salem to find them. You can't make that stuff up."

Paul wove through La Crosse toward Valley View Mall, picked up I-90, which skirted around the city limits of Onalaska, and drove until they came to the southern edge of West Salem. He maneuvered the truck into Brier's Auto, a new and used Chevy dealership off Onshus Road. The lot took up about five acres and had a wide squatting blue and gray pole building situated in the middle of the lot. The front of the building served as the sales headquarters. At the rear of the building were three large bays with extra tall garage doors which led to the mechanical service center.

"What are you stopping here for?" Sam asked, gaping at Paul.

"The Tweedle twins are famous on the local sports scene, so someone inside will probably know who they are and where they are," Paul said, stepping out of the truck. "Besides, I need a Pepsi. You want something?" Sam shook his head. Paul shrugged and walked into the glassed-in front section of the building that served as an office.

Sam watched Paul talking inside the office, pointing toward town, and then waving goodbye. As he walked past the soda machine, he got a Pepsi and walked back to the truck. In the truck, he popped the soda open and slurped a swig.

"They own a farm implement dealership on Highway 16 east of town," Paul said, getting on the ramp to I-90. He drove until he came to the Jefferson Street exit, then traveled across town, picking up Hwy. 16, bearing east for about two miles.

Tweed's Farm Implement was unimpressive even by Midwest standards. Rows of dead and decrepit farm machinery sat in crooked rows behind the main building. Tractors, manure spreaders, balers, haybines, and combines all had impressive layers of rust and peeling paint. Evidently, the machinery had been used and abused into obsolescence. A line of newer farm implements, meant to impress and draw in the younger generation still optimistic about agriculture, stood at shiny attention next to the main highway.

Paul turned in and parked in front of a medium-sized pole building. The front half facing the highway was covered with fake logs, and the sign over the front door had faded substantially, but Sam didn't think the owners or customers really cared. Everybody who was anybody in West Salem knew where Tweed's was. They didn't need a sign.

A late eighties Ford three-quarter-ton pickup was parked in front with a round bale wrapped in netting sitting in the truck box. A border collie sat patiently on the seat, watching the action. Paul noticed a few wrenches, some lug nuts, and a spare tire thrown haphazardly in front of the hay bale. Another newer Dodge truck was parked next to it, some loose hay chaff in the box and a couple hundred-pound sacks of ground corn hunched along the rearview window.

The smell of the implement building was familiar to Sam as soon as they walked in. He'd visited similar places with his dad, the Lutheran pastor, who had served several rural parishes in Minnesota, Iowa, and Wisconsin. The aisles were filled with baler twine, nuts and bolts of all sizes, quarts of motor oil, tires, and a section of farm implement toys. Along the wall, a rack of sweatshirts and plaid work shirts were arranged in piles according to size. The smells took over—rubber, grease and oil, and all things metallic mixed with the lingering scent of cigars, farmer chore gloves, shiny new shirts of stiff material, and a hint of manure. It was a smell you just didn't forget.

Sam and Paul walked up to the parts counter. Flashing their IDs, they asked if the Tweeds were in. The young man glanced at their IDs, their dress slacks, shirts and ties, and backed up slightly.

"John's in the main office, and Del is out back in the yard," the young assistant recited with a hard glint in his eye.

"Would you mind going out back and asking Del to come to the office?" Sam asked, putting a little grit in it.

The assistant looked like he was going to refuse, but he finally grabbed his coat and slipped through the side door to the lot.

"If I'd have known we were coming here, I would have worn my bib overalls and my Red Wing shitkickers," Sam muttered while following Paul to the office at the back of the building.

Paul knocked on the metal frame of the door. John Tweed looked up from his desk.

"Help you?" he asked, but Paul could tell he really didn't want to help anyone. *I sure hope these guys cooperate and don't decide to get bucky, or we're going to get ground up into hamburger,* Paul thought.

Paul and Sam pulled their IDs. John's eyes traveled to their badges. He made a pretense of reading them, and then his gaze slowly returned to their faces. He blinked slowly in a reptilian fashion. Paul's initial assessment of John sitting at his desk was ex-athlete gone to seed. When Tweed stood up, Paul realized he had grossly underestimated his physical prowess.

John Tweed was well over six feet tall, at least 250 pounds, with a massive chest, gigantic shoulders, and a neck that grew in one continuous upward thrust to a huge head that Paul was sure could be classified as a deadly weapon. Biceps like the Hulk. Compared to him, Paul and Sam looked like Willie Wonka of chocolate fame and Tiny Tim tiptoeing through the tulips.

"Well? Whaddya want?" John asked. Paul was still taking in his size.

"Where were you Sunday night?" Sam asked.

John looked at Sam, calculating his answer. "My brother Del and I went into La Crosse for a steak." He rubbed his belly in a slow circular motion with his huge hand. *Must be feeding time for the gorilla,* Sam thought.

"Where in La Crosse?" Sam said, his patience short.

"Lenny's," he answered, crossing his massive arms over his chest.

"We've had a report that a customer from Lenny's was ambushed from behind by two huge wrestling-type guys Sunday night about eleven," Sam recited. "The kid ended up in the hospital—a concussion, a couple of broken ribs, some bruises. The bartender says you were there. Identified you. Why'd you beat up the kid?" Sam made a point not to blink.

"What kid?" a voice said from behind them.

Paul and Sam turned, staring at a carbon copy of John. "You must be Del," Paul said. "Are you guys really twins?"

"Identical," they both said at the same time.

"What kid?" Del repeated.

John jumped in. "These two cops think we beat up some friggin' college kid at Lenny's Sunday night while we were enjoying our twenty-four-ounce steaks."

Del smiled creepily. Sam felt a shiver run up his spine. "We're not in the habit of pounding helpless millennials, or whatever their generation is called now," he said. Del filled the entire doorway, and he seemed to have no intention of moving.

"You guys know Gloria Bjerkes?" Paul asked, looking back and forth from one twin to the other.

"Now there's a subject we're familiar with," Del said, grinning wickedly. "Gloria does get around."

Sam was getting sick of the macho, tough-guy act. "How do you know her?" he asked rudely, fascinated by the facial expressions mirrored from one twin to the other.

"She's a mutual friend," John said vaguely.

"She ever do her massage magic on you guys?" Paul asked.

"We've had a few sessions with her at the U," Del responded, smiling like a lizard.

Sam leaned over the desk, making eye contact with John. "Listen, you bozos. We know you were the two who beat the crap out of Steven Hanratty."

There was a long moment of silence. "Prove it," John said quietly, his snake eyes boring a hole in Sam's forehead.

"We never said the victim was a college kid. You said that," Sam said, his index finger tapping on the top of the laminated desk. Del's eyebrows lifted, and John shrugged nonchalantly. "In case you didn't know, Gloria is the primary suspect in the murder of her husband, Jeremy, and his assistant, Layne McNally. You need to stay out of La Crosse until this case gets cleared up unless you want to get sucked into the whirlwind of suspicion and spend some time in jail." Sam slowly straightened up and headed to the door.

"No more small-town thuggery," Sam hissed as he squeezed past Del.

Paul and Sam walked to the truck and climbed in. Paul looped around the building and turned onto the highway.

"Got your bad cop mojo on today," Paul commented. "Bad cop, good cop. Works for me."

Sam leaned back, ignoring the comment, thinking. "Let's pay a visit to Father Howard's sister. She lives around here," he said, scrolling on his phone. "Genevieve Stamper, 118 West Locust."

Paul reached over and programmed his GPS with the address and followed the directions until they came to the house. A small yellow vinyl-sided residence sat back from the curb. Shaped and trimmed shrubbery hugged the cement steps that led to a cheery bright yellow front door. Paul leaned over and rang the bell.

Waiting on the steps, they finally heard movement inside. A woman dressed in gray scrubs with dark hair styled in a flip answered the door, a stethoscope hanging from her neck. Her name tag read Hillview Home Health Care, Rachel.

"Hello," Paul said. "We were wondering if Genevieve is home? We'd like to speak with her." He displayed his police ID.

"She's just getting out of the shower, but please come in." Rachel stepped aside, pointing them to a small but tidy living room that smelled of mothballs and old magazines. "I'll tell her you're here."

Ten minutes later, Genevieve had pushed herself into the room with her walker and found her favorite recliner. The room was a combination of sixties furniture, including a couch covered in a pale pink fabric, two mint green sitting chairs, a low wooden coffee table, and a leather recliner. In the corner, a hutch was filled with ceramic figures and sets of teacups and saucers. Covering Genevieve's legs with an afghan, Rachel said goodbye and left.

"Now, how can I help you boys?" Genevieve asked. It seemed as if her tiny body had been swallowed in the recliner. Her gray hair was neatly styled, and her eyes were bright with curiosity.

Sam and Paul identified themselves, showing their IDs.

"Ms. Stamper, we talked to your brother, Father Howard, yesterday. We just need to verify that he was here last week. Could you tell us when he visited you?" Sam asked politely, his hazel eyes friendly.

Ms. Stamper blinked, and confusion clouded her eyes.

"Oh, my memory's not what it used to be, but I keep a diary. That way, when I forget, I can look back." She fumbled with a stack of books and magazines piled on the floor next to her chair. Pulling out a spiral-bound weekly planner, she flipped the pages and then stopped. *Must be a family habit,* Paul thought.

Genevieve looked up and said, "Our mother kept a daily diary," as if reading his mind. "She always told us it was the most hopeful thing we could do. Maybe we're just waiting for someone to discover who we really are." She gazed at Sam. He had no idea what she was talking about.

"Last week? Your brother Father Howard? When did he visit you, ma'am?" Sam persisted.

Genevieve continued to flip pages. "Well, it's right here. He came

Monday evening, we had dinner together, and he left at seven-thirty Tuesday morning to visit our father at Hillview Nursing Home here in town. He'll be ninety-six in June."

"Did your brother come back here before he left to go home to Stanley?" Sam asked.

"No, he visited Dad and then left the nursing home and drove to Stanley," she said. She blinked rapidly." Or did he visit Father on Monday evening? My memory isn't what it used to be." By now, her confusion was growing. "Is there some kind of problem?"

"Probably not," Sam said, smiling, trying to reassure the elderly lady.

"What kind of car do you drive?" Paul asked.

"Well, I don't drive anymore. I'm not able," she answered. Then as if revealing a conspiracy, she whispered, "I got lost last year and ended up in Lansing, Iowa."

"Do you own a car?" Paul asked again.

"Yes, it's in the garage. I'm really not good with the makes and models of cars. My memory slips me. But you're more than welcome to check the garage," she said, cheerfully pointing to the kitchen. "Just go through the kitchen. The door to the garage is right there." She turned to Paul and continued her rambling conversation.

Sam got up, walked through the kitchen, and opened the door. The garage was empty. He returned to the living room. Still standing, he looked across the room at Genevieve. "Your garage is empty, ma'am," he said.

"Really?" she said, bringing her hand to her cheek. Now she was truly bewildered. "Well, I thought I had a car. I used to have a car," she said, staring at Sam as if he could solve the problem.

"Do you remember the color of your car?" Paul asked.

"I think it was black, but wait ... " she began rising from her recliner. Paul reached out and assisted her. When she was finally standing, she grabbed her walker and hobbled to a nearby cupboard. Pulling out a gray metal box, she handed it to Paul, who set it on the coffee table. "Look in here," she ordered. "The title should be in there somewhere."

Paul opened the box and began paging through documents. He stopped. "Your car was a 2007 black Chevy Impala." Sam locked eyes with him, a little thrill running up his spine. Paul handed the title to Sam, who copied down the VIN. "Do you know where your car is now?"

Flummoxed, Genevieve said, "Well, I was sure it was in the garage. Where could it be?"

"Ms. Stamper, we're going to try and find out where your car went, okay?" Paul said.

"Oh, that's so nice of you," she said, reaching for Paul's hand and squeezing it.

"Please, don't tell anyone about this right now," Paul explained. "When we find your car, we'll let you know," he said, patting her hand reassuringly.

"Thank you. My lips are sealed," she said, passing her fingers across her mouth.

"Good. Thank you for your time. We'll let ourselves out," Sam said. On the way to the truck, he muttered, "She won't remember we've been here an hour from now. I think dementia has set in big time."

Driving back to La Crosse, Sam began putting together the facts they knew so far. Sam liked to concoct a chain of events, even if they sometimes seemed far-fetched. The possibilities stimulated ideas, and it usually helped them gel all the facts into a cohesive whole. He rolled out a possible murder scenario as Paul drove.

"I'm going to give you my theory about Father Howard and Gloria. Tell me what you think."

"I'm listening," Paul said. "Go ahead."

Sam started. "Gloria meets Father Howard at St. Ignatius Parish, sets her sights on him and hooks her claws in him. With her predatory instincts, that wouldn't have been difficult for her. Church isn't the most common place to seduce someone, but ... "

"When you use the word "hooks",' did you mean she had a

sexual relationship with him?" Paul commented.

"Yeah. She met him somewhere—who knows. Whatever. She wouldn't have any trouble reeling in her prey once she put her mind to it."

"Boy, that's scary if she can seduce a priest," Paul grumped.

"Happens. Priests, pastors, and counselors are generally an empathetic sort. They listen to people's problems and make an emotional connection along the way. From there, it's not that big of a leap to a relationship. That's the hidden danger in that kind of work," Sam said. "Anyway, Jeremy and Gloria can't seem to have kids. Gloria obsesses about it, wants a baby, sees Father Howard as fair game—a means to an end," Sam said, regaining his rhythm.

"Following so far. Keep going," Paul encouraged.

"They begin a relationship. Secret, of course. She gets pregnant but credits the kid to Jeremy. Their 'miracle' baby."

"She must have a huge sexual appetite," Paul commented.

"Not necessarily. From what Leslie told me, she's all about power. The sex probably isn't the main thing. Anyway, that's beside the point. Jeremy finds out somehow that the kid is really Father Howard's, not his. He confronts the priest and threatens to reveal his secret love life to the diocese. They have a huge argument. Jeremy quits the church and forbids Gloria to see him again. Gloria and Father Howard decide to eliminate Jeremy before the news gets out."

"Or Father Howard decides to take him out on his own," Paul adds.

"That's possible, too. His priesthood would've been over. It'd be a pretty big scandal. A lot of dirty secrets would have been exposed, destroying Father Howard's career and reputation, to say nothing about his relationship with God." Sam continued. "You've got to remember he could drive from West Salem with his sister's car to the funeral home in what? Thirty minutes? So he visits his dad to solidify his alibi, then uses his sister's car, drives to the funeral home, shoots Jeremy and Layne, hops in the car and drives the black Impala back to Stanley, dumps the car somewhere, then hitches a ride back to West Salem and picks up his own car."

"Sounds like a lot of rigmarole over a car."

"Not if you killed someone and didn't want to get caught," Sam reminded him.

"Maybe Gloria helped him with the car," Paul suggested. Sam tilted his head and nodded. "One thing's for sure. Genevieve won't remember anything about the car, so we can't rely on her testimony."

"My idea about Gloria helping him ditch the car could work, but right how we're not really sure if Genevieve's car was used in the murder scenario. We don't even know where it is. Her family might have taken it so she didn't go on another trip and get lost. That's just part of my theory at the moment. It'll probably change down the road," Sam said. "But here's the thing—Gloria is probably directly involved, or she planned the whole thing or made the suggestion to Father Skip. Gloria is more than capable of murder. After Leslie's experiences with her psycho boyfriend, Wade Bennett, she can spot a barbarian a mile away. Her antennae were going into overdrive during both interviews."

"Just one problem." Paul glanced at Sam as he drove.

Sam harrumphed. "Yeah, I know—no evidence." Sam's shoulders slumped. "She's mentally unstable, and she has persuasion down to a science. Remember the retracted statements by the three students," Sam finished. "We need some DNA. But it's building. I can feel it. We're getting there. Slowly."

" DNA would be good," Paul said. "The sooner, the better."

"You know it," Sam said, a frown sitting above his eyebrows. ◘

32

Gloria Bjerkes sat in the tiny cabin in Barronett, Wisconsin, wishing she was anywhere but in this little hellhole of a crackerbox Jeremy had built as a deer hunting shack. Well, it wasn't really a shack. But it certainly didn't meet her upper-crust taste in vacation homes.

The twenty-by-forty-foot cabin sat on a concrete foundation in the middle of the woods along a one-lane dirt track off the main gravel road. It had red steel siding and thermal pane windows. A kitchen and living area featured a field-stone fireplace, and the remainder of the cabin was divided into bunk beds for sleeping. The cabin smelled of the woods and old blankets. A screened-in porch faced the north, and a matching red outhouse was discreetly placed behind the cabin. It had served Jeremy and his hunting friends throughout the years. This was the first time Gloria had ever graced the cabin with her presence, and she hated every minute of it. Peeing in an outhouse was as disgusting as it got.

The cabin was located in Barron County, seven miles straight north of Cumberland on Highway 63. It sat next to a one hundred twenty-five acre tract of land the Wisconsin DNR had set aside for hunting. The mature trees had been recently logged off as the result of some bureaucratic decision made by a paper-pushing

SUE BERG

administrator. As a result of the clear-cut operation, it was mostly a marshy wasteland with a few sparsely placed cabins and cottages on its perimeter. The hunting, which had never been that good, was even worse now.

Delbert Tweed, aka Tweedle Dee, the smarter of the two twins of wrestling fame, called Gloria late Tuesday afternoon and filled her in on the visit from the two detectives from the sheriff's department.

"What time were they there?" Gloria asked nervously.

"About ten o'clock this morning," Delbert said in a bored tone.

"Damn. What did you tell them?"

"Told them we didn't know anything about a kid getting beat up. Whaddya think we'd say? We covered for you before," Del informed her. "We know the drill."

"You better, you twit. I'm paying you enough. But this Higgins guy scares me. He's way too persistent. He's one focused individual. He seems to think he's going to find enough evidence to haul me in."

"Well, you didn't kill Jeremy, did you?" Del sounded a little worried now.

"Of course, I didn't kill him. I loved Jeremy." That statement hung in the air, waiting to be challenged. Del did.

"Don't give me that crap, Gloria. We both know you're incapable of a loving, long-term relationship. Your predator instincts are way too keen. You like the hunt and the conquest. The skeletons in your closet are rattling, and they want to get out." He could almost imagine Gloria's cunning smile. She loved a compliment.

"Well, I do have a certain skill set when it comes to the pursuit," she said, her voice low and sexy.

Del chuckled. "Yeah, you betcha. I noticed. Hey, I gotta go. Just wanted you to know we handled it."

After Del called, she arranged for her son, Trevor, to stay overnight at a friend's house. Then she whipped into action. This whole murder investigation was taking its toll. She needed a place to think and plan her next move. Lt. Higgins had proved to be a worthy adversary: intelligent, determined, and disgustingly moral.

But she was good at diversions and she desperately needed one now. A distraction was called for. She was an expert at blowing smoke; she'd been doing it her whole life

She drove straight to the cabin, a four-hour drive. After a few wrong turns on some back gravel roads, Gloria arrived at the cabin about two-thirty in the morning.

At the crack of dawn, when it was just getting light, she hiked about a mile to an abandoned gravel quarry that she'd heard Jeremy talk about once. She'd been lucky and found a map of the area tacked up on one of the walls in the cabin, which helped her get her bearings. Her Glock 43 handgun was tucked into her shoulder holster and had a comfortable heavy feel to it. She wore a light windbreaker in case she met up with somebody in the woods on the way to the quarry. She didn't want to give anyone a reason to be suspicious when they saw a lone female with a gun strapped under her arm.

The morning air was chilly, but once the sun came up, it warmed up quickly. It was quiet, and she seemed to be the only one on the entire tract of land. Luck, or something like it, was with her.

She arrived at the quarry, having worked up a light sweat. She picked out a spot on the wall of the dugout depression, a distance of about a hundred feet, and shot off two magazines. Felt good. Her aim was fair to middling. She liked the feeling of power she got from carrying the gun. She had no idea when she might have to shoot her way out of a problem, but she'd be ready. Her little target practice session got her back into the swing of things and gave her the confidence she needed if she ran into trouble in the next phase of her plan. Hiking back to the cabin, her mood lifted, and she almost felt cheerful. Flipping her phone open, she called a friend in Turtle Lake.

Putting some spunk in her voice, she said, "Judy, I'm in need of a little assistance." ◻

33

By nine o'clock Tuesday morning, Jim had called everyone who really cared with the news of their baby's arrival. Carol was exhausted. Jim kissed her goodbye and promised to bring Lillie in later that evening to see Henri. He drove home, showered, shaved, brushed his teeth, and dressed for work in khaki dress slacks and a soft navy cashmere sweater. He called Sara, wondering what she'd done with Lillie.

"Dad, is everything okay?"

"Yeah. I was just wondering where Lillie is. Have you got her?"

"Of course. She's having a ball in the Pre-K room, wowing everybody with her astute questions and demonstrating her above-average, exceptional Higgins brainpower. The genealogical pool runs deep, Dad."

"I hear you," Jim said, envisioning Lillie causing a commotion. "Listen, I'm running into work for a while. Carol was tired, and she needed a shower and some sleep," he explained. "Can I meet you at the McDonald's on Losey for a bite to eat around five-thirty? I'll pick up Lillie there and take her over to the hospital to see Henri."

With their plan in place, Jim hung up and headed to work. He reviewed the night's events in his mind. If someone had told him he'd be a father again at the age of fifty-three, he'd never have believed it. Henri was a beautiful baby boy, and Carol was mesmerized by him. A wave of gratitude and awe washed over Jim when he thought of the wonderful gift they'd been given. Stopping at the Mormon Coulee Kwik Trip for a cinnamon crunch bagel and a hazelnut coffee, Jim wheeled into the law enforcement parking lot on Vine Street ten minutes later. When he stepped off the elevator at eleven o'clock, the entire team of secretaries applauded and yelled congratulations.

Emily beamed. "I can see the Higgins features. Big eyes that will undoubtedly be blue. Lots of hair and, of course, that intelligent brow," Emily said, pandering to the secretarial pool.

"Intelligent brow?" Jim said, his frown pronounced. "You're mistaken. That's just the confusion that comes with trying to figure out why people do what they do." Jim tilted his head in a reflective pose, and a wistful expression crossed his face. "But Henri is a healthy little bruiser. A beautiful baby." His eyes misted with tears. He cleared his throat and looked at the floor.

"You know, we're all thrilled for you and Carol, Chief," she said. She handed Jim a pile of pink post-it notes scribbled with phone numbers, bits of information, and people he needed to call. "Anyway, you have some messages."

"So, is Leslie here?" he asked, trying to balance the messages in one hand and the bagel and the coffee in the other.

"Yep, she's holed up in her office," Emily said.

Jim turned, stopped in his office to drop the messages on his desk, and headed down the hall chewing on his bagel. He rapped on the door. Leslie swiveled in her desk chair, holding up a finger.

"Thanks for getting back to me," she finished and shut her phone. "Congratulations, Chief. Little Henri looks like a keeper," she said, smiling.

"Thanks. Henri's pretty special, and everybody's fine," he said, taking a sip of coffee. "We're tired, but that might be a regular occurrence for the next few months." He took a sip of coffee and continued. "So, can you fill me in about what's going on around here? I presume Sam and Paul have been busy?" Jim said.

"Yeah, they've been around town."

Leslie began by filling Jim in about the visit to the Tweedle twins. "They claim they didn't beat anyone up. That's the upshot of the whole conversation. Sam told them to stay out of La Crosse until we've figured out this murder, but they definitely know Gloria and have done jobs for her before. Gloria seems to be involved in some questionable activities. She definitely uses her university position as a cover to appear to be a legitimate, educated, upstanding citizen. Who'd have thought?"

"That's not surprising. She's a chameleon," Jim said gruffly. He cringed when he thought about how she'd looked at him like he was fair game. "What else?" he asked impatiently.

"The guys visited Father Howard's sister in West Salem. She has the beginnings of dementia, but she did reveal that she owned a 2007 Black Chevy Impala."

Jim's eyes shot open. "Really?"

"Really. She thought it was in her garage, but when Sam looked, the garage was empty."

His shoulders slumped. "Doesn't sound like she's a very reliable source."

"Well, she might not be, but she trusted Sam and Paul to search through her documents. And guess what?" She held up her index finger in her excitement. "They found the title. They've got the VIN. She has a black Impala somewhere. That's what I'm working on. I've called the DMV, and they're doing a title search to see where and when the car was purchased or if it was sold recently. They gave me the license plate number, too. I'll put out an APB on the car to all the state law enforcement agencies with that information."

"Great. We need to find that car, although we're not really sure whether it was used in the murder – yet, Jim said, straightening his shoulders, feeling encouraged.

"I've been thinking about where Gloria or Father Howard could hide the car if it hasn't been sold," Leslie said. "But that's like … I don't know." She clucked her tongue in frustration. "Finding it seems impossible. They could have driven it down by the river and pushed it in some swamp, or left it on some back logging road somewhere in northern Wisconsin or Minnesota, or hidden it in an old farmer's deserted barn. We may not find it for years."

"Right. But it's worth looking for. We might get lucky. What about Steven Hanratty?"

"Out of the hospital. Recovered enough to go back to work part-time," Leslie said. "He filed a police report after I talked him into it. You know he's still very bitter about the abuse he endured from Gloria. Might be worthwhile to question him about where he was the morning of the murder."

"You think he's got a motive for killing Jeremy? Seems more likely he'd want to hurt Gloria," Jim pondered out loud.

"I don't know, Chief. When it comes to motives, this case, with its sexual implications, stretches the imagination—and theories. Right now, I'm not sure what to think."

"Well, let's keep Hanratty in our sights and on our list of suspects," Jim said. "But right now, I want you to go downstairs and do a title search on all of Jeremy Bjerkes' properties. I want to know what he owns and what his net worth is. Also, do a separate search on Gloria and Father Howard."

Leslie wanted to ask why but Higgins seemed a little stretched. She didn't feel like challenging him over something so straightforward.

"I'm not sure about this yet. I'm kinda grasping at straws. Just trying to shake something loose," Jim said, suddenly feeling tired. "I'm scheduling a press conference for tomorrow morning at nine. I want you there." He'd been leaning against the door frame. Now he turned and walked back to his office. Sitting down at his desk, he took out his phone and called Gladys Hanson. He let it ring a while, knowing she was moving slowly these days with arthritis.

"Hello. This is Gladys," a brisk voice finally said.

"Gladys. It's Jim Higgins. We have a boy, Henri Paul. Born this morning at about three-thirty.

Everything's fine. He's healthy and is sharp like a Higgins is expected to be."

"Wonderful. My prayers were answered. Carol?"

"She was a trooper. Didn't wake me up until her contractions were six minutes apart."

"Well, I'm not surprised. She seems very independent and strong."

"Yes, she is," Jim answered. *Boy, I love that woman ... and my new little son.* After a brief pause, he continued. "Listen, something's come up in one of my investigations, and I was wondering if I could come sometime tomorrow and pick your brain."

"Of course. Not sure I'll be much help, but I'll make a pie. What works for you?" she asked.

"How about three tomorrow afternoon?"

"Sounds good. See you then. Oh ... and congratulations," Gladys said, and she hung up.

Jim called Leslie. "You mentioned Steven Hanratty. Let's drive over to the corporate office and see if we can catch him. I have some questions for him."

"Right. I'll walk down. Just let me finish a call first," she said.

By one o'clock, they were cruising over the George Street viaduct toward the Kwik Trip corporate headquarters. Walking into the building, they stopped at the main desk, where they were directed to the second floor. A secretary called Steven's office, and five minutes later, Hanratty strolled down the hall.

"Detective Brown. What can I help you with?" he asked cordially.

"This is Lieutenant Higgins," Leslie said, turning to Jim. The two men exchanged a handshake. "Is there somewhere we could talk in private?"

"Sure. There's a conference room down the hall. Follow me," Steven said, turning and walking cockily ahead of them. When they settled at a conference table, Jim got right to it.

"How are you feeling?" he asked.

Hanratty gave Jim a penetrating glance. "I'm sore, but I'll be okay, I guess."

Jim asked, "Where were you Tuesday morning, May 14?"

Steven swallowed, gazed through the office window, refocused, and said, "I took the day off."

Jim met his gaze and held it. Leslie said, "Yes, we understood that from talking to the secretary. But what specifically did you do that day? And can anyone corroborate it?"

Steven switched his gaze to Leslie. His eyes were wide, and he swiped his hand through his thick hair. The two detectives waited patiently while Steven squirmed and cleared his throat.

"Well, I like to fish, so I headed to Spring Coulee down by Coon Valley. I didn't meet anyone on the stream, but I did stop in Viroqua at the Driftless Cafe for a bite to eat at about one o'clock. Someone there might remember me," he told them.

"And then what?" Jim asked.

"Drove back to La Crosse. I got home about four and cleaned my apartment."

"What route did you take on the way home?" Jim probed.

"Just drove the back roads. I like to do that sometimes. Wander and discover some new fishing holes and places to hike. My girlfriend and I do a lot of hiking around the area."

"Anyone in your building talk to you that day?" Jim asked.

"No, but my girlfriend was over that night. She came after work about five." Steven's brow creased with confusion. "What's this all about?"

"Just covering our bases, that's all," Leslie said, smiling. "Can you think of anything else you did that day?"

"No, nothing else. I watched a movie with my girlfriend and went to bed about ten. I told you where I was." He rubbed his eyes, then clasped his hands and rested them on the table. "My girlfriend's name is Siri O'Reilly, and her number is 758-3490 if you want to talk to her."

"Thanks, we might do that," Jim said, jotting down the number. He stood and reached his hand toward Steven. "Nice to meet you, Steven," he said, giving him a dimpled smile.

As they walked across the parking lot to the Suburban, Leslie said, "He seemed quite confident and open about sharing his information. Didn't act guilty." She glanced at Jim. "What do you think?"

"It was a pretty poor day for fishing. It rained cats and dogs that morning. Somehow I don't think you'd spend your time fishing in thunder and lightning, getting soaked to the gills on your day off, would you?" Jim asked. His face was stony and hard. "I fish a lot, and that day was a horrible day to go fishing unless you're some kind of fishing fanatic or a glutton for punishment."

Leslie nodded in agreement. "Oh, boy. I wasn't here that morning, so I didn't pick up on the incongruity of the situation."

"Doesn't look good, does it?" Jim said, climbing into the Suburban.

"No. It doesn't," Leslie sighed. ⬖

34

It was early Tuesday evening. Lillie trotted alongside Jim through the corridors of the hospital, taking three steps to his one. The questions bubbled out of her in a continuous stream, and she kept asking them until they stepped off the elevator on the third floor.

Walking down the hallway, Jim stopped at Room #3578. He knocked quietly, then opened the door. Carol had showered, applied a little makeup, and was leaning back in bed dressed in a lacy, light yellow set of lounging pajamas. *Beautiful,* Jim thought. The rolling bassinette was situated next to the bed where little Henri was soundly sleeping. Suddenly, Lillie became extremely shy, hiding behind Jim's leg. Jim leaned over and kissed Carol, running his index finger across her cheek.

"How're you doing?" he asked, his blue eyes scanning her face. "Had a lot of company?"

"Yeah, John and Jenny just left, and Vivian and Craig were here. Boy, the night is catching up to me. I'm tired, but I'm glad it's all over, and everything went well." Gazing lovingly toward the baby bed, she said, "I can't believe I'm really a mom." Jim noticed her eyes misting over.

"Hey!" a little demanding voice complained, patting Jim's leg. "When can I see my baby brother?"

Jim leaned down, picked up Miss Lillie, and nestled her in next to Carol.

"Hi, Lillie," Carol said, tenderly kissing her cheek and holding her little hand.

"Mommy, where'd your big belly go?" Her blue eyes were wide with fascination as if Carol had performed some magic abracadabra trick.

Carol laughed. "That's where baby Henri was and now ... "

Jim had leaned over and plucked little Henri from the bassinette. He gave the baby a gentle kiss and laid him in Carol's arms. Lillie stretched her neck to gape at the newborn.

"Is this my baby brother?" she whispered, staring up at Jim.

Carol said, "He can be if that's what you want."

"He's really tiny and red. Why's he so red? Is he mad?" Lillie demanded.

"No, that's just what new babies look like," Carol said, rolling her eyes at Jim.

"I think he needs a big sister like me to take care of him," Lillie said assertively, carefully petting his little head and winding his little hand around her own chubby finger.

"I think you're right," Jim said smiling, standing next to the bed with his arms folded across his chest.

For the next half an hour, Lillie bombarded Carol with questions while Jim tuned in to the evening news on FOXX. An hour later, Jim lifted Lillie out of the bed and announced it was time to go home.

"But Mommy and Henri have to come, too," she said, starting to whimper.

"I sense a full-blown meltdown coming down the pike," Jim said. Carol tipped her head at his use of the old-fashioned phrase. He knelt in front of Lillie. "No, Mommy and Henri have to stay one more night," he stated firmly. "They'll come home tomorrow."

Lillie's whimpering quickly turned into wailing. Jim kissed Carol good night, took one more peek at Henri patting his little back, picked up Lillie, and left the hospital. Lillie's wails lasted all the way through the hospital corridors to the car. She finally cried herself to sleep on the ride home.

After tucking Lillie into bed, Jim thought, *I hope I'm up for this.* Although it was only nine o'clock, he was exhausted. He undressed down to his boxers, pulled out his novel, but he woke with a start fifteen minutes later, the book resting on his chest. Tossing it on the nightstand, he turned out the light and fell asleep. ◘

WEDNESDAY,
MAY 22

35

By ten o'clock Wednesday morning, Jim and Leslie were facing a throng of reporters in the lobby of the Law Enforcement Center on Vine Street.

"We're asking for the public's help in the murder investigation of Jeremy Bjerkes and Layne McNally," Jim's deep baritone voice rumbled. Leslie stood discreetly behind him, watching the reporters. Her eyes scanned the crowd, and she nodded to a few reporters she knew.

"On Tuesday, May 14, an unknown person entered the Bjerkes and Oates Funeral Home on Fifth Street on the south side of La Crosse and brutally shot and killed Mr. Bjerkes and Mr. McNally. A witness has come forward who said that a dark vehicle, possibly a Chevy Impala, was parked in the visitor's lot at the funeral home around ten o'clock the morning of the killings. We are asking for the public's help in locating the car and driver of this vehicle."

As Jim talked, his anger fired up. He put some bite in his words, emphasizing the ruthlessness and coldblooded spontaneity of the killer. "This was a heinous, brutal crime that resulted in the deaths of two innocent people in our community. If you have any information—if you saw anything around the funeral home that morning—we are asking you to come forward and do the right thing. You may call the La Crosse County Sheriff's Office or the Crime Stopper's hotline. You can remain anonymous. Thank you," Jim concluded, his face solemn as he stepped away from the mike.

Mike Callahan, a reporter from the *St. Paul Pioneer Press,* who covered Wisconsin news stories for the paper, shouted, "Lieutenant Higgins, is it true Bjerkes' wife is a primary suspect in this case?"

Jim stepped back to the mike, adjusting his tie. "The spouse of any murder victim is always a prime suspect," he answered in a neutral tone.

"But doesn't she have some dubious history involving sexual misconduct at the University of La Crosse?" Callahan badgered.

"To our knowledge, those charges have been dismissed due to victims who recanted their allegations." Jim turned and began leaving the lobby of the Law Enforcement Center where the news conference had been held. Reporters crowded around Leslie and Jim, jostling and jabbing each other for a favored position. Pushing the elevator button, Jim turned when Callahan rushed up to him through the crush of bodies.

"Hey, Higgins, off the record, what about this Gloria Bjerkes? Is she a suspect or not?"

"I can't comment at this point in the investigation." Jim eyed the young disheveled reporter. "We're trying to uncover any clues that will give us a better picture of the perpetrator, but it's been slim pickin's."

"You mean, you've got zilch," Callahan said disgustedly.

"I wouldn't go quite that far," Jim said, stepping into the elevator. As the door closed, he waved to the frustrated reporter. Leslie, who'd accompanied Jim to the news conference, kept her eyes on the floor numbers blipping past as they shot upward.

"Boy, he's persistent," she said quietly.

"One of the most stubborn. Gotta be careful with the press. I didn't give them much. The news conference was more of a fishing expedition than anything. Something might pop to the surface. Besides, I wouldn't say we have enough evidence to even speculate about the killer. Although some strong indications point to Gloria's involvement, we're not anywhere close to arresting someone."

"It's not too promising … so far," Leslie said despondently.

Walking off the elevator, Jim headed to his office. He hung his suit coat over the back of his chair, then turned to Leslie, who'd followed him.

"What did you find out about Bjerkes' property and net worth?" he asked as he got comfortable at his desk.

Turning and walking to the door, she said over her shoulder, "I'll go get that stuff in my office."

Jim's phone beeped.

"Jim, Luke here. The DNA on Gloria Bjerkes and Trevor will take a while yet."

"We need a rush on it. Can't you get it faster?" Jim asked, frustrated as he shuffled through his pile of papers. "Those samples from Gloria and her son, Trevor, are crucial to the possible motives in this case. And the DNA from that ribbon could break everything wide open. You have to emphasize the importance that the DNA plays in this investigation," he said forcefully, emphasizing the obvious.

"Yeah, I know, Chief. You and every other investigator in the state say that. All the time. I'll try again. Talk to you later." Luke clicked off.

Leslie walked back in, laying a file folder on Jim's desk. Flipping the folder open, she withdrew a sheet of notes and began explaining what she'd found.

"Jeremy Bjerkes owns the funeral home on Fifth Street, which is no big surprise. It's valued at $400,000 and was paid off in 2014. Their home in Dunwoody Estates is titled to Gloria. Value—$600,000. Whether her dad paid for it or she inherited it isn't clear from the records."

Jim listened carefully, leaned back, and stared at the ceiling. "She's probably quite wealthy; her dad was rich," he commented. "Doc invented a number of heart surgery-related tools, some robotic stuff. His royalties on those alone would make us look like paupers.

There's no way that Jeremy or Gloria could afford a house like that on their salaries." Making a circular motion with his index finger, he gestured for her to continue.

"Jeremy also has a small parcel of land—a couple of acres—east of Barronett, Wisconsin, with a small structure on it. Probably some kind of hunting cabin, from what I can tell from the description. Valued at $50,000," Leslie continued.

"Huh. Keep going," Jim muttered.

"Bjerkes also has a number of rental properties on the north side of La Crosse near Logan High School on North, Moore, Prospect, and Salem. It's set up under Bjerkes Holdings and is run separately from the funeral business. All the rentals together are valued at around $400,000. So all total with his business, the cabin up in Barronett, and his rentals, he's got real estate valued well over a million dollars."

"What about Gloria? She own any property?"

"Just the house that we know of. Of course, we haven't seen her savings, checking, or investments," Leslie said.

"Well, I know one thing," Jim said, letting out a sigh.

"What's that, sir?"

"Can't prove it, but I don't think Jeremy was killed for money. There's some sexual stuff going on. Some secrets. Power. Control. Abuse. Something. Gloria is used to money, and I get the distinct impression money doesn't interest her—as long as she has plenty of it, which she probably does. If she's the predator we know her to be, she's interested in power. Power over people. Power to intimidate with secrets. Power over her victims by getting them hooked sexually and then dangling them over a barrel. To her, it's all a control game. She's a real piece of work, that's for sure." Jim tapped a pencil on his teeth as he thought out loud.

"Exactly my thoughts, sir," Leslie commented.

"Listen, I want you and Paul to check out those rental units. Go to Jeremy's office. Shake some trees. Talk to the renters. See if they have any insights about Jeremy or any dealings with Gloria."

"Right. I'll grab Paul, and we'll get on it."

Jim got up and walked down the hall to Sam's office. He knocked, then sat down in a chair near his desk.

"Mornin', Chief," Sam said pleasantly.

"Tell me about your impressions of Father Howard," Jim said, getting right to the point. He leaned back, resting an ankle on his knee, and listened to Sam rattle on about his visit to Stanley.

He absorbed everything he said without interrupting Sam, silently agreeing with his conclusions.

After a moment, he said, "On Saturday, Father Howard might make an appearance in Genoa, and you and Leslie are going to be at the St. Ignatius Catholic School picnic and celebration to watch it play out."

"We are?" Sam said, scrunching up his face.

"Yep. Apparently, one hundred ten years of continuous Catholic education in Genoa is something to celebrate. I'll be there, too."

"How'd a Lutheran like you get invited to that?" Sam asked, his curiosity piqued. Then his eyes lit up. "Oh, wait. Your daughter, Sara, right?"

"You got it," Jim said, pointing to Sam. "The picnic will give us a chance to see the delightful aspects of Father Howard's personality in action—if he shows up."

"Gloria going to be there?"

"Maybe. Maybe not. At any rate, it should be interesting, don't you think?" Jim said, cocking his head at a jaunty angle. ◘

36

Paul and Leslie had visited three of the four rental units that Jeremy Bjerkes owned in the Logan neighborhood of north La Crosse as well as a visit to the office of Bjerkes Holdings, Inc. By three o'clock, they'd talked to the renters in three of the four units. They'd heard nothing but good reports about Bjerkes, the landlord. It seemed he charged reasonable rents, and his company was quick to maintain the units and fix the myriad of problems that regularly plagued buildings in a Midwestern climate. His tenants were satisfied with him as a landlord.

A secretary at the rental office told them that Bjerkes regularly attended the Logan North Neighborhood Association meetings and made suggestions for improvements to its parks and playgrounds. He sponsored a Little League baseball team in the summer and a midget hockey team in the winter. He was very community-minded and took his civic responsibilities seriously. On the walls of the office, a number of mayoral and city council awards were displayed. His concerns about the welfare of La Crosse families and neighborhoods was evident and sincere.

Paul pulled the Ford F-150 truck into the shade of an ancient oak as they approached the rental unit on Prospect Street. The duplex was a two-story stucco affair with a front porch that ran the front span of the building and connected the two units. Each duplex was book-ended by a single-car garage.

Leslie hopped out of the truck and wandered up to the duplex on the right. Ringing the bell and not getting an answer, Paul peeked in the front windows.

"This unit's empty," he said. "Let's try the other one."

The duplex on the left was occupied by a small Hmong lady who answered the door. She studied Leslie and Paul seriously when they presented their IDs.

"Yes? What do you need?" she asked politely, primly folding her hands in front of her. She was tiny—short and fine-boned with blue-black hair and delicate features. A yellow sweater was draped over her shoulders, and underneath she wore an aqua cotton house dress.

"We're wondering if you've had contact with your landlord recently?" Paul asked. Seeing her confused expression, he clarified. "Mr. Bjerkes? Have you seen him lately?"

"No. But I usually don't. He comes around sometimes with maintenance crews. I heard about his death from neighbors. Too bad," she said sympathetically, shaking her head back and forth.

"What about the unit next door? It seems strange that it's sitting empty," Leslie commented.

"The renters were thrown out last month. They were selling drugs or something," she said with a disgusted tone. "Bad stuff." She paused.

Have you ever met Mrs. Bjerkes?" Leslie asked.

"No, I've never seen her," Mrs Xiong said.

"Thanks. Here are our cards. Please call if you think of anything else," Paul said.

Mrs. Xiong nodded energetically. "I will. I will do that," she said, smiling.

Walking down the shaded sidewalk, Leslie said, "Well, that was another dead end."

Paul blew out a little huff of air. "Happens in every case. We've just have to push through. Something will turn up."

"That's a good bet,"Leslie said seriously. She walked to the garage door, shielded her eyes with her hand cupped over her brow, and pressed her face to the small glass window. "There's no car here," Leslie told Paul. Walking back to the truck, she hopped in. "Let's get back to the office. Higgins will be interested in this." ◙

37

Jim went to the hospital to pick up Carol and Henri at one o'clock. After several trips up and down the elevator with baby gifts, flower arrangements, Carol's overnight bag and finally, Carol and Henri, it was two o'clock. Jim turned out of the hospital parking lot and headed south on U.S. 35 to Chipmunk Coulee Road. The day had warmed considerably. The sky was clear, and the river sparkled with promise. Jim cranked the window down slightly. The air had a fruity scent mixed with hot tar and car exhaust odors.

"Gorgeous day to take our little Henri home," Carol said, glancing at the car seat in the back.

"Yes, it's beautiful today," Jim commented. "And we have a beautiful new son." He paused a moment, then glanced at Carol. She was dressed in a colorful floral top, capris, and a pair of Sketchers. "You okay, babe?" he asked, grabbing her hand.

"I'm tired, but I'm fine. Why?"

"Well, once I get you settled, I've got to go see Gladys and have that conversation I've been putting off about Juliette." Jim felt a pang of anxiety at the thought of what else he might uncover about his family.

"Oh." Carol seemed disappointed.

"You okay with that?" She didn't respond, so he continued.

"Vivian called and said she was bringing some food for dinner. She'll come around five."

"Oh, that's good," Carol said, visibly relaxing. She was quiet for a few minutes as Jim drove through Chipmunk Coulee in the dappled afternoon light. "You need to find out about this whole deal with Juliette sooner or later. Somehow I think sooner is better."

Jim drove down the driveway, flicked the garage door opener, and parked the Suburban inside. He helped Carol into the house, got her settled comfortably in the bedroom, laying baby Henri in his bassinet. Then he unloaded all the cargo and set it in the hallway. *Vivian can put that away later,* he thought.

"You'll be okay for an hour or so?" Jim asked, leaning over her and pulling off her shoes.

"Yeah, I'm just going to rest until Lillie gets home. I'll be fine," Carol said sleepily. She pulled Jim to her and kissed him. "Love you," she said softly, rubbing his back. She rolled to her side and closed her eyes.

"I'll be back soon. Your cell is right here if you need to call me," Jim said as he tucked it next to her.,but she was already sleeping. Jim checked Henri, and he was also sleeping soundly in his bassinet.

He crept out of the house and slipped into the Suburban. At the end of the driveway, he turned left on Chipmunk Coulee Road and drove through the winding coulee until he hooked up with County K. The spring day was balmy, washed clean from any lingering trace of winter. Trees popped with that brilliant new green growth only seen in the spring. The lilacs were in full bloom, filling the air with their intensely sweet fragrance. Birds fluttered from branch to branch, building nests, and preparing for their young. Suddenly in front of him, a doe and her tiny spotted fawn leaped from the edge of the road, the fawn wobbly on its long legs. Jim braked, rolling slowly to a stop to let them pass. He drove into Gladys' farmyard a couple of minutes before three o'clock. Gladys was a stickler about time. He shut off the engine, then sighed, and leaned his head on the headrest for a minute, trying to calm the queasiness in his stomach.

Despite her profession as a social worker, Gladys was a farm wife at heart. She lived modestly since her husband Otis had died five years ago. She had managed to keep the farm buildings in good shape by hiring carpenters now and then. The red hip-roofed barn and white chicken coop were outdated but well-kept. She'd sold Otis' beef cattle but retained some goats and her flock of laying hens. Jim and Carol bought fresh farm eggs from her every couple of weeks.

Climbing out of the truck, Jim sauntered toward the white clapboard house. A couple of leghorn chickens strutted across the driveway, their black beady eyes nervously following his movements. Gladys appeared at the door, her white hair floating around her face like a cloud. Jim knew her perceptive eyes missed nothing. Gladys was very intelligent. He'd decided on the drive over to lay out the story without any pretension. Waving him in, she disappeared into the house. Jim entered a small alcove, then took the two steps up into the kitchen.

The house was simple but welcoming. The kitchen had a long wall of painted mint green cupboards interrupted in the middle by an antique porcelain sink under a window that gave a view of Cedar Valley. A sturdy square oak table and matching ladder back chairs sat in the middle of the room. Jim's eyes settled on the far wall where a treasured hutch filled with heirloom dishes sat prominently along the wall opposite the cupboards. The smell of freshly perked coffee relaxed Jim. *I'm in the presence of a cherished friend. How bad can this be?* he thought. He was about to find out.

"Mmm, I smell blueberry pie," he said, seating himself at the kitchen table, "and coffee."

"Comin' up," Gladys remarked, cutting pie and putting a piece in front of him with a fork. She served him coffee, poured a cup for herself, and sat down.

"How are Carol and the baby?" she asked politely, pushing a strand of loose hair away from her lined face.

"Fine, fine. Henri is healthy, a beautiful baby, and Carol is just tired. Pretty typical," Jim said dryly, taking a bite of pie, bursts of blueberries waking up his mouth. He sipped his coffee, savoring the flavor.

"Jim," Gladys started, "I'm not going to beat around the bush. Something's troubling you. I could hear it in your voice when you called. What's going on? How can I help?"

Her intensity always made him edgy, but he understood that was just her Type A personality coming through. The love and care she'd shown Jim's family over the years was solid and reliable, a port in a storm.

Jim savored another bite of pie, then laid his fork across the plate. "Well, this isn't easy to explain and probably harder to believe," he started. "But let me tell you about the events that have happened in the last week."

Gladys listened carefully as Jim laid out the unbelievable scenario of his lost sister. How she was found dead in Riverside Park with a four-year-old child in tow who'd suffered through the trauma of homelessness and witnessed the death of her very ill grandmother. How Jim and Carol had been granted custody and had taken the delightful Miss Lillie into their home. Gladys maintained a steely reserve during the account, occasionally nodding to indicate she was listening. If she was shocked, she didn't let on, but Jim noticed a pain in her eyes she couldn't hide.

"We're committed to loving and raising her as if she were our own," Jim said seriously, locking eyes with Gladys.

She nodded politely. "That's no surprise," she commented brusquely.

Jim paused a moment, drawing on some invisible courage. "When I examined Juliette's adoption papers, I noticed that you were the foster parent for her before the actual adoption took place. You've always been a straight shooter with me, Gladys, and I need you to fill in some blanks if you can," Jim finished, his blue eyes hopeful. He studied her aging, wrinkled face. Beneath the tough exterior of her feisty personality beat a heart of gold. He was counting on her balance of goodness and truthfulness. *Speak the truth in love,* he thought. *I need to hear it.*

Gladys cleared her throat, uncomfortable with the details of Jim's account. "Well, I don't really know where to start, but I think you know that I've fostered many kids in my day as a social worker," Gladys began. "Fostering is a tough thing to do. You have to balance your love and welfare for the child with the understanding that you have to let them go when a home is found for them," she explained in her rather curt manner. "It's easy to get too attached." She lifted her chin and looked Jim squarely in the eye.

"I know all that," Jim said impatiently with a wave of his hand, sweeping the generalizations away. "What about Juliette?"

Gladys held up her hand, sighed, and began again. "Your mother came into the hospital to have her baby. By now, you've figured out she was single and rather desperate. When Juliette was born, she was barely four pounds—tiny and extremely vulnerable to infection and sickness. She'd had a rough time being born. Your mother decided to give her up for adoption since she had no way of supporting a baby." She sympathetically watched Jim's confused expression. "Lutheran Social Services called me to see if I'd foster the baby until she was well enough to be adopted. I really didn't expect Juliette to live out the first week of her life. But, you know me," Gladys lifted her chin, and her face was resolute with determination. "I wouldn't take no for an answer. I fed her every two hours, rocked and nurtured her as best as I could. Gradually over two months, she came around and developed into a strong, healthy baby. I couldn't have done it without Otis, God bless him. He did all the chores."

"But, couldn't my mother have kept her? Why didn't she keep her?" Jim blurted, his frustration tinging his words. He laid his big hands on the table and leaned back in his chair. His blue eyes danced with exasperation. All the tension of his unknown past threatened to throw him into a tailspin.

Gladys refused to be badgered. She calmly started again. "Your mother had a very difficult delivery. By the time she delivered Juliette, she was exhausted. Then she hemorrhaged, and the doctors thought

SUE BERG

they'd lose her. She pulled through, but she was in very rough shape. Your mom made the decision to give up Juliette to provide her with a loving home. Juliette's chances of survival were pretty grim." Gladys said. When Jim stayed silent, Gladys continued. "She bravely made a decision to give Juliette was she couldn't give her—a chance at a good life in a home with both a mom and a dad." She'd been watching Jim, aware of the anguish he was feeling at hearing this hidden, buried story.

Jim turned, leaned over, and put his elbows on his knees, holding his head in his hands.

"Jim, listen to me," Gladys said, leaning forward, her voice tremulous with emotion. "Your mother was a very brave woman. Her decision was hers to make. It was very rough for her to give up her child. She did what she thought was best at the time."

Jim turned back to Gladys, his eyes filling with tears despite his anger. "Did my mom ever see Juliette again?"

"No. In that era, when an adoption was final, all ties to the child by the mother were severed. Your mom carried a tremendous secret all the years she lived. That's not an easy thing to do," Gladys said. "I know it seems wrong to you, but I believe she did it out of love for her daughter." Jim noticed her wrinkled hands and her old apron with decorative butterflies fluttering across the outdated fabric.

"That's probably what killed her at fifty-one," Jim said sadly, turning back to the table, leaning his chin on his clasped hands. "A hidden secret and a bad heart."

"I'm sure it contributed to her early death. I'm sorry, Jim. Really I am," Gladys said. Her face was lined with deep and genuine sadness. "Your mom did what she thought was best at the time. I don't fault her for it, and you shouldn't either."

It was quiet in the kitchen then. It seemed there was nothing more to say. The day outside was bright, and a slight breeze swished the needles of the huge white pine outside the window. Jim could hear the antique kitchen clock ticking the minutes away. An image of baby Henri came into his head and the way Carol had gazed at him with wonder when she'd first laid eyes on him. He couldn't imagine the weight of his mom's decision. *It must have been awful*, he thought, *to live with that secret all those years.*

Finally, Gladys spoke. "I've always had a soft spot in my heart for you, Jim," she whispered softly, her eyes filling with tears, "because I knew your untold story. I've hoped all these years that you'd never have to discover the truth, especially in this way." She reached across the table to grasp his big hand. "There's one thing I'm glad you're doing."

Jim looked over at Gladys, his eyes reflecting the sad realities of his family history.

"What's that?" he asked hoarsely.

"You've rebuilt your life with Carol after Margie's death, and now you're raising your sister's granddaughter. I can't think of anyone who'll do a better job."

Jim nodded, but the flood of emotion that had been building now spilled over. He sat at the table and quietly grieved for his sister and the pain she'd endured to bring Lillie to him. He thought about the sorrow she must have felt when she discovered she had two brothers whom she would never know. And he lamented the loneliness and agony of Juliette, dying in a forgotten corner of a city park with the uncertain future of a granddaughter weighing her down. Regret and sorrow overwhelmed him. He didn't know how long he sat there, letting himself fall apart. Gladys didn't rush him; rather, she let all the pent-up frustration and confusion he'd hidden the last few weeks surge out in one gigantic wave of emotion.

Jim finally glanced at the time. "I should go," he said, wiping away the tears on his cheeks. He felt like he'd been wrung through a knothole. Gladys clasped his big hand in both of hers. "Thank you for telling me the truth," Jim said, his voice cracking. "Now I know why you prayed for me all these years."

"I've always loved you as if you were my own son," she said with a sad smile.

Jim kissed her lightly on her soft wrinkled cheek, turned quietly, and left the house. ◖

38

Sam Birkstein sat hunched down in the seat of his black Jeep, waiting for Gloria Bjerkes to exit Halloway Hall on the UW–La Crosse campus. He was sweating, and his crisply ironed dress shirt had melted into a soggy, limp affair. He loosened his tie, wrangled it up over his head, and threw it on the seat. *What I wouldn't give for a T-shirt, shorts, and sandals right about now,* he thought. Opening his phone, he glanced at the time: 4:45 p.m. *She should be coming out soon.* Running his fingers through his brown curls, he took another swig of bottled water and scrolled through his messages. The phone beeped.

"Birkstein."

"Hi. What are you doing?" Leslie's voice sounded soft, and he realized how much her voice meant to him, especially at the end of a very humdrum, boring day of investigative work.

"Mmm. Just waiting for Gloria to come out of her office at the U. Thought I'd follow her and see where she goes and what she does." *Something might happen,* he thought.

"Okay," Leslie asked, sounding confused. "And you're doing this because—"

"Because Paul told me that Higgins expects me to strike out on my own and not just do what I'm told," Sam rambled on. "He said

I'm supposed to display some independence and creative thinking, so that's what I'm trying to do. Be independent and think. Create some opportu—oops, here she comes."

"Whatever," Leslie replied. "Should I make dinner for one or two?"

"Two. I'll be there by seven."

"I'll plan on it. I might go for a run with Paco up in Hixon Forest," she added.

"Yeah, catch you later." Sam clicked off, keeping his eyes glued on Gloria.

As she strolled to her car, he noticed the confidence in her swagger. A woman in charge. *Maybe she's trolling for a new victim,* he thought. Her pencil skirt hugged her hips and the loose, flowing blouse hinted at firm breasts and a flat tummy. Sam had to admit she was a sight that could get a man thinking about *things*. He closed his eyes briefly, feeling guilty at the lustful ideas creeping into his head. Before Gloria got to the car, she donned a pair of sunglasses, scanned the area, unlocked the door of the red Audi A6 sedan, and slid into the front seat. Sam started his Jeep and kept her in his sights.

Easing her car out of the university parking lot near Halloway Hall, Gloria turned left on Main until she came to Losey Boulevard. Sam followed at a discreet distance. Proceeding north on Losey toward Valley View Mall, she turned west on Gillette, then worked her way to a parking lot within the Kwik Trip corporate complex. Sam turned into the parking lot but drove past her to the far side. He parked his Jeep some distance away but close enough that he'd have a good view of her vehicle. Then he hunkered down in his seat, watching Gloria's car. Within a few minutes, Sam saw a young, well-dressed man texting on his phone as he walked toward a newer model pickup truck.

Sam texted Leslie. *Need a pic of Steven H. Can U send one? Sam.* A moment later, his cell buzzed, and he opened up a photo of Hanratty. Sam observed Gloria step out of her car and walk briskly to a dark blue Chevy Silverado truck that the young man had just climbed into. *Hanratty*, Sam thought. Slapping her hand on the passenger side window of the Silverado, Gloria made a circular motion with her finger to indicate the driver should roll down the window. Nothing about her movements was friendly.

Sam quietly opened his door and began walking toward the truck. As he got closer, he could hear the argument ramping up in intensity.

"Listen, Steven. You're not in charge. I am!" she blustered, jabbing her index finger in the air.

"Screw you, Gloria! You need to get a life and leave me alone!" Hanratty yelled back, red-faced. "I'm not talking to you—not now—not ever!" He reached over and started the truck.

"I hear you had a little run-in over to Lenny's the other night," she yelled. "There's more where that came from. You can count on it! I'm sick of your friggin' whining to the cops ... "

Sam walked up behind Gloria, his red Badger hat shading his eyes from the late afternoon sun.

Gloria and Steven continued to exchange hostile barbs.

"Is there a problem here?" Sam asked politely, his hands on his hips.

"No, I'm leaving," Hanratty said as he rolled up his window. He drove his truck out of the parking lot.

"Who the hell do you think you are?" Gloria asked, turning her full attention to Sam. Her face was flushed, and her eyes were snapping with anger.

Sam whipped out his ID. "La Crosse Sheriff's Department. I'm a detective. Having a little problem with Mr. Hanratty?"

"So what if I am? It's none of your business, so butt out!" she said, the spit flying.

"Why don't you hop back in your Audi and move along?" Sam suggested reasonably.

"Don't tell me what to do! You have no idea who you're dealing with!" Gloria hissed, her green eyes flashing.

SUE BERG

"Oh, but I do know who I'm dealing with. I know all about you, Gloria," Sam said softly. He ratcheted up the intensity in his voice. "You're Jeremy Bjerkes' widow, a potential suspect in his murder, and the one who hired the Tweedle twins to beat the crap out of Steven Hanratty because he had the guts to tell his story of sexual abuse. Is that what's bothering you? Your little minions are rising up and defying your control?"

Gloria sputtered, then shouted, jabbing her finger toward Sam's chest. "You have no right to follow me! This is harassment!" Her body coiled like a tight spring, her fists clenched in tight balls at her sides.

Sam moved in closer. Gloria backed up a few steps. "Now you listen to me," he said quietly, his eyes blazing with righteous anger. "What I just saw here was intimidation and harassment. I heard repeated threats. You can go on your way peacefully in the next minute, or you can spend a night in jail. I'll be happy to accommodate you and call a squad car to take you in. Your choice."

Gloria stepped back a few steps, taking stock of Sam for a long minute. Then she turned on her heel and walked to her Audi. Sam's heart was pounding, and his face was flushed. He watched Gloria spin her car around and drive out of the lot.

Well, she certainly doesn't disappoint, he thought as he strode back to his Jeep. *She's everything everybody said she was ... and more. Wait 'til Leslie hears this.* ◘

39

The evening sun was setting over the huge maples and oaks in Jim's backyard casting elongated shadows on the manicured lawn. As dusk fell, the birds' raucous chattering ceased for the night. Jim sat slumped in an Adirondack chair by the fire pit, sipping a Leinenkugel's beer.

Dinner had been a noisy affair with Carol and Vivian chattering, Lillie bombarding everyone with questions, and Sara regaling them with tales of fifth-grade antics. Henri was the only one who seemed oblivious to the chaos. Now the house had quieted. Vivian had cleaned up the kitchen and departed for Holmen leaving a mountain of food behind that would feed them for a week. Bathing Lillie and reading to her, Sara had tucked her into bed and retreated to the confines of her new apartment in the basement. Carol was nursing Henri in the living room and promised to join him on the patio when the baby was settled in.

Jim's cell buzzed.

Groaning, he saw it was Sam.

"Yeah, what's going on?"

"I followed Gloria late this afternoon. She had another confrontation with Steven Hanratty in the corporate parking lot at Kwik Trip."

"Her claws are coming out," Jim grumped. "We might want to start some surveillance on her."

Sam continued. "Also, Paul and Leslie talked to the lady who lives at the duplex on Prospect—a Mrs. Xiong—but she's never met Gloria. Didn't know her at all so that was a dead-end."

"I'll make a phone call up to the Barron County sheriff. Jeremy has a cabin up there somewhere. Maybe she hid the car there. It's a long shot, but it's worth a try."

"Sounds good. See you tomorrow."

Jim found the number of the Barron County Sheriff's office and called. He told them what he was looking for.

"A black car—an Impala?" the officer on duty asked. "There are lots of those around."

"Yeah. I know. It's a long shot, but Jeremy Bjerkes has a cabin somewhere around Barronett."

"How do you spell the last name?"

Jim spelled it. "We're wondering if the car is hidden somewhere on his property," he explained.

"We'll check on it. There are lots of cabins up by Barronett, so it'll take a while. Won't be 'til tomorrow," the officer said casually.

"The sooner, the better. This involves a double homicide, so let me know as quickly as you can."

Jim leaned forward and stirred the coals of the fire, lost in his thoughts about his family history. He'd always assumed that stories of lost siblings who were found would be cause for great happiness and celebration like the biblical tale of the prodigal son returning to his waiting father. But the story Gladys had told him revealed a side of his family history that made his mind swim with unresolved confusion and sadness. He sighed heavily. A rustling sound of feet on the fieldstone patio broke into his thoughts. Carol walked over and sat down next to him. She grabbed his hand, studying the side of his face as he stared into the coals of the fire.

"So what'd you find out today, honey?" she asked. "You were awfully quiet at dinner."

Jim told her about the family secret that had been hidden for so many years. Carol listened carefully, not interrupting, knowing Jim's emotions were close to the surface. When he finished, she sat mesmerized by the red and blue coals radiating warmth and heat into the night air.

"Oh, my. That's a lot to absorb in one session," she said, her brown eyes warm with concern. "How are you doing?" She reached out and gently stroked his arm.

"Overwhelmed. Angry. Disappointed." Jim let out a pent-up sigh. "I don't know ... " He leaned his head back and gazed at the myriad of stars overhead, twinkling so steadily in the inky sky. "Confused doesn't even come close to describing it."

"Give it time to percolate and settle into your soul. I'll be here for you whenever you're ready to process it. But right now, I need you to come to bed with me," she said, reaching out to take his hand.

Needs. Everybody's got needs, he thought. *What about my needs?* He stood up, and they walked through the darkness into the house, shutting off lights as they went down the hall to their bedroom. Henri was sleeping in his bedside bassinet. The lights in the bedroom were turned low. Jim stripped down to his boxers and crawled in beside Carol, grateful for clean sheets and the cool night air softly flowing through the window.

"I'd like to rewrite the past, but nobody can do that," he said, pulling Carol close. "Hey, you're skinny again," Jim commented, running his hands over her stomach.

Carol groaned. "Not skinny enough. You should see my stretch marks." She cuddled next to him, laying her head on his chest. "But they're worth it considering the wonderful result."

"When I look at you, the last thing I see is stretch marks, honey," Jim said, chuckling. "Thanks for listening. I'm glad you're right next to me." He reached up and turned out the lamp.

"Mmm, my favorite place in the whole world ... other than Paris," Carol mumbled sleepily. She rolled over, and soon Jim heard her quiet breathing. He lay there in her presence, the warmth of her body cradled next to him. He wondered why God had privileged him with such a woman. He whispered a litany of thanks, surrendered the present circumstances to the mysterious ways of the Almighty, and drifted off to sleep. ◘

THURSDAY,
MAY 23

40

Paco barked loudly as he ran ahead of Sam, coaxing him along Oak Trail in Hixon Forest, which paralleled Bliss Road. Traffic was light. Sam huffed along, basking in the early morning mist, the promise of a brand new day laid out before him. Running energetically, he passed a scenic overlook on the bluff trail, the morning fog floating in wisps in the valley below. The views he normally enjoyed of the city and the Mississippi River in the distance peeked in and out of the haze.

Often, Bible verses would come to him on these early morning jogs, similar to how the surroundings materialized on the trail up ahead. His mother had helped him commit scripture to memory when he was just a child, and now a verse popped into his thoughts: "I will lift mine eyes to the hills, from whence cometh my help. My help comes from the Lord."

Paco, Leslie's black lab, was in his glory. With his nose to the ground, the scents of spring had sent him into high-tailed ecstasy. He sniffed at the base of an ancient oak tree, barking wildly when a squirrel tore off into the underbrush. Sam called him several times, and when he finally came, Sam clipped on his leash. They eased into a brisk walk toward the end of the trail, Paco tugging Sam along the sidewalk. It was quiet as they made their way back to Cliffwood and Leslie's apartment.

Taking the front porch stairs by twos, he picked up the *La Crosse Sentinel* and unlocked the front door. The caption on the front page caught his attention: "Police Ask for Help in Double Homicide." He hung Paco's leash in the back hallway, threw the paper on the kitchen table, and started the coffee before heading for the bedroom.

Leslie was still sleeping. Stripping off his sweaty clothes, Sam stood over the bed in his boxers, watching her tranquil face. Her beauty mesmerized him. Her long blonde hair was unfurled on the pillow, golden and thick. The room smelled of talcum powder, and a light cool breeze moved through the open window, fluttering the sheer curtains. Despite the rough-and-tumble past of military service in Iraq and sexual and physical abuse by her sniper boyfriend, Wade Bennett, Leslie was a lovely and decent woman with some serious baggage.

Sam stood there for a few minutes thinking about their future. *Where are we going to end up?* he thought. He didn't believe in extrasensory perception or that someone's thoughts could wake somebody from a dead sleep, but Leslie must have sensed his presence somehow. She rolled on her back, the sheet and quilt barely covering her breasts. Opening her eyes, she jerked when she saw him staring at her. Then she smiled.

"Hey, you go for a run?" she asked, her voice husky with sleep.

"Yeah, in Hixon. Just an easy jog on Oak Trail," he said, leaning over her.

She pulled him down to her, then pushed him away. "Ew! You stink, and you're all sweaty."

"Well, I was heading for the shower. You could join me," he suggested as he stood up, his dark hair rearranging itself around his expressive hazel eyes.

"Too bad we don't have a big soaking tub like Higgins," Leslie commented, her blue eyes meeting Sam's. "I never thought of him as such a romantic, did you?" she asked, crinkling her nose.

"No, but if I have as much sex appeal and energy as he seems to have at fifty-two, I'll be more than happy with my lot in life."

"That'd be something to aim for, wouldn't it? Sex appeal when you're fifty. A life goal?" She smiled subtlely, eyeing his muscular shoulders and strong arms. "Start the shower. I'll be there in a few minutes."

Sam was about to head to the bathroom when the doorbell rang.

Looking at the clock, he wondered who would be stupid enough to come uninvited to someone's house at six-thirty in the morning. *Well, if they're that dumb, then they're going to get the whole load— boxers and nothing else.* He smiled wickedly. *That oughta teach 'em not to knock on someone's door so early in the morning.*

"This better be good," he muttered to himself. Walking to the front door, he grabbed the handle and swung the door open.

"Dad!" Sam said loudly. "Dad, what are you doing here?" he asked, peeking around him, noticing the gray Cadillac in the driveway behind his Jeep. He thought about Leslie in the shower. He felt like his heart was going to blast out of his chest. *Please, Leslie. Don't come out here now in a towel,* he thought, hoping she would miraculously receive his message via telepathy, even though he didn't believe in it.

"Hi, son. We didn't mean to startle you," Pastor Birkstein said, his voice calm and well-modulated. His father was immaculately groomed, his dark hair trimmed, his mustache expertly clipped. He wore a crisp white shirt, dark gray dress trousers, and a maroon tie with tiny sheep wandering across its surface.

His mother began getting out of the car. "Hi, honey. Surprise!" She did a cutesy wave.

At that moment, excited by the unfamiliar voices, Paco decided to come through the duplex from the back hallway at breakneck speed. Barking a warning, he plowed past Sam and tore over Pastor Birkstein's polished wingtips, almost knocking him over. Propelling himself down the front steps, Paco focused his black lab energy on Mrs. Birkstein.

"Paco! Paco!" Sam yelled as he slammed the front door shut and ran down the stairs in his boxers. Paco dug in, his barks unfriendly and threatening. "Paco! Come here," Sam yelled, grabbing his collar.

"We didn't know you had a dog, Sam," Mrs. Birkstein said, holding her hand on her chest. "He doesn't bite, does he?" Her eyes were wide with trepidation. Backing up several steps, she stopped when her butt smacked against the car door with a thud.

Standing in front of her, Paco growled ominously. "Hey! Stop it!" Sam warned, pulling the dog toward the porch. He looked up at his mother, who was cringing against the car. "He doesn't bite, Mom. He's pretty good most of the time, although he can be somewhat protective with new people."

"Where are your clothes, Sam?" his mother asked, embarrassed, her eyes scanning his body.

"I was just about to jump in the shower after my run when the doorbell rang," Sam explained.

"Well, can we come in? We'd love to see your new place," Mrs. Birkstein said in her light, airy voice. Her smile waffled as she continued chattering. "Your roommate told us you'd moved. It's really nice on the outside. Do you have a new roommate, honey?"

Oh, boy. Sam stopped on the sidewalk, looking back and forth at his parents.

"Mom, Dad. I'm sorry, but I'm working a double homicide case, and I've got to get to the office. I'm late already, and I still have to shower, shave, and eat breakfast," Sam said apologetically. Seeing their disappointment, he tried to make amends. "But listen, I'll meet you for dinner tonight. Seven o'clock. The Waterfront down by Riverside. How's that sound?"

"That sounds fine," Pastor Birkstein said, his perceptive gaze taking in Sam's apparent discomfort. "We're at the Free Lutheran Convention over at the Radisson. The Waterfront is close by there, isn't it?"

"Yeah, yeah, it is," Sam said, still standing in his boxers on the sidewalk, holding Paco's collar.

SUE BERG

"That sounds good, son. We'll meet you at seven," Pastor Birkstein said, frowning at Paco as he walked carefully around the dog and retreated to the car.

Sam turned and started climbing the stairs. When he got to the top step, he turned and waved as the Cadillac backed down the driveway. "Seven at the Waterfront," he said weakly. He let himself into the apartment and leaned against the front door. *This is going to be a disaster,* he thought. Leslie came out of the bathroom wearing nothing but a towel. "Who was that so early in the morning?"

"You'll never believe it," Sam groaned. ⧉

41

Judy Orbeck sat in her 2017 Toyota Corolla hatchback in a patch of scrub oaks near a turnout at the Hoffman Hills State Recreational Park near Colfax, Wisconsin. She cracked her window open and lit a cigarette, disgusted with her addiction since she'd promised herself she wouldn't smoke in her new car.

Taking a drag, she thought about the phone call from Gloria Bjerkes. *Huh. She just can't rein in her excessive appetites.* Judy smiled. *Nothing's really changed since college. Wild then, wild now.* She sat for a while, fidgeted with the radio, then flicked it off. She thought back to all the escapades they'd had together—sexual flings with a lot of athletic studs, selling a little dope, ski trips out West, a couple of local small-time robberies that the cops had never solved, a little extortion here and there. *Let the good times roll, baby.*

Finally, a red Jeep Grand Cherokee pulled up ahead of her. Judy could see the familiar silhouette of Gloria as she primped in the rearview mirror. Stepping out of the Jeep, she came around the hood and climbed into the front passenger seat of Judy's Toyota.

"Hey, how's it goin'?" Gloria asked, pecking Judy on the cheek.

"It'll be going better when I get the specifics on this deal you need my help with," she pouted, running her tongue over her glossy lips, giving Gloria a hostile stare.

Gloria looked worried, shifting her gaze to the scenery outside. "Well, I've gotten entangled in a big mess. Bigger than usual. But once you do this little job for me, hopefully things will settle down," she said confidently.

"First things first. I gotta know—just for my own peace of mind—you didn't kill Jeremy, did you?" she asked, staring straight out the front windshield. Her voice sounded gritty like sandpaper. Judy didn't look at Gloria; she was way too manipulative. Instead, she listened to the tone of her voice and gleaned the truth from what she heard.

"Come on! I could never have killed Jeremy. Number one, I was in my office when he was killed. That's an established fact. Even the police know that," Gloria said flatly. "Number Two, I loved my husband."

Judy believed the first part. There was no drama and no whining. Just facts. The last part about loving Jeremy—no way. The only person Gloria loved was herself. Judy cleared her throat self-consciously. "Okay. You've got the money?" she asked, getting down to business.

"Right here. A thousand like we talked about and agreed to," Gloria said, handing her an envelope thick with bills. "Just take the blonde detective down a few notches. I didn't like her attitude during my interview at the police station, and I need to get close to Higgins without actually messing with him. Don't kill her, and don't get caught. Just shake her up a little. Here's her address. Supposedly she lives with another cop, so be careful."

"How do you want me to do it?"

"Be creative. That's why I hired you."

"At least someone recognizes my hidden talents," Judy said. Then she smiled and glanced at Gloria, holding her gaze. "How come other people don't appreciate that quality about me?"

"Because you're way too scary," Gloria said, smiling back. "Now gimme one of those cigarettes." ◘

42

Leslie was confused about Sam's dinner arrangements with his parents. The day had flown by, and now she was nervously combing her long, blonde hair, watching Sam carefully in the full-length mirror.

"So, what is the purpose of my presence at this dinner tonight? And don't tell me I'm some kind of symbolic trophy. Mild-mannered pastor's son snags glamorous noir detective," she finished. She noticed Sam's shaking hands as he fumbled with the clasp on her mother-of-pearl necklace. "That's a joke, Sam," she said with a deadpan expression.

"Lez," he said tenderly, turning her toward him and away from the mirror. "You are the woman I love. Trophies have nothing to do with it, although I'm sure you deserve more than one. I want you to meet my parents. Your suspicious tendencies are getting way ahead of you." He kissed her tenderly.

"And you are beautiful, by the way," he finished, his eyes running over her dress. *What a knockout. Kind, sensitive, and smart. What's not to love?* he thought. *Don't screw this up.*

"Well, how could I refuse you this simple request?" she asked. But her lingering nervousness invaded her outward calm. Parading her pedigree for Sam's very Lutheran parents seemed like a proposition bound to fail.

Leslie had dressed carefully. The aqua sundress she'd forgotten about in the back of her closet seemed like a perfect choice to impress Sam's parents. She studied herself in the mirror. The delicate floral motifs and long flowing skirt emphasized her lithe, graceful figure and long legs. Feminine strappy sandals adorned her feet, and her long blonde hair shone with a lustrous sheen. She'd never worn much makeup, but she made sure it was understated and tasteful tonight. All in all, she had to admit she did feel special.

Sam gently pulled her close to him and looked into her eyes. "Just relax. My parents are wonderful people. They're not going to be happy that I'm living with you, but for tonight, I just want you to meet them. We'll deal with the fallout later." *And that will be the beginning of several long, moral lectures, complete with scriptural references,* he thought. *All well-deserved.*

"That does nothing to calm my nerves. And the fallout might be worse than you think, buddy," Leslie reminded him. "But, to echo Higgins' sentiments, it is what it is," Leslie said, raising her eyebrows, smiling shyly. She held up her index finger. "On second thought, I think Higgins would say that they're adults. They'll have to figure it out." Sam smiled at her nervously.

The drive across town to the Waterfront was harried and busy. Traffic was congested downtown. People were desperate to get home, everyone breathing a collective sigh of relief that the weekend was almost here. The beautiful weather had brought out bikers, families with children, the perpetual joggers and fitness freaks, and lovers holding hands. Everyone was relishing the warm romantic mood of the city. Sam hurriedly parked his Jeep on Front Street and scrambled around the truck to help Leslie out.

"How're the nerves?" he asked, grabbing her hand.

"Fine. How are yours?" she asked, smoothing her skirt.

"Fine, just fine," Sam said a little too quickly.

"The only thing missing is Paco," Leslie said wistfully.

"If my mom ever sees Paco again, it'll be too soon," Sam reminded her. He began walking rapidly toward the restaurant as Leslie teetered beside him in her flimsy sandals.

They found Sam's parents on the patio, the Waterfront's outdoor dining area. It was lovely right next to the river. Boats were cruising up and down the waterway, and the air was thick with the smell of grilling steaks. The trees were lush and green with spring growth. The manicured lawn was like a beautiful carpet of green. The patio had a louvered roof in a pergola style, and sprawled beneath it were black wrought iron tables and chairs with white cushions. Long-stemmed red roses on each table and twinkling white lights draped in the canopy added a touch of elegance. Everything was comfortably Midwestern—relaxed, welcoming, and understated.

After introductions, they ordered drinks and appetizers and fell into easy conversation.

Leslie described her family and background to Pastor and Mrs. Birkstein. As she talked, she felt herself relaxing. Sam was attentive and charming in a funny sort of way. More than once, she caught him gazing at her in that tender way, his eyes filled with affection— the way he looked at her after they'd made love. She felt her stomach turn over.

Across the table, Leslie noticed Mrs. Birkstein's dark, coiffed hair, her pristine clothing and jewelry. She projected a distinct image of perfectionism—something that left Leslie feeling substandard, despite the care she'd spent on her makeup, clothing, and jewelry. Chewing on a blue cheese-stuffed fig, Mrs. Birkstein watched Leslie with discriminating intuition. Exchanging a glance with her, Leslie could see where Sam got his expressive, hazel eyes.

"So you're an Army veteran, dear. Is that right?" Mrs. Birkstein asked. She'd picked up the undercurrents between Leslie and Sam. *This is more than a girlfriend thing,* she thought.

Leslie smiled and answered, "Yes, I was a military dog trainer. Paco, my black lab, was my partner. We were embedded with a couple of different companies in Iraq and worked together as a team to root out various explosives. Paco sniffed out and alerted our battalion to IEDs hidden in vehicles or the terrain. He's highly trained and has won numerous awards for his work in the field. Of course, he's retired now after he took some shrapnel in his hip. But we were always the first to lead the company when we were on reconnaissance," Leslie explained.

"Wow! That sounds dangerous," Pastor Birkstein remarked, sipping his Pepsi. *Now I know who Paco belongs to,* he thought.

"Yes, it was very dangerous," Leslie confirmed. "I saw some pretty bad stuff. We had a saying posted on the entrance of our compound. 'You only have today. Live it to the fullest.' I lost a lot of friends and comrades." She stopped a moment, swallowed, and continued. "That was tough. I still suffer from PTSD associated with my service, but I'm learning to manage it with help from my therapist," she said.

"Good for you," Pastor Birkstein said quietly. He lifted his eyes to hers. "Thank you for your service," he finished seriously, his dark eyes shining.

Leslie nodded. "It was an honor, sir," she said.

The food came, and the conversation slowed down. Everything was delicious, but Sam seemed to be picking at his entree.

Leslie leaned over and whispered, "What's the matter with your food, hon?"

"Nothing. It's great," he said distractedly, cutting into his steak.

"Well, you're acting weird. Is something wrong?" whispered Leslie.

"No, nothing's wrong. Everything's great."

"Sam, can you tell us about the case you mentioned this morning—the double homicide?" Mr. Birkstein asked, trying to spark some conversation,

"Oh, sure. Our team has been busy with that," Sam said, laying down his napkin and becoming animated.

Leslie interrupted him. "Well, we think this priest was messing around with this physical therapist from the college, and the husband found out and … " Leslie began explaining, setting her fork down on the table, ready to launch into it.

Pastor Birkstein's eyes widened. "Excuse me. A priest?" he said. He seemed confused. His eyes wandered to Sam and then back to Leslie. "How would you know about that?" he asked, focusing his perplexed gaze on Leslie.

Leslie stopped abruptly. "Oh, I'm sorry. I thought you knew. I'm a detective, too. I work with Sam every day."

"Well, I guess I missed that piece of information along the way," Pastor Birkstein said, smiling testily at Sam. "You didn't tell us Leslie was a colleague, Sam."

"Yeah, we've been working together for a while. Listen, I'm not sure we want to go into all the details of the case anyway," Sam said, hurrying on. "It's pretty gruesome and not really appropriate dinner talk. Besides, nothing's solved yet anyway, so we really shouldn't be discussing it. Right, Lez?" Leslie turned and gave Sam an inexplicable stare.

"Yeah, if you say so," Leslie said, confused, her eyebrows wrinkled in befuddlement.

Sam rushed on, filling the void. He turned to his parents, noticing their mystified expressions. "Listen, I want you to know that Leslie is very good at what she does. She's been through a lot in her military service and personal life. She's made great strides."

There was a strained silence in which Mr. and Mrs. Birkstein stared at Leslie, trying to reconcile Sam's strange comments with the woman in front of them. The quiet bustle of the wait staff provided a buffer of neutrality to the blooming animosity between Sam and Leslie. Sam's comments felt like a wet blanket had been thrown over the evening's festivities.

"I don't need you to explain my problems, Sam," Leslie said, nonplussed. A chill had crept into her voice. "Or justify them."

"No, No, you're taking me the wrong way. That's not what I meant." Sam blundered on, blinking. Leslie's eyebrows raised conspicuously. Sam hurried on. "I just meant that I admire you for the way you've dealt with your issues."

"Everybody has issues, Sam. You included," Leslie said, her tone icy.

Mrs. Birkstein wedged her way into the discussion. "Well, I'm not sure you really understand women, Sam," she said with an accusing undertone. "After all, you've never really had a girlfriend." She blinked rapidly, laying her hand on Pastor Birkstein's arm. He turned to her and whispered something in her ear. Mrs. Birkstein blushed. Sam felt like he'd been slapped.

"Don't remind me, Mom," he said huffily, staring at his plate. Leslie was taken aback by his response. *What in the world is going to come out of his mouth next?* she thought. Totally confused, she said, "I … Can we talk about this later?"

He leaned over and placed his hand on her neck under her hair, pulling her to him. He kissed her tenderly. *Who's the needy one now?* Leslie thought. *You've got issues, too, bud.*

Pastor and Mrs. Birkstein stared unabashedly. Sam noticed it had suddenly become very quiet. He gave Leslie another quick kiss.

"Absolutely, we'll talk later," he said. "I was being stupid. I'm sorry."

The ride home from the restaurant was icy. Leslie refused to bite on Sam's weak attempts at conversation, but when they got in the apartment, she turned on Sam and expressed the built-up rage she'd stuffed earlier in the evening.

"I can't believe you did that to me in front of your parents!" Leslie yelled, slamming the front door. Paco had rambled out of the back hallway. Sam and Leslie squared off in the living room, facing each other. While they argued, the dog's head bobbed back and forth between them as if he were refereeing their disagreement.

"Lez, please forgive me. I know I'm a screwup, but I was nervous. I love you. I just wanted my parents to see how much you mean to me."

"Sam, that conversation was so random, I can't even explain it." In a singsong voice, she said, "My issues. Look how far she's come."

Leslie stopped and parked her hands on her hips. "Like I'm some kind of a psychological freak in a museum somewhere." She stared at Sam, wondering if he was understanding her point. She held out her hands in a beckoning gesture. "I don't want your parents' pity."

"That wasn't my point," he said huffily. "That's not why I said it! What's wrong with admiring someone for overcoming adversity?"

She wilted and looked up at the ceiling as if there were answers written there. She felt like screaming. *Were men always this dumb?* Leveling her eyes back on Sam, she said, "I guess there was nothing wrong with it. It was just a very awkward exchange." She sighed, defeated. "I just think it was too soon in our relationship to display my dirty laundry. That probably didn't make a very good impression."

He grabbed her hands and pulled her into an embrace. "I apologize," he said sincerely into her hair. Then he pulled back and stroked her hair gently. "If the evening was a failure, it was because of my asinine antics. I just wanted them to see how really great you are and how much I love you."

Leslie smiled shyly. She sat on the couch and unbuckled her sandals, rubbing her feet. "I'm ready for bed." She stood up, leaned over and kissed him ardently. He let out a little groan. "You coming?"

"Whew! You had me worried for a minute. I thought I'd be sleeping on the back steps or in my Jeep."

"You better watch it," Leslie warned him, reaching down to ruffle Paco's ears who was stationed at her feet. "Paco's waiting to reclaim his status as the alpha male." Paco woofed as Leslie continued to pet him.

"If I keep saying stupid things like I did tonight, that won't take long," Sam said softly. ◘

SUE BERG

FRIDAY,
MAY 24

43

Friday morning started out chaotic. Lillie was being stubborn about getting dressed, and then she refused to eat her scrambled eggs and toast. *Four-year-olds. Go figure,* Jim thought, messing around in the kitchen, spreading jam on her toast, hoping she'd eat it.

She was wearing only a pair of panties, and she gave Jim her very worst scowl. "I wanted Cheerios, Bapa!" she whined, crossing her arms over her bare chest, her lips turned down in a pout.

"Take it or leave it, Lillie. I'm already late, sweet pea," he said, rushing into the bedroom to finish dressing. Pulling the closet door open, he stepped out of his sweatpants and grabbed a shirt with tiny gray checks. He began buttoning his shirt. He chose a subtle burgundy Brooks Brothers tie, pulled on a pair of dark gray dress slacks, and topped everything with a light wool navy blazer.

"Bapa? Why are you so mad?"

Jim stopped what he was doing. He knelt down in front of Lillie. "I'm not mad, honey. I'm just trying to get ready for work. Come here," he said, opening his arms. Her little body cuddled against his chest. "I need you to help Mommy take care of Henri this morning. Can you do that for me?" he asked, burying his nose in her curls.

Lillie squirmed out of his grasp and gave him a serious stare. She sighed, tapping her little foot in a self-righteous pose. "Okay. But I don't think Mommy wants my help."

"What's going on in here?" Carol asked, poking her head around the door frame. Henri was cradled in the crook of her arm.

"I was just telling Lillie how much you need her help," Jim said, catching her eye, hoping Carol would pick up on the suggestion.

"Oh, Lillie, I can't get through the day without you," Carol said, winking at Jim.

"Can I hold baby Henri now?" Lillie asked, walking toward Carol with her arms open wide. Carol kept talking. Jim kept dressing.

"First, you need to get dressed. And then we'll go out to the living room, and you can hold Henri for a little bit, okay?" Carol said.

Negotiating with Lillie is pointless, Jim thought, *but she'll figure that out pretty soon.* Jim finished his tie and then pulled on his socks. Scrambling in the bottom of the closet, he found a pair of dress shoes. He sat on the edge of the bed and slipped them on. He stood, grabbed Carol's hand, pulled her in for a kiss, kissed little Henri on the cheek, gave Lillie a fist bump and kiss, and scrambled to the door.

"Love you," he shouted over his shoulder, wrestling on his suit coat. "I should be home by five or so." He ducked swiftly into the garage and was on his way.

A half an hour later, Jim pulled into the Vine Street parking lot. He glanced at the dashboard clock in the Suburban: 8:10. He was running late. He rushed into the building and went straight to his office and called Luke Evers.

"Luke, any DNA results?"

"Hey, I was just about to head up there. Gimme five minutes."

Jim headed down the hall and gathered up the team. Just as they entered his office, Luke came off the elevator and joined them. He was his usual calm, unflappable self. His dark hair was neatly combed, his blue dress shirt covered by his white medical jacket. He stood in the center of the office, and the team stared at him intently, their hopes pinned on some kind of evidence—any kind of evidence.

"All right, Luke. What have you got for us?" Jim asked, taking a seat behind his desk. He was still rattled by the morning circus with Lillie. *That little imp,* he thought, but his heart warmed at the thought of her.

"Well, some interesting things have turned up," he said, referring to some stapled sheets in his hand. "First of all, and this probably won't surprise you, Trevor Bjerkes is not Jeremy's son. I don't know whose son he is, but ... " Luke's voice trailed off. He locked eyes with Jim. "That might be important, right?"

Jim nodded. "We've got some ideas about that."

"Secondly, the hair sample from Father Howard didn't include any root, so we couldn't get any DNA from it."

"Shit," Sam said under his breath.

"Sorry, Sam. It's not the shaft of the hair but the flesh where it's attached to the head that we need for a good sampling. However, we did get some touch DNA from the red ribbon found in the funeral home office," Luke explained.

"Touch DNA?" Paul asked, running his hand across his cheek, suppressing a yawn. "What's that again?"

Leslie spoke up. "Skin cells can be left on the surface of an object. Techs use it when fingerprints are hard to lift. They extract the skin cells that have been left on textured or rough surfaces. It's what they call low-level DNA—not usually admissible in court as evidence."

"Exactly," Luke said, eyeing Leslie with respect. "Apparently, the ribbon was grosgrain. It has little ridges, so fingerprints couldn't be lifted, but skin cells were retrieved. That's good. So when you find the killer, we'll have a sample on file if the ribbon came from the killer— if the judge will allow it as admissible evidence."

"So let me get this straight. We don't have a sample of Father Howard's DNA since the hair was a washout, right?" Sam asked.

"Right. The only other hope of DNA from Father Howard would be an elimination sample, or you could ask him for one outright," Luke continued to explain. "If he refuses, well, you can get a court order. Elimination samples are collected from EMTs, police officers, crime scene techs, and others. Was he ever an EMT?"

"Don't know, but I doubt it," Jim said, shrugging his shoulders. Everyone thought about that information for a few moments.

"Anything else?" Jim asked, moving the conversation along.

"Wait a minute. Back to Father Howard. Why don't you just get a cheek swab from him?" Luke asked, puzzled.

"He's skittish," Jim explained. "I don't want him disappearing. If we get more conclusive evidence of his involvement in the murders, we can get the Stanley police to run over and arrest him, but we're not ready for that yet." Jim turned and faced Leslie. "I want you to check Father Howard's background. See if he was ever in a car accident or was an EMT." Leslie wondered how she was supposed to do that.

Luke continued. "Of course, we have good DNA from Gloria and Trevor. Establishing paternity is still problematic if she's been sexually active with other partners. We've got the right mother, but we don't know who Trevor's father is." Luke shrugged. "Sorry, but that's the reality."

Jim waved off Luke's apology. "We're making progress. We'll get there," he said, but the frustration and disappointment made Jim feel like they were wading through thick mud. Every step seemed bogged down with roadblocks.

"Anything else you need from me?" Luke asked, looking at the group, handing the stapled paper to Jim.

"Not right now. Thanks," Jim said. Luke turned, gave a backward wave, and left the office.

"Leslie, I want you to turn over every rock you can to see if we can find a DNA sample from Father Howard," Jim said brusquely.

Leslie stood and turned. "I'm on it, sir," she said crisply. She walked down the hall to her office, thinking she had no idea what she was doing.

The morning slid by in report writing and the reviewing of witness testimonies which were few and far between. Sam sat at his desk, hunched in concentration while reading the testimony of Mrs. Walsh, the close neighbor across the alley from the funeral home.

Picking up his phone, he dialed her number.

"Mrs. Walsh?"

"Yes. Who's calling, please?" a voice asked rather formally.

"Sam Birkstein. I'm a detective with the La Crosse Sheriff's Department. I've read your statement that you gave police the morning of the murder at the Bjerkes Funeral Home on May 14."

Mrs. Walsh interrupted. "Oh, my. That was a horrible event. Just horrible."

"Yes. Yes, it was," Sam agreed. "I noticed you said a blue car left the funeral home parking lot at nine-thirty. Is that correct?"

"A blue car left. Yes, I believe it was Lyle's car—Lyle Oates—the co-owner of the funeral home. I've noticed it there many times."

"But you didn't see any other vehicles come or go during the morning hours. Is that right?" Sam asked.

"That's right. I just happened to look out my window at that specific time. Normally I don't even pay attention to what goes on over there."

"Do any of your neighbors happen to have surveillance cameras on their properties?" Sam asked.

"Well, my neighbor Joe McDonald is kind of a tech geek. He might have some equipment I don't know about."

Sam jotted down Mrs. Walsh's address, hung up, headed down the hall, and walked into Paul's office. He was busy at his computer. A box stuffed with documents sat next to him. Sam came up beside him and randomly flipped through some of the files.

"What?" Paul asked gruffly, continuing to type. "You need something?"

"There's a geeky type dude over by the funeral home that might have some surveillance stuff. I'm going to lunch and then headin' over there to check it out. Wanna come?"

"Oh man, do I. Let's get out of here." He grabbed his suit jacket, headed for the door, and turned out the lights. ◘

SUE BERG

44

Jim was crunching on an apple, reading through some bureaucratic paperwork he needed to finish about a past case that would soon be coming to trial, getting his ducks in a row. As he worked through the piles, he thought about Lyle Oates, got up, and walked down the hall to Leslie's office. She was on the phone.

"Finding those blood samples for Father Howard will be hard," she said when she noticed him at the door. "I really don't know what I'm doing. Did you need something, sir?"

Jim shuffled his feet impatiently and took another bite of apple. "Would Lyle Oates have known about Jeremy's argument with Father Howard? He worked with him for twenty-five years. Usually, at some point, when you know someone that well, you get into personal conversations about life, personal stuff," Jim said. "Stuff that bugs you, problems, whatever."

"I hadn't thought about that. Wanna go talk to him?"

"Yeah. Let's go over there and see if he knows anything."

Within twenty minutes, Jim and Leslie were walking through the front door of the Bjerkes funeral home. Wandering down the main hallway, they found the formal viewing area, a large room decorated with tasteful couches, love seats, chairs, and standard off-the-rack artwork. In the center of the room, rows of padded folding chairs had been set up in front of a lectern. Lyle was off to one side, arranging floral bouquets for a funeral the next day.

"Mr. Oates?" Jim said, approaching him.

Lyle turned. "Yes, I'm Lyle Oates. How can I help you?"

Jim appraised the mortician with a critical eye. From a distance, he was dressed professionally and seemed well-groomed with a decent haircut. *Maybe he turned over a new leaf since the murder.* But when Jim got closer, the lingering repercussions of a life of alcoholic tendencies were evident—a bluish cast to the skin, the tremor of his hand that hung loosely at his side, the red, enlarged veins that formed tiny spider webs on his nose and cheeks, and a funky breath that smelled like the reek of whiskey.

Flashing their IDs, Leslie began. "We'd like to ask you some questions about Jeremy if we could."

"Sure, let's go in here." He pointed to a small kitchenette area off the main room. "We use this room for the grieving families during a viewing. Coffee, snacks, and such. Have a seat," he said with a friendly tone. They sat down at a dining table. Lyle offered them coffee, but they declined.

Jim leaned forward and asked, "We'd like to know if you were ever aware of an argument that Jeremy might have had with a Father Howard from the St. Ignatius parish in Genoa?"

Lyle was silent for a moment. "Yes, he did mention that he'd had a disagreement with a priest. He didn't mention his name, though. Why? Is it important?" He leaned back in the chair. His tie was askew, revealing a missing button on his wrinkled shirt.

"It might be," Jim said. "We're not sure yet. When did Jeremy tell you about this argument?"

Lyle thought carefully. "Oh, that was a while ago. Maybe two or three years ago, at least. Maybe longer." He waved at the air like he was swatting an invisible fly.

"Do you remember any details about the argument? Did he mention anything specific that you can remember?" Leslie asked.

Lyle's shoulders slumped, and he studied the floor, trying to remember. "I didn't actually hear the argument," he repeated. "I just remember him saying he'd had a verbal confrontation with his priest. Jeremy made a comment about what lengths people will go to deceive someone … or something like that," he finished, making a disgruntled face. "It didn't mean anything to me then. Still doesn't, for that matter."

"What can you tell me about Jeremy's relationship with his wife, Gloria?" Jim asked.

Suddenly Lyle snapped to attention. His eyes popped open wide, and he began energetically pointing his finger at Jim. "She tried to have me fired! She's a royal bitch!" Lyle's flashing anger was genuine and interesting. He momentarily glanced away, lowering his finger, then continued his tirade. "She's a real pain; I can tell you that," he sputtered, glaring. "Nobody can please her. Jeremy tried, but she's … what do they call it?" He snapped his fingers. "High maintenance. Yeah, that's it. She's high maintenance." He was glad he'd remembered the term. It described Gloria perfectly. He continued scowling at Jim and Leslie.

Jim thought Lyle's description of Gloria was accurate. Lyle's anger was certainly notable, but Jim was discovering that Gloria made a lot of people angry. He asked, "Anything else you can recall?"

"No, the argument was quite a while ago. If you've ever met Gloria, you know what I mean," Lyle finished sourly.

Yes, I do, Jim thought. *I know exactly what you mean.* He gave Leslie a quick, perceptive glance.

"Where were you the morning of the murder?" Leslie asked.

Lyle pulled his head back, offended. "I was at home. I told that to the other detectives."

"Yes, we know that, but the other two detectives haven't been able to corroborate your story," Jim said. "We understand you argued with Jeremy the morning of the murders."

"Yeah, we argued, but that was ongoing—had been for a while. Jeremy wanted me to retire, and I wasn't interested in retirement yet. I got mad, walked out, and went home. I guess nobody saw me. I don't know what else to tell you," he said, flopping back in his chair. "I went straight to a bar near my house about eleven o'clock and started drinking."

"Did you kill Jeremy Bjerkes in a fit of anger?" Jim asked quietly, staring at the aging undertaker.

Lyle shook his head slowly. "No, absolutely not. I disagreed with Jeremy, and he certainly didn't understand my alcoholic problems, but I didn't kill him. He was my friend and business partner for twenty-five years. I would never have killed him, although sometimes he could really tick me off." Lyle sat with his head in his hands, his posture sagging with the seriousness of the conversation.

"If you think of anything else, please let us know. Thanks for your time," Jim said, offering his hand.

"No problem," Lyle said despondently as he shook Jim's hand. Jim and Leslie got up and began walking to the car. They were almost to the front door of the funeral home when they heard Lyle shout to them.

"Detective Higgins! Wait!" Lyle rushed up to them. "I just remembered something else," he said.

"What is it?" Jim asked.

"About three months ago, a young guy came in the office and confronted Jeremy. They had a heated argument—lots of yelling. Jeremy kicked him out of his office, which surprised me because he's normally pretty level-headed."

"Describe this guy. What'd he look like?" Jim asked.

"Dark hair, medium build but in good shape like an athlete, mid-thirties maybe," Lyle said, concentrating on some invisible picture in his mind.

Leslie scrolled through her phone and brought up Steven Hanratty's photo. She handed it to Lyle. "Is this the guy?" she asked.

Lyle studied the photo carefully. "Might be, but I couldn't swear to it in court. I just got a brief look at the guy."

"What kind of car did he drive?" Jim asked.

"Couldn't tell you. I was working in the main room setting up a visitation, and I just heard the commotion and caught a glimpse of the guy when he left. Sorry," Lyle apologized. "I just thought it might be important."

"Hey, we appreciate it. Give us a call if you think of anything else," Jim said, pointing to the card in Lyle's hand.

Jim's phone beeped as he walked to the car. Plucking it from his suit jacket, he answered.

"Jim Higgins."

"Dad?"

"Yeah, sweetheart. What's going on?"

"Something's come up. I think you better come down to the school," she said.

"I'm pretty busy, honey," Jim said, perturbed at this unexpected request. "Is this something about Lillie?"

"No, no. I have a student here who thinks he saw something suspicious on the day of those murders in La Crosse," she said seriously.

"What?" Jim's heart rate ticked up a few notches. "How old is this kid?"

"He's ten, Dad. He's one of my fifth graders."

"We'll be there in twenty minutes," Jim said, clicking off. ⬛

45

The afternoon weather was unseasonably warm, the temperatures climbing into the upper seventies. As Jim and Leslie drove through the south side of town and rolled along U.S. Highway 35 along the river, Leslie thought about Rocky's, the supper club where Sam had taken her on their first real date. Then she recalled the dinner they'd had last night with Sam's parents at the Waterfront. Sam had been a little unhinged to see his parents on the doorstep of the duplex yesterday morning. But, in all fairness, Pastor and Mrs. Birkstein were from Minot, North Dakota, so she could understand his surprise at finding them perched in his driveway at six-thirty in the morning. She giggled to herself when she thought of Paco pinning Mrs. Birkstein against the car door. The dog's protective sensibilities had come in handy several times since she'd joined the police force, but his timing and targets were a little off.

"What's funny?" Higgins asked, picking up speed out of La Crosse.

"Oh, yesterday morning was something else." She told him the story of the incident in the driveway.

"Oh boy. What did his parents say when they found out he was sleeping at his girlfriend's house?" Jim asked, giving her a sideways glance. It was quiet for a moment as Jim turned his attention back to his driving.

Leslie studied the side of his face. "You sure know how to suck the humor out of a good story, Chief," she said sourly, staring through the windshield as they blew down the road.

"It is what it is. Isn't that what kids say today?" Jim shrugged his shoulders, hiding a grin.

"Yeah, whatever," Leslie grumped. Then turning to him, she said, "Sam's parents don't know he's staying at my house. They think he moved to a new apartment and has a new roommate. Of course, after last night, they've probably figured it out."

"Well, he does have a new roommate. You," Jim said. "Do you want some advice on that?"

"No," Leslie said sourly

"Fair enough. You're adults. You'll have to figure it out."

Leslie slumped in the seat. "That's exactly what Sam said you would say."

When they arrived at Goose Island Park, Jim pulled the Suburban into the turnout close to the backwater where Sara had parked her car. They got out. Sara was standing along the shore of a deep quiet pool of water, conversing with a dark-haired boy dressed in a La Crosse Loggers T-shirt and black sweat pants. Jim and Leslie walked up to her and her young student.

"Hi, guys." She lifted a hand in greeting and turned to the boy. "This is Bobby Rude. He's a student of mine."

Bobby had intelligent brown eyes set in a serious, expressive face framed by dark brown hair. He reminded Jim of a lost waif, like a character from a Charles Dickens novel. Jim decided the boy had seen a whole lot more of life's harsh realities than he should have. While Jim was drawing his own conclusions about Bobby, the perceptive boy closely scrutinized the two detectives, carefully sizing them up. His wariness spiked as they walked toward him, and he looked apprehensively at Sara. She gently laid her hand on his shoulder.

"It's okay, Bobby," she said softly, her blue eyes kind. "They're here to help."

Rather than tower over the child, Jim stood about six feet away and casually crossed his arms. He locked eyes with the young boy and gave him a dimpled smile. "Miss Higgins says you have something to tell us," he started out. He kept his voice calm and friendly. His demeanor invited the boy's trust, what little there was of it.

"Could I see your badge first?" Bobby asked shyly.

Jim's eyebrows raised a notch, and he smiled. "Sure." He grinned and opened his ID, handing it to Bobby.

"Wow! You're a real detective!" the young boy exclaimed. His eyes studied every detail of the police ID card. Then a puzzled expression crossed his face, replacing the wary one that had been there at the beginning of the conversation. His eyebrows crinkled together in a frown. "Wait a minute. Your name is Higgins, too?"

Jim's smile grew wider. "Yes, Miss Higgins is my daughter."

"Really?" Bobby looked at Sara with awe. "You never told me your dad was a detective."

"You never asked, buddy," Sara said smiling, patting his back.

"So, getting back to my question. What did you want to tell us?" Jim asked patiently as Bobby handed back his ID.

"I saw a man throw something in the river here on Goose Island," Bobby blurted, pointing behind him toward the backwater pond just fifty feet away. *Oh boy, this might take a while,* Leslie thought.

"When did this happen?" Leslie asked quietly.

"Tuesday. It was Tuesday. I skipped school that day because ... " He hesitated. He glanced at Sara with a pleading expression for help.

Sara nodded. "It's all right, Bobby. They won't tell anyone." She smiled sadly at Jim.

Bobby started again. "I skipped school that day because my dad came home drunk the night before, and he fell in the kitchen. I had to clean him up and help him to bed. I was tired that morning, and I slept in." *That's why his eyes are old,* Jim thought. Bobby continued. "Then, about nine o'clock, I rode my bike up to Goose Island Park to do a little fishin'." A soft breeze blew through the trees and ruffled the boy's dark hair.

Sara interrupted the narrative. "We checked the calendar. It was the fourteenth."

"So you saw this man after you got here to Goose Island," Jim said.

"Yes, sir. I got here about nine-thirty, I 'spose, and the man drove up a little later."

"Do you think you could show us exactly what happened and maybe recreate the scene as you remember it?" Leslie asked. Bobby nodded vigorously and began walking out on the land that jutted into the backwaters.

"So you saw this man, and then what?" Jim asked, following the boy. The grass squished under their feet as they approached the fishing hole. Bobby continued walking and stopped abruptly near the shore.

"This is my favorite fishin' hole," he said as he extended his arm and pointed to an area where a large submerged tree had fallen in the water. "I was fishin' right here," he pointed at the ground where he stood, "and I saw the car coming over there. The man slowed down and parked right about where your car is now." Bobby's finger indicated the access road about one hundred feet away. The adults looked that way.

"What happened then?" asked Leslie.

Bobby continued. "Well, when the man got out of his car, he looked over my way, but he didn't see me 'cause I hid in the bullrushes over there as soon as I saw the car. I got a bad feeling about him even though I didn't know him. He walked toward the fishin' hole," Bobby paused, remembering the moment, "and he just stood there a while. I stayed real still. I thought he might hurt me if he saw me. He was crying, and he seemed really upset. Like something had made him really sad. After a few minutes, he tossed something in the river," Bobby finished, letting out a big sigh. His body relaxed. Jim could see his shoulders fall as if a huge weight had been lifted from them.

"What do you think he threw in the river?" Jim asked quietly.

It was silent for a moment. The iridescence of a dragonfly hovering on the water caught Bobby's attention. After a moment, the boy looked over to Jim and continued.

"Whatever it was, it wasn't big. It was a black color, and it made a big splash." Bobby's eyes squinted as he recalled the event. He shook his head as if he were arguing with himself. "No, it was more like a *ploop* when it went in the water."

Jim studied the young boy's face. As odd as the boy's description sounded, Jim could imagine the difference in sound from a *splash* to a *ploop*. Then he thought, *He's smart enough to sense danger and stay quiet. His story seems reasonable. Could it have been a gun? That makes a plooping sound in water. So does a rock. Would he lie? For what reason? He told the truth about his alcoholic father.* Jim knew kids like Bobby developed a sixth sense when it came to threatening situations. He was pretty sure the kid was telling the truth.

"About how far did he throw it?" Jim asked.

Bobby thought a moment. "See that crooked branch that makes a Y right by the surface of the water?"

"Yep," Jim nodded. *The kid has an eye for detail*, he thought.

"Whatever it was went in real close to that branch," Bobby said confidently. Jim played the scenario in his head as Bobby had described it. All of it could have happened, and he found himself believing Bobby's account.

"Would you recognize this man if you saw him again?" Jim asked.

"Well, I didn't know him—never saw him before—but yeah, I think I could pick him out of a crowd," Bobby said. Jim doubted it.

"What color was his car?"

"Dark, maybe black."

"Thank you for this information," Jim said sincerely, placing his hand on his frail shoulder.

"No problem," Bobby said, narrowing his eyes, gazing at Jim in the dappled light. "Hey, Miss Higgins told our class she goes fishin' with you sometimes. Do you think you could take me trout fishin' down in Timber Coulee someday?"

"We'll make that a date, buddy," Jim said, smiling widely.

After Bobby and Sara left, Jim and Leslie sat in the car discussing Bobby's story.

Leslie said, "I don't know, Chief. Kids' stories can be pretty unreliable. Do you really think he saw the murderer?" Her skepticism was based on her experience in Iraq, where she'd discovered most children's accounts of specific events were usually peppered with hyperbole and exaggeration, especially if a reward was involved.

"He's seen a lot of stuff in his young life. He didn't seem to be trying to impress us. I get the feeling he was being honest and giving a good account of what he saw happen. I think he'd have trouble making up a story with that much detail," Jim answered.

"Well, you've been at this longer than I have," Leslie said dubiously. "It's your call."

Jim thought for a moment and then said, "I'm calling the La Crosse Dive Team. See if they can find the gun. The one good thing about this area is that there's little or no current here, so the gun shouldn't have drifted. It might have sunk in the mud, but we've got a specific area to search. It should be pretty much where the guy threw it. If it's there, it shouldn't take too long to find," Jim explained. "You call the firearms unit of the Justice Department and see what they have on Father Howard. Maybe he has a background check on file, or he might have registered a gun, although I doubt it."

"Right," Leslie said, opening her phone to locate the number.

The La Crosse Dive Team was a volunteer group of citizens responsible for swift water and flood rescue, ice rescue, and underwater rescue and recovery. Jim had used their services a number of times in his investigations. He called around and finally found a diver who was home and available. While they waited for him to show up with his equipment, Jim called Carol and told her to go ahead with dinner. He'd eat when he got home.

Using his cell phone, Jim snapped pictures of the tree and the jutting section of land. He walked around the area, trying to imagine the scene the day Bobby had been there. Heading south out of La Crosse after the murders made sense to Jim since the funeral home was in a southside neighborhood. After getting rid of the weapon, the murderer could have crossed U.S. 35 and used a different route to make his way undetected across the coulees and bluffs until he hit a main highway.

Leslie's call to the Justice Department went to voicemail—another thing she'd have to do Monday. She crawled out of the car and called Sam. Leaning against the back passenger door, she explained the afternoon discovery.

"We're waiting for the diver. It's four-thirty now. I should be back there around six unless you want to run down here and watch," she said. "What've you been doing this afternoon?"

"Went back over to that witness by the funeral home and then to her supposedly high-tech neighbor. He was kinda high tech, a little bit of a geek, but he didn't have any video or anything that would help sort out the murder. Dead end."

"So, are you coming down here?" Leslie asked again.

"Yeah, I'll be there in twenty minutes," he said.

Marty Hooverson, a volunteer member of the La Crosse Dive Team, drove up next to Jim's Suburban in a Chevy pickup a half-hour later, the truck bed loaded with a small inflatable raft and his scuba gear. Jim explained what he was trying to locate, using the submerged tree as a reference point.

"Let me get my gear on, and we'll see what we've got. It's gonna be pretty dark down on the bottom, but I can use my headlamp," Marty said. He wrangled himself into his scuba outfit and strapped on his tank, adjusting his underwater torchlight on his head. Waiting on shore, Leslie and Jim watched him slide into the water and disappear from sight. In the meantime, Sam arrived.

"What's going on?" he asked, staring at the dark, murky water.

Leslie explained the interview with Bobby. After about fifteen minutes, Marty, the diver, returned to the surface with the gun in hand.

"Yes!" Leslie shouted, pumping her fist.

"Looks like a small-caliber Ruger," Jim said, handing Marty a plastic evidence bag. Marty dropped the gun in and handed it back to Jim. "I doubt it's registered, but we'll put a trace on it," Jim said, his face grim. "There might be DNA or prints—sometimes they can survive underwater—but there will be rifling in the barrel. If the rifling matches our bullets, we know we have the murder weapon. The closest forensic firearm examiner I know of is Jeff Sloan over in Rochester. I'll get a squad car to take the weapon and bullets over and see if we can hurry this thing along."

Jim made a quick call to Sheriff Davey Jones, explaining their find. Turning to Sam and Leslie, he said, "You guys drop the gun at the sheriff's department, and they'll run it over to Rochester with a squad car. Hopefully, by Monday, we'll have some results."

"Got it," Sam said, taking the gun in the bag. They climbed into his Jeep. Jim watched them drive off, and then he rang Sara.

"Dad? Did you find anything?" she asked.

"We retrieved a gun. It's headed to a lab in Rochester as we speak. We might get results by Monday," Jim said.

"Wow! Bobby will be glad to hear that," she said, excitement in her voice.

"Listen, keep this quiet for now. Don't tell Bobby yet. The killer is still out there, after all. I was wondering if Bobby would be at the school picnic tomorrow," Jim said.

"I don't know."

"Is there any way you can get him there?"

"Maybe. Let me work on that. I think I can convince him to come. Why do you want him there, Dad?"

"I'll explain tomorrow. You go have some fun tonight. Talk to you later," Jim said.

He jumped in the truck, and on the drive through Chipmunk Coulee, he thought about criminals. Jim considered his conversations with Gloria Bjerkes over the last week. It seemed unusual that she would aim her sights on a priest, but Father Skip was a charming guy, according to Sam and Paul. Movie star good looks, too. He was the kind of prey that Gloria simply couldn't resist.

Did she initiate an affair out of boredom with her husband, Jeremy? Or did she want to have a trophy like Father Howard, the forbidden fruit that Mabel Zabolio talked about? *Maybe a little bit of both,* Jim mused.

He was becoming more convinced that Gloria did not kill her husband. But her attitude of calloused nonchalance toward his horrible, untimely death angered him. However, her reactions were typical of her sociopathic tendencies.

What about Father Howard as the murderer? Jim knew jealousy, betrayal, and secrets were powerful motives, and this murder seemed to have all the touchstones of rage and passion.

Then he considered Steven Hanratty. Was his alibi on the day of the murder believable? No. Fishing in a thunderstorm? Eating at the Driftless Cafe? Something to check out. As he drove into his garage, he wondered what the school picnic would reveal tomorrow. ◘

SATURDAY,
MAY 25

46

Leslie woke up before Sam. She silently rolled out of bed and found some panties, a pair of jogging pants, a sports bra, and a cotton hoodie. Sneaking out of the room, she shut the door and got dressed. Paco greeted her with a cold, wet nose, his toenails clicking on the hardwood floor of the living room. Leslie found her favorite running shoes by the rear entrance and slipped them on.

She noted the time: 6:05 a.m. Paco woofed and slobbered, his dark eyes urging her to hurry up. Before she went out the front door, she hung the lanyard with the duplex key around her neck and tucked it into the hoodie, grabbed her cell phone, and slipped on Paco's leash.

They warmed up slowly, walking north on 28th Street. When they came to Ebner Coulee Road, Leslie turned right, picking up speed, bearing east. The road wound through a wooded section of residential housing, which muffled the sound from the street. Everything was quiet and shuttered in the early morning light. They jogged at a brisk pace until they came to the Dobson Tract, part of the Mississippi Valley Conservancy, an area crisscrossed with dirt hiking trails. Although it was against regulations, Leslie reached down and unclipped Paco's leash.

As they ran, Leslie's thoughts turned to her relationship with Sam. She loved him for his innocence and goodness. But she knew in the struggle against crime and violence that he would change. She would, too. It was inevitable. In the metamorphosis, she wondered if their relationship would survive. So many cops' love lives were disasters. She didn't want that. She'd already hurt Sam once— seriously. She didn't want either of them to experience the pain of another separation.

In her heart, she knew Sam was good for her, even though she wasn't always good to herself.

Giving someone permission to love her and enter the territory of her walled-off, scarred heart felt frightening. Leslie knew most people found it challenging to understand what she'd been through. Recalling her list of failed relationships, she felt worthless and unlovable. In her deeply wounded state, she'd lashed out and hurt Sam. His heart still held the scars of their separation, and she frequently felt the guilt of injuring him. Usually, the feelings blindsided her when she was tired, vulnerable, or lonely. She knew you couldn't base your feelings for another person on guilt, but the alternative of forgiving herself was new territory.

Despite the conflict they'd experienced in their relationship, Sam continued to cling to his pollyannish beliefs that they would always be happy since they were together again. Leslie had to admit it was a deceptively simple way to view things, but she couldn't resist muddying everything up. The dark angst she carried with her was like a stinking albatross hanging around her neck.

The naked truth was that Sam made love easy; she made love hard. She grumped to herself in frustration. *You're the one who's damaged. Don't blame Sam for that.* Could she heal? She didn't know. But she was beginning to think God could restore her. At least, that's what Sam kept telling her.

Her scars were real. She'd seen awful things in Iraq. She'd been beaten and raped, and the stresses of her job as a detective sometimes threatened to undo her. But despite all of that, she'd also experienced acceptance. Sam accepted her, understanding the frailties of the human condition. His love was like a sponge; he soaked up her pain and squeezed it out, leaving her cleansed and purged, able to find new beginnings.

Hitting a comfortable stride, Leslie and Paco entered the wooded sanctuary. Winding their way through the valley at the base of Grandad Bluff, Leslie inhaled the clean, crisp air and drew it deep into her lungs. Dew hung on the vegetation like diamonds, reflecting rays of sunlight, glinting and sparkling. The trails were challenging—hilly in certain parts, flat in others. Rounding corners where chimneys of sandstone peeked out between wooded sections of land, Leslie's shoes made a dull thwacking sound on the dirt trail as the coulee spread out before them. Birds were waking up after the dark, silent night, filling the air with song.

Leslie was concentrating on an area of rough, patchy ground strewn with loose sandstone gravel and tufts of June grass and timothy. Yesterday she had tripped here and almost fell when a rock had gotten wedged under her shoe. Paco was close by somewhere chasing rabbits, but his efforts were unproductive. He didn't have enough speed, resulting in frustrated barks and snorts. Leslie noticed his dark head bobbing in a large patch of bracken ferns and meadow grasses off in the distance, about seventy-five feet away.

An outcropping of limestone rock loomed ahead, rising into the air about ten feet above the trail, peppered with pockmarks and loose slices of blonde, sandy rock. Leslie ran down the path and was just below the exposed rock when someone jumped from above, landing directly on her back. She was knocked violently to the ground. Her chin dug into the gravel, but her knees and elbows absorbed the brunt of the blow. She slid on her stomach and then rolled down a slight incline. Reeling from the surprise attack, she rolled onto her back and kicked her feet under herself. She sprang up to face the assailant, gasping for air.

"Paco! Here boy! Paco!" Leslie yelled, ending with a piercing whistle.

SUE BERG

The assailant was smaller than her. Leslie had a fleeting thought it might be a woman, although it was hard to tell since a nylon stocking had been pulled down over the head. Whoever it was, their features were smashed into an unrecognizable blob.

Crouching low, keeping her feet in a wide stance, Leslie faced the thug. In an instant, the attacker ran up to her and kicked her leg toward Leslie's groin. At that very moment, out of the corner of her eye, Leslie could see Paco running full bore toward them, moving fast and furious. She grabbed the leg and pulled it upward, flipping the assailant on her back. By this time, Paco had arrived. He tore into the arm of the downed attacker, growling and pulling aggressively, whipping his head back and forth in a frenzied motion.

The assailant yelled and swore, trying to dislodge her arm from Paco's jaw. But the black lab would have none of it. Paco hung on, vigorously holding the assailant down despite screams of agony. He snarled and drooled on the jacket, his grip like a steel vice.

"Call off your dog!" a woman's voice yelled.

"Not until you tell me who you are and why you jumped me!" Leslie snarled, reaching over and pulling the nylon stocking off the head of the attacker.

"Call him off!" the attacker yelled desperately. The more she resisted, the harder Paco hung on.

"You know the drill. Tell me who you are and what your business is with me!" Leslie said, wiping the blood from her scraped chin onto the sleeve of her jacket, the nylon sock dangling from her hand. She grimaced as she checked her knees and elbows, which were bleeding and beginning to throb with pain.

"I'm Judy Orbeck. I'm a friend of Gloria Bjerkes," she said through gritted teeth.

"You should be a little more careful about picking your friends," Leslie retorted loudly, taking hold of Paco's collar. "Paco, down," she said quietly to the dog. He released his hold, but the hair on the back of his neck stood up. Showing his teeth, he growled at the woman with a curled lip. Leslie clipped on his leash, but the black lab remained in a heightened state of alertness, his body erect and tense with aggression.

"Easy, Paco," Leslie said. "Shhh, Paco. It's okay, boy," she said, reassuring the agitated dog.

Judy gradually sat up, rubbing her arm where blood was beginning to seep through her lightweight jacket. She slowly got to her feet. Leslie patted her down, searching for weapons while Paco stood at attention near Leslie's side.

Judy was a small, compact woman, intensely fit and agile. Her carefully coiffed, short brown hair was messy now, and it stood out in all directions. Leslie could see her brown eyes sparking with anxiety. Judy's gaze never left Paco. Returning her stare, he gave a sharp, piercing bark and continued growling ominously.

Judy had vastly underestimated Leslie, a strong, athletic, quick formidable opponent. *Military,* she guessed, disgusted. *So much for Gloria's information.* And then there was the dog. Another factor conveniently ignored by Gloria. Judy felt anger swelling inside. When she thought about the trouble she'd gone through to ambush Leslie, it hardly seemed worth it. *A thousand bucks to get chewed up by a dog. Definitely not worth it,* she thought. Paco growled a warning again as she locked eyes with the agitated canine.

"You do know that if you try anything, I'll sic Paco on you. You don't stand a chance," Leslie warned in a quiet voice. "He's 105 pounds of dog dynamite, especially when he's ticked like he is right now."

"I didn't know you could get a lab to be that protective," Judy said, panting. She grimaced as she cradled her arm next to her body. Pale and sweating, she stayed like that for a few moments, trying to regain her equilibrium.

Leslie patted Paco's side while she kept her eyes on Judy. "We served in Iraq together, sniffing out IEDs. We're very attached to each other. He'd protect me with his life."

"Yes, I see that now. My bad."

"So, what's the deal? Attacking a police officer is not a very smart strategy, but ... for some information, I won't haul you downtown," Leslie said, still huffing from the encounter. "So, tell me. What's with the ambush?"

"Gloria wanted to scare you off the investigation. She's got something against some Higgins guy—whoever that is." Judy ran her fingers through her tousled hair, wincing from the pain in her arm.

"That would be my boss," Leslie told her. "She's frustrated because he refused to take her bait. Did she kill her husband?"

"She told me she didn't, and I believe her. But Gloria has trouble reining in her obsessive behaviors. When she's bored or threatened, she's more than capable of criminal activity," Judy said, disgusted. "I should know. She's been my friend since college."

"So she gets her hired hands to do it?"

"Yeah, sometimes," Judy said.

"Would she have put out a contract on her husband?"

"Maybe. She's capable of that, and much more."

"What about her son? Do you know who the father is?"

"Could be a number of people. Gloria operates in a morally loose world," Judy said offhandedly.

"Do you know anything about a relationship she might have had with a Father Skip Howard?"

Leslie questioned, her breathing settling down.

Oh, boy. I'm not going there, Judy thought. "She's had a lot of flings over the years. I don't recall her talking about him," she said brusquely. "Her problems usually stem from control issues."

"Yeah, I already figured that out." Leslie took a few deep breaths and felt her heart returning to its normal pace. "Hey, I'll give you a head start back. Maybe you should think about finding another line of work. You're not very good at this."

Judy began walking back to the street. Turning around, she looked over her shoulder as she started to walk. "I'll think about that. This didn't turn out like I thought it would. I know one thing—I don't want to meet another dog like that guy," she said, her eyes flicking toward Paco.

Paco growled ominously. Leslie nodded, waiting until Judy had a good head start. Then she continued down the trail with Paco by her side, watching the woman painfully crawl into her Toyota parked along Ebner Coulee Road. Leslie jotted down her license plate number on her hand. As soon as Judy had driven out of sight, she felt her knees buckle. She stopped walking, knelt down next to Paco, and gazed into his eyes.

"What would I ever do without you, buddy?" she asked, roughing up his ears. "For once, your protective instincts were right on target." His warm brown eyes acknowledged her compliment, and he licked her face affectionately.

Back at the apartment, Sam had a fit.

"What? You were attacked!" Sam yelled, his eyes wide with alarm.

Leslie limped to the couch, laying out the first aid supplies.

"Well, where is he?" he asked anxiously, pushing the drapes back and peering out into the street. He turned back to her. "Where is this guy?" Leslie sat calmly on the couch, inspecting her wounds. She noticed Sam's panic-stricken expression.

"It wasn't a guy. It was some woman who thought she had some street skills. She tried to scare me off the investigation of Gloria Bjerkes," Leslie said disgustedly, dabbing the scrapes on her knees with a damp washcloth and antiseptic. "As if that would work."

"That's about the stupidest thing I've ever heard of," Sam sputtered. "Who even thinks they could get away with that?"

"Judy, apparently," Leslie said. "And Gloria." She began to swab the damage on her skinned elbows. Sam's expression softened when Leslie screwed up her face in pain.

"Here, let me help you," he said gently as he applied some ointment to her wounds. "What was that idiot thinking?" Sam said, his voice ramping up again. His anger came in little puffs until he sounded like a steam engine warming up.

"Gloria probably paid her some hefty cash. Thank God for Paco, or it might have gotten ugly."

"Whaddya mean? It did get ugly," Sam yelled, jumping up from the couch and parking his hands on his hips. "This is just stupid. And why did you let her go without arresting her?" Sam asked angrily. His eyes, normally calm and kind, were blazing with frustration.

"It was a trade-off for information, but sadly, she didn't tell me anything I didn't already know. Although she did say Gloria was capable of putting out a contract for Jeremy's murder. We need to check her bank accounts and look at her withdrawals. She's got to be paying out some questionable funds for all this thuggery. First Steven Hanratty, now me." She paused a moment while Sam stared at her with disbelief. "What? I was hurting," Leslie continued, "and I wasn't in the mood to file a complaint downtown and go through all that rigmarole. Besides, negotiating with the enemy is familiar territory to me. We did it in Iraq more than I like to remember."

"Well, this isn't Iraq. This is the United States!" Sam shouted.

Leslie tipped her head and said, "Duh! I already know that."

"Lez, you can't just let people jump you and get away with it. You're a police officer," Sam said, walking in a tight little circle in front of her. "Damn."

"Settle down. I'm okay," she said, pumping her hands up and down in a gesture that was meant to reassure him. "I've experienced a whole lot worse," she said dejectedly.

"That doesn't justify or excuse her behavior. Higgins is going to be furious on a number of fronts. You do realize that, don't you?" Sam lectured.

"It was a very clumsy attempt at bullying, and need I remind you, it didn't work. I'll deal with Higgins and the fallout. But I'm gonna be sore." She leaned back on the couch, the box of Band-Aids scattered on the cushion. Sam sighed and sat down, pulling her closer to him. "I'd like to get my hands on him," he said, kissing her on the cheek.

"Her."

"Right. Her." ◘

47

Carol lay in bed Saturday morning nursing Henri, stroking his little cheek with her finger. She loved these quiet moments when everyone else was sleeping, and she could treasure the miracle in her arms. *How did this happen?* She chuckled to herself. Well, she knew how it *happened*. She just couldn't believe it *had* happened.

The baby in her arms was a living love letter that God had a plan for their lives. When she thought about her life over the last year, it was like watching a merry-go-round—a kaleidoscope of swirling colors and shapes spinning wildly. She was stationary, but everything else whirled past in a vortex. Snippets of events streamed by, reappearing again and again.

Their wedding at International Gardens in La Crosse, wandering around Paris on their romantic honeymoon, moving to Jim's house on Chipmunk Coulee, a crazy bomber who left a note in their mailbox, camping on remote islands in the Mississippi, lovemaking here, there, and everywhere, Lillie's surprise arrival, driving through the thunderstorm while in labor, the intense feelings of love and blessing with Jim and Henri immediately after their son's birth. Quiet moments like these gave her a chance to stop the memory merry-go-round. For just a moment, the noisy calliope lost its steam; the strident music faded and retreated. Becoming someone's

SUE BERG

wife and lover, then becoming a mother twice in the same week. Unbelievable. Incredible. *This is your amazing life,* she thought. This fast-paced reality was the new norm.

Jim stirred next to her. With her free hand, she played with his graying hair.

"Mornin'," he said groggily. He scooted himself to a semi-seated position against the upholstered headboard, rubbing his eyes, slowly waking up. "How was Monsieur Henri last night?" he asked, stuffing his pillow under his neck, rolling toward her, playing with Henri's toes. He loved watching his son nurse at Carol's breast. It was such a tender reality of what God had given them.

"Ate every three hours. He's a stickler—on a schedule already," Carol informed him. She elbowed him gently, joking, "Some help you were. Obviously, you heard nothing."

"You're welcome to wake me up in the middle of the night, but it won't do much good. I can't feed him." Jim kissed her lightly on the cheek, then turned her face toward him and kissed her tenderly on the lips. "Right now, I'd like to have a good romp in the hay with my beautiful wife." Carol rolled her eyes, shaking her head, "But that's not going to happen. But when it does, baby, it's gonna be *so* good." He rolled out of bed and headed for the shower.

Ten minutes later, Jim came back into the bedroom and took Henri from Carol. He sat propped against the headboard, pillows stuffed behind him, comfortable in his boxers and T-shirt. Laying Henri on his chest, he sniffed his little head, gently patting his tiny back to release a burp.

The early morning aura outside the bedroom window filled Jim with wonder. The lawn sparkled with dew, and through the open window, he could hear the frantic awakening of songbirds calling and chirping. Sunshine blazed through the leafy trees in golden shafts, leaving blocks of yellow on the thick grass along the wooded lot at the back of the house. Tulips were blooming—flashes of fuchsia, scarlet, yellow, and purple creating a mosaic of color, leftovers from Margie's gardening ruminations. He could hear the shower running. He imagined Carol's body in his mind. He smiled, his dimples prominent as he envisioned her soft curves and lovely legs. He drifted off in a doze. Fifteen minutes later, Carol lifted Henri from his chest, and he took a deep breath.

"I was having a dinosaur moment imagining the victorious conquest of your lovely body," he said, grinning. He could smell something wonderful—lilac, lavender or maybe both—something French. It reminded him of their lovemaking in Paris. *Would there ever be anything like that again?* he thought. *Oh yeah. I'll see to it.*

"Dream on, buddy," Carol said mockingly. Seeing his disappointment, she giggled. "Be brave, my lionheart. Good things are on the horizon. Breakfast in twenty minutes."

Jim hoped Lillie would sleep for a while so they could enjoy a quiet breakfast without a backdrop of constant chatter and questions. He slid out of bed, pulled on a pair of blue jeans, and traded his white T-shirt for a Milwaukee Brewers one.

Jim and Carol were still adjusting to the drastic changes in their sedate, calm household. It seemed every waking moment now teemed with activity and noise. *Better get used to it, buddy,* he thought, sauntering down the hallway to the kitchen. *It'll be this way for the next twenty years.* Another thought. *In twenty years, I'll be seventy-two if I don't get killed or drop dead of a heart attack.* He sobered suddenly, remembering his sister Juliette's final plight to La Crosse to secure a home for Lillie. Vowing to appreciate how very fortunate he was, he thanked God for a loving wife and beautiful children to comfort him as he headed toward old age.

He sat down at the sunny dining room table, sipped his coffee, and enjoyed a stack of pancakes with bacon. Leaning over the baby bouncy seat, he studied little Henri's face and took another bite of pancake. "So I'm going to the school picnic around noon. Do you want to bring Henri and show him off? Mrs. Zabolio would love to meet him."

"Actually, I thought I might drive up to Vivian's this morning for a visit. Can you take Lillie with you?"

Jim frowned. "Well, no, I wasn't planning on it. I'm only attending the picnic to meet Father Howard and see him in action. I was hoping Bobby Rude would be able to identify him as the one who threw the gun in the river. So maybe Sara can handle Lillie?"

Carol stopped eating. "Jim, there won't be trouble at the picnic, will there?" Her fork was poised in mid-air, pancake syrup dripping onto her plate.

Jim shook his head. "Shouldn't be. I'm just there to observe. We're trying to get a handle on this priest." He paused when he noticed her look of doubt, took a bite of bacon, then reiterated, "Everything should be fine. Father Howard doesn't even know who I am. Like I said, it's just basic surveillance," Jim finished calmly.

Carol relaxed. "Wear your vest," she advised. Jim scowled, then nodded when he saw Carol's determined expression. "You have more people to consider now than just me." Her brown eyes were usually inviting and warm, except for how they looked at him right now. He was familiar with that determination and firmness. He'd seen it before on other occasions. None of those times brought back pleasant memories.

"Jim? Are you listening?" Carol asked persistently, a little flash of impatience.

"Yup. I'll wear my vest," he said, frustrated. He didn't like the part when his investigations spilled into their everyday lives.

"Good. Otherwise, Lillie could come with me."

"It'll be fine, honey," Jim said, trying to reassure her. "Besides, Lillie will be very disappointed if she can't go to the picnic. Sara's been telling her about it for at least a week," Jim said, trying to defuse the situation. Picking up the paper, he read an editorial in the *Wisconsin State Journal* about the president's proposed border wall and the congressional funding needed to build it. His phone buzzed on the kitchen counter. He got up to answer it, put the cell to his ear, and sat back down at the table.

"Jim Higgins."

"Chief. It's Sam."

"Yeah, you guys planning on being in Genoa by noon, right?"

"Yeah, but there's been an *incident*," he said, emphasizing the word. "Leslie got ambushed while she was running this morning near Grandad Bluff. Some woman jumped her from a ledge along one of the trails."

Jim sat up straight and let the newspaper flop onto the dining table. "What?! How does this stuff happen?" he asked loudly, alarming Carol. At that moment, Lillie appeared in her pajamas and crawled into Jim's lap, where she cuddled against his chest. He could smell the sleep in her hair. "Did she talk to this guy?"

"Woman. It was a woman. Some gal named Judy Orbeck. Gloria hired her to try and convince Leslie to stop the investigation or something stupid like that. Part of the motivation was to get back at you as if that could deter us," Sam said testily, getting fired up again.

"Is Leslie all right?" Jim asked, worry creeping into his voice. *When was she going to quit getting beat up?*

"Yeah, she's tough. Got banged up and scraped her chin, knees, and elbows, but Paco gave Judy a run for her money. That damn dog is always showing me up," he complained sarcastically.

"Are you gettin' mad yet?" Jim snarled. Lillie looked at Jim with frightened eyes. He toned his voice down. "She didn't let her go, did she?"

Carol had stopped drinking her coffee, listening intently.

"Yeah, she did. She agreed to let her go if she'd give her some information. I ripped into her about that already, so you might not want to go there," Sam explained.

Jim groaned. "Oh, brother!" A pause. "Well, what's done is done. The picnic starts at noon. Meet me at the Citgo gas station on U.S. 35 at eleven-thirty so we can make a plan. It's right at the turn-off to Genoa." *Things might be heating up,* he thought.

"Right. We'll be there," Sam said.

Carol stood near the table, one hand on her cocked hip, one hand holding her cup of coffee. "Well, after listening to that, I'm not sure Lillie should go to the picnic," Carol said anxiously.

"Honey," Jim said with exaggerated patience, "there will be a whole bunch of kids there."

Lillie interrupted. "Yeah, Mommy. All my friends will be there."

"Plus, there will be lots of adults to supervise," Jim finished confidently. Lillie gazed at Jim with her big blue eyes. "Trust me. She'll be fine," Jim said, kissing her on the nose.

"She better be fine, or you'll be answering to me!" Carol snapped, turning abruptly and walking to the sink.

By eleven o'clock, Jim and Lillie were downstairs in Sara's apartment.

"Bapa, will you be at the picnic?" Lillie grabbed the leg of his jeans as he started to leave. Her little face was pinched with worry. It was easy for Jim to forget how much trauma Lillie had already experienced. After all, she'd only been with them for two weeks, although it seemed like it had been much longer. Separations, especially from Jim, were still difficult and teary.

"Yep. I'll be there," he said, kneeling down to look into her eyes. "We'll have a hot dog together, okay?"

"Okay. What about Mommy and Henri?"

"They went to Holmen to see Aunt Vivian. It's just you and me, toots," Jim teased, pecking her on the cheek.

"And Sara?"

"Yep. And Sara," Jim said, glancing up at his daughter.

"We'll be fine, Dad," Sara said confidently. "I'll have my eye on her every second." ◘

48

"Gloria, you screwed me over!" Judy yelled as she beat on the back entry door of Gloria Bjerkes' swanky home in Dunwoody Estates. She continued hammering, her anger building with each tight-fisted knock. "Open up! I need to talk to—"

"What's goin' on?" Gloria yelled as she unlocked the door. Judy pushed through the door, slamming Gloria to the nearest wall, shoving her good arm under her neck until Gloria was flopping like a fish reeled in on a hook. The impact with the wall and the arm shoved against her windpipe cut off her oxygen and stunned Gloria into submission. Judy was sizzling, her eyes threatening and dark. "What were you thinking hanging me out to dry with that blonde femi-Nazi? Huh?"

Gloria's eyes bulged in her head, and puny, pathetic sounds escaped from her throat as Judy kept the pressure up. Judy's breath was coming in huge raspy waves. "When I let go, you better have some answers!" Judy eased up, and Gloria slumped against the wall, holding her neck and swallowing huge gulps of air.

"What's with the blonde cop?" Judy demanded, roughly grabbing Gloria's blouse, jerking her upright, slapping her across the face.

Shocked at Judy's vehement, violent actions, Gloria began crying unexpectedly—a peculiar, irritating whine.

"You sold me out. You embarrassed me," Judy screamed, spittle flying in Gloria's face. She let loose with a string of obscenities. "And I got my arm chewed up by a vicious dog in the process. Your information on that cop was pathetic!" Judy continued her diatribe, still clutching Gloria's blouse in her fist.

Terrified, Gloria held her hands in front of her face. Judy released her, and Gloria slowly slid down the wall until she was seated on the floor. She sighed a pathetic whimper. "It's all coming apart. Everything's coming down like a house of cards," she whispered, croaking out the words.

Judy knelt down in front of Gloria, her eyes blazing with betrayal and anger. Stabbing her finger in Gloria's chest, she hissed, "Don't you ever call me again for anything. I'm done with you and your stupid screwups! We're done!" Judy jumped up, turned, and briskly charged through the door, slamming it so hard that the pictures on the wall jumped in alarm. Gloria heard her tires squeal down the driveway.

The quiet of the house following the intense confrontation with Judy rattled Gloria to the core. She didn't know what to do with the unfamiliar feelings of isolation and vulnerability. They were alien to her. She heard the television in the background as she lay on her back and stared at the ceiling. She began crying again.

Lying there helplessly, Gloria thought about her life with Jeremy. He'd been a good man. They'd had their moments of happiness. Why wasn't that enough? Why couldn't she enjoy a normal relationship? Her uncontrolled, unrestrained desires always got in the way. She was the drama queen par excellence, but now that role seemed ridiculous—like something she'd pulled out of the closet for Halloween.

Who am I anyway? she asked. Whatever she once was had faded into the background with each new criminal foray. She had no authentic sense of self. *I am the shell of a former drama queen and sexual pervert who got in over her head.*

Now she was truly alone. Her former goons and thugs had

deserted her. She swallowed the bitter bile that rose in her throat. There wasn't much that scared Gloria, but being alone was one of them. Sadly, she had no other real friends to count on. She bit her lip as she debated her next move.

Skip. Maybe he'll help me. He helped me before. He still loves me, doesn't he? It was worth a try.

She slowly got up from the floor and stumbled to the breakfast nook, where she poured herself three fingers of brandy topped with some hot coffee. She drank deeply, feeling the warmth of the alcohol spread through her and calm her nerves. She picked up her phone from the table. Scrolling through her contacts, she found Skip's number. With shaking fingers, she punched it in, tenderly rubbing her face where Judy had slapped her. Wiping her tears away, she waited for an answer.

"Gloria? Why are you calling me? We agreed to let things settle down." Father Skip's voice sounded hard and brittle. "What do you want?" he demanded rudely.

"I'm scared," she said like a mewing kitten. Father Skip had to admit she certainly didn't sound like the Gloria he knew. He closed his eyes and leaned against the back of the car seat. There were no seductive pleadings or sexual philandering now. "Everything's falling apart," Gloria whined, her voice grating on Father Skip. "This Higgins guy is figuring things out."

"Whadda ya mean? Figuring out what?" Father Skip asked, fighting the rising panic in his chest. When Gloria didn't answer, his anger threatened to boil over. "What's he figuring out? Tell me!" he demanded roughly.

There was a sniffling sound. "That we were lovers. That Trevor is really your son. That you killed Jeremy," she said in a sad, muted voice.

"Gloria, that is just about the stupidest thing you have ever said! You and I both know I didn't kill Jeremy! Now listen to me. I'm going to the school picnic at St. Ignatius at noon today. I'll drive over after that, and we'll talk about this." He hung up before she could respond with some pathetic platitude. With each passing moment, his choices were fewer. Desperation and regret stalked him.

Looking in the rearview mirror, he straightened his clerical collar and ran a brush through his hair. *A man's gotta do what a man's gotta do,* he thought. *Gloria, be damned.* He wished he'd never met her. ◻

49

The expansive grounds of Our Lady of Guadalupe on the outskirts of La Crosse, Wisconsin, was the destination of many faithful Catholics from the United States and other parts of the world who regularly made spiritual pilgrimages to the shrine. The Italianate-designed complex on one hundred acres of donated land south of La Crosse was built as a place of worship—a refuge for faithful believers who sought peace from a combative and stressful world—a place of contemplation and fervent prayer. The Guadalupe gave devoted followers a hallowed respite in a depraved and degenerate world.

On Saturday, the grounds of the shrine were glorious in spring splendor. The brilliant May sunshine brightened the breathtaking flower beds that lined the winding walkways of the verdant grounds. Paved stone pathways, flitting birds, and impressive statuary lent an air of peaceful repose, inspiring visitors to meditate and earnestly seek the Lord. Surrounding the shrine, the hushed, heavily wooded hills and bluffs muffled the sounds of the outside world, insulating the gardens from the discordant zoom of traffic and the exhausting bustle of everyday life. Here things were slow, purposeful, and serene.

The stone and brick edifices seemed to grow from the ground, swelling and filling nature with their majestic presence. Beautiful stained glass windows with their brilliant images and colors in the main chapel enhanced the praise of the congregation as their songs soared upward to God in ardent adoration and exaltation.

Father Skip Howard sat in the Saint Tekakwitha devotional area, but he found no peace despite the beautiful surroundings. He kept a lonely vigil, his desperate prayers falling flat and lifeless as he stared pensively at the bronze statue of the saint known as the Lily of the Mohawks. She was dressed simply in native buckskin, and she knelt before a rough, homemade cross. The three sisters, the Native American crops of corn, beans, and squash grew around her, and a basket of strawberries lay at her feet.

O for a life of simplicity and devotion, Father Howard thought. *The life that I used to aspire to but so foolishly threw away in the lure of seduction and the heat of passion.* His eyes filled with tears of regret at the life he'd wasted, exchanged for moments of lust with a godless, heartless woman.

The bench beneath Father Skip felt hard and uncompromising as he studied the intense, worshipful expression of the native woman's statue. He'd prayed here before. He'd probably end up here again, but even now, the quiet and solitude of this place wasn't the balm for his soul that he'd hoped. Father Howard thought of the writer Fulton Oursler and his cryptic words: "Many of us crucify ourselves between two thieves—regret for the past and fear of the future." *That certainly describes me,* he thought bitterly.

The sound of swishing fabric and heavy footsteps crunching on the gravel walkway brought him out of his tortured daydream. He looked beyond the statue to see the Most Reverend Phillip William Strahan approaching him along the shaded pathway. A simple, wooden cross swung back and forth across his chest, his cream-colored vestments rippling softly as he walked. Father Skip stood as his superior approached the bench. *It's so easy to wear the cross and appear committed,* Father Skip thought, fingering the cross hanging around his neck.

"Good morning, Father Skip," Strahan said, grasping his arms. He noticed Skip's parched, dry skin, the dark shadows under his intense eyes, the nervous way he fingered his crucifix, the slight aroma of cologne. "It's good to see you again."

Father Skip dipped his head in a reverential bow. "You, too, Father Strahan," he intoned.

"How are things going at your parish in Stanley?" Reverend Strahan asked, his eyes studying the troubled priest.

"Fine. I just wanted a moment of your time. I know you're very busy," Father Skip said breathlessly.

"Never too busy to encourage another servant of Christ," Father Strahan counseled patiently. He tilted his head and studied the man in front of him carefully. His eyes seemed too big, like he was in a state of hypervigilance. His expressions were wooden and stilted. *Why is he so perturbed? Maybe because the rumors about him and the Bjerkes woman are true,* he pondered, answering his own question.

It was a difficult time to be a faithful Catholic priest when the actions of so many church authorities had come under suspicion and accusation. The church's reputation was sliding toward the gutter, with the horrible sexual abuses being revealed almost daily by victimized parishioners. They sat down on the bench. Father Skip brushed his hair away from his forehead in a nervous gesture.

"I'm sorry to tell you that the ugly business at St. Ignatius is apparently still simmering. I'd hoped that when I left, things would settle down."

"I'm not sure I understand what you're saying," Father Strahan said, confused. His soft white hands lay relaxed in his lap. "I've heard nothing but good reports about Father Knight and the St. Ignatius Parish."

"I'm sure you have. I don't mean to tarnish Father Knight's reputation. He's a fine priest." Father Skip said. He hesitated. "But a couple of detectives from the La Crosse Sheriff's Department drove up to see me on Monday, questioning me about the Jeremy Bjerkes murder, and more specifically, about my relationship with his wife, Gloria." Father Skip's nostrils flared, and worry creased his wide forehead. His hands were clenched together as if in prayer, but his

SUE BERG

attitude was anything but prayerful. *Desperate and defiant,* thought Strahan.

"Oh, I'm sorry to hear that," Father Strahan said sympathetically. Then he toughened his voice, and his eyes took on a hard sheen. "But you know that Satan is not easily defeated. He will continue his attacks unabated unless we spend much time in sincere prayer and devote ourselves to fasting and repentance. We need to quiet our busy lives and learn to listen to the Savior's voice."

"Yes, I know all that," Father Skip said impatiently. Father Strahan didn't appreciate the brusque intonation of his answer. With more self-restraint, Father Skip continued. This time his tone was more penitent. "I'm attending the St. Ignatius school celebration today. I wanted you to know that my attendance there will, once and for all, put these ridiculous rumors to rest."

"That's good, my son. Is there anything else you want to tell me?"

Father Skip noticed his superior's skeptical expression, and his eyes seemed hard and unapologetic. "No. Should there be?" he asked testily.

That attitude. That belligerence. Maybe he deserves the title of Accused, thought Strahan. "No, not unless you're burdened with unconfessed sin."

"I'm fine," he said arrogantly. "But would you pray with me?"

"Of course. I'd consider it a privilege," Father Strahan said humbly.

As the prayers began, Father Skip bowed his head, his shoulders slumped slightly. He leaned forward, resting his elbows on his knees, his head perched on his tightly clasped hands. *When is this all going to end?* he thought. *I can't take much more.* ◘

50

Jim sat in his Suburban at the Citgo station just off Highway 35, speculating about Father Howard. He was uneasy about the conclusions they had reached about the priest. However, Jim's understanding of the human heart left him with no doubts about criminal intent and behavior, even among the clergy. *The heart is desperately wicked,* he thought. *The prophet Jeremiah certainly had that right.* On that point, he agreed with the farseeing ancient truth. Sam pulled up behind him. Opening his door, Jim jumped out and walked back to the Jeep Patriot.

"What's the plan, Chief?" Sam asked before Jim could explain.

Jim glanced at Leslie. Her chin was mangled, and she appeared ornery.

"Don't ask," she said, pouting.

Jim looked at the ground and shook his head. "I'm going to keep an eye on Father Howard. I might push him if I get the chance, but we don't want a confrontation at the picnic. If I confront him, it'll be away from the main event. If things get dicey, be ready to go. He might bolt if he feels boxed in, so be careful. Leslie, I want you to hang with Bobby Rude and see if he can identify Father Howard. Don't lead him, though. He has to recognize him on his own, or his testimony won't stand up in court. And be smart. Don't draw in any bystanders."

"We got it, Chief," Sam said seriously.

Jim parked his Suburban in the school lot. As he stood there, he noticed the red brick school and the children gathering around the grill in the parking lot, lined up to get a hot dog. Small clusters of congregants and parents stood in groups and watched the games being organized. The place gave off a casual, friendly vibration. Some of the children formed the starting line for a three-legged gunny sack race out of the spacious lawn, while others organized a tug-of-war nearby. Jim caught Sara's eye, and she brought Lillie over. Jim ate a hot dog with her. While they were eating, Father Knight settled at the picnic table across from Jim.

"So what's a staunch Lutheran doing at a Catholic school picnic?" he asked.

"Considering school prospects for Lillie. She seems to like it here, so Sara suggested I come and meet some of the staff and parents," Jim explained. His dimpled smile put Father Knight at ease. "You do accept Lutherans into your midst, don't you?" Jim asked, delivering a mild barb.

"Absolutely," Father Jerome said confidently. "The wayward and deceived are always welcome at St. Ignatius."

Jim laughed heartily. Sara was organizing a game of duck, duck, goose, and Lillie hurried in that direction. "See you later, Bapa!" she yelled. She was having a blast with the other little kids, and her breathless excitement and sparkling eyes filled Jim with optimism.

Peering over Jim's shoulder toward the parking lot, Father Knight stood suddenly and said, "Oh, excuse me, please. I have to greet a special visitor." Jim turned to see a handsome, athletic man strolling toward the school grounds. *Father Howard,* Jim assumed. He finished his hot dog and sipped his Pepsi as his eyes scanned the crowd. Spotting Mabel Zabolio, he threw his trash in a nearby can and strolled over to talk to her.

"Hey, how's my favorite informant?" he said quietly, easing up to her, grinning.

"Couldn't be better," Mabel whispered. "Anything new?"

"A few things. And one very important breakthrough."

"Will you let me know how things turn out?" she said, looking up at Jim with her bright, perceptive eyes.

Jim nodded. "Absolutely," he said.

"Is your wife here?" Mabel asked. "I was hoping to meet her and that new baby."

"No, she went to visit her sister in Holmen. But we'll get together when things settle down. Nice to see you, Mabel."

He'd been keeping his eye on Leslie as he conversed with Mabel. Bobby Rude was pulling on Leslie's sleeve, whispering something in her ear. From across the school lawn, she locked eyes with Jim and tipped her chin up. Making his way through clumps of parents, he stopped in front of Bobby, Sam, and Leslie.

"Bobby, recognize someone?" Jim asked. Bobby shook his head.

"No, I don't see the man who threw the gun in the river," Bobby said remorsefully.

"Really? Well, if he's not here, he's not here," Jim said calmly. He thought of the many times witnesses fingered someone they thought they'd seen at some specific location only to have it turn out to be inaccurate. Bobby anxiously studied the three detectives. Having only seen the man once, Jim wasn't surprised at the disappointing result.

"Bobby, look at me," Jim instructed seriously. Bobby's eyes snapped to Jim's face. "I want you to know how much we appreciate all of your help. You go play now. If you need anything, you talk to Miss Higgins." Bobby ran off to the ball diamond where a pick-up baseball game was starting.

"Well, that was a dead end," Sam muttered, running his hand through his dark hair in frustration.

"It's not surprising," Leslie commented. "Most people can't identify someone again when they've only seen them at a distance for just a couple of minutes."

"Well, Father Howard is still the man we have in our sights, so

I'm going to speak to him. If he leaves, I want you to follow him. I'll be right behind you."

"Okay," Leslie said. Jim casually strolled over to a group of parents who were giving Father Skip Howard their rapt attention.

"… and we love Father Knight," a woman said. "But it just isn't the same since you left."

Father Howard smiled at the group of admirers as Jim hovered at the edge of the group. Fidgeting, the priest studied Jim, nervously wondering if this was the detective that Gloria had mentioned. Father Howard's friendly mood suddenly evaporated. He broke through the women's admiration club and extended his hand to Jim.

"New parent at St. Ignatius?" he asked, gripping Jim's hand. The gesture was meant to be friendly, but his eyes were distrustful.

"Checking out the school for my daughter," Jim said carefully. "Do you have a moment for a word in private?" he asked. His phone vibrated in his pocket.

"Jim Higgins," he answered, shifting on his feet. He held up a finger to Father Howard, and stepped away.

"This is Officer Shelby Rankin calling from the Barron County Sheriff's Department. We've scoured the area you mentioned around Barronette, specifically the area with the cabins near the DNR tract of land. Sorry, but we didn't find a black Impala.""

"We were hoping it would show up somewhere."

"Well it might be here somewhere, but we haven't found it yet. We'll keep looking, though. If we spot it, we'll call you.?"

"Sounds good. I'll call you later. I'm busy right now," Jim said, turning back to Father Howard, who was walking briskly to his car in the parking lot. I gotta go," he said, flipping his phone shut.

Father Howard reached his car and roared the engine to life. By the time Jim jogged to his Suburban, Father Howard had squealed his car from the parking lot and was boring up Main Street in Genoa, making a run for U.S. 35. Sam and Leslie were already in the Jeep, following him closely. Jim speed-dialed Sam.

"Yeah, Chief," Sam said, his cell phone to his ear, pulling his Jeep onto the street.

"Don't lose him, Sam! He's running. I'm right behind you. I'll call in some help," Jim said as he stepped on the gas. Calling 911, he gave a terse description of their predicament. "This is Lt. Jim Higgins. We're in pursuit of a murder suspect driving a dark green Ford Focus, license WI6984. We're heading north on 35 from Genoa. We need assistance. We'll do our best to stop him before he gets into the city," Jim ordered succinctly.

Sam surged onto the highway, clicking his seatbelt as he drove. Weaving in and out of traffic, Father Howard torpedoed down 35. Sam glanced at the speedometer—eighty miles per hour. He did some quick mental math. At these speeds, they'd be in La Crosse in less than five minutes. The village of Stoddard blew past like a blip on the radar.

"Hang on!" Sam yelled to Leslie. "Shits and giggles time!" he warned loudly. He threw his cell on the seat. "Get Higgins on your phone," he ordered.

Father Howard tore past a slower car, forcing another oncoming vehicle into the ditch. Sam braked. Dust billowed. Cars spun and slid to recover. Sam looked quickly in his rearview mirror. Higgins tore through the haze of gravel and dust, dodging disaster, coming out on the other side unscathed.

Father Howard's vehicle fishtailed, but he maintained control. He stepped on the gas, recklessly thundering north up the river road.

Sam saw the La Crosse city limits sign flash by—then Bluffview Elementary School, the Highway 14 turnoff, the bridge over the train tracks, and the two Kwik Trips. Howard slowed as two squad cars screamed toward them, sirens wailing.

Stop. Please stop! Leslie prayed silently.

One squad car did a 180 at the nearest intersection and joined the chase; the other screamed to a stop, then turned off on a side street.

"Cut him off! Cut him off!" Sam shouted, pounding his steering wheel in frustration. Leslie gripped the overhead strap with one hand, her eyes wide with concern, the cell phone plastered to her ear with her free hand.

A block ahead, Sam saw the light change from green to red. A car pulled out from a side street. Father Howard ran the red light, clipped the car's front end, and sent it into an out-of-control spin. It crashed into a bus stop shelter. Glass shattered. Metal flew. Pedestrians scattered. Father Howard wobbled precariously back into the lane of traffic, the crunch of glass beneath his tires putting Leslie's teeth on edge.

Sam slid through the red light, narrowly missing a pickup. Cars huddled along the road as police sirens howled a warning to traffic.

"He's headin' downtown or across the big, blue bridge," Sam yelled, panicked. "God! Not the bridge!"

Leslie relayed the message to Jim. Howard turned left, skidding through the intersection on Fourth and Cass, barreling up on the sidewalk, narrowly missing a biker who jumped out of the way at the last second.

"He's going over the big blue bridge heading to La Crescent!" Leslie hollered into the phone. In an instant, Sam floored it onto the bridge, roaring next to Father Howard in an attempt to cut him off. Leslie threw the phone on the seat. She rolled down her window, her blonde hair sailing behind her in the wind. Pointing her revolver at Howard, she screamed, "You need to stop! You're under arrest! Stop the car now!" Howard looked over and saw the gun. His eyes widened, and he snarled, yelling something Leslie couldn't hear.

"STOP THE CAR!" she screamed again.

Father Howard slumped forward. His car slowed as he got to the middle of the bridge. Sam hooked Father Howard's front fender, ramming it onto the bridge abutment. Sam and Leslie bounced side to side in the Jeep as Sam forced the compact car over. Howard crashed through the pedestrian fence. The crunch of metal on metal seared the air. His car crumpled to a sideways stop, the bumper hanging limply like a wet noodle on the pedestrian sidewalk.

Everyone screeched to a halt as Jim squeezed in from behind.

Leaning over, Jim pulled his revolver out of his glove box. Two squad cars tore around them and slammed to a stop, hemming in Howard's car. The officers jumped out but hunkered down behind their doors. They were the only ones on the bridge; police had blockaded traffic from the Minnesota side.

It suddenly became very quiet. The river seemed incredibly far down from the bridge's vantage point, although it was only sixty-seven feet to the water's surface. Still, it was high.

Jim approached Howard's car carefully, easing up from the rear along the driver's side, his revolver drawn. Sam and Leslie crouched behind their doors, waiting, wondering what Howard would do.

"Give it up, Father. You're surrounded," Jim said loudly, his baritone voice booming in the quiet atmosphere. Jim noticed the barges and pleasure boats cruising up and down the river. Such a beautiful summer day. The boaters seemed oblivious to the drama unfolding above them.

Howard collapsed and leaned his head on the steering wheel. Jim knew better than to trust his demeanor. He hadn't surrendered—yet. Jim pumped his left hand in a stop motion, warning the cops to hold off as he inched forward. Suddenly, Father Howard slid over to the passenger side. Flinging the door open, he jumped through the mangled fence and scrambled like a monkey onto the beams of the bridge. He turned and faced the police, grasping the bridge structure with white-knuckled fists. He peered over his shoulder at the water below. His eyes were wild; his hair disheveled.

Stunned, Jim saw something move on the floor in the back seat. In a second, Gloria Bjerkes burst through the back passenger door, jumping next to Father Howard, angrily brandishing a pistol at Jim.

"Drop the gun!" Jim instructed loudly. When she continued to point the gun at Jim, he lowered his voice but kept his gun in front of him, attempting to deescalate the situation. He repeated his warning, "Drop the gun, Gloria!"

The desperate duo appeared shell-shocked. Jim said quietly, "Give it up, Gloria." Locking eyes with the anguished woman, he aimed his gun at her chest. Gloria stared into the barrel of the gun, the black dot boring a hole in her subconscious, causing her to freeze in fear. She suddenly understood the profound terror that her husband had experienced the morning he'd been shot in the funeral home.

"Think of Trevor. He'll be all alone in this world if you die. Don't do this," Jim implored, his voice hushed and intense.

Father Howard gave Gloria a pitiful glance. "Put the gun down, Gloria. You have to be there for our son," he entreated.

Gloria began crying softly, lowering the gun slowly until it hung limply at her side. "Why did you kill Jeremy?" she asked, turning to Father Howard. "Why?" she begged, trying to understand.

"I didn't kill him! I didn't! " the priest screamed at Gloria. "Trevor belongs to me! He's my son!" Father Howard squinted in the bright sunshine, and a breeze gently blew his hair away from his anguished face.

" Jeremy didn't deserve to die," Gloria cried pathetically.

"You told Jeremy that Trevor was his son! That's on you, Gloria. But he's mine! Trevor's my flesh and blood!" Father Howard rasped, his face a mask of regret and sorrow. Sobbing and grasping the beams, he turned and leaned precariously over the river.

"No! No!" Jim shouted as he scaled the wreckage and leaped forward. But Father Howard pushed off and jumped, hitting the water with a tremendous splash. Jim watched him disappear from sight beneath the swirling currents. Jim grabbed Gloria and wrestled the gun from her grasp. City police moved in and cuffed her, taking her into custody. Walking away, she gave Jim a stunned look of disbelief.

Suddenly, Jim felt undone. Leaning over the bridge framework, he searched frantically for any sign of Father Howard in the rippling current. Not seeing any trace of him, he climbed over the wrecked fence and sat down on the curb, holding his head in his hands. His heart was pounding in his chest like a big bass drum. After a few moments, he tipped his face toward the sky. His hands began shaking, and he felt nauseous. Stunned, he sat with his eyes closed. He lost track of time until he heard Sam next to him.

"Chief … Chief … " Sam said, kneeling in front of him, getting his attention. Jim opened his eyes. He wasn't sure how much time had passed. He'd been in a world of his own. "It's over. He's gone. We haven't spotted him. He hasn't come up. I've called the dive team out to recover the body."

Leslie appeared at Jim's side while he sat crumpled on the curb, buzzed and lightheaded, feeling the adrenaline stepping down. Leslie put her arm around his shoulder, and he leaned into her.

"Thanks," he said simply.

"Not a problem, Chief," she said softly. "Not a problem." ◘

51

By the time the scene was processed and the wreckage removed from the bridge, it was early evening. Traffic was reduced to one lane on the east and westbound sides of the highway, which had caused something of a jam on the big blue bridge. People slowed and stared at the smashed hulks of vehicles and the shattered glass being cleaned up by a county highway crew. The news of Father Howard's suicide jump had already exploded on social media.

"They're still searching for Father Howard, but they haven't spotted him yet. It might be hours or days before he washes up. They'll probably find him pretty far downriver," Sam said, slouching in a chair in Jim's office. Jim answered his phone and talked for a while. Sam figured it was Carol. Leslie walked into the office with Paul, who'd come to help process Gloria Bjerkes into jail on reckless endangerment charges. She'd be held over the weekend and questioned on Tuesday.

When Jim finally hung up, Paul spoke up.

"So there's no question then that Father Howard murdered Jeremy Bjerkes?" he asked.

Sam answered. "Oh, that's not an established fact yet. Father Howard vehemently denied killing Jeremy, even when he was going to jump off the bridge, but Gloria was somehow involved. We might find some evidence at the house. It'll be a long twisted road trying to untangle all the lies and deception." Sam continued to watch Jim carefully. "She won't go down easily." Noticing Jim's gray complexion, Sam asked, "You okay, Chief?" The team studied Jim with concerned expressions.

"Yeah, I'm all right, but I'm going home," Jim said, standing up and walking to the door. He stopped suddenly and pivoted to face them. His face was haggard, but his eyes were hard and uncompromising.

"Just remember, we still don't know who Trevor Bjerkes' father *really* is," Jim stated firmly. "Keep that in mind. There's something about that scene today that strikes me as odd. I think Sam's right. Gloria accused Father Howard of killing Jeremy, but he denied it before he jumped to his death. That whole scenario just doesn't sit right with me. We haven't located the black Impala and frankly, we may never find it and until we do, we'll get no DNA there, but since Howard committed suicide, we can get his DNA if we recover his body from the river. Don't hold your breath, people. I seriously doubt that Trevor is Father Howard's son. I don't think we've solved anything yet—not to my satisfaction. The evidence just isn't there—at least evidence that will hold up in a court of law."

Sam, Leslie, and Paul listened carefully to Jim's conclusions. They began filing out of the office, heading to the elevator.

"Well, that's depressing. How come we all put our lives on the line, and then everything falls in the ditch? Just once, I'd like it to be nice and simple," Paul said bleakly as he punched the elevator floor button.

"Deal with it, people," Jim said, frowning. "Everybody needs to go home and get some rest, but we need to meet briefly on Monday. We've got a lot more work to do next week."

The other three followed Jim out of the elevator. "Get some rest, Chief," Leslie said kindly as they walked into the evening dusk of the empty Vine Street parking lot. "Let Carol take care of you."

"I will," he said wearily as he climbed in his Suburban. ◘

52

Les Aspenson was a salesman at the Mound Ridge Chevy dealership on the northern edge of Richland Center. Since selling the agency to his middle son, Shawn, he only worked part-time. He thought about Shawn. *That kid could sell snow to an Eskimo,* he thought, letting out a little chuckle.

He waved to the couple who had just purchased a midsized Chevy Traverse SUV. As they drove out of the lot, he walked into the showroom and went to the office to finish the paperwork on the purchase. He'd seen the television press conference by Lt. Jim Higgins a few days ago about the May 14 double homicide in La Crosse. He squirmed uneasily in his chair. He couldn't get the black Chevy Malibu sitting in the back lot out of his head. His conscience had been causing him significant consternation. He leaned back at his desk watching the traffic on Hwy. 14 and considered his options.

What was it that was so different about the customer who had traded up for a beautiful, dark blue Chevy Silverado? Nothing really. He seemed like a nice young guy. Certainly handsome and well-spoken except for that stupid remark he'd made when Les had asked him why he wanted to trade. His answer seemed flippant and crude, but some people had a strange sense of humor. Les had dealt with all types of people during his lifetime as a car salesman, and sometimes customers said off-the-wall things that they later regretted. Still, a chill raised the hair on his arms when he thought about the comment.

"Well, if I ever want to murder somebody, a pickup box would be a great place to haul the body, don't you think?" he'd said, grinning.

Who goes around saying stuff like that? Les thought.

Still, he'd feel stupid reporting the car to Higgins, especially if it turned out to be a false alarm. Cops were busy enough nowadays without citizens giving them false leads that resulted in a wild goose chase. But the vehicle was still on the lot, and he knew they could get DNA from it. *Most criminals were nailed by DNA, weren't they?* He'd think about it over the weekend. Maybe Monday, he'd make a call to Higgins. ◘

53

" So you decided to take Lillie into a potentially lethal situation? How does that work?" Carol asked Jim, her brown eyes blazing.

Jim was sprawled on the couch, exhausted from the confrontation on the bridge. The memory of the car chase and suicide was catching up to him. He'd assisted with plenty of suicides after the fact, but he'd never been present when someone jumped off a bridge and drowned right before his eyes. He could still see Father Howard's determined expression as he fell into the river. Carol's tirade continued, and he made a halfhearted attempt to pay attention.

"Jim, she could have been hurt, abducted, or run over when this priest made a mad dash to escape," Carol criticized. "She's seen enough bad things, and to expose her to something like this is just ... well ... it's pretty irresponsible."

Carol's interrogation made Jim squirm uncomfortably. She'd been chewing on the subject since he'd gotten home, and he was in no mood for it. She hadn't even been there, for Pete's sake. He frowned at her accusations since they were exaggerations of what really happened. But, she had a valid point, he supposed. He inhaled a deep breath while she waited for his explanations to begin.

"I'm sorry it turned out that way, but we didn't believe Father Howard was a danger to anyone except himself," he started calmly.

"All of the action was pretty far away from Lillie. Sara did a beautiful job of keeping her close and out of harm's way. She had her eye on her constantly." Carol threw Jim an exasperated look. Jim leaned back, unintimidated by her disapproval.

"Really, honey, we can't protect Lillie from everything," Jim continued, hoping she'd back off with her criticisms. "Only God can do that. He has his eye on her, and He knows the number of hairs on her beautiful little head. Think about it. Three weeks ago, she was homeless, living on the street with her grandma, who was dying of pancreatic cancer in the—"

"I already know all that," Carol interrupted impatiently, putting up her hands to stop him. "You're right, but the mother in me protests."

More like Tiger Mom, Jim thought.

"And don't use her homelessness and compare it with this so you can downplay the whole thing," Carol continued. "They're two totally different situations."

Jim tipped his head, conceding the point. "Okay, I won't. And your instincts are noble," he said, his blue eyes shimmering with feeling.

"We've been given a trust, Jim," Carol said, tearing up, wiping her cheeks with her hand, "and it's an awesome responsibility. We have two beautiful little people to raise."

Jim nodded in agreement and went on. "Your innate protective senses kicked in, which is how it's supposed to work. That's how God created us. So I completely understand because I feel the same way about Lillie and Henri," Jim said, reaching over to Carol and pulling her closer to him. He tenderly ran his forefinger along her wet cheek. "And you ... well ... I love you. Don't worry. We'll figure this out. It's all new to both of us," he said softly, kissing her forehead.

"You're right, but at the same time, I don't want you to skate around this subject. It's far from over, but right now, you look like death warmed over, and you don't smell so good either, so come on," she said, standing and pulling him to his feet. "You need a shower, some tea—"

"A brandy," Jim interrupted.

"Whatever. A brandy and bed," she finished. Jim pulled her to his chest and engulfed her in his arms. "Orders of the queen in residence," she said into his T-shirt. "That would be me."

"Am I protesting?" he asked as she turned her face up to him. He kissed her tenderly.

"No, but I am. You *really* need a shower," Carol said, untangling herself and gently pushing him down the hall to the bathroom. ▢

SUNDAY,
MAY 26

54

Sam and Leslie had taken off early Sunday morning with their bikes, a picnic lunch, and Paco, who was crammed in the back seat of Sam's Jeep Patriot. They'd decided to point the car in the direction of Devil's Lake near Baraboo, but when Leslie read that the largest natural land bridge in Wisconsin was located right on Highway 80, about ten miles from Devil's Lake, they headed that way.

Sam parked the Jeep on a turn-out along Rustic Road 21 northeast of the park, and they climbed out and unloaded their bikes from the rack on the back. Sam frowned at the deep scratches on the front fender of his vehicle—the result of the frantic chase after Father Howard. He'd call the insurance company on Tuesday.

After the rough and tumble chase and the suicidal situation on the blue bridge yesterday, the challenge of pumping along the hilly terrain cleansed Sam's and Leslie's lungs and relieved some of their pent-up anxiety. Pedaling down the road, Paco trotted happily next to them. Although the gravel roads were rougher, the hilly terrain of Orchard Drive and Slotty Road was worth it in terms of scenery.

Eventually, they traversed a high ridge peppered with huge, old trees and fantastic views.

Dropping down into the bottoms, they pedaled through ancient sandstone formations that stood frozen in time above the rolling greenery like giant mystical castles complete with mysterious cracks, deep crevices, and jagged fault lines. Sculpted into a half-mile-long finger of blocked and layered rock, the land bridge rose sixty feet above the floodplain of two merging valleys. The narrow outcropping was topped by tall pines and covered with green shrubbery.

Sam and Leslie parked their bikes near the hiking trail. Natural Bridge State Park stretched out before them. Paco bounded up the graveled paths through beautiful upland areas filled with oak and maple hardwoods. Within the shade along the trails, bracken and maidenhair ferns swayed in a gently undulating motion, and underneath them, trilliums and violets bloomed in profusion. An Eastern Phoebe balanced on a shrub near the forest's edge and bobbed its tail, calling out a burry *fee-bee* song.

"Oh! Look here, Sam!" Leslie exclaimed, bending down to inspect a delicate plant in the shade of the rock wall. "According to Wikipedia, this is a rare type of goldenrod," she narrated, scrolling on her phone. "It says there are even small cacti on the top of the formations here and another rare purple plant called a cliffbrake."

She looked up at Sam from her kneeling position, and he noticed her cool, blue eyes. *How can you think about a friggin' flower at a time like this?* he thought. His mind was frantically turning over the facts of the murders. He was having a hard time accepting Father Howard as the killer. Too many things were not adding up.

"Rare, huh?" Sam said distractedly, gazing off into the distance.

"Yeah. Are you all right?" Leslie asked. "You seem distracted. Are you thinking about the murders?"

"And you're not?" he asked, irritated and grouchy. Leslie wondered at his cantankerous mood. Usually, Sam was so even-keeled.

"Well, it's percolating in the back of my mind, but Sam," she said, getting up and standing in front of him, "sometimes things come to you when you relax and chill—like now. This place is spectacular, and you're missing the whole thing," she said, watching him with concern.

"Yeah, I guess," he said huffily, breaking away from her and walking quickly along the trail.

They turned a wide corner on the hiking path and came upon a natural arch with its window and prehistoric rock shelter. Although it couldn't compare to the triumphant, iconic rock formations of the Desert Southwest, it was still a very impressive ancient geologic structure in Wisconsin. Leslie was admiring the quiet majesty of the place, petting Paco's head, watching Sam.

"Historians say that humans occupied this area 8,000 years ago," Leslie said, continuing in her tour guide mode. "I can just about imagine Native Americans perched on the rocks, surveying the area for deer and buffalo." She struck an alert pose, her hand to her brow. Sam looked at her, his mood petulant. After a moment, he stared at her with a stunned expression.

"We've been chasing the wrong person, Lez," he said, a feeling of horror engulfing him. Leslie's face creased in confusion. "The killer wasn't Father Howard. And it's not Gloria."

Leslie puffed in exasperation. "Sam, you are acting very strange. What are you talking about?" She waited for an explanation, but Sam's thoughts were racing. "It's going to come together," she continued. "We just don't have all the evidence yet, but we'll catch the killer, whoever did it. You just have to have a little patience."

Sam frantically waved his hands back and forth as if brushing away her comments. "Who's the only other person we know of who had sexual relations with Gloria? Who else was manipulated and coerced by Gloria into doing despicable things?"

Leslie turned and faced him. She noticed the pupils of his eyes were tiny and black, and he seemed sweaty and clammy.

"Well, I guess that would be Steven Hanratty. Maybe he's Trevor's dad," she said, matter-of-factly. "Crazier things have happened."

Sam nodded and plowed right on. "What if the black car at the funeral home wasn't Father Howard's black car but somebody else's?"

"You mean Steven Hanratty's?" Leslie suggested, trying to make sense of his ramblings.

"Yeah."

"But Sam, you said he drives a Chevy Silverado pickup. You saw him get in it at the Kwik Trip corporate parking lot," Leslie reminded him.

"Yeah, I know that's what I said, but that's what he drives *now*," Sam said emphatically, pointing his index finger to the ground. "Maybe he drove some other vehicle when he went to the funeral home. Or he traded the black vehicle for a new truck. Or he walked there. The black car could have been somebody else's—somebody who wasn't even involved in the murder," he finished, hoping she could follow his meandering thought processes.

"Well, it's possible, I guess, but it's a pretty slim chance."

"Well, what about the possibility that Father Howard and Gloria were planning on running away together to start a new life? Sam asked. "It wouldn't be the first time a priest left his calling for a woman." He shook his head in disgust. "And to think we swallowed it hook, line, and sinker."

Leslie was full of doubt. "I don't know, Sam. That sounds pretty far-fetched. But I'll play along with your idea." She squared her shoulders and began again. "So if your scenario is true, then explain to me why Father Howard would fling himself off the bridge if they were going to run away? People don't kill themselves on a whim unless they're depressed or agitated or desperately afraid of something."

Sam was staring at the ground, thinking. He lifted his head, and his eyes widened. "Are you kidding? He's a Catholic priest who had a sexual fling with some hot-to-trot physical therapist. He felt all of those rollercoaster emotions associated with a forbidden fling—love, sexual desire, guilt, and disappointment in his failure as a man of God. I could go on and on. There are plenty of motives to choose from. Take your pick." He stopped for a moment, and Leslie watched him carefully. He continued his rationale.

"First, if he had any spiritual backbone at all, he'd be terribly saddened by his failure and fall from God's favor. That alone would be enough to unhinge someone who had once taken his vows seriously. And then there's Gloria—that witch." Sam's mouth curled in a snarl. "Besides, who wouldn't be depressed after dealing with that woman every day?" Sam asked, his arms gesturing in the air. Leslie stayed silent, wondering about his new passionate theory. She listened carefully as he continued.

"You said it yourself, Lez. Gloria is a damned snake charmer." His voice was loud, and his face flushed as he drove his justifications home. "She's convinced a lot of people to do things that go against their innate sense of right and wrong. She tried to seduce Higgins, for God's sake, and he's the most stable person I know. And she successfully seduced a Catholic priest. She doesn't respect people's moral framework. Do you think she could have convinced Father Howard that Trevor was his son?" He didn't wait for her response. "Of course she could—and she did. But he's not."

"Come again?"

Sam grabbed her hand and kissed her roughly. "Thanks, Lez. You just helped me figure out who the killer is. Come on. We've got to get back and talk to Higgins."

"What about our picnic?"

"We'll eat it in the car," he said, walking swiftly down the trail toward their bikes.

"There's just one thing wrong with your theory," Leslie said quietly. Sam turned abruptly and stared at her. She held up two fingers. "Well, actually two." Another finger went up. "Well, maybe three." She waited for his frustrated outburst.

"Well, let's hear it then," he said impatiently, rooted to the trail. Leslie lowered her fingers into a fist.

She tilted her head provocatively and held up a finger. "First, Steven Hanratty's motive?"

"Yeah?" Sam sneered. "What about it?"

"There's little or no evidence to support your theory that he's the killer. What was his motive in killing Jeremy? If he wanted to kill anyone, I'd think it would have been Gloria." Silence. Another finger went up. "Second, the only evidence we have to support this Hanratty theory of yours is that he took a vacation day on the day of the murders. Pretty innocuous." Sam continued to stare, his jaw slack with amazement. "And third, we still don't know for sure who Trevor's father is, so to speculate that Hanratty might be the father is pretty far out there," she said, lowering her hand gingerly to her side. "Although, in your defense, they did have sexual intercourse about ten years ago, so maybe he could be the dad." She was waiting for him to give her the finger. Her dissection of his dubious theory did not discourage Sam in the least.

"Yeah, I know, but I have a hunch we're on the right track," Sam said, ever the optimist. "We'll get DNA from Father Howard, and if I'm right, he'll be eliminated from Trevor's parental line. But we need to get a court order to get DNA from Steven Hanratty. We need to get that—like now!" He turned and began jogging down the trail. Leslie and Paco followed behind, trying to catch up. ⬛

MONDAY,
MAY 27

55

Although it was Memorial Day and Carol had planned a picnic in the backyard at noon, Jim called the team in for a session to review their evidence and construct a plausible theory for Jeremy Bjerkes' murder. Their disjunct facts frustrated everyone. It seemed they'd been on the right trail, but now that trail had gone surprisingly dead. They were right back at square one, minus their lead suspect, Father Howard. The case was falling apart before their eyes.

"Whoa, whoa, whoa!" Jim said when Sam started reeling out his scenario. "Let me get this straight. You think Hanratty is the murderer?" His expression of disbelief made Sam squirm.

Leslie was frustrated as well, eyeing Sam with skepticism. Jim had heard her in the background when Sam phoned last night, trying to tamp down his overzealous conjectures. Leslie's romantic involvement with Sam would make it hard for her to stay objective about Sam's latest speculations. Jim was hoping her innate common sense would come through.

He glanced at Paul standing against the wall, arms crossed, watching Sam with conspicuous doubt. His eyebrows were cocked together in confusion, and his arms crossed over his chest suggested anything but open-mindedness. Since the shooting last November in which he'd been seriously wounded, he was more careful in his conclusions and reticent in revealing his thoughts. What that meant for their investigations, Jim wasn't sure.

Sam had plenty of enthusiasm for the job, but balanced, logical thinking sometimes eluded him. Still, if there was one thing Sam could do, it was spark creative ideas. Since creative thinking was necessary in solving crimes, Jim gave him the courtesy of his full attention.

Sam stood up from his chair and began pacing. His voice was intense like last night when he'd called at seven wanting to come over and lay out his theory. Jim had listened patiently, but in the end, he decided the theories could wait until today. So here they were.

Sam's face reflected resolve and single-mindedness as he turned to face his boss. Jim shifted uncomfortably, and his chair creaked loudly. From the expression on Sam's face, Jim felt like he was going to get a hell and damnation sermon, something he had heard once in a while from Pastor Berge while he sat in a pew at the Hamburg Lutheran Church. Sam surprised him, however. As he began, his voice was surprisingly moderate and even.

"From the conversation between Gloria and Father Howard on the bridge Saturday, we could conclude that Father Howard did not kill Jeremy Bjerkes. Gloria accused him of it, but he denied it not just once, but twice. Can we agree on that?" Sam asked as if he were taking a poll.

Everyone stared at him. Jim finally spoke up.

"For argument's sake, we'll postpone judgment and agree. Go ahead with your theory," Jim stated patiently.

"So if Father Howard didn't kill Jeremy, then who did?" Sam's hazel eyes moved around the room, engaging each person. He waited a few moments, then continued. "I propose that Steven Hanratty had as much justification for killing Jeremy Bjerkes as any of the other suspects. Sexually abused, bullied, and badgered by Gloria, his feelings of hatred for her ran deep. He'd lost his girlfriend over the whole sexual scandal, not to mention the embarrassment of retracting his original allegations. When Leslie interviewed him, he was still deeply affected by the incident despite the fact that ten years had passed since the abuses occurred. Over the years, Gloria certainly gave him several reasons to despise her. I'm guessing that his rage led to a tremendous desire to hurt Gloria and the people she loved—namely her husband and son."

Paul spoke up. "So Steven's motivation is hatred and revenge?"

"Yep," Sam quipped. "He saw himself as powerless, so he decided to hurt Gloria like she'd hurt him ... or something like that," Sam said.

"All right. Where's the evidence for your theory?" Jim asked patiently.

Sam colored with embarrassment. "Well, that's the problem. I don't have any, but his alibi for the day of the murder—"

"—is weak, to say the least," Jim finished.

Paul rolled his eyes. "So what the hell are we doing here if we haven't got any evidence?" he asked.

"Just hear me out," Sam began again. "The black vehicle at the funeral home has been a problem from the get-go. We assumed it was the killer's car, and it could have been. But it could just as easily have been someone else, say a customer or acquaintance of Jeremy's, who stopped in briefly and talked to him, then left again. Or the killer could have walked there, shot the victims, and walked away again unseen."

"Yeah, I see what you're saying, and that could be true," Jim said.

"Any news on Father Howard's DNA? " Leslie asked.

"Not yet," Paul said. "And we still haven't found Genevieve Stamper's car anywhere.

"I don't know where that car is," Sam said. "Maybe Gloria knows something about that. We can ask her when we interrogate her tomorrow." For someone with such a random theory, he was surprisingly calm in his deliberations and questioning from the team.

Jim's cell rang, and he frowned. "Don't people know it's a holiday?" he asked, irritated. He answered, leaning his elbows on his desk. Suddenly he stiffened and sat up straight, alarmed.

"When did this happen?" He listened some more. "You still have the car?" More listening.

"Don't let anyone touch it or move it," Jim ordered. "I'll send a wrecker down, and we'll impound it. One more thing. Are you at the office? What's your cell number?" He listened carefully, scribbling down the number. "I'm going to send a picture of a man I want you to identify if you can. As soon as you get it, study it closely and call me back," he finished and hung up.

Jim shifted his gaze and said, "Leslie, I want you to send a picture of Steven Hanratty to this cell number. Now," he ordered, handing her a slip of paper.

"Sure, Chief," she replied, getting out her phone. Her thumbs flew, and soon her phone rang.

Sam and Paul exchanged an inscrutable glance. Leslie handed her phone to Jim.

"Higgins." Jim listened carefully. "Thanks so much. This is very important. But please keep this information to yourself." He clicked off.

"Well, what's going on?" Sam asked, frustrated.

"Steven Hanratty traded a black Chevy Malibu for a dark blue Chevy Silverado pickup at Mound Ridge Chevy dealership in Richland Center on Wednesday, May 15. The owner has the car on his lot, and he identified Steven Hanratty from Leslie's photo."

The silence in the office was deafening. ◘

TUESDAY,
MAY 28

56

Gloria Bjerkes was feeling lousy. Her hair was greasy. Her orange jumpsuit was wrinkled and sweat-stained. Despite her attempt to eat breakfast earlier, she'd pushed away the tasteless food. Now her stomach rolled with hunger. Her pale complexion and short cropped hair gave the impression of a lost orphan. For once in her life, she wasn't putting on an act. She felt utterly abandoned and alone.

The La Crosse County Jail was an inhospitable place, and since Saturday night, it had become almost intolerable. Toilets flushing, the clang of metal doors, inmates who demanded services they didn't deserve. The reality of her incarceration was nothing like she'd imagined it might be.

Gloria was waiting for her lawyer, Vincent Palachecky, to show up in the early afternoon and post bail before Judge Benson. Jumpy at the unfamiliar, harsh sounds around her, she tensed when a jailer stood outside her cell. The female jailer gave her a careful once-over, her eyes traveling along the rumpled gaudy jumpsuit. The jailer seemed to understand how difficult this situation was for Gloria, and she gave her a weak smile. Gloria glanced at the clock on the wall: 9:30 a.m. The morning yawned like an open chasm before her. Four hours seemed like an eternity to wait until she could get out of this hole.

Gloria considered the many hurdles she would have to overcome if she didn't want to get charged with conspiracy to commit murder. Bargaining was not her style, but she knew that's exactly what she'd have to do—plead for lesser charges. All of it was unbelievable. That she couldn't buy her way out of a sure prison sentence sent her deflated ego into an abyss of insecurity and depression. It was just a matter of time before Higgins began gathering enough evidence to file some serious charges that would stick.

She lay on her narrow cot, staring up at the cinder block ceiling. No one had come to commiserate with her in her predicament. She thought of her son, Trevor, and her conversation with him during the supervised recorded phone call on Saturday night.

"Hi, Mom. When are you coming home?" he'd asked, his quiet sobs echoing over the line.

Gloria closed her eyes at the sound of his crying, gathering what little strength she had to comfort him. "Don't worry, Trev. I'll be out of here by Tuesday afternoon," she'd said more confidently than she really felt. "We'll be together again, and we'll figure this out."

"Really? Promise?"

For a moment, Gloria couldn't find her voice. She cleared her throat, surprised at the lump that had formed there.

"Yeah, I promise," she said, her voice cracking, the tears beginning to silently streak her face.

"I miss Dad," Trevor said sadly. He sobbed quietly as Gloria listened, her heart breaking for all the tragedy she had brought on her young son. *He doesn't deserve this*, she thought. But she had willfully and deliberately done it to him, skidding through every warning sign, not stopping until she'd found herself at the edge of a cliff.

"I know. I miss Dad, too. Listen, I have to go. You stay strong, and we'll make a plan, okay?" she said regretfully, tears wetting her cheeks.

"Okay. I love you, Mom," he whispered bravely.

"I know," Gloria said. She hung up the phone but continued to cling to the receiver, hanging her head in the crook of her arm. The tears she had previously held in now flowed freely, sympathy for her young son crashing over her in waves. She sobbed loudly. Regret flooded her, and she wondered if she could ever be forgiven.

She felt a light touch on her shoulder. Woodenly, she rose from the telephone area and shuffled back to her cell ahead of the jailer, falling on the cot in utter exhaustion. ◙

57

On Tuesday morning, Jim and Paul stood in the impound center on Vine Street, assessing the black Chevy Malibu that had been brought in from Mound Ridge Chevy in Richland Center. They watched the crime scene techs going over it, collecting fibers and possible DNA. If the DNA from the Malibu matched the DNA from Steven Hanratty, then Sam's theory could actually be plausible. Jim turned to Paul.

"Once we establish Trevor's paternity, then we can get Hanratty in here and interrogate him, although paternity alone doesn't prove he killed Jeremy and Layne. But it makes him a stronger suspect. That bullshit about fishing the day of the murder doesn't fly with me. I don't know one fisherman—even dedicated ones—who would fish in a raging thunderstorm. We're going to go over and talk to him again today and confront him about his activities on the day of the murder. Sam seems really sure that Steven is the killer, but I don't know. What do you think?" Jim asked, tilting his head sideways, watching Paul's reaction.

Paul placed his hands on his hips as he watched the crew work on the vehicle. "Truth is often stranger than fiction, Chief. Sam is like a dog gnawing on his favorite bone when he gets an idea in his head. I'll give him credit; he thinks of stuff I'd never think of, but

SUE BERG

this latest idea seems pretty far out there." He sighed tellingly, then pursed his lips. "I'll be surprised if it actually works out the way he thinks it will."

Jim listened, then rubbed the back of his neck. "Sometimes, he forgets to develop his theories based on evidence. But you're right. He does think up some corkers. Let's head over to the morgue and see if Luke's got any DNA from Father Howard yet."

Jim and Paul stepped onto the third floor of the investigative department mid-morning on Tuesday after their visit to the impound center. Late Monday afternoon, Father Skip Howard had been pulled from the Mississippi River near Lansing, Iowa. A fisherman was casting toward shore under the Lansing bridge when a piece of clothing caught his eye. He investigated, discovered the body, and called it in. Luke Evers drove a DNA cheek swab to Rochester within hours of finding the body. Now they were waiting for results.

"Morning, Emily. Any word from Luke yet?" Jim asked, hoping for something they could bank on—something believable.

"Nothing yet, Jim. I'll call you if I hear anything," she remarked seriously.

They walked down the hall to Jim's office. He flicked on the lights, walked to the window, propped it open, then turned and sat down at his desk while Paul settled into a chair.

"Forgot to tell you, Chief. We bought a house over on Market Street, so we'll be collecting a return favor from you when we get ready to move toward the end of the month."

Jim smiled. "Hey, congratulations! Welcome to the world of monthly payments. Now the home repairs and improvements begin—and never end." He leaned back in his chair and studied Paul, noticing the bright, hopeful sparkle in his eyes.

Paul grinned. "The house is in pretty good shape. It's been really well-cared for. Ruby's so excited."

"I remember when Margie and I bought our place. We were pretty excited, too," Jim said, a wistful shadow crossing his face. Despite the happiness and joy he'd found with Carol, he still missed Margie. The memories were sharp and intense and left him somewhere between nostalgia and melancholy.

"Oh, and the other news. We're pregnant again. December."

Jim leaned forward and placed his arms on his desk. "Wow! That's great. Really great." He smiled widely and listened with one ear while Paul rattled on about names and other baby stuff. Then during a lull in the conversation, Jim said, "So, not to detract from your exciting news, but could you get together about six photos from our files and a current photo of Hanratty and print them? I want you to make a trip down to Genoa to talk to Bobby Rude. See if he can identify Hanratty as the guy who threw the gun in the river. I talked to Sara, and she'll go with you over to his house. Bobby's a little skittish, but if she's there, he'll be more relaxed."

"Sure. I'll get right on it," he said, standing. "Does Sara know I'll be coming?"

"No, I'll call her. You can meet her at the Mobil station in Genoa."

After Paul left, Jim buzzed Leslie and asked her to come down to his office. "You and I are going over to Kwik Trip headquarters and question Steven Hanratty about his whereabouts on the day of the murder.

"I'm ready whenever you are," Leslie said, standing in front of Jim's desk.

Jim glanced at the time. "Call the office first and make sure he's there, but don't let him know we're coming. How's ten o'clock sound?"

"Great."

Jim continued working at his desk, but his thoughts were turning over the facts of the case and the nagging issues at the perimeter. Snippets of conversations and other nubs of information rolled around in his head. What had he missed that his conclusions had been so off? Part of it had been the missed opportunity to interrogate Father Howard. That was on Jim. He felt a deep sense of remorse that perhaps a conversation could have preempted his suicide. Except for the information Paul and Sam had extracted during their talk with him, Jim was at a loss. How had a priest fallen so far from grace? The old biblical wisdom still proved true; all have sinned and fallen short of the glory of God.

But he was even more confused about the reason behind his suicide. What was really eating at Father Howard? If Trevor was his son, then why'd he kill himself? Had Gloria refused him access to Trevor and he felt shut out? Did he simply crack and mentally go over the edge because of his spiritual failures? It happened more than anyone would like to admit. Or had he lost his way back to God and no longer believed in the power of forgiveness? Whatever it was, now they'd never know.

He leaned back in his chair, releasing a pent-up sigh. His phone burred.

"Higgins."

"Sir, Hanratty never came to work today. Didn't call in, didn't notify anybody," Leslie informed him. "His supervisor says that's totally out of character. I've been trying his cell, but he's not answering."

Jim felt a cold hardness in his stomach. "Oh boy. That's not good. Let's run over to his apartment and see if we can find him."

Jim and Leslie were about to leave the office when his phone buzzed again. Irritated, he glanced at the caller and felt a surge of hope.

"Luke? What do you have?"

"The priest is not Trevor's father." There was a long pause. "Chief? You there?"

"Yeah. So do you have anything from the Hanratty vehicle that will give us DNA?"

"Actually, yes. We've gotten good samples from the steering wheel. And there was a Mountain Dew can on the floor of the vehicle under the passenger seat. We'll get good samples from that, too, but it might take a while."

"No, no, it can't take that long. It has to be today," he said hurriedly, the authority ramping up in his voice. "We're closing in, but without DNA, our theory is very tentative. It's got to happen today," he insisted.

"Well, someone could run it over to Rochester, wait for the results, and run it back. That's still going to take four or five hours," Luke said.

"Let me call Davy Jones and see if he can get an officer to run it over and wait while they run it," Jim suggested.

Talking while he walked, Jim rang Jones, and he got the go-ahead for the DNA to be taken to Rochester. With that settled, Jim and Leslie hurried out of the Vine Street parking lot and drove to the Logan Northside neighborhood where Hanratty lived. In ten minutes, they were at the Rublee Community Apartments complex. They went inside the lobby and took the elevator to the second floor, walking down the hall to #232. Leslie knocked and waited. The apartment was quiet. More knocking, which turned into pounding. No answer.

Finally, a young girl came out of #234, peeved by the commotion in the hall.

"Are you looking for Steven?" she asked brusquely, her brows wrinkled in a frown.

Jim answered, "Yes, have you seen him today?"

"No, but I did talk to him briefly last night about nine o'clock. He said he wasn't going to work today because he had somebody to visit at the county jail." She looked back and forth at Jim and Leslie. "That seemed a little strange to me, but it's wasn't my business so—"

Leslie looked at Jim, her eyes wide with panic.

"Gloria," they both said at the same time. Hollering a thanks over their shoulders, they pivoted quickly, took the stairs two by two, and blew through the lobby doors. Running to the Suburban, Leslie called the jail.

"Listen, this is Detective Leslie Brown. Gloria Bjerkes is being released today when she posts bond." The voice on the other end of the line began arguing, but she impatiently interrupted. "No, no, don't take the time to go look. She's there, and she's scheduled to be released around two. This is very important. We believe Steven Hanratty may ask to visit her. Under no circumstances should you let him do that. In fact, if he shows up, restrain him and hold him until we get there. Put him in a cell if you have to. Understand?"

Leslie clicked off.

"Call Jones and fill him in," Jim ordered tersely, speeding down Lang Drive, whipping recklessly around slower drivers. Leslie talked to Jones as Jim barreled toward the Law Enforcement Center. Hurtling into the parking lot, they jogged to the building, trotting briskly to the jail. Sheriff Davey Jones met them at the front desk. He took one look at their tense faces and held up his hands.

"What's going on? This Hanratty—you think he's a threat?" he asked brusquely.

"Oh, he's a threat," Jim said, huffing considerably from his jog into the building. "We think he may be waiting for Gloria Bjerkes to be released from jail so he can ambush her. We have reasons to believe he may have murdered Bjerkes and McNally. He didn't show up for work today, and he told a neighbor at his apartment complex he had business at the jail."

"Got it. Let's proceed with a shelter-in-place lockdown. I'll start the chain of command. No one goes anywhere until we see where this is headed," Sheriff Jones ordered as he began texting. "I'll send a text to the officers on patrol to see if they can spot this guy somewhere around town."

Jim and Leslie stepped into the nearest elevator and punched the number for the third floor. As they rode up, Leslie texted Sam and Paul and gave them the details of their discovery. When they stepped off the elevator, the atmosphere in the secretarial pool was ominously quiet. In fact, no one seemed to be around. Emily and her coworkers were huddled in the breakroom despite the sheriff's text warning everyone to remain at their stations and continue to engage in normal activities while the building was locked down. When Jim came through the door, he noticed their wary eyes and panicked expressions.

"Ladies? Is there a problem other than the shelter in place?"

Emily rose to the challenge. "No, sir. We were just reviewing what we would do if someone came on our floor and threatened us with a weapon."

"Isn't that covered in your mandatory training when you're hired here?" Jim asked snappily. "Let's get everyone back out onto the floor," he said, pointing his arm toward the outer office. The younger secretaries scurried by him in timid silence. Focusing on Emily, he said, "Could I have a word in my office?"

Emily cringed inwardly but maintained her cool outward demeanor. She had never been asked by Jim to "have a word." She followed him, feeling like a kid going to the principal after a hallway fight. Leslie continued down the hall. Jim stood ramrod straight by the door as Emily came in and parked herself before his desk. He quietly shut the door, walked around her, and pivoted to face her.

"Explain what you were doing just now," he said tersely, his voice flat. His hands rested on his hips. At times like this, Emily hated those cool, blue eyes.

"Some of the girls were a little freaked by the sheriff's message. I was trying to calm them down and review our procedures to shelter in place. That's all," she explained weakly. Her excuse sounded pathetic.

"Okay, I get that. But, Emily, in an emergency, everyone is supposed to be able to carry on their duties within the procedural framework we've established. If your girls can't do that, they're putting the rest of us at risk," Jim said. Emily remained mute like a prisoner receiving a sentence. "You're their leader—so lead by example," he finished sharply.

"Yes, sir. I promise that we will review and practice the procedures until they are confident they can carry them out, sir. I apologize," Emily said, tears welling up in her eyes.

Jim's shoulders relaxed, and he sat down in his office chair. He leaned back and stared at the ceiling, then aimed another gaze at her. "Oh, hell. Listen, I realize in this day and age of mass shootings that this can be upsetting. But really, Emily, we, of all people, should be able to handle these kinds of threats." A few tense moments passed. Emily refused to dissolve in a puddle of tears. Finally, Jim said more gently, "I know you meant well. Review and practice, okay?"

"Yes, sir. That's what we'll do in the next few weeks. I promise," she said. She turned to go, then stopped.

"What is it?" he said, not unkindly.

"It's just that Margo was in a school shooting three years ago, and the shelter-in-place warning left her feeling a little insecure, sir," she said quietly. She left the office, closing the door quietly behind her.

"Oh, boy," Jim said. He covered his eyes with his hand and slid it down his face plopping his hand in his lap. Feeling like a heel for giving her a hard time, Jim thought about it, then reconsidered. Threatening situations could happen at any moment. Keeping your head and knowing procedures was crucial to a better, if not good, ending.

His phone buzzed.

"Sam. Where are you?"

"I was headed back to the office after checking in with one of my informants up on the north side. I got the messages about Hanratty, and I noticed Steven's truck up ahead in traffic. I'm sure it's him. I'm following him. He's almost to the Vine Street parking lot. I think his threat is a serious one. We're going to need some backup officers outside the building. I'll stay in my truck, get my vest on, and wait for orders, but if he tries to enter the building, I will have to confront him."

"Right. Be careful. I'm on it. I'll get you backup. Keep your phone on," Jim said quietly, the dread rising in his chest like a hard ball.

Jim relayed the message to Sheriff Jones and Police Chief Pedretti while Sam drove past Hanratty to the second parking lot entrance. He parked his Jeep Patriot in the farthest corner of the lot opposite Hanratty. Leaning over the back seat, Sam grabbed his Kevlar vest, placed it over his dress shirt, and holstered his standard-issue weapon. His heart was banging in his chest like a gong, and his mouth had gone dry and pasty. He had a perfect view of Hanratty's truck in his rearview mirror. He hunkered down, watching him. *Please God, let him abandon his ideas,* he prayed. Then he thought, *That's not going to happen. If he's here, he has a plan.* Then another thought. *He who dwells in the shelter of the Most High will rest in the shadow of the Almighty.*

Hanratty moved around in his truck, fussing with something, then he stepped out on the pavement. The truck door slamming filled Sam with a dread he could not explain. It settled deep in his guts and stayed there. The parking lot was extremely quiet. Sam crawled out of his Jeep, breathing deeply. He could feel the dead weight of his gun in the shoulder holster, but it provided little comfort. He felt the hair raise up on his arms and the back of his neck.

Approaching Steven slowly and calmly, Sam began crossing the large parking lot. He noticed two armed, uniformed cops coming around the building walking toward Steven. The officers were in full protective gear, and one of them called out in a loud voice which echoed off the building into the parking lot.

"Steven Hanratty, if you are armed, drop your weapon!" the officer shouted, assuming the position. "The building is in lockdown. You will not be able to get in," he said assertively. "I repeat, drop your weapon!"

In an instant, Hanratty's gun came up and the officer fired. Hanratty went down but he continued shooting. Time warped to a sickening crawl, but in reality only a few seconds had passed. Sam ran toward Hanratty who was lying on his stomach on the pavement. Sam's legs churned like he was plowing through a field of thick mud, each step harder than the last. Sam was about twenty feet from Hanratty when he rolled over.

In a split second, Hanratty aimed, pulled the trigger, and shot Sam in the chest. Sam saw Hanratty's body jerk from the kick of the gun. He smelled the acrid smoke of the gunshot. Simultaneously, he felt a tremendous pain in his chest like he'd been hit by a baseball bat. Knocked off his feet, the pain traveled through his body until he felt it would blow through his back and leave a big hole in the parking lot beneath him. For just a second, Sam felt like silly putty being stretched and elongated through a tiny hole as if he were being squeezed into an alternate universe. The events happening around him drifted away to the edges of his consciousness. He lost track of time. He floated somewhere in space, and silence followed him there.

"Sam! Sam! Wake up!" Leslie screamed. Her hands shook as she ripped the Kevlar vest off over his head and unbuttoned his shirt. Sam slowly came to. He was sprawled on the parking lot, his arms extended on the pavement, his gun still in his hand. He focused on Leslie's agonized face with a stupified, shocked expression.

"Hurts. God, it hurts," he whispered. Leslie bent over him, stroking his dark hair, kissing his cheek. Higgins appeared. His hair was disheveled, and his tie hung at an awkward angle. His face was ashen with fear and concern.

"Help's on the way. Hang on, Sam," Higgins was saying, grasping his hand. A siren began wailing in the distance, getting louder and louder.

Sam thought everyone seemed so far away. He was fading, fading ... ◘

58

A couple of hours later, Sam woke up to the beep of machines. The air in the hospital room smelled of rubbing alcohol and bleached cotton sheets. He tried to move, but pain shot through his chest. He went still again. Wiggling his toes, he thought, *I must not be hurt too bad.* He forced his eyes open, but the light's brightness made him squeeze them shut again. He moaned quietly.

"Hey, Sam."

He opened his eyes. Leslie was leaning over the bed, reaching for his hand. Her long blond hair was messy, and she had been crying.

"You scared the shit out of us," she said, tears coursing down her cheeks.

"You going to give me a damage report?" he whispered, although it hurt even to talk. He heard other deep male voices mumbling in the room somewhere. *Must be Higgins and Saner,* he thought.

"Well, thank God you wore your vest, or you wouldn't be here right now," Leslie said. She lost her composure and began crying again. After a few moments, she started her litany of his injuries. "You've got a cracked sternum, a bruised heart and right lung, and a couple of displaced ribs. The bruises are impressive—very similar to your dog bite in the butt, except they're on your chest. They're really ugly." She smiled tenderly and touched his cheek. "They checked for lung punctures, but you didn't have any. If you feel sleepy, it's because they gave you a sedative. You can go home later today, providing you have adequate care. You've got me, so you're good on that one." She leaned down and kissed him on the mouth.

"What about Hanratty?" he whispered.

"Died on the table about an hour ago. Officer Malhoune was shot in the leg but should make a full recovery. Everybody else is okay."

Sam nodded and whispered, "Good. That's good." Then he slipped off to sleep. ◘

59

In the days that followed the shooting incident in the Law Enforcement Center parking lot, Jim and his team began putting together the confusing puzzle of the murders of Jeremy Bjerkes and Layne McNally.

They had DNA to prove that Trevor Bjerkes was Steven Hanratty's son. Following the shooting death of Steven Hanratty in the Vine Street parking lot, Gloria Bjerkes broke down when she was charged with assaulting an officer of the law, extortion, and conspiracy. She could not hide her bewilderment when she found out that Trevor was Steven Hanratty's son. Her lies and twisted machinations had snuck up and ambushed her, leaving her dazed with surprise.

Hanratty had committed the heinous crimes. The red grosgrain ribbon found in the mortuary office the morning of the murder had Hanratty's DNA all over it, proving he had been there that day. What the significance of the ribbon was, they didn't know. The ballistics test from the Ruger pistol matched the riflings on the bullets found at the crime scene. Finding the receipt for the handgun in Hanratty's apartment clinched the fact that the gun belonged to him.

Paul had been in Genoa when the shooting at the Vine Street parking lot went down. Bobby Rude had carefully considered the eight photos Paul had prepared for viewing, taking several minutes to compare and inspect them. Then he had confidently picked out Steven Hanratty as the man who had tossed the gun in the river. Turning his dark eyes to Sara, Bobby held up the photo and said, "That's him, Miss Higgins. I'm one hundred percent sure, and I'll swear to it." That was good enough for Jim.

Sam was placed on administrative leave for a few weeks to rest and recuperate under Leslie and Paco's watchful eye. Physically sore and emotionally shaken, he agreed to go to Vivian's counseling service in Holmen when Jim insisted he receive psychological treatment.

"No arguing, Sam, you will go—orders from the sheriff. Paul went when he was shot. You may not be hurt as badly as Paul physically, but being shot damages your emotions and sense of well-being. So don't even try arguing with me," Jim finished giving him an uncompromising stare.

"Right, Chief," he muttered unceremoniously.

Everyone got back to their lives as best they could. Things were slow, and that gave them all time to recover and gather the evidence they needed to hand over to the district attorney. ◘

MID-JULY

60

Juliette's tiny house on Camden Street in Wausau, Wisconsin, sat forlornly beneath a towering white pine, its siding covered in some kind of creeping black mold. The front steps tilted precariously, and the tire swing in the pine tree swayed back and forth in the morning breeze. Jim sat in his Suburban for a few minutes, gathering his thoughts. When he finally inserted the key in the front door and turned the knob, odors of dust, mildew, and Listerine floated to him in the stuffy atmosphere. He had avoided wading through Juliette's possessions for weeks, but the Wausau Clerk of Courts wanted to settle the estate, and Jim finally conceded. Standing inside his sister's neglected home, the view from here told a story he wished he'd never uncovered.

How was it that a person he had not known about until a month ago could so radically change his inner emotional landscape? Trying to decipher his feelings about all of it had left him in a blue funk. He thought of Socrates' statement that the unexamined life was not worth living, but he was sure there were plenty of people who'd never bothered to do that. He, on the other hand, had lived his life fully, without regrets, deliberate in his intentions, and he knew he'd been blessed beyond anything he deserved. If he'd never considered his mortality, he probably never would have become a cop.

When Margie died, things changed. Left alone, standing at the edge of his mortal existence, the vastness of eternity stepped up beside him. Rather than becoming frozen with fear, it galvanized his faith and determination to make his life count. If that didn't qualify as an examined life, he didn't know what did.

He breathed in the stale surroundings of Juliette's home. It was like viewing an aging time capsule. Everything was just as Juliette had left it when she was evicted and became a homeless person. Shuffling throughout the tiny house, he shifted through the detritus of a poor, divorced, disease-ridden woman. A cracked coffee cup in the kitchen sink, a can of Comet cleanser on the bathroom vanity, an alarm clock on the dusty nightstand whose hands were frozen in time.

He thought of Lillie. Juliette had done the best she could with what little she had. Lillie had been loved, and all the trappings of this world could not begin to compare with the acceptance and unconditional love that Juliette had so willingly poured into her little granddaughter.

Jim plopped down on the couch, a balloon of dust rising from it that made him cough and sneeze. He turned and picked up a picture from a scruffy end table, one in which Juliette and Lillie smiled back at him. He set the picture back on the table and absentmindedly picked up a photo album near it, paging through the contents. He stopped here and there, lingering on a picture, trying to paste together the life of the lost sister he'd never known and his newly adopted daughter.

Finally, in exasperation, he walked back to the truck, opened the back passenger door, and grabbed the cardboard boxes he had brought to pack up what he thought might be valuable to his family. In a few hours, he'd gathered photos, a few embroidered handkerchiefs in Juliette's top dresser drawer, her wedding ring, and a tiny toy tiger that was well-worn from Lillie's hugs and kisses. He came across a couple of articles from the *La Crosse Sentinel* about himself, noticing the dates. Five years ago. Things had certainly changed since then.

He thought about his own life. When people sorted through the leftovers of his possessions, what conclusions would they draw from them? He hoped his possessions had nothing to do with the legacy he left behind. Instead, he hoped the people who loved him would be able to point to qualities that lived beyond things—love, patience, kindness, integrity, and faith.

Jim gathered up the boxes, walked them to the truck, then turned back to lock the door. As he stood on the narrow sidewalk outside the home, his eyes roamed over the residence and yard that supposedly defined his sister's existence. But he knew he'd never be able to relegate her to the scrap heap of society. Her spirit had been large and generous. If Lillie was the product of Juliette's efforts and love, then he was far richer than he deserved to be.

"Thanks, Juliette," he whispered, "for bringing Lillie to us. We can never repay you for protecting and loving her when you were so vulnerable and desperate." Tears stung his eyes as he slowly turned and walked down the cracked sidewalk. When he turned out onto the street, he took one last look at the dilapidated house. For just an instant, he could see Lillie running and laughing beneath the tall pine tree that shaded the postage stamp yard. The frayed rope swing hung crookedly now, but in his mind's eye, he could see Lillie swinging, high and free. He smiled through his tears and drove away, knowing he'd never return. But he had Lillie, the living embodiment of the power of love. And he knew you couldn't beat that with a stick. ◘

LATE AUGUST

61

The heat of the early afternoon sunshine beat down on the sparse crowd gathered at the Hamburg Lutheran Church cemetery on Hamburg Ridge Road. The gentle swishing of the silky pines in the breeze and their sharp, tangy fragrance left Jim feeling wistful. He gazed at the rolling hills and craggy limestone bluffs that soared upward from the vibrant green of the woods and fields. Holstein cattle browsed contentedly across the road from the churchyard, always moving in search of greener pastures.

This little piece of earth on top of the hill seemed like the perfect place to lay Juliette to rest.

It had been a couple of tough months emotionally. Jim had hoped the bitterness of his heart would gradually unravel and give him some relief. But the peace that he sought after the death of Juliette eluded him. His heart was stubborn and wouldn't let go of the heavy weight that had moved in and sat in his chest like a bar of steel, alienating him from Carol and his family. Lately, the only people he didn't resent were Lillie and Henri. They were innocent in this whole big family mess.

He'd had ample time to rethink the truth of his family history. Death was a familiar reality in his personal life and his job. But this felt different. Juliette left a hole that nothing seemed to fill. The whole sad story of his sister's spiral into homelessness left him feeling defeated. For once in his life, he couldn't do anything to rectify the circumstances and bring a better ending.

More than once, he'd retreated to the back acres of his property, cleaning up brush and throwing it in the John Deere gator in a madding search to find some kind of deliverance from the anger in his soul. He built huge piles of dead shrubbery and burned them. Watching the flickering flames, he wished he could rewrite the sad saga of Juliette's broken life. But he came away empty without answers. He built an impregnable wall around himself, and he fortified it with the stones of regret, anger, and guilt.

Carol watched him with apprehensive concern. This was new territory in their relationship, and she was weighed down by the sorrow and angst he was experiencing. More than once, she said she was praying for him. Jim silently appraised her, keeping to himself, not willing to bare his soul. Even their return to lovemaking was tinged with something new and different. There was passion and release, but the joy they'd once experienced had diminished as if a shadow had fallen.

Recently Carol had asked him how long he intended to wage his private war.

"For as damn long as I want to," he'd said bitterly. Carol's eyes teared up, but Jim stoically refused her offers to listen and empathize. Although Vivian tried to convince him to get counseling, punishing himself was all he was interested in doing.

Now on this hot afternoon, they gathered to spread Juliette's ashes over the gravesite. Lillie, as usual, was filled with questions. She pulled on Jim's pant leg impatiently.

"What are these rocks for, Bapa?" she asked, squinting up at him in the hot sun.

"They're markers with people's names. It tells us that someone loved them once, and they don't want them to be forgotten," Jim said simply. He noticed the rays of sunshine reflecting from Lillie's golden curls. Her little nose was sunburned, and her quizzical expression filled him with tenderness. *Thank you, God. She's the only good thing that came out of this mess.* He knelt down in front of her and kissed her cheek.

"We won't forget Grandma, will we?" she asked, worry coloring the expression of her innocent voice. Her little hand gently stroked Jim's cheek.

"No, we won't forget Grandma, Lillie," Jim said softly, his throat tightening with a lump. Baby Henri squawked in hunger, so Carol walked through the graveyard to sit on a bench under a massive pine tree where she nursed him. Her expression of sadness and isolation filled Jim with guilt. *I've shut her out, and she feels useless.*

Pastor Berge, Sara, John and Jenny, and Jim's brother Dave stood in a little group talking in low, quiet voices. Off by herself, Gladys Hanson stood alone, stoic and sober. Later, she was joined by Paul, Sam, and Leslie, who walked up silently just as the memorial service was about to start. The plain bronze urn tucked under Jim's arm felt heavy. *Ashes to ashes, dust to dust,* he thought. *Eventually, our lives boil down to that.* He walked to the grave and placed the urn near the headstone engraved with his sister's name. Then he joined the group of mourners. Lillie stood next to him. Placing Henri in his stroller, Carol walked back over to them, firmly clasping Jim's hand.

"The Lord is my Shepard, I shall not want," Pastor Berge began. His deep voice resonated among the gravestones. The wind had died down, and the silence seemed profound but comforting. It was as if all of nature was taking a moment to remember Juliette's life.

Jim had struggled to find a reading or poem that would adequately describe the essence of Juliette. He felt incompetent, like a bumbling fool. He didn't know her, and in the end, when she'd needed him the most, he'd failed her. He spent long hours in his study trying to reconcile his guilt. He'd prayed and asked for God's help, but his prayers seemed to bounce off the ceiling. He wasn't sure anymore if God heard him or even cared.

Finally, one day when he was browsing online, he found a poem that seemed apropos. Jim read it now. His strong voice carried in the silence of the little cemetery, but his heart fluttered wildly, and tears misted his eyes and wet his cheeks.

Weep not for me though I have gone into the gentle night,

Grieve if you will, but not for long, upon my soul's sweet flight.

I am at peace, my soul's at rest, there is no need for tears, There is

no pain, I suffer not, gone now are all my fears. Remember not my

fight for breath, remember not the strife,

Please do not dwell upon my death, but celebrate my life.

Everyone stood rooted to the ground, their heads bowed, lost in thought. Jim quietly wept. Carol hugged him gently, and he kissed her tenderly. Reaching down, he picked up Lillie, who gave him a baffling stare. It was as if she could see down into his heart and the guilt crouching there. Her blue eyes focused on him.

"Bapa?"

"Uh-huh," he said, clumsily wiping away his tears.

"Remember the pretty lady in white?"

Jim's face scrunched in confusion. "The lady in white?" Carol listened carefully, exchanging an inscrutable glance with Jim.

Lillie nodded her head confidently. "She came the night Grandma died. She took Grandma home and showed her the way. Remember?"

Jim nodded perceptively, his face brightening. "Oh, yeah. I remember you telling me that."

"I saw her again. Right here," Lillie said, her eyes wide and somber. She caught Jim's brief expression of disbelief. "She came. And look! She left me this feather."

Jim and Carol were awestruck. Lying in Lillie's little palm was a tiny, pure white feather of exquisite and delicate beauty.

"Isn't it pretty?" Lillie asked. "I know Grandma is happy and loves us very much. You believe me, don't you, Bapa?" When Jim

SUE BERG

didn't answer, she raised her innocent face to Jim's. "Bapa?"

"Yes, I believe you, Lillie." A snippet of scripture came to him. *And he shall give his angels charge over Thee to keep Thee in all Thy ways.* "Yes, I believe you," he repeated firmly. He didn't know if he meant he believed Lillie or God—he wasn't sure. Maybe it was both.

"I love you, Bapa," Lillie said, carefully clasping the feather in her hand.

"I know. I love you, too," he said, drawing her close.

Throwing her arms around Jim's neck, she squeezed with surprising strength, and he felt something release deep inside. Whatever it was, it hovered above him and then it was gone. He couldn't believe it, but the pain that had burrowed into his heart had vanished. In its place was acceptance and forgiveness; a path that had been rocky now seemed smooth. It was as if Lillie's love had released him from the prison of his own making. Jim tilted his head back and whispered to no one in particular, "We'll take good care of her, Juliette. We'll do our best."

At that very moment, a slight wisp of wind moved through the trees and seemed to whisper back, "I know you will." ⬛

THE END

If you have enjoyed this book, I would be so grateful if you would consider writing a review. I love hearing from readers who enjoyed my stories, and reviews play a big part in other readers discovering my books. If you bought a book online from Amazon or Barnes & Noble, you may leave a reader review there. Otherwise, you may message me on Facebook (Sue Berg-Luepke) or at my email: bergsue@hotmail.com

ABOUT THE AUTHOR

Sue Berg is the author of the Driftless Mystery Series. She is a former teacher, and enjoys many hobbies including writing, watercolor painting, quilting, cooking and gardening. She lives with her husband, Alan, near Viroqua, Wisconsin. ◘

COMING IN
JUNE 2023

JIM HIGGINS'
ADVENTURES
CONTINUE...

Look to the opposite page for
an excerpt from *Driftless Desperation*.

1

The sound of slapping waves on the sides of the *Geechee Girl* houseboat in Pettibone Harbor near La Crosse, Wisconsin, created a gentle, rhythmic cadence that was comforting. The houseboat swayed with an undulation that felt natural—a motion as old as the river itself. It reminded DeDe Deverioux of the river currents that rocked her grandfather's shrimping boat as they met the ocean tides in the early morning light. When she was a small child in the Gullah country of Beaufort County, South Carolina, that movement had become a way of life flowing through her veins. Now, as she sprawled in her chaise lounge chair under the flickering stars of a velvety black night on the Mississippi River near LaCrosse, Wisconsin, she wondered what the next chapter in her life would bring.

Raised by her grandparents, Lorenzo and Hettie Deverioux, on the bayous and tidal creeks of South Carolina, the smell of the river water and the life that teemed beneath it filled DeDe with a deep longing for home—home in the low country near Morgan Island with its simple food, natural beauty, and unpretentious living.

She puffed lazily on her pipe—a habit she'd picked up from her

Grandma Hettie. Wisps of fragrant smoke rose into the air spiraling into weird gray shapes that swirled in the cool September night and then disappeared. In the distance, the bluffs along the Mississippi huddled like overgrown pouting children crouched along the shore. The light from a sliver of the gibbous moon shone on the dark surface of the water, leaving a rippling yellow crescent. Somewhere in the stillness of the night, a cackle of laughter and soft jazz music made DeDe remember the sultry nights patrolling the parishes of New Orleans as a city cop.

At age thirty-two, DeDe was still searching for a place to land. She tried teaching, but that had lasted barely a year. Her inquisitive mind was restless, searching for some great mystery that needed a solution. She drifted from one low-paying job to another until a friend suggested police work. Though it seemed an odd career choice at first, the suggestion ended up matching her insatiable curiosity about people and what made them tick. Restless, her intellectual energy found its match in the challenges of detective work. Puzzling out the tangled tentacles of motive and opportunity focused her restless mind, gave her a purpose, and added meaning to her life.

Enrolling in the police academy was a cultural shock after her quiet and simple existence in the isolated surroundings of Wilkins on the riverbanks, where she lived with her grandparents on their small vegetable farm. River life was in her bones. She'd spent her Saturdays and summer months on her grandfather's small fishing boat trolling the tidal creeks, pulling in crabs and shrimp. DeDe could throw a cast net into a creek and retrieve a *ketch uh da day* as good or better than any man.

But as important as the survival skills she'd learned from Grandpa Lorenzo, she soon discovered that her calm and deliberate manner in tense situations was crucial to surviving the streets as a cop in New Orleans. Whether it was her simple, unsophisticated philosophy of life or her hardheaded, practical approach to problem solving, she thrived in difficult, challenging predicaments. She had found her life's work, and there was no turning back.

SUE BERG

With three years of policing in New Orleans under her belt, she forged ahead with night classes until she became a detective. But her wanderlust poked her in the ribs, and a few months ago, she'd decided to pull up stakes in her beloved south and move north since Grandpa Lorenzo and Grandma Hettie had passed on. She used her small inheritance from her grandparents to buy a 1993 Harbor Master fifty-two-foot houseboat and began navigating her way north on the Mississippi River.

Maneuvering through locks and dams, she became an expert at traversing the currents and avoiding the dangers of the largest river in the United States. She'd been traveling now for almost three months—an extended and unintended vacation. Along the way, she fished and stopped periodically at farmers' markets along the river to stock up on fresh fruits and vegetables. With her fifty-pound bag of rice on hand, she could cook up a pot of gumbo or hoppin' john any night of the week.

Sitting in the blackness of the night, she wondered at the wisdom of moving this far north. September had already arrived, and the nights were cool and crisp. The brilliant colors of the hardwood trees and the sandstone bluffs that towered along the shores of the Mississippi complimented the cooler weather. However, living on a houseboat would not be feasible for much longer. She groaned with anxiety as she thought about what might face her in this northern climate. The winters were notorious for heavy snow, bitter cold, and ice. *What do people do around here when it's that cold?* she thought. *Dat's enough to freeze da titties offa da witch.*

She'd applied for a detective position online at the La Crosse Sheriff's Department, resulting in a scheduled interview with Lieutenant Jim Higgins and Sheriff Davey Jones on Monday. The interview was only two days away. Now she wondered what she'd gotten herself into.

The river she understood; the people she wasn't so sure about, and the weather scared the bejesus out of her. She tapped the tobacco out of her pipe on the edge of the boat. The red coals hissed as they hit the water. She could still feel the heat in the bowl of the pipe as she cradled it in her hand and stuck it in the pocket of her sweatshirt. It was the most treasured possession she owned from her beloved grandmother.

Standing near the bow, she stretched her six-foot frame upward, her arms reaching for the stars. Silently she prayed a familiar Gullah prayer. *Twas mercy brought me from my Pagan land, taught my benighted soul to understand there's a God, and there's a savior, too.* Then her voice broke through the dark night. "Well, Lord, you be watchin' over me," she finished solemnly, remembering the words spoken by her wrinkled grandma Hettie when she was just a child. DeDe knew who she was and who she wasn't and knew what she would bring to the job interview. She hoped it would be enough. ◘

2

SEPTEMBER 7

The evening sun was just beginning to sink behind Lt. Jim Higgin's house on Chipmunk Coulee Road south of La Crosse, Wisconsin. The woods that bordered the manicured lawn left odd elongated shadows on the thick green grass. As the wind blew gently through the trees, the shadows moved and swayed as if they were dancing to a rhythm all their own. Covered with cracks and crevices, the irregularly shaped sandstone formations at the back of the property provided excellent cover. A chipmunk scampered out from under a rock, trilled a warning at the man in camo, and scurried back into its underground burrow again.

The evening sun was just beginning to sink behind Lt. Jim Higgin's house on Chipmunk Coulee Road south of La Crosse, Wisconsin. The woods that bordered the manicured lawn left odd elongated shadows on the thick green grass. As the wind blew gently through the trees, the shadows moved and swayed as if they were dancing to their own rhythm. Covered with cracks and crevices, the irregularly shaped sandstone formations at the back of the property provided excellent cover. A chipmunk scampered out from under a rock, trilled a warning at the man in camo, and scurried back into its underground burrow again.

Rolf 'Maddog' Pierson leaned against the limestone rock outcropping, thankful for anything solid that would support his shaking legs. The irony that he had to lean on a slab of unforgiving rock for support instead of on his own two feet was not lost on him. *The story of my life*, he thought. He'd promised himself he wouldn't drink while he was doing reconnaissance, but as he gathered up what little courage he had, he pulled a half-pint of vodka from the pocket of his camo vest and took a huge gulp. His eyes watered as the burn of the alcohol slid down his throat and belly spreading its warmth throughout his body. He needed something to steady his shaking hands and calm the wild beating of his heart.

He had thoroughly checked out Higgin's place when no one was around. The sophisticated camera mounted on a tree by the driveway aimed at the house's front entry was a problem he hadn't anticipated. It was some kind of expensive surveillance. The camera was too high to easily disengage, and Chipmunk Coulee Road was too busy with traffic to risk taking it down. The surveillance system meant he'd have to come up with another plan.

The reputation of Higgins as a determined investigator with the La Crosse Sheriff's Department was another foreboding factor. From everything Maddog had heard and read on the internet, he was the synthesis of persistence and intelligence. He'd come after him with both guns blazing if Lillie went missing. Pierson had no illusions. Higgins would never give up his niece now that he'd bonded with her so completely.

Although he was a burned-out druggie and alcoholic, he wasn't stupid. However, a drug-addled brain could override an intelligent mind. Fully-informed, coherent decisions often became a crap shoot. After all, the proof was in the pudding. Here he was hiding behind some rocks doing surveillance on his own daughter. That fact alone made his situation hard to face in the light of day.

He was full of regret and anger and a remorse so deep it felt like a hot coal burning a hole in his stomach. Walking out of the Wausau hospital higher than a kite almost six years ago, he'd left the baby girl behind without even signing the birth certificate. At the time, he was strung out on meth and knew the desperation of having no choices left except your next fix. Addiction was the monster who stalked his waking and sleeping moments. The demon strangled every good decision he'd made except the bad one to get high. Meth skewed your judgments until the only words to describe yourself were a harebrained loser. It left you a hideous mess with your personhood splattered on the walls of deceit and shame with no place to go. No one, except another addict, could ever understand.

Quietly he picked up his binoculars, turned toward the house, and knelt behind his rock perch. A hundred yards away, he watched the scene unfold. The squealing laughter of the little girl was infectious as she ran and chased a squirrel up a nearby tree. The innocence of youth. He adjusted the lens to see her clearly—the blue eyes, the golden locks of curly hair, the obvious intelligence and curiosity that seeped from every pore. The little girl was so beautiful it hurt him to look at her. That's my girl, he thought wistfully. Tears burned his eyes as he watched the impish figure turn toward the dark-haired woman on the patio who was holding another little toddler, a curly-haired blonde baby boy. They exchanged smiles and words. Higgins lounged in relaxed contentment next to the woman. The little girl tilted her head back and laughed spontaneously with pure joy.

Lowering the binoculars, Maddog sat in his lair. Hiding was a familiar methodology in his drug operation. His criminal forays required stealth and secrecy. After all, he ran one of the biggest meth labs in central Wisconsin on his old man's 200-acre farm. The tentacles of his operation spread far beyond Marathon County, Wisconsin. Camouflage and subterfuge were his trademarks. He wasn't called Maddog for nothing. He'd earned his nickname eluding police and making drug drops in out-of-the-way places, and he'd killed a few men. One of the hazards of his work.

He lifted the binoculars to his red, bloodshot eyes again. Now another younger woman had joined the group. He scanned the house and lawn. The property was pristine and well-kept, with beautiful places for a child to run and explore. A creek, rocks to climb, trees in which to build a treehouse, a lush green lawn bordered by beautiful flowerbeds, and just outside the perimeter of the lawn lay the mysteries and wonders of nature—a perfect environment for an inquisitive child.

Once again, remorse stalked him, poked him, ridiculed him. What do you have to offer her? What could you possibly give her that she doesn't already have? That was the dilemma that tormented him. He had nothing to give her except one thing—he was her real father. She was his blood. And by God, somehow she would be his again.

He laid his binoculars down and stood hunched like an old man against the coming darkness. Then glancing back over his shoulder for one last glimpse of the little girl, he snuck quietly into the woods, his plan gelling in his mind. He would return for the girl but not tonight. Later, under cover of another night, the time would come. ◘

CPSIA information can be obtained
at www.ICGtesting.com
Printed in the USA
JSHW052245250722
28533JS00006B/13

9 781955 656313